UNTOLD
ADVENTURES

DUNGEONS & DRAGONS®

UNTOLD ADVENTURES

ALAN DEAN FOSTER · KEVIN J. ANDERSON
JOHN SHIRLEY · LISA SMEDMAN
MIKE RESNICK · JAY LAKE
AND MANY MORE

Dungeons & Dragons

Untold Adventures
©2011 Wizards of the Coast LLC

Published by Wizards of the Coast LLC. WIZARDS OF THE COAST, DUNGEONS & DRAGONS, D&D and their respective logos are trademarks of Wizards of the Coast LLC in the U.S.A. and other countries. Other trademarks are property of their respective owners.

Printed in the U.S.A.

Cover art by Android Jones

First Printing: June 2011

9 8 7 6 5 4 3 2 1

ISBN: 978-0-7869-5837-5
ISBN: 978-0-7869-5934-1 (e-book)
620-33275000-001-EN

U.S., CANADA,
ASIA, PACIFIC, & LATIN AMERICA
Wizards of the Coast LLC
P.O. Box 707
Renton, WA 98057-0707
+1-800-324-6496

EUROPEAN HEADQUARTERS
Hasbro UK Ltd
Caswell Way
Newport, Gwent NP9 0YH
GREAT BRITAIN
Save this address for your records.

Visit our web site at www.dungeonsanddragons.com

CONTENTS

UNDER THE PLAINS OF RUST
JOHN SHIRLEY

1.

It was daylight outside the Nentir Inn, but in this windowless garret it might have been night. The dying warlock's chamber was lit by a single feeble lamp dangling from the darkened ceiling; it swayed slightly, though there was no reason it should.

A slender young steward in close-fitting black garments, Gnarl stood just inside the doorway, an empty tray in his hands, wondering what exactly the warlock wanted. He had refused all service but a little broth and wine. The shadows darkening the chamber seemed to have substance, and personality, as if they'd gathered in the room to observe the tiefling's decline. He was, after all, no ordinary tiefling—Sernos was quite a famous worker of magic.

"Come closer, young man," said the warlock hoarsely, shifting on the small bed in the corner of the dank, shadowy room. "And close the door. I have a mission for you . . ." The tiefling's rasping voice reminded Gnarl of the filing of old swords. Seeing Gnarl's hesitation, the warlock scowled, the glow of his crimson eyes quickening like embers blown on a cold night. Trying to prop himself up on his pillows, Sernos gave an agonized grunt and pushed back his hood. Gnarl saw that the tiefling's head was crowned by horns; his elongated features, always the color of a sunburn, were both noble and infernal.

Reluctantly, Gnarl closed the door and took a step into the room. He feared a malediction should he refuse to approach. "May I fetch you a tonic?" Gnarl suggested. "For your injuries . . . Perhaps a soothing solution of the poppy—?"

"Trying to put me to sleep, boy—so some assassin can slit my throat?" grated the warlock, eyes narrowing to fiery slits. "Has someone paid you to drug me?"

Gnarl licked his lips. "I am thinly paid, and all gold is welcome, but I wouldn't take a pot of it to poison a warlock. My papa did not raise a poltroon. I have no wish to be magicked into the Abyss."

"It's curious you should mention the Abyss," growled the warlock, grimacing in pain as he shifted again. "The wretch who passes for a healer to this inn mentioned you might moonlight as something of a thief. Is this"—he paused to take a shuddering breath—"is this indeed the case?"

Gnarl cleared his throat. "I prefer the term 'retrieval specialist.' I have sometimes journeyed out and about to . . . *cull* special objects for guests of the inn—without the knowledge of our proprietor. I . . . *re-appropriate*. But never from anyone within these walls."

"The proprietor—ah, Zemoar!" said the warlock, glancing toward the door. "I am especially concerned you do not tell Zemoar about this. I mistrust elves, and half-elves. If you wish to undertake this quest for me, say nothing to anyone about it—except to those who might accompany you."

Gnarl bowed—slightly. He didn't like the sound of the term "quest." It implied long distances and unknown dangers. Truth be told, Gnarl was not half so good a thief as he supposed himself. But admitting failure was becoming painful to him. He had failed at being an apprentice to his uncle, a low-level wizard, though he'd gotten something of an education. He had earned only a pocketful of gold as a "retrieval specialist"—he could not afford to quit his day job. Still . . .

"Quests are risky," Gnarl said. "That's on one side of the scales. What enticement's on the other? What balances my risk?"

"*Wealth!*" the tiefling hissed. "Wealth and land; shining castles and supple maidens to grace them. All can be yours, boy, if you undertake the task I set for you. The journey entails a trifling risk or two, but if you do as I say, you shall have your just desserts, and I shall have my own heart's desire. You will no longer concern yourself with pouring pots of ale for belching merchants and—inevitably—emptying pots of piss!"

Despite persistent rumors to the contrary, Gnarl was not entirely without common sense. It was true that one balmy evening he had "borrowed" a fine, silken costume from a snoring grandee at the inn and disguised himself for entry into the masquerade at the Kamroth Estate. He'd intended to try his hand, as it were, at pick-pocketing the celebrants—but he was sidetracked by Armos Kamroth's drunken mistress. He narrowly escaped from Telia's clutching hands—and the mailed fists of the enraged Kamroth—but the getaway entailed Gnarl sprinting through the cobbled streets naked from the waist down. His harlequinade mask protected his identity until a couple of milkmaids recognized other distinctive features. His reputation as a slick operator had suffered grievously.

He was older now—all of three months older—and was moved to caution. "Sir, you are a great worker of magic—

you must know someone better qualified."

The warlock grunted. "I threw the seeing bones—they see you as favorable. Of all those I could reach from here, only you might succeed . . ." He broke off, his face twisting into a contortion that made Gnarl wince with sympathetic pain. "There is no one else suitable. Hence" —the warlock paused to gasp before continuing—"hence, your epochal opportunity. I am crippled, and I am dying—I have little time. You know me as Sernos. But I have chosen a greater name. Time runs short . . . that name must be fulfilled soon. Look here."

He swept his bedclothes aside. Gnarl saw that all of the warlock's body, below the breast, down to his knees, was tightly encased in metal, the interlocked plates incised with runes. It was like a partial suit of gray armor—one that was far too small for the tiefling. Beads of blood and purulence showed where metal compressed flesh; hideous purple swellings, like grotesque flower patterns in relief, marked his skin above and below the tightening metal sheath. As Gnarl watched, stomach twisting at the sight, he saw the enchanted sheath of gray metal contract further, moving of itself, the metal squeezing tighter by a few hairs' width, making a little *crick* sound that had a certain smug satisfaction about it.

"There," groaned the warlock, "you see my bane, my curse, and what may soon be my end. It is Ermlock's Grip, the malediction of a certain hateful wizard, who has hidden himself somewhere in this very settlement. The villain wishes me to die slowly, thinking of him all the time. Seven days are required for Ermlock's Grip to finish its squeezing. In three days and a half, it will squeeze out the final drops of my blood like the last wine from a wineskin. Already blood starts from my ears!"

"But surely a powerful warlock such as yourself—"

"Do you not think I would remove Ermlock's Grip if I

could?" Sernos growled. "It is fixed in place with potent magical seals. The first blacksmith to attempt to remove it will die instantly—and horribly." He made a tiefling sign of disgust with his fingers. "I was overconfident—taken by surprise as I traveled through Harken Forest. A harpy, hired by my enemy, swooped down and dropped a purple orb containing the spell—the orb struck me square. Once struck . . ." He sighed, and let his head drop back onto his pillow. "I scarcely made it to this bed; I can go no farther. My powers are at an ebb. But I have knowledge of a secret under the Plains of Rust, deep in the Abyss." He pointed a talonlike finger at Gnarl. "Activate the magical device you will find there, in a place I will describe, and your glory will come, Gnarl—and so will mine. The device will set up mystic reverberations that will undo this spell, unbuckling Ermlock's Grip, while opening up the realm of Glorysade—a realm of order that you, Gnarl, will rule, safe from the eruptions of chaos."

Now he had Gnarl's attention. *Glorysade.* Could there be truth in it? "I have heard a little of Glorysade. It's just a legend. My uncle mentioned it to me . . ." The tiefling hesitated. Then he asked gruffly, "And what have you heard?"

Gnarl shrugged. "That there are dark deep places in the Elemental Chaos—the Abyss, for one. And somewhere is hidden an artifact that can bind together a part of the Elemental Chaos, forge it magically into an order that will make a man lord of a new realm. Glorysade. My uncle told me my destiny might be mingled with Glorysade—if it were true . . ."

"The tale is true! You have heard of me—you know I was once a warlock of power. If you will only trust me."

Gnarl cleared his throat. "Ah, trust." He smiled apologetically and made a gallant flourish with his hand. "A term resonant of reliability, assurance, certitude—how I'd love to feel all of that! But 'trust' also raises the possibility of the opposite . . . mistrust. Unreliability. Lack of assurance—"

He could hear Sernos gritting his fangs. "Set aside this affected glibness and give me your answer! Think of your life as it is now—and think of what it could be! Yes, yes, you must trust me—but if you trust no one, you will never cease having to empty chamber pots in this ramshackle inn! Will you undertake the mission—or won't you?"

Gnarl was a person of outsized ambitions, which was why he'd left the sleepy hamlet Desul Torey and the doubtful protection of Baron Stockmer. But *this*—should he risk it? He'd never entered the Abyss—the Abyss was itself a legend, and the legend was a grim one. But if Glorysade was real—if he could transform the Chaos into a land over which he could rule—it would be worth the risk. It *was* true, after all, that Sernos was a famed warlock, well known in Fallcrest—and Glorysade seemed to Gnarl a name that tingled with destiny, just as his uncle had said.

He was known for grandiose speaking—and impulsiveness. He said, "Very well. Blow the trumpets of Glorysade! The time for rejoicing is here. Gnarl the Cull will undertake the mission!"

"Then—there is much more I must tell you. A certain dwarf and his adopted sister are visiting Fallcrest . . ."

2.

"Young fellow, whenever they say 'mission' or 'quest,' " declared Rorik the dwarf, clanking his tankard down on the oak table, "watch out! What they really mean is 'a miserable, unrewarding trudge through the Nine Hells.' " Rorik gave a contemptuous snort and set about braiding his long red beard. They were silent for a moment—the muted roar of the falls could be heard outside.

Gnarl leaned against the open doorway of the dwarf's rented hut and looked questioningly at Miriam, who lounged in a rude chair across from Rorik. She was drinking ale as enthusiastically as Rorik.

Gnarl's gaze lingered on her: she was lithe, with long raven-wing black hair; her comely features were mostly human but she had the pointed ears and arched eyebrows of a half-elf. Rorik, in previous dealings, had told him something of her. She was the daughter of rangers killed in a skirmish with hobgoblins in the Dawnforge Mountains. A mere girl of seven, she'd fled into a cave. Dwarves found her, a starved child wandering in the mazy tunnels, and took her into their city of Hammerfast where she was adopted by Rorik's family; a rare thing, as the clannish dwarves were known for fierce loyalty to their own kind.

Gnarl had not been surprised when the warlock had recommend Rorik to accompany him—the dwarf artisan was known for his skill with magical items—but he'd never met Rorik's adopted sister before, and it seemed strange that Sernos had suggested they take this sinuous beauty along. True, a dragonhide quiver of arrows hung on the back of her chair, the longbow leaning against the wall within reach. She wore a dragonhide kilt and a warrior's tight-fitting top of chain mail—but her long, tanned arms and legs were bare, and her fingernails were painted with flecks of crushed jade. She turned him a cool appraisal with her dusky olive eyes, then returned her attention to her ale, draining the brass tankard. When she moved, he glimpsed emerald lights in her hair.

Strangely stirred, he looked away from her. Out the open door, the mist of the falls rose, prismatic in the late afternoon sun. An idea was forming. He looked back at Rorik, wondering how he could set the trap.

"So you see, Gnarl," said Rorik, shooting him a look of warning from under his bushy brows, "we are absolutely, and completely, *not* interested in signing on to your mission. Particularly as you mention the Plains of Rust. I doubt you know anything about the place!"

"Just the little that the warlock told me," Gnarl admitted. "Not much. I've heard of the Abyss—but I know little of that either." He put on his best look of heroic defiance. "I'm equal to anything that might claw and scrabble in the bottommost pit of any abyss you can name!"

Miriam covered a smile with her hand at that—but it seemed to Gnarl that his bravado pleased her, too.

Rorik spat into a brass urn on the floor. "Ridiculous! Oh, yes, many in Hammerfast have dreamed of visiting the Plains of Rust—but it is too dangerous, even for our heroes. If you'd done your homework when you were an apprentice, you'd know it is secreted within the Abyss of the Elemental Chaos! It's said to be awash in howling ghosts and the vilest demons. Even a casual trip to its fringes would be lunacy. I don't care who your warlock is. And I don't have time, anyway—we're going back to Hammerfast. If you were a clansman, I *might* consider it. But a young human, a punkling such as yourself—"

"Punkling!" Gnarl bridled.

Miriam laughed lightly, catching the tip of her tongue between her teeth. "You've offended him, Rorik!"

"What of it! I scarcely know him! He shouldn't be inviting me on suicide missions! It's true he *did* get a ceremonial cup back for the clan, once—but I could have done the job myself." He shrugged, and looked into a clay jug for more beer. "Wasn't politic for me to do it. I come here for my work—like to stay on the right side of the locals."

Gnarl decided to make his move, and damn the consequences. The warlock was dying inch by inch, as the hours passed; Gnarl had sworn to restore him, as well as claim the prize: Glorysade. "You speak of working here," Gnarl said, with a skeptical oiliness he knew was offensive. "I've heard you boast that the local wizards summon you to work special enchantments on devices."

"Boast?" Rorik scowled at him. "What do you mean, boast? I am the best worker of enchanted items this side of Hammerfast!"

"Come, come, only the best work for the local wizards. But dwarves? They know about simple swordmaking, tunneling through mountains—useful skills, in a minor way, but hardly fit for fine work; dwarves haven't got the insight, the intelligence—"

Though Rorik was only four and a half feet tall, the little wooden domicile shook when he jumped from the chair to thud to the floor heavily in his armored boots. "You insult my intelligence, punkling?" The hue of the dwarf's face darkened to match his beard.

Gnarl was afraid he'd have to run. Rorik was short—but powerful. While Gnarl thought of himself as wiry, others thought of him as spindly, and it was true that the dwarf could easily bowl him over. And easily jump on his chest. And then quite as easily jump on his head.

Suddenly, Rorik spun around and stalked toward the opposite wall. Hanging beside a shelf was a battlehammer. But just as Gnarl was about to take flight, he saw that Rorik, on tiptoes, was reaching for a box on the shelf instead. He drew down the little silver casket, ten inches by six, and carried it back to Gnarl, the shack trembling with every booted stomp. He snapped the box open. "Look at this!"

Within, on black velvet, was a many-tool, forged of a precious platinum-based alloy. Its ends divided into gadgets—wedges, sockets, spirals, all angling this way and that. Red and blue gems shimmering with magical energies ran down its length, each gem pulsing in turn. "Do you know what this is?" Rorik demanded. "I'll tell you! Why, it's nothing much—it's *only* a master artificer's many-tool, that's all! This one is especially rare—and doubtless some of the reason your sickly warlock sent you to me. But do you suppose I would risk it in the Plains of Rust? It took seven years to make, by seven toolsmiths, seven hundred years ago! I toil with exquisite precision with this tool! Nothing else will serve!"

"I'm sorry for doubting you! May I . . ." Gnarl did a credible simulation of awe, gaping at the many-tool wide-eyed. "May I just hold it for a moment? I revere such items!"

Slightly mollified, Rorik growled, "No—but you can look a little closer."

Gnarl pointed at the battlehammer on the opposite wall. "Is that hammer also of such fine quality?"

Rorik turned to look. "What, that old thing? It's just a skullbasher I carry around—"

"Don't look away, Rorik!" Miriam cried. But she was too late. Gnarl had taken the opportunity to snatch up the many-tool. He backed out the door, thrusting it in his cloak pocket.

"I thank you for the loan of the tool!" he shouted. "I'll bring it back!" Then he turned and ran. Shouting erupted behind him, a roar of invectives. An arrow sped past his right shoulder. Gnarl ran around the corner of a sausage shop and into the cobblestone street, heading toward the House of the Sun.

Probably the long-legged Miriam would be close behind. The dwarf had short legs, but he was strong and would not relent. Gnarl was counting on that.

3.

Across the road from the triangular, three-towered temple called the House of the Sun lay the northern arm of the Tombwood.

Lightfooted, Gnarl sprinted along the road, past the three-spired temple, and cut east into the woods, ignoring the laughing taunt of Miriam not far behind him. He suspected that she was not running full out—she was taking her time, enjoying the pursuit.

He ran onward and into the cool shadows of the thicket; boughs of resinous trees overhanging the path switched at his face. A whining sound behind him was followed by the *chuk* of an arrow burying its head in a tree trunk just to his left.

"Oh ho, almost pierced an ear with that one!" shouted Miriam.

Gnarl broke into a clearing cloaked in ground fog, and immediately stumbled over a stone jutting from the old cemetery. He caught himself and ran on, angling toward the age-eroded statue of a winged angel standing before a tumble-down crypt. It was just as Sernos had described.

The door of the crypt stood open and he skidded inside, gasping. *Open the sarcophagus,* Sernos had said, far too blithely, *and climb within.*

This was no time to give in to the dread clutching at him. He pushed back the lid of the sarcophagus—it was hinged, and surprisingly light—and saw a narrow iron ladder descending into the rectangular block on which the sarcophagus rested. He climbed onto the block, stepped into the opening, placed his feet on the top rung, gripped the rim of the pit, and—

And froze, hearing Miriam's voice. "Don't move, punkling, or I'll split you with an arrow! I could have killed you twice already if I'd wanted to."

Gnarl looked over his shoulder and saw her backlit by the

light outside the crypt's doorway, bow drawn, an arrow nocked, her bosom heaving but her hands steady. She chuckled and said, "This has been fun—I do get so bored, visiting Fallcrest. Now, climb out of there. Hurry! Rorik will be here in a moment. I suppose he'll want to break your fingers with his battlehammer after he takes the tool back—but they'll heal. Come along. It's better than getting an arrow through the spine!"

"Very well," Gnarl said. He braced himself, putting his weight on his hands, and removed both feet from the ladder rung. Knowing that he might fall ten feet or a hundred, he let go.

An arrow flashed over his head as he fell—literally parting his hair—and then he was in darkness. His feet struck a packed-earth floor about twenty feet down. He sprawled into clinging cobwebs and rat droppings, cursing under his breath. He got to his feet, dusted himself off, and glanced up at Miriam—she was peering down at him, her long hair like drapery as she leaned over the shaft. He couldn't see her face well enough to read her expression. "Sorry!" he called up to her. "Well—I'm off!"

Then Gnarl turned down the murky passage, wincing at the bruises on the balls of his feet.

Gnarl paced rapidly toward the signal lantern in the distance. He pushed through tenuous curtains of cobweb, strode thirty yards past stacks of strangely-shaped phosphorescent skulls, beckoned by the lantern. It was held high by a pear-shaped man, the eunuch whom the warlock had described: Sernos's minion, Qalimar. "Hurry!" Qalimar wheedled in a piping voice, as Gnarl strode up to him. The minion wore a long, intricately sewn caftan; he had a bisected nose and pendulously long earlobes. His head was shaved, eyebrows scraped away.

"Go through the door, into the portal!" Qalimar cried. "Quick, before something comes through it from the other side and finds me down here! Sernos does not pay me enough for the risk. How many times have I let mad suicides through this portal . . ."

"Two others will be coming!" Gnarl gasped, pushing past him. "Let them through!"

Then he stepped into the old dungeon under the forgotten, buried temple of Tharizdun, where a whirling dark purple energy lit up the rectangular stone chamber. He sprinted to the glowing portal, speaking the necessary words the warlock had taught him, hearing Rorik bellowing behind. An arrow clattered against a wall—and then he plunged into purple luminosity.

Passing through the portal, Gnarl was stretched out, remade into the form a portal required—he was an arrow himself, shot by the "bow" of the portal through space and outside time. His stomach contracted, his instincts protested.

Then he arrived at his first stop on the way to the Plains of Rust.

He tottered through another whorl of dark purple shimmer, out onto a small island of craggy stone floating in space itself. The air swirled around him, smelling of cinnamon and fish and daffodils and sulfur. The island was shifting under his feet, like a raft between waves, and he struggled to keep his footing. Then it stabilized, and he was able to look around—he saw that he was on the frontier of the Elemental Chaos.

Shapes formed and dissolved in the distance; the horizon rushed toward him, then recoiled—and then vanished completely. Spinning asteroids gouted fire from craters, spitting fireballs that contracted to become blue-red balls of frozen gas hissing randomly through space, capriciously changing direction. Melancholy melodies rose and fell on the troubled wind, music that spontaneously composed itself—and then decomposed. Great sunlike orbs of flame formed, igniting with a roar—only to stretch like taffy and burst apart into iridescent confetti, which then rearranged into living helixes—that were sucked away into nothingness.

He looked around at the stony island, and wondered if he'd been misdirected. Perhaps he was doomed to die there.

But a gleam of curving blue caught his eye. There, at the far end of the drifting island, was the bridge of water Sernos had described; it arced out over empty space, ending in a whirlpool of coruscating energy.

"Shoot him!" bellowed Rorik, behind him.

He turned to see Miriam stepping through the portal behind Rorik. The dwarf shook his iron battlehammer at him, teeth bared.

"This way!" Gnarl shouted, gesturing for them to follow. "Come on!" He waved the many-tool at Rorik, tucked it into a pocket of his cloak, and ran toward the watery bridge.

It's impossible to cross a bridge of water, he told himself, even as he stepped out on it.

And it would be impossible, were this not the Elemental Chaos. But the pressure of rushing water, forced through some invisible sluice, dragged him onto the bridge—and he was sucked forward, pulled horizontally, tugged feet first across the translucent blue arc, and launched out into space—flung willy-nilly through another portal.

4.

Deep within the Abyss, beyond the Plain of a Thousand Portals, concealing the forgotten depths of a primeval swamp, lay the Plains of Rust.

Gnarl jumped from the portal onto the rust-colored plain. He steadied himself and looked around.

The Plains of Rust, at first sight, perpetually affected visitors in the same fashion, always bringing about gloom and depression. Gnarl was no exception. "Why did I even come here?" he muttered.

Stretching relentlessly under an unnatural light was a wind-scoured plain the color of dried blood. It was chilly, but not strikingly cold. Flat and shadowless, it went on forever. No need to take lanterns, the warlock had told him, for a perpetual twilight prevails there.

Gnarl took a deep breath with the wind in his face—and regretted it, coughing from a mouthful of powdered rust. It gritted between his teeth, tasting of iron.

Turning from the chilly wind, rubbing rust particles from his eyes, he surveyed the prospect. Here and there the vermillion flatness was broken by angular red projections and rolling crimson dunes. The wind keened with a particularly high, metallic note. He continued turning, looking for a certain landmark—and saw it almost immediately. Some distance away, harsh lines spiked against the horizon. It was a ruined citadel of angled, leaning towers, their edges corroded like forgotten knives—just as Sernos had described it. That was his destination.

Completing his survey, Gnarl turned left, noting an angry dwarf coming at him with a battlehammer and a woman with pointed ears about to shoot him with a bow and arrow. Beyond them was—

He collected himself and dropped flat as the hammer, swung by the furious Rorik, whistled through the space he'd just occupied.

"Now I've got you!" roared the short but unnervingly muscular Rorik, raising the hammer again for a killing blow.

"Rorik—don't kill him!" Miriam shouted.

That made Rorik hesitate just long enough for Gnarl to roll to one side, scramble to his feet, and raise his hands in front of him. "I'm unarmed, except for a dagger and a couple of spells I'm not even sure I can use! You wouldn't want the shame of killing someone so defenseless, Rorik! Think of how the dwarves will shake their heads over it in the tavern!"

"In your case, thief, I'll live with it!" Rorik snapped, slapping the hammer in his horny palm. "But—I could be merciful. I might simply break your legs and leave you here to die—if you hand over the many-tool now!"

"It's all yours!" Gnarl drew the tool and, with a bow, set it ceremoniously on the rusty ground, stepping quickly back. "Take it! But I feel bound to point out, I won't be able to lead you home if you break my legs! And you can't go back without a portal!"

Rorik picked up the many-tool—then a startled look passed over his face. "What did you say about the portal?" The dwarf turned and looked back the way they'd come. The portal they'd all come through—was gone. "Treachery!" Rorik snarled.

Miriam's characteristic expression of amusement faded as she looked around at the rusty wasteland. "The Raven Queen save us," she murmured. She turned angrily to the dwarf. "We are lost in the Abyss, Rorik! I told you not to run through that portal!"

"You—Gnarl!" the dwarf said, shaking the battlehammer at him. "Where is the portal we came through?"

"Gone," said Gnarl, spreading his hands apologetically. "Sernos opened it only temporarily. To return, we must do his bidding. He swore to me, swore a mighty oath—a really, *really* mighty oath—that we'd return to our world if we complete the mission!"

"But—how do we know where to begin in this wasteland?" Miriam asked doubtfully, looking around.

"I know how. We must find our way to a dungeon beneath that fortress." Gnarl pointed at the spiky, rusting towers in the distance. "Underneath it, a certain device awaits activation. And there is more good news—if you work with me, and help me on my mission, I will reward you when I am the High Potentate of Glorysade!"

Rorik gaped at him. "Sernos! Did you say *Sernos*? Is that who sent you to me?"

Miriam groaned. "*That* scoundrel? Now I know why you didn't tell us his name!"

Gnarl shrugged. "He did suggest I shouldn't mention his name. But he is a famous warlock—you must admit that. And he did get us here—expediently! I've heard the legend of Glorysade myself! I always felt I might find my way to it . . ."

"Glorysade—I don't know that one," said Miriam, lowering her bow and arrow. She returned the arrow to its quiver.

Rorik snorted. "Glorysade! It was a dream! The notion that a glorious utopia could be forged from the rawest parts of Elemental Chaos! Ludicrous!"

Gnarl looked toward the bent, pitted towers of the old fortress. "It is a persistent tale. My uncle Verle was a minor wizard—he told me how an angelic being built a magical device that would turn chaos into order. Devils attacked to stop him from using it—and he was forced to hide the artifact somewhere in the Abyss. They struck him down—and its whereabouts were lost. The story says that a great ripple, a reverberation, will set up from the creation of Glorysade"— he gestured grandly at the sky—"and this wave of order will destroy dark spells in many places, our world included. Sernos says it will set him free from his curse. And"—he smiled benevolently at them—"whoever triggers the creation of Glorysade becomes its master." He cleared his throat and looked modestly at Miriam. "If his heart is sufficiently . . . ah . . . good."

"Sufficiently good?" She seemed once more amused. "You mean—as in pure of heart? Being a thief, you would not qualify! But for now, I suppose we'd better hope the warlock's oath is good."

Rorik grunted. "I don't see what other choice we have without a portal." He stuck his battlehammer into his belt and growled, "Lead on—punkling."

5.

"And I'm to activate this device, am I?" Rorik asked suspiciously as he trudged along beside Gnarl and Miriam, approaching a great dune of sandy rust. "How exactly?"

"Once we're there, we'll know," Gnarl said. "Or so I'm told. You'll do it with your many-tool—if we can win past any demonic guardians that may protect it."

"Oh— is *that* all we have to do?" Rorik growled.

"But what *is* this crimson desert?" Miriam asked, shielding her eyes from the metal edged wind. "It doesn't seem to be sand, exactly—is it really rust?"

Rorik spat into the dune of oxidized particles as they trudged up its slippery face. "It is! A desert of rust—and rusting hulks. During the Blood War, the devils of Asmodeus built strongholds here, in this very plane, around the nameless swamp. Fortresses of solid iron, they were, outposts for attacks on demon rivals, through the Gates of the Nine Hells. There was a nasty pair of demon lords who made poisonous vapors steam up from the local swamps. The fortresses corroded, quick as a dice throw, and fell around the horns of their enemies. The rust was blown into the air and came down like bloody snow! And the devils who built the fortresses were either buried alive, or fled." He shook his bushy head grimly. "Now you see all that remains, a world of rust and dried blood."

"You know a deal about it," Gnarl observed.

"Dwarves take an interest in all things metallic," Rorik said. "And in magical devices. It is said there are many curious treasures buried hereabouts. Questers have sought them before . . . ah, I believe we see some of those courageous seekers now. They got here before us."

Jutting from the crest of the dune, impaled on tall spikes of rusty metal, were five mummified bodies: human travelers, their eyeless, leathery faces contorted in eternal agony, withered arms akimbo like scarecrows.

Gnarl grimaced, remembering what the warlock's minion had said: *How many times have I let mad suicides through this portal . . .*

"Look—we're almost at the old fortress!" Miriam said, pointing. "We're a bow shot away from its outer walls."

Gnarl nodded, gazing down on the spires, obelisks, and jagged-edged bulwarks of pocked and rusted iron rising starkly from the dull crimson plane. No shadows should exist in that place, with the light so eerily uniform—yet he spotted one, an inky stain at the base of a tower angling crookedly from the desert. As he watched, the shadow moved, detaching from the tower's base to seep into the sand, vanishing. He suspected a phantom, perhaps a wailing ghost. But the trapped spirits of demons were said to wander these plains, too . . .

"You didn't perchance have the good sense to bring any water with you, Gnarl?" Rorik asked, wiping rust-grit from his mouth.

"I had not planned to come here yet," Gnarl answered ruefully. "I thought we'd spend an hour or two outfitting—but as you refused to come any other way, I was forced to bring you . . . suddenly."

"No water." Rorik looked at Miriam. "Miriam? Can't I just crush him a little? Perhaps a few fingers? Or his nose?"

She shook her head. "He may need his fingers to do magic—and I rather like his nose. But what defenses have we, Gnarl, before we enter the old fortress? Surely the warlock gave you something."

Gnarl licked his dry, dusty lips, tasting iron, and took from the pocket of his cloak the two attack spells the warlock had given him. "Only these." One was an ivory tube no bigger than an index finger. The other, a glass ball about the size of a plum, was wrapped in purple silk. It seemed to mutter something as he held it in his hand. "Sernos said to use this one only in dire circumstances. Its name is Porphyros. This tube projects a spell that causes ghostly befuddlement—or some such thing, and can be used only once. It's not a lot, I'm afraid. It's all he could manage in his weakened state."

Gnarl replaced the glass ball and the ivory tube, and drew his dagger to keep it ready. He frowned, seeing the dagger had turned a strange reddish hue. He tapped it experimentally with a finger and the blade crumbled into red dust, blowing into nothingness. It had rusted through.

"Whoa ho!" crowed Rorik. "There you see how the Plains of Rust treat unmagicked metalwork! I just hope these spells that the warlock has sent with you are of better quality. But perhaps he simply wanted you to die here, punkling. Could be that your family angered him in the distant past. Consider the special name Sernos has chosen for himself, after the manner of tieflings!"

"Ah . . . he did not reveal that name to me."

"No? His name is Revenge, young fellow! *Revenge!*"

Gnarl remembered, then, the warlock's cryptic remark: *Time runs short . . . my name must be fulfilled soon.*

Rorik turned to Miriam. "I came unprepared. What of you? Any magic in that quiver?"

She shrugged. "My arrowheads are of elven steel—they'll resist the rust vapors. I have a healing gem, and one magic arrow that might apply—its arrowhead is treated with demonbane. I've carried it for two years and never had occasion to use it."

"One magic arrow!" Rorik groaned. "Not enough. The place stinks of necrotic energy. Listen—the very wind is revolted by the spirits who flit through it!"

They listened, for a moment, to the keening of the wind—and its metallic soughing carried a note of horror.

"Still," Miriam ventured, "we must try the fortress. Perhaps there's water there . . ."

"Poisonous water, if any at all," the dwarf grumbled. "No food, no water, few weapons. A fine mess. Come along, let's get this over with—we'll parch up here in the wind."

They descended the far face of the dune, half stepping, half sliding down until they reached the flatter ground below.

Rorik stumped impatiently ahead, battlehammer in hand, and Gnarl murmured to Miriam, "You said you could have killed me with your arrows, but somehow you missed. How did that happen?"

"Perhaps I wasn't trying too hard to aim."

"Does that mean that you pity me—or you like me?"

She rolled her eyes. But he saw she was smiling. "Well—"

But up ahead of them, Rorik gave out a howl of dismay. He was sinking in the coating of rust particles as in quicksand. It was a sinkhole over the Bloody Fen. The sinkhole could be seen now that Rorik thrashed in it, up to his armpits in rusty muck.

Gnarl ran to him, knelt near the edge of the sinkhole, and reached one hand toward Rorik, the other to Miriam. "Take my hand, Miriam!" She braced herself, digging her bow into the rusty sand, and they clasped hands to wrists. The touch thrilled him, but he concentrated on pulling Rorik out. Miriam pulled Gnarl, and Gnarl pulled Rorik by the battlehammer's head. Grunting, they dragged the dwarf out of the sinkhole.

Rorik got to his feet, swearing blackly as he brushed damp rust from his short legs. "Damn it to the reeking depths of the Ninth Hell!"

Gnarl noticed a juddering turmoil in the red scum on the sinkhole—a kind of corroded metal shark's fin surfaced, wending back and forth. Then something reared up out of the sinkhole, a bestial face made of rust on a framework of necrotic energies, a gigantic feral visage, seven feet high with red-iron jaws like a bear trap, snapping at Rorik. The dwarf shouted in mingled fear and fury and swung his battlehammer—it struck deep, and the bestial face exploded into a sparkling cloud of rust particles, some of which the dwarf inhaled, sputtering as he backed away.

Rorik wiped his eyes, then looked in puzzlement at his battlehammer. "What's wrong with my hammer?"

Gnarl saw that the hammer's iron head was steaming, seething within itself—and then it buckled inward, crumbling into a streamer of red powder. The rust was blown away on the wind, leaving only the hardened oak handle.

"Will you look at this!" Rorik snarled. "I've had this hammer for—" He broke off, shivering, blinking rapidly. His eyes glazed over and his mouth opened wide with a demonic howl. A harsh, sibilant voice issued from his mouth. "*This one shall replace me in the red pit!*" And Rorik began to walk toward the sinkhole, as if determined to plunge into it.

"No!" Miriam cried out. "Stop him!" She jumped toward Rorik and tried to pull him back. He struck at her shoulder with his hammer handle, knocking her sprawling.

Gnarl drew his ivory tube—it was in fact the hollow finger bone of a wizard—and he stepped between Rorik and the hidden pit. Face twisted, the possessed dwarf raised the hammer's handle to strike at him—but Gnarl blew hard through the tube, directing it at Rorik's head. A jet of brilliant green mist issued from the ivory tube and formed a ghostly cobra in the air. The green, transparent cobra struck at Rorik's forehead—sinking fangs into his skull without drawing blood, striking only the possessing spirit. The fiend was driven out, showing itself as a visible shriek emitting from the dwarf's mouth, and it rushed at Gnarl.

Gnarl ducked, warding the apparition off with the ivory tube. The ghost cobra still had hold of the spirit—it whirled overhead once, then dived down into the pit. Gnarl glimpsed the dark spirit's horrified ectoplasmic face as it was pulled down in a whirlpool whipped up by the ghost snake, both apparitions vanishing into the red murk with a final sucking sound. Rorik squatted on the scarlet sand, gasping, rubbing his eyes. Then he shook himself and stood, stretching. "Thought I was going to drown in that stuff," he muttered. "Couldn't control myself."

"Rorik," Miriam said, as Gnarl helped her up, "you might consider thanking Gnarl for saving your life."

"Bah!" Rorik snorted, glaring at Gnarl. "Rubbish! I would not have been here to sink in sinkholes if not for his theft, his deception—his foolish truck with tiefling warlocks!"

"He has a point," Gnarl allowed. "Miriam, are you hurt?"

"Nothing broken. Rorik, if we are to proceed, let's use what's left of that hammer to prod the ground, find the way through."

Using the hammer handle, they soon found a hidden shore, curving along the edge of the fen under the ferrous crust. They kept to the shoreline and at last found themselves standing on solid ground within the rusty spines and the leaning, red-crusted towers of the old fortress.

Gnarl decided he'd better keep them moving. He looked around for the landmark the warlock had described. "There's supposed to be an entrance under the tower that leans farthest toward the horizon," Gnarl said. "There it is!"

The half-fallen tower was like a great corroded sword two hundred feet high, thrusting up diagonally from the metallic sands at a sharp angle, pointing to their left. Gnarl led the way, almost excited about the quest again, wondering if he could really be close to triggering the creation of Glorysade.

Then he saw a crescent-shaped opening at the base of the swordlike tower. "There! Look, Miriam!" His destiny seemed to call to him—and he ran toward it, dimly aware of the others shouting for him to be more cautious. He stopped at the entrance. It was dim, but not truly dark within. Rusty sand had blown through the entrance, covering the floor. A muted reek of decay and alien musk wafted from somewhere inside.

There was no turning back. He stepped through the entrance, feeling a drumlike hollowness under the thin, rusty floor beneath his feet, before his upper arms were grabbed from above. He felt himself dragged upward, into the air. He looked up and felt ice where his heart should be. A vrock! His uncle had told him of these winged, vulturelike demons—and had given him nightmares with the telling. Now he was living the nightmare as he shouted and writhed in the vrock's grasp. With his arms pinioned, he could not reach a weapon.

The vrock's body was humanoid but with a raptor's claws for feet, a vulturine head, and silvery eyes glittering with intelligence under stubby horns. The creature had a twenty-foot wingspan and a lean, muscular body far more powerful than Gnarl's own. It squeaked at him. "Ceeeease to struuuuugle! I will lift you to my aerie and tear you to pieeeeces at my leisure—be pleeeeeased to feed your betters!" Gnarl struggled in its grip as it lifted him into the dimly lit interior of the high, narrowing, rusted shaft. He recoiled from the reeking tongue that issued from its snapping, fang-lined beak to taste his face.

"They like to eat the face first," his uncle had said matter-of-factly.

"But why wait to rend, to tear," the creature creaked as it flapped its great wings to lift him higher. "I shall pull you apart and watch as you feeeeel it all!"

And then he heard Miriam shout from beneath, "Stop moving, you fool! I can't get a shot!"

He made himself go limp. The yellow beak gaped to encompass his face—and then an arrow swished from below, buried itself in the base of the vrock's long neck. It squealed, the shrieking so close his ears ached with it, and his face was sprayed with rancid spittle. Black blood spurted about the fletch of the arrow—and more spurted about the second and third arrows shot from below, each shaft burying itself deeply. But something else issued from the beast, like motes into the air. Gnarl's mind clouded, his limbs suddenly heavy from the spores, his thoughts veering wildly.

Thrashing in the air, the vrock squeezed him brutally, vindictive in its death throes, so he could hardly breathe—and then it gasped and its grip relaxed. He was slipping free, falling, plummeting toward the dusty floor of the chamber. He seemed to fall in slow motion.

He lost sight of the expiring demon as he crashed through the rust-eaten iron of the floor and into the subchamber beneath.

6.

Sitting up on the dusty floor of the subchamber, Gnarl heard the demons stalking through the darkness toward him, but he found that he didn't much care. A seductive numbness was upon him—the effects of the spores of madness. Lunatic thoughts flashed through his mind, tumbling his senses in hellish ecstasy; it was as if the Elemental Chaos occupied his skull. As laughing faces of fire lit his brain he found he could scarcely move; it was as if his arms and legs each weighed hundreds of pounds. Why not just lie here, and get it over with? It might be interesting to be torn to pieces.

Yes, why not? And he watched the skulking silhouettes of the approaching demons, recognizing them from his uncle's grimoire; evistro, newly awakened by his intrusion. How long had they waited in dormancy here? He supposed someone had placed them to guard against the activation of the Glorysade device. He found it all very interesting, in an abstract sort of way.

Hunched over, clutching the air with their oversized, pawlike hands spread wide for tearing, the seven evistro approached him. They were hairless, thickly muscular crimson demons, their tooth-lined maws as oversized as their hands and three-toed feet. The grimoire had said the carnage demons usually came in larger numbers, swarming and rending—unless some wizard sent a group of them on a specific mission. It seemed that Sernos wasn't the only sorcery worker concerned with Glorysade.

The seven demons encircled him, a couple of strides away, their mouths gaping in great slavering grimaces. Gnarl was captivated. Fascinating creatures, he thought. Wonder what it'll be like to be eaten alive? Missed my chance with the vrock.

He heard Miriam in the chamber above, shouting at Rorik.

"The vrock has struck him with spore madness! He's paralyzed, he's not in his right mind! We have to, Rorik!"

"But it stinks of demons down there! I hate demons!"

But just as the evistro reached for Gnarl, Rorik leaped down into the subchamber, swinging his hammer handle—braining one of the demons before he'd even touched the floor. The demon flailed, falling back, and the others retreated a few steps, squalling in confusion. An arrow whickered into the subchamber from above, and then another, and two demons fell writhing. But the other five slashed at Rorik with their clawed paws. He swung the handle of his hammer furiously, using it as a club to drive them back. He's quite a little dynamo, thought Gnarl, sitting on the floor. It can't go on, though. They'll overwhelm him soon and we'll both be eaten. How their jaws drip with saliva . . . intriguing.

Then he was aware that someone had dropped down behind him, was pressing a small circle of cold to the back of his neck, over his spine. A cleansing fire flashed through him, then a wave of nausea, swept away by a surge of energy. Miriam had used her healing gem to save him.

His head clearing, Gnarl jumped to his feet and plucked the glass ball from his cloak pocket, even as Miriam loosed two of her three remaining arrows. The demons were circling them, leaping, slashing—and her arrows missed their marks, striking one in the shoulder. The wounded demon screamed in fury and snapped at the dwarf, who was nearer. Rorik dashed some of its teeth out with his club.

Gnarl exposed the glass globe—and almost dropped it in his startlement as he saw the grisly face staring out at him: a lich vestige. The lich's skullish face pressed eagerly against the curve of the little glass sphere, distorted and leering. "Release me!" hissed the diabolic face, bony jaws gnashing, empty eye sockets shining, "so that I may destroy all!"

He swallowed. "Kill only demons, in the name of Vecna!" he ordered.

It sighed in disappointment. "Very well. Only demons . . . if you insist!"

The demons chose that moment to rush—but Gnarl threw the glass ball at their feet. It burst, and they scattered before the bleak effulgence that blossomed out of it. Porphyros, the gaunt, skull-faced spirit warrior, expanded from the shards and leaped at them with extended claws, ripping into the demons, gibbering happily as it tore them to pieces.

"Come on!" Rorik shouted. "Let's get out of here before it turns on us!"

Head still swimming from the departing effects of the spores, Gnarl followed Rorik and Miriam through a narrow passage, onto a descending ramp of rusted iron. The warlock's words drifted in Gnarl's mind. *Once inside, if you win so far—descend!*

They descended the ramp between pitted metal walls, traipsing down a gentle slope that clanged softly with their tread. On they went, the passageway lit by the same unnatural light as the surface. Gnarl found himself imagining how he would build his castle in Glorysade—seven spires, perhaps, each a different color, inlaid with semiprecious metals. A fountain—no, seven fountains! Would he have a seraglio? But stealing a glance at Miriam, he thought perhaps he wouldn't want one.

"I like this less with each step we take," Rorik grumbled. "And that vrock, the evistro, so closely placed, waiting almost."

"I had the same thought," Gnarl admitted. "Someone arrayed them to protect this device—and Sernos gave me no real warning."

"You were a fool to blunder into this!" Rorik declared.

Gnarl shrugged. "My uncle said my destiny was connected with Glorysade. I always thought he meant a good destiny. So here I am. But now . . . I'm not so sure."

"We're committed," Miriam said, shrugging. "Looks like a doorway ahead."

They stepped through a door frame into a low-ceilinged chamber cut into the naked gray stone that underpinned the Plains of Rust. The walls were granite, but the ceiling was rusted iron.

In the middle of the chamber was a glinting dome about seven feet high, sixty in diameter, not quite a perfect circle, made of unblemished silvery metal. In its curving side was an open doorway. Excited by its shiny metallic promise, Rorik scurried eagerly through the low door—he didn't have to stoop, as Gnarl and Miriam did.

Inside, rising up from a silvery floor, they found a large, glistening artifact shaped outwardly like a polyhedron, some of its panels transparent; it was almost big enough to fill the roughly circular chamber, leaving just a little space to move around its edges. On one facet, partway up, was an opening, within which several curious knobs and studs crackled with miniature bursts of lightning.

"Marvelous!" Rorik exclaimed. "These shapes seem formed to match the many-tool." He had the magical utensil in his hand, and he tinkered within the device, muttering to himself in a grumbling voice. "Yes, the hexagonal knob asks to be turned *this* way; the next one requires that I reverse the tool, turning it the opposite way . . . I seem to hear a whispering suggestion that I press the cool-energy glim"—here he activated one of the magical jewels in the tool, pressing the blue crystal with his thumb, making it shine with a mystical emerald light—"and that would seem to call out for . . . Yes! And now if I turn this . . ."

Gnarl felt an odd mix of elation and anxiety at the possibility of Glorysade. Why indeed had the vrock and the evistro been set to guard the interior of the rusty tower? What did he know of Sernos, really?

"Wait, Rorik," Miriam said worriedly. "Aren't you being a bit hasty? *Who* is telling you how to use the tool? Don't you wonder? Perhaps . . ."

But it was done: Rorik stepped back as the artifact was fully activated. Clockworks and magical energies intersected, revolving within it, linking and shifting, armatures rotating.

And suddenly the floor beneath their feet shook. They were knocked flat by the shuddering, Rorik clutching the many-tool, all three of them sprawling on the floor of the little dome-shaped chamber, their teeth clattering with the vibrations as the entire structure lifted itself from the floor, rising up and up, the silvery dome smashing through the rusted iron ceiling. Instinctively, Gnarl looked for the door—but it had sealed shut, quite seamlessly. Two windows opened, opposite, shaped like gigantic eyes—eyes looking outward. The floor continued to rollick and vibrate so he had to crawl to look out one of the windows of translucent blue glass—and he saw that the dome was no longer underground.

They had risen up, out of the underground, smashed up through the crust of the Plains of Rust, lifted high, towering above the scarlet desert. The chamber swayed and Gnarl heard gigantic footsteps—*thump, thump, boom, thump*. Through the windows he glimpsed giant metal hands and arms, swinging. He realized that he was looking out through the eyes of a gargantuan head. He looked down—saw a nose, cheekbones, the lineaments of a diabolic metal face. The enormous creation was stalking toward the rusted old fort. It reached the towers, paused, squatted, and thrust its jointed metal fingers into the desert of oxidation. The fingers fished around, and then the construct straightened up. As the giant stood, it pulled out the tower that they'd entered to arrive at their current place. It was actually a gigantic sword—its hilt had been buried in the red sands, its semi-rusted blade angling toward the sky.

"A colossus!" Rorik shouted over the rumbling, crawling to look out the eye-window beside Gnarl. "We're in its skull! It was buried under the plains! You've activated the biggest colossus ever made!"

"*I* activated it? You're the one who—"

He broke off, thrown onto his back by the acceleration as the colossus leaped into the sky. It flew straight up, rocketing with magical force, piercing the gray overcast. Lifting his head to look through its eyes, Gnarl saw that the metal giant, as it flew, was emanating rays of dark purple from its outstretched arms—the rays seemed to pierce space itself, so that a whirlpool formed, a circular gate, big enough for the giant.

"It's opening a portal!" Rorik exclaimed.

They felt themselves compressed, transmuted, transformed—as, carried inside the giant, they passed through the portal. They traveled through the churning uncertainties of the Elemental Chaos, and through another portal—leaving the Abyss, coming out into the natural world, flying through the sky. Clouds flashed past. A glimpse of a river appeared below.

A great thundering, bone-jarring, double *thump*—and they were left dazed. After a moment Gnarl forced himself achily to his feet beside Rorik and Miriam, the three of them staring with astonishment out the window-eyes. The colossus stood upon the soil of their own world, awaiting a command.

Five hundred feet below them was Fallcrest.

"Ah, you've done it!" It was the voice of the warlock Sernos—whom Gnarl now understood was also known as

Revenge. It emanated from the magical device behind them. "You've animated Glorysade, the greatest colossus, built by the Demon Chark himself—all have failed till you! You will be rewarded with the orderly world you find . . . locked forever inside the head of the colossus!" He chuckled dryly. "That is your Glorysade!"

Miriam shook her head. "Sernos must have made up the legend—he must've been trying to get at this colossus for years! It's no surprise he lied to you, Gnarl!"

"I'm a fool!" Gnarl muttered sourly. "But what is Sernos's intention here?" He turned to the device within the metal skull. "Sernos—can you hear me? Will you grant an answer or two?"

"I hear! Speak quickly—I am about to exact revenge on my enemy and cement my name as one of the greatest warlocks the world has known! Glorysade is nearly drained from its journey—it gathers full power from the dark energies. When that is done, I strike!"

"Then if we're doomed to be trapped here, tell me at least—why destroy Fallcrest? Why not destroy your enemy alone? Couldn't you let the town go?"

"Fallcrest protected him! My enemy knew what I would do if I succeeded in animating Glorysade. And I was close! So he set demonic guardians around it—and then he struck me down with Ermlock's Grip. The pain of the Grip makes a man mad! Now I will send that pain upon the world! Listen, as I speak to the land—and learn."

And in a voice boomed from Glorysade, psychically transmitted by the warlock Sernos, he addressed the township below. "People of Fallcrest! You have sheltered amongst you my enemy, Kraik the Necromancer." The voice echoed over the houses and old keeps; over the roar of the falls and the screams of people gaping up at the giant, holding a great pitted sword in its jointed metal hand. "Kraik hides in Fallcrest even now, enjoying your wine, your women—and my slow destruction. But behold, I now have control of the colossus towering over you! In order to destroy Kraik—I will destroy Fallcrest. And all the world will know whose power is greatest. I have been Sernos . . . I am now—Revenge!"

As he listened, Gnarl circled the magical device in the center of the giant's skull, examining it closely.

"No one will stand before me when they hear what happened to Fallcrest," thundered the warlock. "Take comfort in knowing your sacrifice will be the start of a grand empire. The power of Glorysade is almost complete! The moment comes! Try to enjoy it!"

Rorik groaned. "Thousands of innocents will die because of us!"

The magical steel colossus raised its pitted, gigantic sword—poised to set about destroying the city. It paused. Screams of terror floated up from below.

"That last arrow of yours, Miriam!" Gnarl said, turning to her. "Your only magic arrow! Bring it here!"

She hurried to him, handing over the arrow, and he used its demonbane tip to pry at an opening, scarcely visible, in the floor beside the humming, glowing device. Magical seals tried to resist—but the demonbane overcame them, crackling with dark blue sparks, and the trap door popped open with a groan. Gnarl climbed through, still holding the arrow, and dropped down to a landing from which spiral stairs descended in a steely vertebral column, like a twisting staircase in a light-house. The vertebrae shivered with dark energies as the giant soaked power from the atmosphere itself. Glorysade shifted on its gigantic legs—he could feel its eagerness, an extension of the warlock's hunger to strike at the town. Hiding the arrow in his cloak, Gnarl hurried down the staircase and reached a heart-shaped chamber.

He stepped through a door into the chamber—a small room throbbing with heat where a humanoid being made of blue flame pulsed with life. Its arms were extended into gauntlets, its feet into metal boots; it gazed into a glass panel which allowed it to see what the colossus saw—through these extensions it directed Glorysade.

Its face was that of Sernos—superimposed by his psychic control.

Seeking to distract and delay Sernos, Gnarl stepped around on the circular catwalk to face the creature. He knew instinctively he had to be in just the right position. "Sernos—you control this being and it controls the colossus. But not so fast!" He edged closer, wincing at the heat. "Soon Ermlock's Grip will squeeze you dry!"

"No!" The voice of Sernos roared from the air about the blue-flame humanoid. "When I destroy Kraik, in a handful of moments, I destroy Ermlock's Grip. There are minutes yet before it completes compression. But what do you want here? I swore you would return and live—but if you do not go back to the chamber above, you will die in this one." The proxy Sernos drew its left hand from the gauntlet—a thing of flame that mocked flesh—and the blue flame hand began to fulminate warningly with red energies. "Go or die!"

Gnarl bowed, as if in acquiescence. He turned away, drawing the arrow from his cloak as he turned—then he spun around and drove it like a dagger between the creature's blue-fire eyes. The arrow shaft burst into flame and charred away, but the magical arrowhead remained, spinning in place.

Sernos screamed, the scream reverberating in the metal carapace like a ringing in a great bell. The mystically charged arrowhead of demonbane turned the fiery magic back upon itself, and the resulting explosion threw Gnarl back against the metal wall. He fell, stunned—but he made himself crawl to the door, out and up the stairway as the colossus rollicked about. He clambered up and up, sometimes on hands and knees as cracks appeared in Glorysade, daylight glimmering through. He clambered up to the landing, struggling to continue as the colossus wrenched about, struggling with a chaotic unleashing of its own magical energies.

The trap door was open—and an arm, lean but strong, stretched down. Miriam took his hand, helped Gnarl climb up.

But there was no standing, not up there. Rorik, Miriam, and Gnarl were thrown to the floor of the silvery skull as the colossus staggered and as it leaped wailing into the sky. The device within its skull was beginning to melt, coming apart in the heat of a blue flame. The creature that guided the colossus seemed in torment, and Glorysade flew up through layers of atmosphere as it tried to escape the destructive force Gnarl had loosed within it. It dropped its sword, which fell, end over end, to vanish into Lake Nen. On and on Glorysade flew—until, trying to escape its agony, it created a portal, blindly flying through it. But it learned what men, too, learn: no one can run from the pain within.

As the colossus passed through the Elemental Chaos, it exploded, its head and chest and arms flying asunder. Gnarl and Rorik and Miriam, within the skull, were spinning through white light. Miriam fell into Gnarl's arms.

The gigantic skull, carrying them with it, spun through space—and crashed into darkness.

7.

They did not expect to awaken. But they did. It must have been several hours later. Their noses were bloodied; they were battered and worn. But they were intact.

They got to their feet—and found that the back of the metal skull had cracked open, and they tottered through it, Gnarl leading the way.

They emerged onto a dawn-lit beach in an unknown land. The body of the colossus was gone. Glorysade's head was there, skewed, stuck in the sand—a devilish face, glaring lifelessly up at the gray-blue sky, the fading stars.

Gnarl and Miriam and Rorik walked up to the edge of the sea. It hissed its mysterious mantra. "What sea is this?" Rorik asked, tugging his beard.

Miriam shook her head. "I don't know. I am not sure if we are in our own world—or another."

Rorik turned angrily to Gnarl. "I should take you apart for what you've put us through!"

"We are alive," Gnarl pointed out. "And we averted the worst. Also—by now, Sernos is dead, crushed by Ermlock's Grip! When we saved Fallcrest we saved Kraik—and saving Kraik destroys Sernos."

"That's something, anyway," Miriam said, combing her hair in place with her fingers.

Gnarl nodded. "I would suggest that if we are to find out where we are—and how to get home—we'd better set off up the beach. I see a crystalline tower in the distance. We might go that way. And I would further like to point out, if I might, before you rashly dismember me with your bare hands, Rorik, that our chances of surviving and returning home are better . . ." he turned to look at Miriam, catching her gaze, "if we put aside our quarrel. If we . . ."

She smiled wryly and nodded. "If we stay together."

Rorik groaned and shook his shaggy head in exasperation. "Oh, come on. Let's get started."

And they headed for the crystalline tower, far away along the unknown shore.

John Shirley is the author of numerous books and many, many short stories. His novels include *Bleak History, Crawlers, Demons,* and the seminal cyberpunk works *City ComeA-Walkin'.* His collections include the Bram Stoker and International Horror Guild award-winning *Black Butterflies and Living Shadows: Stories: New & Pre-owned.* He also writes for screen (*The Crow*) and television. As a musician Shirley has fronted his own bands and written lyrics for Blue Öyster Cult and others. "Under the Plains of Rust" is his first venture into the world of the DUNGEONS & DRAGONS® game.

THE STEEL PRINCESS
ALAN DEAN FOSTER

The well-dressed, powerfully built stranger was tired, hungry, and angry. It was not necessary for him to hold up a sign attesting to these facts. They were plain enough to see in his hunched-over posture as he sat at the heavy wooden table, and in his face as he glared in the direction of the back bar.

The bartender and temporary innkeeper, a heavy-set dwarf like much of the population of Hammerfast, dutifully continued to polish a gilded wide-mouthed goblet he held in his thick fingers. The fact that it gleamed like a gold mirror from having undergone this process nonstop for the previous ten minutes in no way induced him to put it down. It was a useful way for his hands to keep busy when they were not engaged in stroking his beard. Besides, if trouble was brewing, it would double as an excellent missile.

And trouble, like the fine local Crackkeg Ale, was brewing aplenty.

It took the form of Kot, Grerg, and Mulk, the three ogres who were making their way toward the stranger's table. They had been drinking too much—never a good situation. Norgen, the bartender, had continued to serve them because they had continued to overpay, and in gold. Each time he had suggested to them that they'd had enough, they doubled his tip. The fact that they might tear up the place if they became sufficiently inebriated didn't bother him. His second cousin's elder sister was getting married in Fallcrest next week, and Norgen was perfectly prepared to quit his job anyway.

But there was the matter of a severance bonus, and the possibility that he might want to return to work at Fiveleague House some day. Plus he considered the not incidental fact that if he simply stood back and watched while destruction ensued, his boss might kill him, which would complicate his attendance at the wedding. But what could one dwarf do against three ogres, except stand and watch and goblet-polish? For that matter, what could the stranger do?

As the ogres confronted the newcomer, an increasingly edgy Norgen became increasingly convinced that, willing or not, he was about to find out.

"Hoy, traveler!" Kot grunted. "What are you doing here, anyway? This be the Nentir Vale. We don't see your kind here." He grinned, showing ragged, sharp teeth. One massive hand suggestively fingered the mace slung at his belt.

The stranger looked up. Norgen gazed into pale, watery blue slitted eyes that peered out from the wholly feline face, but it was difficult for the dwarf to tell if the stranger was more angry or bored. Dark spots marked his white fur where it was visible on his face. He had backward facing clawed hands and broad feet, not to mention an unusually long and large black-spotted white tail. He wore a single-button black singlet shot through with gold thread over loose-fitting black pants. From his shoulders hung a cape that seemed fashioned of woven silver.

"Really?" His voice was a muted growl. "What kind that you don't see would I be?"

"You're a rakshasa," Grerg replied. As the ogre pronounced it, it emerged sounding like an obscenity. "We're honest folk here. No mind-twisters." He was holding a huge club in front of him. "When we fight, 'tis honest and straightforward, and no shifty magic."

"Get gone, demon-spawn." The third ogre, Mulk, clutched a spiked ball and chain. "This be a clean establishment."

The stranger looked past them, toward the bar. "How about that, innkeeper? Should I leave?"

"Eh, what's that?" Reaching up with one hand, Norgen stuck a sausagelike finger deep into his oversized left ear. "Bit hard of hearing, I am." He returned to his increasingly frantic polishing, though by then the goblet shone so as to take a place of pride in a dragon's hoard. As he continued to mine unpleasant detritus from one ear, the barkeep surreptitiously took small steps in the direction of the exit.

He didn't quite make it before all the hells broke loose.

"We'll help you on your way!" Kot bellowed as he swung his mace out, up, and down.

Intended to split the seated rakshasa, the forceful blow splintered only the innocent table. Other patrons scrambled for cover, diving under tables, bolting for the door, and in the case of one especially prescient elf, springing out the nearest open window.

"Fast—but not fast enough!" roared the third ogre as he swung the heavy spiked iron ball on the end of its chain. It struck the stranger square in the midsection—only to pass completely through him. Reeling from the absence of any resistance, Mulk took a wary step backward.

"Phantom image! 'Ware your selves, brothers!"

" 'Ware indeed," a warning voice growled.

All three ogres whirled. Having drawn a longsword, their opponent stood behind them. Each time the weapon moved through the air, it seemed to emit a soft but audible snarl, and when the diffuse light of the inn caught the blade, the metal seemed to change color—from silver to gold to bronze, and back again. Its hilt twisted slightly in its owner's grasp. It was as if the stranger was gripping the tail of a live thing instead of a shaft of mere metal. Engraved in the metal hilt guard, two cats' faces glared at one another around the shaft of the sword. The more the owner moved it around, the more animated the hilt's faces became.

"I am Ruhan Bijendra, a rakshasa Dhanesh. I have come to the Nentir Vale from my homeland in search of a legend. There are many such here, but the tale of the one I seek was spun to me from an early age by a voluble mage, and I have vowed not to return home until I have ascertained the truth or the lie of it and made it do my bidding."

"Of your speaking, one thing's certain," snorted Kot, the leader of the ogre trio. "You're not going to be returning home." Tightening his grip on his mace, he let out a howl that shook mugs from the rafters, then charged.

Bijendra did not run. He did not try to dodge. He did not even employ the innate magic for which his kind was known. Instead, he simply raised his longsword high above his head and held it parallel to the floor.

Brought down by the full weight and strength of the ogre, the heavy iron mace slammed into the sword. The blade did not shatter. Nor did the arm of the one who wielded it. Instead, the rakshasa twisted his sword just enough at the moment of impact so that the much heavier mace slid sideways along the guiding blade. Sparks flew as the parried head of the bulky weapon smashed into the floor. From where he presently crouched behind the bar, Norgen looked on in amazement. What kind of rakshasa noble was this, who fought with blade as well as with magic? An explanation was forthcoming.

"I am Ruhan Bijendra, and in addition to being of noble blood, I am also by choice—a ranger."

Clearly confused, Grerg paused as he was about to swing his club. "Your lies multiply. There is no such thing as a rakshasa ranger."

Sliding his right foot back to firm his fighting stance, Bijendra's frown was fraught with mock seriousness. "Then how can I possibly be standing here before you? Or perhaps I am not here at all. Perhaps I am only a figment of imaginations as dim as your wits."

Growling, Mulk readied his ball and chain for a second swing. "For a small traveler with backward hands, you have a big mouth. We will close it for you."

Gesturing with his reversed left palm, Bijendra beckoned. "Then come and seek. Oblivion awaits. As a rakshasa noble I would rather not fight—but as a ranger, a melee is as good exercise as counting coin. I will defeat all three of you with only my one sword."

They came at him from two sides this time, intending to catch the haughty cat face between them. As one swung his club and the other his mace, the rakshasa spun. His sword was a blur. At the last possible instant, so was he. Descending mace connected with onrushing skull at the same time as swinging club met out-thrust face. Blood and jumbo dentition went flying as the weapons of the charging ogres connected not with the head of the stranger but with each other. Kot and Grerg went down in separate but equally bloody heaps. As the only one of the belligerent trio to retain consciousness, the last member standing clutched his ball and chain nervously. His small, glaring eyes sought danger in every shadow and corner.

"Some illusion again!" Outrage, as well as the first inklings of fear, filled the ogre's voice. "You said you would use only your sword!"

From behind him, a powerful feline shape stepped forward and gestured. A pale essence coalesced around Mulk, engulfing him in otherness. As a strand of it grew dense around his throat, the frightened ogre spun and swung wildly, striking at the smoke. As soon as he faced the ogre, Bijendra swung his enchanted sword around in a wide, powerful arc, striking—

With the flat of his blade. As it made contact with the side of the ogre's skull, Mulk let out a gurgle. His eyes rolled backward into his head and he collapsed into a pile of unconscious, motionless meat. Stepping forward, Bijendra stared down at the unmoving body.

"I lied. It's clear you don't know much of anything about my kind or you would be aware that we are known for deception in word as well as in image." Wiping clean the gore-streaked blade on the ogre's backside, he slid it neatly into the sheath slung against his back as he turned and strode toward the bar. Brave and confident dwarf that he was, Norgen was ready for him.

"Drink?" the dwarf mumbled, swallowing hard as he held out the sloshing goblet. "On the house."

Bijendra looked over his shoulder and said, "Three mighty ogres in a heap, who upon awakening will wish that they were dead. I could oblige them that, but I must not linger here. I have leagues to cross still, and they would be better traversed without having to always look behind me."

Norgen knew what the rakshasa was getting at, and said, "The ogres have other kinsfolk in Hammerfast. And there's always the outside chance that Goldspinner, the leader of the

Merchant Guild and the current High Master of the town, might take an official's interest in the brawl—though we dwarves tend to look first after our own."

"That being the case," Bijendra said, "I'll content myself that I have one friendly witness to the fight on my side. It would be easy enough to persuade the individual in question." The ranger reached in the direction of his longsword.

Sensible coward that he was, Norgen tried to bury himself in the lower reaches of the back bar. "Please, noble sir! I beg of you, mind twist me if you must, but spare my life! I am but a day removed from departing hence for the wedding of my second cousin's eldest sister, and if my body arrives without its head it will most surely put a damper on the nuptials!"

Stopping well short of his sword, Bijendra's hand dipped into a purse sequestered in his belt sash. He flung a couple of gold pieces onto the bar. "Calm yourself, good innkeeper. I seek your silence and possibly your witnessing, not your blood."

Peeping tentatively out from his hasty hiding place, Norgen eyed the stranger uncertainly. Then he spotted the glint of gold on the bar and emerged the rest of the way. The coins looked real enough. So did the stranger's grin, though it revealed all too many teeth for the dwarf's liking.

"Silence you shall have, noble rakshasa." He quickly scooped the coins off the scarred and gouged wood. "Are you truly a ranger?"

His long thick tail switching sharply back and forth, the visitor with the face and body of a backward-handed snow leopard and the bearing of a knight paused at the entrance to the inn.

"I go where I will, unconstrained by house, family, or friend. I journey freely and without encumbrance. No obligation lies upon my head as I travel to the Gray Downs."

Norgen emerged further from behind the bar. "The Gray Downs! You'll find nothing there but bare rock and cold memories. Why would a nobleman such as yourself seek such a place when temptation and good comfort lie the same distance away to the south in Fallcrest?"

"You may have heard me say that I seek a legend, told to me since youth of a place in the Gray Downs. It is called the Sword Barrow, and I would seek it out to learn the truth of the story. For I am on a journey on behalf of another more so than for myself."

"Sword Barrow." Norgen shook his head sadly as he regarded the stranger. "You have come a long way in search of a trash heap. Nothing lies there but rusting blades of ancient design."

"Then I will return home satisfied in self and content in mind that I have done my best to learn that truth. Your concern is touching, innkeeper."

"As is your gold." One thick-fingered fist clutched the two coins the stranger had given him. "Journey well, then, noble cat-face. Journey safe. And beware the ancient warding magic they say lingers about that place like an outhouse stink."

"I will be careful." Bijendra indicated the unconscious ogres. "Will you be able to manage this lot? When they wake up, they will be discontented."

Norgen smiled through his beard as he turned to take a sip from the untouched goblet. No sense in wasting good ale. "I have excellent clean-up people. Do not worry yourself on that score, stranger. Stranger?"

But in an elegant swirl of silks and scent, money and musk, the rakshasa ranger had disappeared.

On the southern edge of the Winterbole Forest, the Gray Downs formed an unhappy bulge between the Nentir and

Winter Rivers. All soil fled, little but tough grass and determined bracken grew on the otherwise bare stone. Diced and broken by the contortions of a disturbed geology, the Downs promised a visitor rough walking and the likely prospect of a turned ankle.

Hailing from higher mountains, Bijendra was not intimidated by the crushed terrain. Picking his way westward, he soon found himself in the depths of the Downs themselves. Around him there was no sign of higher life, no calling of boars or bugling of deer—far less that of civilized conversation. Even the rats and mice, of whose presence there was ample evidence, were reluctant to show themselves in that place.

The Downs presented a prospect that was bleak enough during the day. Night was worse. The nearly treeless, rolling landscape lay barren and silent beneath a full moon, as if the spirit of life itself lay chained and jailed beneath the rocks. He had timed his traveling to be there on just such a night, because the legend told that it was then that She might appear.

It was when he entered the Sword Barrow that his hitherto austere surrounds for the first time took on a quietly threatening tone. Without having to search, his footsteps turned up first one half-buried blade, then another, and still another. Of ancient design and still retaining hints of superb workmanship, they lay scattered wherever he looked. Blades broken and whole poked out of the turned ground from among pockets of gravel or between split stones. At first they appeared to have nothing in common. On closer inspection, he saw that regardless of size or shape, design or composition, all pointed toward the center of the barrow.

That made it easier for him to find it.

So did the dozen or so rotting, disarticulating skeletons of those who had come before him.

Choosing a level platform among the rocks, he drew Furcleave. Holding it vertically before him with its point aimed straight at the ground, he murmured a soft incantation. Though the handle twisted violently in his clenched hands, he held it firmly. On the hilt, the two cat-faces ceased arguing. After a pause of consideration, they realigned themselves so that both were facing in the same direction.

Opening his eyes, Bijendra started in the direction they were staring and searched carefully until he found what he was looking for. By the light of the full moon it was easy enough to locate: a slot between two slabs of stone where he could carefully insert the blade, point first. Once that was done, he stepped back, stretched out both hands, and backward clawed the night air as he recited the words he had been told to say.

"I, Ruhan Bijendra, call upon the savants of the swords in the name of my brother Layak Bijendra, gravely wounded in battle at Giriraj Keep! Remove the sliver of metal that lies deep in his side and that the chirurgeons cannot touch for fear of cutting his heart. The metal splinter has been thrice bellicose-blessed, and if it kills him, he will not be able to reincarnate. Do this and I will promise my own blood for the quenching of a sacred blade to be dedicated to the brotherhood of swords everywhere!" Dropping to his knees, he brought his knuckles together. One tear escaped the corner of a reluctant eye to moisten the fur of his left cheek.

When he opened his eyes again, something was stirring.

Under the light of the moon, the ancient, buried weapons that encircled the barrow were in motion. Twitching, jerking, heaving, one by one they pulled or yanked or drew themselves from the stones and gravel in which they were entombed. Each imbued with a pale blue glow, they rose softly and silently into the air. While the awed yet alert noble looked on, they sloughed off the rust of ages like so many snakes shedding their skins. As he rose to his feet, the circle they formed began to close in around him. Before his eyes, Furcleave was likewise glowing. It had partaken unbidden of the magic of the place.

Then She appeared.

The Steel Princess. Mistress of the Old Blades. Her legs were longswords melded together, her face all angles and sharpness. Spikes protruded from the helmeted metal hills of breasts and her fingers were tapered stilettos. In place of wrists and ankles were sword hilts. As she came toward him, her intricately arabesqued metal limbs made faint scraping sounds, and the moonlight made of her a walking armory. Light glinted off her polished body from the swords and sabers, daggers and dirks of which she was composed. The long, silvery hair that fell swaying to her waist was fashioned of hundreds of strangler's cables.

Truly, Bijendra thought as he stayed close to Furcleave but made no attempt to draw it forth from the rocks, a hard-edged woman.

She halted barely an arm's length away. Around them the storm of swords circled closer, their intense blue phosphorescence brighter than before. Her right hand rose and the index finger extended toward him. As sharp as a poet's tongue, the tip was aimed directly at his heart. When she spoke, the moonlight shining from her eyes like a blacksmith's fever dream, even her words were cutting.

"Whoever comes to this place with hope or supplication leaves fallow. Whoever comes on the night of the full moon when I assemble myself and perform my rounds, must die. So say I, Jiriyel, Wardress of the Weapons."

Back ramrod straight, Bijendra met her metallic gaze without flinching. "Beautiful dreamer, I come on behalf of my brother, who is already dying. You who command the ancient blades, who know their ways and moods, could draw the broken metal from his body as a chirurgeon would draw a poison. You can save his life." For the second time that night he spread his arms wide, the fingers of the backward-facing palms opening outward as he lowered his head. "I offer mine in exchange. Pierce me as you will. Cut me quick or slow, as is your pleasure. But do that which is necessary to spare him." He lowered his head and waited for whatever might come.

Faultless metal in the moonlight, the lethal finger moved forward—to stop a thumb's length from the noble's chest.

"You could fight me, Ruhan Bijendra." From her throat sounded a grinding as of gears. "Your longsword is near. Yet you forgo your own weapon."

He raised his eyes to meet hers anew. "I would not insult the Steel Princess by presuming to assault her with one of her own. I come to you as a supplicant, not as a challenger."

"Even if it is to mean your life?" she queried him.

"Even if so," he replied, resigned.

Around them, the halo of drifting swords—short and long, single-edged and double, slim and broad—rotated like a pulsing blue ring around a distant planet. The deep turquoise light that shone forth from them was bright enough to outshine the moon. Occasionally one blade would make contact with another. At such moments a swift *zinging* sound would sting the otherwise silent night air. It reminded Bijendra of the sound of blades being drawn from metal scabbards.

The swords were whispering among themselves.

Her index finger continued to hover a hand's breadth from his heart, but the fatal thrust continued to be withheld.

"You are unlike any of the many who have come this way and dared to confront me. You are without fear, yet you are

prepared to spend your courage and life on behalf of another."
Fluttering steel eyelids made the faintest of cymbal sounds.
"Were I not cursed to forever serve as wardress to these blades,
I would do for you what I might wish. But I am as you see me,
and can do naught but continue to fulfill my sorrowful destiny."

His tone turned curious. "What were you before you were
cursed, woman of sharp edges?"

"I was once a princess of the eladrin. Unknowing, I gravely
offended the greatest witch of the hill folk who lived in these
Downs. As you know, eladrin do not sleep but must enter
trance for several hours each day. Catching me helpless in
such a state, she cursed me to watch over the orphaned swords
of this place until I should rust away to nothing, as will they
all eventually. She made me of them, and so I am as you see
me." The finger pointed at his chest trembled. "Nothing can
break this curse or return me to flesh. And as Wardress of the
Weapons, when I make my rounds beneath the light of the
full moon, I am compelled to slay any who trespass here."

He could have run, but Bijendra did not flee. Not even from
death. He held his ground. "I am rakshasa. You are eladrin.
As rakshasa I can do nothing for you. As eladrin you can do
nothing for yourself. But I have traveled wide and spoken to
many outstandingly knowledgeable representatives of many
races. More important than talking, I have listened. Among
the humans there is one thing, one gesture, one magic that can
sometimes break the strongest curse. It is uncommon—nay,
largely unknown—among my kind. But I have learned it."

She was beyond doubtful. Her tone was spiteful. "There is
no spell that can release me. Symbols do not touch my feet.
Potions make me rust. You are wasting your time, rakshasa."

Black-blotched white ears flicked in the moonlight. "Then
if I am to die anyway . . ."

Thrusting himself forward, he planted his mouth directly over hers. Eyes like polished silver pieces widened. Her left arm was flung backward while the right continued to hover in the vicinity of his heart. Sharpened small steel shutters closed halfway over her eyes. He held the kiss as long as he could before the pain made him draw back. Blood trickled from his mouth to stain the white fur of his chin. He had cut himself on her scalpel of a tongue.

She stared at him, for the first time wordless, her right hand still extended in his direction. Around them, the risen sword blades whirled so fast that the two figures appeared to be encircled by a solid ring of blue luminance. The princess staggered backward another step, recovered her balance, and started toward him anew. Then she looked down at herself.

Dull steel gray was fading to a pale pinkish white. Edges formerly cutting softened and flowed. From the tips of her fingers, life surged backward to replace steel. Her ears remained pointed but were no longer deadly sharp. From metal eyes, a bright, pupilless eladrin green spread forth as though they had been stained with the dye of life.

Around them, the singing of the sword circle had risen to an overpowering metallic hum.

She stood before him, unclothed but no longer shining, her pale flesh glistening rather than reflective in the moonlight. Shining—and shivering. Removing his gleaming argent cape, he placed it around her shoulders. She drew the fine soft fabric close around her, not to hide her nakedness but to ward off the chill.

"You—you broke the curse." Standing as tall as him, she did not have to look up to meet his gaze. "So many years . . . it is not possible!" While one hand held the cape snug around her, the fingers of the other touched here and there, as if to confirm that she was once again a woman of flesh and blood and not of cold, unfeeling steel.

"Among the humans, many strange things are possible." Bijendra stood looking back at her. "I do not seek out their company, but neither do I forswear it." Moving to his left, he drew Furcleave from where he had placed it in the crack in the rocks. All but powerless and still in shock, she stared at him uncertainly.

"I am no longer Mistress of Steel, Wardress of the Sword Barrow. At the very last instant, before the beginning of the changing, I whispered a word to the weapons. The message was carried instantly. Whether it arrived at your keep whole and in time to do any good I do not know." She dropped her head. "I tried. I owe you everything, but I can do no more. Kill me if you will."

"You did not kill me. Why would I kill you? Come with me to my home and we will see together if you have saved him. I would never slay one who tried. If he lives, he will want to thank you himself. Afterward, if you wish, I will escort you safely to a feyhold, where you may dwell in happiness for what remains of your natural life. Without fear of rust."

Her eyes fluttered again—noiselessly, this time. "I owe you my true life, Ruhan Bijendra."

"And I owe you the life of my brother—I hope. Come, Princess. It is dark, it is cold, and I am hungry from this night's work."

A furry, muscular arm went around her shoulders, drawing her forward. With the other he held Furcleave stiffly out before him. As they approached the fading but still glowing circle of floating swords, the ring parted to let them pass. As soon as Jiriyel had stepped through, the blue lambency vanished. Inanimate metal once again, the ancient blades fell to the ground. The single loud, unified clanging of their fall resounded across the Downs—a vast metal sigh. Together, the two figures strode with lengthening steps in the direction of distant Hammerfast. Eyes half shut, the eladrin Jiriyel leaned close against the protective bulk of Ruhan Bijendra.

"You know," she whispered softly, "I had a kitten once . . ."

Alan Dean Foster is the *New York Times* best-selling, award-winning author of more than 110 books. Having spent time in more than a hundred countries, he is most comfortable when writing about strange places, climes, and characters.

TALLFOLK TALES
A Tale of the FORGOTTEN REALMS

LISA SMEDMAN

So it's a guide you're wanting, is it? Well, if it's Araumycos you're going to, that guide won't be me. Regardless of the rumors you may have heard around town, I've had my fill of that place. Why, even the smell of mushroom wine—

Now hold on, elf. Don't be so hasty to leave. I didn't say there wasn't a guide to be had. You've come to the right person. I know someone who's as familiar with the twists and turns of Araumycos as that barkeep over there is with this tavern. And best of all, she won't cost you a sack of coin, the way someone from the guides' guild will—assuming they'd even take you there. No, she won't charge a thing. And reliable? Well, listen to my tale and you'll see that Rook is the person you want one pace ahead of you, if you're venturing into Araumycos. And I'm the one who can tell you how to find her.

Fetch me some ale and sit down here at my table, and I'll tell you my tale. But none of that spitfroth the humans try to pass off as lager, mind. Nor any of that honeyed cider you elves seem to love so much. Make it dwarven Samman ale, bitter and brown.

Ah. That's the stuff. A meal in a glass, as they say.

You'll be wondering at my taste in drink and my thick red beard. I've seen you note the silver hammers braided into it and my iron bracers. The star on them, just above the wrist, is part of my clan name. It's Morndin you're talking to, son of . . . well, son of Moradin, you might say. It was the Dwarffather who forged my soul anew, after whoever I was in my last lifetime died. He took my dwarf soul and cast it in a human mold, this time. Although if you ask me, it's likely Vergadain had a hand in it too. They don't call him the trickster god for nothing.

So here I am in this lifetime, a human. That's why my shield brothers call me Morndin. Compared to them, I'm high as a mountain.

Now don't raise that eyebrow. Just because it's odd doesn't mean it isn't so. The Dwarffather must have decided there's something I had to learn in this lifetime, something I could only discover in this body. Or perhaps there was some deed he wanted done. Something it would take this towering, narrow-chested human body to accomplish.

I see that smile you're trying to hide. I know what you'll be asking next: how is it I came to believe such foolishness. You'll be wondering if someone cast a befuddlement spell on me, or some such. The short answer is no. The long answer has to do with that footman's mace leaning against the wall beside me here.

My parents—also human—had a provisions store in Hammergate, down by the Rift. They often took items in trade. I'm told that, a year or two before I was born, a creaky old longbeard said his adventuring days were behind him, and asked my father if he'd like to buy this mace. It's pretty battered looking, isn't it, with that slight bend in the handle and one of the flanges missing from the head? My father thought so, too. He didn't want to take it in trade, but the longbeard said coin would comfort him in his final years more than any weapon would. And so my father bought the mace, tucked it away in the storeroom, and forgot all about it.

Turns out it was a magical weapon forged by the Ironstar clan—light as a feather, and capable of dealing a blow that calls down Moradin's thunder, if you know the right word to say. But I'm getting ahead of myself.

Years later, when I was seven, a half-orc tried to rob the store. He held my mother at knife-point and demanded all the coin in the lockbox. I was in the storeroom, and heard the commotion out front. The mace was the closest weapon to hand. I rushed into the shop, swinging it like a *kuldjargh*— that's Dwarvish, by the way, for "beserker." They say I wielded the weapon like I was born with it in my hand. And here's the part that will lift that other eyebrow of yours. As the mace cracked against that half-orc's head, I shouted a word that filled the room with magical, booming thunder. The crack of it split his head wide open.

Once I recovered from the surprise, I wondered how I'd done it. I knew a little Dwarvish; I'd grown on the Rift's edge, in a shop that catered to dwarves, after all. Both of my human parents spoke Dwarvish, if a bit brokenly, and could read a little. But there was no explaining how I knew what word to shout that day. It wasn't a word you'd expect, like *corl* or *raugh* or *rorn*. It—

Yes, yes, I'll tell you about the guide in a moment. It's just that you need to know this piece of it, so you'll understand all that follows.

Could I have another Samman? My ale cup's gone dry.

Ah. That's better.

You're obviously an elf of the surface realms, judging by that longbow you carry. That won't be much use to you, down here in the Underchasm. And that leafmottle cloak won't be much use either. Not here in Gracklstugh, where the buildings are as gray and gloomy as the duergar who built them. Nor will it aid you within the musky embrace of Araumycos. Most of the fungus is gray-white, dotted with orange puffballs. That's what you have to watch out for, by the way. Blunder into one of those, and you'll die a slow, choking death with spores that clog your nostrils and fruit deep in your lungs. Even a little whiff of it's enough to scar the lungs for life. And a man whose body is erupting from the inside out with puffballs is a shuddersome sight, I'll tell you.

But Rook will steer you clear of those.

You obviously have some passing familiarity with the Underchasm, to have made it this far down. And I see by that shield ring on your finger that you know a little about Araumycos's strange pull. The closer you get to Araumycos, the more vivid those nightmares become. Even with magical protection, they root in your mind by night and fill it with strange whispers by day, telling you to join with . . . something. Whatever's at the heart of the thing. Some say it's a patch of the fungus that's afire with spellplague and needs live fuel to stoke it. I couldn't say if that's true, myself. I just know you have to beware of the *golhyrrl'fhaazht*.

I see that frown. You're wondering why I speak Drow. Short answer is, I don't. They're a race that's evil through and through—cruel and depraved—but that word they coined is the best fit I know.

"Dream trap." That's Araumycos, all right.

Given their fear of it, the drow normally avoid Araumycos like the spellplague. That's why we never expected to—

Yes, yes, I'm getting to the part where I tell you about Rook. But first I have to set the stage.

I won't ask why you want to venture into Araumycos. Your reasons are your own affair. The reason we went in, my shield brothers and I, is best told by what's in this pocket, here.

You ever seen one of these? It's a rock gourd—a tiny one, no bigger than a walnut. They're usually much bigger, at least the size of your head. Shake 'em like this . . . and there you go. See the water dripping from the stone? That's what makes a rock gourd so valuable. Get lost in the Labyrinth, or trapped by a cave-in—or, I suppose, get lost in one of those deserts you have up there on the surface—and you'll at least have all the water you need until you find your way out again.

'Course, this one's too little to be worth much. Takes half a day to fill a thimble. But you get the idea.

Sad thing is, it's the only one I was able to bring back with me.

Rock gourds are the reason we ventured into Araumycos. A patch of Araumycos had died off, and Gamlin and Farrik—two dwarves I once counted as shield brothers—figured they'd make their fortune before it grew back again.

Gamlin was the one who knew there'd be rock gourds there. He can sense things like that. He's spellscarred, you see. Blundered into a patch of spellplague a few years back, and came out with feet that crackle with blue fire. Turned out to be a blessing in disguise. That spellscar roots him to the earth—roots him deep. Most of the time it just lets him stand firm on stone—long as he's barefoot—and not be pushed around. But stone whispers to stone, as they say, revealing secrets buried deep.

Anyhow, Gamlin talked his brother Farrik into venturing into Araumycos. Told him they could carry out their own weight in rock gourds several times over and be set for life. Which is where I came into the scheme.

After I came north, looking for my clan, I apprenticed as a stonemason. Swinging a mallet all day's what gave me these arms. I was still living on the surface, in those days—still saving up for these darkvision goggles. One day, as I watched two earthmotes grind together, casting off a drift of splinters that thudded to the ground in their wake, I found myself wondering why the broken-off pieces lost their magic and fell, rather than staying aloft. I wondered if there might be some way to restore their magic.

I thought of an earth node I'd heard about—one that, if you enter it, creates an invisible, floating disk that follows you around. Handy, if you've got a heavy load you need to move. Trouble was, the magical energy fizzles out after about a day, so the node isn't much use unless you live close by.

I knew the node didn't make regular stones float, but I got to wondering what would happen if I took a broken-off chunk of earthmote and carried it into that node. It worked—beautifully. The chip of earthmote began to float as soon as I entered the node—and kept on floating for more than a month! It's probably bobbing around somewhere near the quarry, to this day.

The next step was to find an earthmote of flint or obsidian or chert—stone that would knap into nice, thin sheets. I needed the quarrymaster's help with that one. Once we located one that was just right, I knapped off a big piece and rounded the edges, then carried it to the node. It floated on its own, just like one of those driftdiscs the drow are so fond of. But better, because I didn't need magic to control it. Just a simple nudge of the—

That's right. You're talking to the man who invented the motedisc. Ryordin Hammerfist is the man who took credit for it—even though all he did was help me locate an earthmote of the right type and provide the labor to mine it. Hammerfist claimed the motedisc was all his idea, but it was actually me who dreamed it up, back when I was his apprentice. And did he give me anything for it? Hah! If he did, don't you think I'd be the one buying the drinks?

Anyway, motediscs. One day, Gamlin and Farrik came to one of my master's floating quarries. Not to buy—Farrik always keeps his coin pouch tightly tied, and Gamlin's purse is seldom full for long—but to offer Ryordin a deal. Said they'd cut him in on a third of the profits if he'd fund their prospecting.

Ryordin turned them down stone cold. Actually laughed at them when they told him they were from the Ironstar clan. Said he supposed they were ghosts, then, since the last of the Ironstars had vanished centuries ago.

Ironstars. The same clan that made my mace.

Their meeting with Ryordin had been behind closed doors—protective of their future claim, Farrik and Gamlin were. I blundered into the room just long enough to hear them name their clan, and hear them ask for motediscs.

An elf like you might scoff, but I saw the hand of Moradin in it. Farrik, Gamlin, and I were fated to meet. And when I offered to slide a few motediscs their way if they told me more about my clan, they jumped at the chance.

There's that eyebrow again. Of course you would think they were lying about being Ironstars, taking advantage of me. People often take me for a fool when I tell them my life story, but I know when someone's tugging my beard. And they weren't lying—not really. All dwarf are clan, when you go far enough back past the time of Bhaerynden.

What's more important to my tale is this: I demanded a one-third share in the venture, in return for me "borrowing" as many motediscs from the quarry as I could spirit away. And I insisted on going along.

Yes, yes, I'm getting to the part where I tell you about Rook. Almost there, in fact. In the meantime, could I trouble you for just one more ale? Tale-telling's such thirsty work.

Much obliged.

We went down into the Underchasm—Gamlin, Farrik, and I—and made our way to the spot where Araumycos had died back. We found a shaft that had, just days before, been filled to the rim with fungus. That shaft was deep, I'll tell you, and of natural-worn stone—likely carved by a thundering waterfall long ago. A trickle of water still fell, starting from a point in mid air, just above the place where the shaft met the tunnel we'd followed in. Obviously a portal to the plane of water that had been shrinking for millennia. A portal that had all but closed by the time we found it.

As I was staring up at the spot the water fell from, I saw a flash of something black. I figured it was just one of the bats we'd stirred up earlier, on our way in. Only later did I realize it had been Rook.

What remained of Araumycos was a soggy mess at the bottom of the shaft. Foul-smelling muck. We slip-shuffled through it for the better part of a day, collecting the rock gourds Gamlin ferreted out with his spellscar.

Before I say what happened next, there's a thing or two you should know about Farrik and Gamlin. They're twins—that's been commonplace, among the dwarves, since the time of the Thunder Blessing. But although Moradin cast them in the same mold, they're different as the surface is from the Underchasm.

Both of them are black bearded and heavy browed. And both are fiercely proud of our race. But Farrik's not the cleanest, to put it politely. You don't want to stand downwind of him. He's always covered in dust, even when he's not prospecting, and his beard's always a terrible tangle. He says he's just too busy to tend to it. That a man who works hard should look like he works hard—dirt under the nails, and sweat stains. But you'd think he could at least take a bath, now and again.

Gamlin's the clean one. He was the one taught me to braid my beard like this—and to develop a taste for the finer, oak-barrel ales. Gamlin's coin pouch is pretty flat, most days, because when he has coin, he spends it. Doesn't matter if you're clan or not—if you're someone he's taken a liking to, Gamlin's always ready to fill your cup.

He didn't like me much at first. Nor did Farrik. I could see that. But the motediscs I got for them fixed that, soon enough.

So there we were at the bottom of the shaft, sliding around in ankle-deep rotting fungus, our noses filled with the stench, but grinning away because each stubbed toe was another prize in what turned out to be the motherlode of rock gourds. I'd been able to spirit out six motediscs from the quarry and each was heaped high with rock gourds.

The twins insisted we collect every last rock gourd, until the motediscs were sagging under the weight. I thought that was foolish, that it would slow us down—but they were the prospectors and I was the lowly apprentice, so I did as I was told.

Farrik was tying the last of the nets in place to hold the rocks down, and Gamlin was off in a fissure in the wall, relieving himself of some of the ale he'd drunk along the march. I was bending down to pick up the rock gourd I just showed you. After I got my share, I'd hang on to it as a keepsake, I figured, of our expedition.

I was tucking it into my pocket when a crossbow bolt whistled past my ear.

My first thought, I'm ashamed to say, was that the twins had betrayed me. Then I heard Farrik cry out in alarm and clasp his arm. He'd been hit by a bolt shot from above. Even though it was a shallow wound, little more than a graze, the poison took him in a matter of heartbeats. He twisted, sagged, and splashed flat on his back in the muck.

I glanced up and saw a lone drow, levitating perhaps a dozen paces overhead. She shifted her wristbow, aiming at me. I dived under an overhang and heard the bolt splinter against it. I fumbled for my mace, praying to Moradin that I'd live long enough to use it.

Then the light pellet went off.

I'd been hoping Gamlin might surprise the drow from behind when she landed, take her down. She hadn't seen him yet, after all. But when the light pellet exploded with such brilliance, I knew it was all over. Gamlin would be completely light-dazzled. Blind as a bat.

An apt comparison, as it turned out.

The overhang of rock blocked the drow's aim; she couldn't hit me without descending right to the floor. That would bring her within mace range, but trouble was, I still couldn't see. My goggles were crackling with dazzle from the light pellet, and taking them off would leave me completely unable to see in the utter blackness. A dwarf I might be, but my eyes are still human, more's the pity.

I wasn't about to give up without a fight, however. As soon as I heard her squelch down into the muck, I leaped out of my hiding place. I swung my mace blindly in the direction the sound had come from.

I missed.

Her wristbow bolt took me in the thigh.

I staggered, my leg awash in pain. I crashed into the wall and my goggles were knocked off kilter. As my human vision returned, I spotted the faint blue glow of Gamlin's spellscar; it crackled around his feet, which were buried in muck. He stood at the far side of the shaft, behind the drow, his eyes wide and staring. Streaks of blue fire raced across the floor as I watched, questing out the spot where the drow stood. Its light briefly silhouetted a large round object on the floor—a rock gourd we'd somehow overlooked. But that didn't matter just then.

The drow spotted the streaks of blue fire just as Gamlin drew back his hand, preparing to throw a dagger. She whirled and shot a bolt. It plunged into Gamlin's chest. His chainmail vest stopped it, but the point penetrated the links of chain just enough to let the poison enter his blood. He wavered, blinked—then fell and didn't get up again.

His blue fire lasted a heartbeat more. Even with my weak human vision, the dim flicker was enough to show me where the drow was. I hurled my mace and shouted. Thunder filled the shaft as it connected with the drow's head.

She died instantly, her skull shattering like lightning-struck stone.

I felt myself sagging. I managed to twist around just enough that I wouldn't land face-down in the muck. That was no way for a dwarf to die, I thought. Then everything went black.

Rook? Yes, yes. Be patient. Her part in this saga comes next. Truly. But just one more ale . . .? Certainly this tale's worth that? Thanks.

So there I was, dead of drow poison. Or so you'd expect. But it wasn't a lethal potion the drow had coated her bolts with—just one that places its victims in a deep slumber. She was after slaves, not corpses.

I woke up with a jolt, screaming at the agony of Gamlin binding my wound. The bolt had passed completely through the muscle of my thigh, he told me. I'd lost blood, but not enough to kill me.

As he worked on my leg, Gamlin gave me the bad news. While we'd lain unconscious, Araumycos had started to grow back. Already the upper portion of the shaft was thick with new growth that was starting to weave itself together up near the top. If we were going to escape, we had to hurry. Even with the magical rings that were shielding our minds—purchased at great expense, and with great complaint from Farrik—I could feel the tickle of Araumycos trying to take root in my thoughts.

Farrik, meanwhile, was beside himself. As Gamlin tended me, Farrik sloshed back and forth through the muck, shouting that I was in league with the drow, that I'd deliberately led him and his brother into a trap so I could claim all the rock gourds. I shouted back as best I was able, in my weakened state. If that had been true, I pointed out, I'd have helped her finish off the two of them, not taken a wound that came near to crippling me.

He shot back that I was a stupid human who'd underestimated my accomplice. That drow always turn on their allies, and can never be trusted. I shouted back that I was a dwarf. And so on.

It was Gamlin who told the two of us to shut up, that we were wasting valuable time. I glanced at where he was pointing. Above us, some of the strands of fungus had grown as thick as my arm. One had sprouted a puffball. As Farrik also turned his glance upward, it darkened from white to orange and then burst, releasing a tiny puff of spores. Each of us held his breath as long as we could, but eventually we were forced to gasp for air. The spores were spread pretty thin by the time they reached us. Even so, that gasp of breath had an aftertaste like blue cheese. Some of them rooted. I can feel the scars from them still, every time I draw too deep a breath, despite the healing draughts we drank. If I ever were to venture back into Araumycos, I'd wheeze like an old man. Like I was telling you when I first began this tale, even the smell of a mushroom—

All right, all right. Don't be so impatient. Let me finish.

So there we were at the bottom of the shaft, with the fungus growing back fast. There was still a gap in the growth overhead, but it would be a tight squeeze at the top. Worst of all, we'd have to leave the motediscs behind. We had a fortune right in front of us, neatly piled up—and no way to get it home.

I couldn't believe my eyes—my future lay at the bottom of a fungus-encrusted shaft. I couldn't return to my apprenticeship at the quarry—not without returning the missing motediscs. That wouldn't have mattered quite so much if I'd struck it rich, of course. I would have paid for them—double their value. But now I'd be branded a thief.

It was enough to make even the stoutest dwarf weep.

While Farrik complained and I tried to shout sense into him, Gamlin searched the drow's body, trying to figure out which of her trinkets had allowed her to levitate. He found one of those medallions the drow are so fond of, but couldn't make it work. Little wonder; even if he had been able to speak the language, he didn't know the command word. Meanwhile, Araumycos continued to grow. By the time Farrik sputtered to a stop, the opening at the top of the shaft was even narrower. We'd have to hack our way out.

There was one consolation, I told the twins. They could each carry a couple of rock gourds out if they emptied their packs. Enough to cover the cost of the mind-shielding rings and healing draughts Farrik had purchased for our expedition, plus a little profit for each of us on the side. Enough to keep us fed and in ale for a month or two, while we figured out what to do next.

Farrik asked what I'd be carrying. I pointed out I'd have a tough enough climb without a heavy pack on my back. My injured leg was going to give me trouble. In fact, it was already stiffening up. If they wanted to reduce my share as a result, I told them, that was just fine with me.

Farrik looked ready to agree, but Gamlin shook his head and said we'd better hurry, or none of us would get out of there with anything.

The brothers set to work, emptying their packs and filling them with rock gourds. Meanwhile, I felt around for the rock gourd I'd spotted by the light of Gamlin's blue fire—the one we'd missed. Might as well add it to the pile, I figured. One day, if we were lucky, Araumycos might die back again. Then we could come back and collect our reward.

My hand brushed something solid. I felt holes in its smooth, rounded surface. It was lighter than it should have been, I thought, as I pulled it from the muck. It felt thin and hollow. A moment later, I saw why. It wasn't a rock gourd I'd found, but a skull. Slimy fungus dribbled out of the eye sockets and down my arm. The jawbone hung by a thread.

I nearly dropped the skull in disgust. Then I looked a little closer. The skull had a thick forehead, broad cheekbones, and a squarish look.

He—or she—had been a dwarf. Whoever it was had died some time ago, for there wasn't a scrap of flesh or beard clinging to the bone.

If we didn't get moving, we'd wind up just like him.

I placed the skull on top of one of the piles of gourds while Gamlin and Farrik were busy tying their packs shut.

They glanced at it, but didn't say anything. They were too busy grunting under the load in their packs. I wondered how they'd be able to climb.

They managed it somehow, sweating under the strain. I had a harder time of it. Even without a pack, I spent my climb gritting my teeth at the pain of my wounded leg and trying not to faint.

At the top, we had to cut our way through. Having no pack to impede me, I clambered over the edge first, squeezing through what opening there was. Behind me, Gamlin and Farrik struggled, their bulging packs caught on the lattice of fungus. I looked down the corridor that led out—and saw that it was completely plugged. We were trapped!

I was starting to shout this to Gamlin and Farrik when something strange happened. The fungus that plugged the corridor quivered, then suddenly died back, leaving a gap.

Out of it stepped a drow. Black-skinned, gaunt-faced, she stared down at me with all the solemnity of a Deep Lord about to make a judgment.

I struggled to my feet, convinced for the second time that day that I was about to die. My mace was on my belt; I'd needed both hands for the climb. There was no way I'd undo the lashings in time.

Instead of attacking, however, she beckoned me forward. So startling was it, I took a step back, nearly going over the edge.

Behind me, I could hear Gamlin and Farrik sawing their way through the fungus. Getting out with their backpacks on was more important, it seemed, than hastening to my aid. Or maybe they hadn't spotted the drow yet.

I noticed that she carried no weapons, wore no armor. And she'd still made no move to harm me. Nor did she look exactly as a drow should. Drow women are tall, but this one somehow seemed stretched thin, oddly jointed. Her white hair stood out from her head like old straw, but her hands disturbed me most. They were all wrong: only three fingers, the outer two more like hooks, the middle one straight, and all tipped with claws.

I suddenly realized what she must be. Not a drow at all. A soul, taken at the moment of death, kept warm for days or years or centuries in Bane's chill embrace, and spawned in a new form that was wholly unlike whatever body it had inhabited before.

She nodded, as if she'd heard my thoughts. "Will you help me, Daffyd? Lay at least part of me to rest?"

I asked how she knew my name. It was one I'd left behind when I departed the Rift. Even Gamlin and Farrik didn't know it.

She touched her chest with a claw. "Ironstar," she whispered. Then she pointed at me. "Ironstar."

I shivered as I realized we must have been fated to meet. Just like me, she'd been . . . reforged. But not by Moradin. Instead she'd been cast in the form of a race any dwarf would attack on sight.

Bane had played an even crueler joke on her than Vergadain had on me.

"Will you help me?" she repeated.

I wet my lips. Helping her would mean climbing back down that shaft. If it had been Gamlin's or Farrik's body lying at the bottom of it, I wouldn't have given it a moment's thought. But she was a stranger to me.

I stared at the revenant, wondering what kind of person she'd been as a dwarf. Had there been kin who'd mourned her, or had she been a clanless outlaw? An honest person or a rogue? Then I realized that I might as well ask the same questions of myself.

Whatever she'd been, it didn't matter. Dwarves take care of their own.

"You deserve better," I said. "I'll see that you get it. By Moradin's beard, I swear I'll see your skull laid properly to rest."

Her mouth stretched to a thin smile. She turned and pressed on a section of the wall. A hidden door swung open. Behind it was a staircase, leading up. The air that rushed from it smelled sweet. It was obviously a way back to the surface. One we'd missed on our way in.

I asked if she was going to lead us out.

She shook her head. "Not until the rest of my bones are recovered can I rest," she told me. "The orcs scattered them far and wide when Delzoun fell—a final insult to my people. But one day I will find them."

"Delzoun!" I repeated, incredulous. "But that was . . . How long have you been searching?"

"Too long," she said wearily. "And yet, not long enough. The dwarf body has so many bones . . ." Her words trailed off in a sigh.

Behind me, I heard a shout of triumph. I turned and saw that Gamlin and Farrik had hacked their way through. If they saw me talking to a "drow," Farrik's suspicions would be rekindled. But I had to know one thing more. "Who—"

Rook was gone. Already, the hole she'd parted in the fungus was closing.

Gamlin and Farrik struggled up over the edge with their packs and shouted in dismay when they saw the corridor blocked. I showed them the staircase up, and told them it was our way out. They were so relieved they didn't even ask how I knew. Then I told them what I needed to do: recover the skull, take it to a priest, and give it the last rites.

They thought I was joking. Gamlin actually guffawed. Then they realized I was serious.

Gamlin said there wasn't time. Farrik said the dead dwarf was no clan of his. When I said the skull had belonged to an Ironstar and that it was our duty, he slid a look at Gamlin. Both rolled their eyes.

They turned toward the staircase, as if there was nothing more to say.

Fine, I told them. They could go on ahead, but I was going back for the skull. I'd catch up to them later, and collect my share then.

I see by your look you can guess what came next. I never did see either of them again. Not during that long, painful climb back up the stairs to the surface, nor back at the town we'd set out from. I waited there for tendays, but they never came.

Maybe someday, I'll see them again, but if I don't, it doesn't really matter. That's what Moradin's trying to teach me in this life, you see—to choose my shield brothers more carefully. Or something like that.

Well now. Would you look at that? My glass is dry again. Could you . . .?

No?

That's all right. My tale is done.

I know what you're thinking. You'll be wondering, about now, why I would tell you all about a fortune in rock gourds that's just lying there for the taking. Short answer: it doesn't matter anymore. Gamlin and Farrik will likely try to go back to recover them—assuming they haven't tried already, which might explain what happened to them. Without Rook's help it will be impossible. With each step I took up those stairs toward the surface, Araumycos followed. By the time I reached the top, the staircase was plugged solid. Anyone who finds it now will set off puffballs every step of the way.

A revenant isn't bothered by any of that, of course. And

Rook, of course, has some way of making Araumycos die back. Wherever it has, that's where you'll find her. If you promise to bring whichever of her bones are there to a dwarf priest, and see that they're given the last rites—or maybe it's whichever of *his* bones; I never did get the chance to ask—Rook will likely guide you to wherever it is you need to go.

All I ask is that, if you do find Rook, you put in a good word for me. Tell her I laid her skull to rest, and had a priest say the proper words over the pyre. Ask her, on my behalf, if she'd mind fetching me a rock gourd or two from that cache, in return for me sending her way someone else who'll help.

What's that? The name Rook? Oh, it's just a name I gave her. Those curved, black fingers of hers, with their claws, reminded me of a rook's toes. I don't know what her real name is—was. I'll bet she doesn't know, either. That's the way revenants are, you see. A little vague on the details of their past lives. Kind of like me.

I see you getting to your feet. You're going? So soon? No more questions?

Ah. I see. You think I spun this tale just to cadge a pint or two of the good stuff.

Not so, my good elf. Not so. Every word I've just told you is true.

I wasn't tugging your beard—not that you have one. What I just told you is the truth. If you want a guide who knows every pace of Araumycos, find Rook's bones. Help her, and she'll help you—and maybe me, too, in the bargain.

Just remember one thing. Don't let her appearance fool you. Regardless of what she looks like, she's a dwarf.

Just like me.

Lisa Smedman is the author of novels and stories set in the Forgotten Realms, Dark Sun, Shadowrun, and Deadlands universes. A reporter by profession, she also teaches game theory and video game history at the Art Institute of Vancouver. She also writes history books, children's books, plays, and screenplays, and has designed dozens of adventures and sourcebooks for various role-playing games over the years. Her website is www.lisasmedman.topcities.com.

THE FOUNDLING
MIKE RESNICK

Charybole was twenty-two years, three months, and six days old when she heard the screams.

She had been grieving, not just recently but for most of her life. A githzerai, her father had been killed by the githyanki when she was seven years old. Her mother had died beneath the awesome gaze of a cyclopean beholder two years later, her body literally melted before the glare of its single eye. Somehow she had survived to adulthood, living in the southern fringes of the Nentir Vale. In the fullness of time she had produced a daughter, a tiny thing on which she lavished all of the pent-up love and attention for which she had never found a recipient.

When her daughter was still an unnamed infant in her arms, she laid her down on the ground, just for a moment, while she filled a gourd full of water with which to bathe her from a nearby stream. She heard the screams a moment later, but arrived too late. An immature, but still heavily armored bulette, that half-snake, half-monster lizard that dwells and travels in the underground, had sensed the infant's presence and broken through the surface, where it was tearing the child to shreds. She threw herself on the creature fearlessly, but its heavy armor protected it, and after a moment there were no more shrieks from the child. When the bulette finished its grisly feast it turned its attention to the githzerai female who was flailing away at its back and head, and realizing her child was past saving, Charybole backed away. The bulette stared coldly at her for a moment, as if deciding whether she was worth the effort, decided she wasn't, and disappeared back down its subterranean burrow.

Charybole left the few remains of her child where they were, thereby guaranteeing that some scavenger or other would chance upon them and develop a taste for githzerai flesh. It made no difference to her. Every single thing she had cared about was dead, and she hoped to join them soon, to see if the next life held more joy and promise than this one did.

Yet the same instinct that makes even a prey animal sell its life as dearly as possible kept her alive, made her go through the motions of living, of eating, of sleeping, so that she could live and eat and sleep through another purposeless day. This continued, day in and day out, week in and month out—

—until the day she heard the wails and discovered a new purpose in life.

It was certainly not one she had anticipated, nor was it one she had prepared for. Had anyone mentioned what she was about to do a year ago, she would have thought they were crazy. But a year ago she had not seen a bulette rip her infant daughter limb from limb.

The cries came from a baby. Curious but cautious, she gingerly approached the source of the sound, and found a baby lying in the grass. At first it looked like a githzerai infant, but then she saw the yellow tint to its skin, and knew it was githyanki. She looked around for its mother, but there was no one to be seen.

They were near a stream, and she wandered over to it to see if the mother was washing herself in the cool, rapidly flowing water. No one was there . . . but then she saw a single blood-soaked sandal, and she knew what had happened. It was a warm day. The mother had set her baby down in the tall grasses for just a moment while she went to the stream to rinse the sweat from her body. Clearly she had not seen an approaching crocodile as the beast glided toward her beneath the surface, possibly had not known that the local streams were filled with them, and one bite would have been all it would have taken. Most of the local crocs were fourteen to eighteen feet in length, weighing well over a ton, and she'd have been dead, probably bitten in half, before she knew what hit her.

Charybole's reconstruction of the tragedy was interrupted by increased screaming from the child. She walked over and looked down at it. She had just lost her own baby to a bulette. She knew if she left this one here for more than a few minutes, it would suffer the same fate—or worse, for hideous as it was, the bulette was far from the top of the food chain. It wasn't its fault that it was born of the githyanki. It needed care, and love, and shelter, and she had all three to give. Finally she picked it up and walked off with it, all but daring any of the creatures of the Witchlight Fens to try to take it from her.

She arrived home, clutching the baby boy. She fed him, and when she went to sleep at night she did so with her arms wrapped around the little foundling.

Come morning the baby cried again, and this time it attracted not predators, but other githzerai, neighbors who knew that Charybole had lost her infant the week before.

"This is a dangerous idea," said Baryomis, her closest friend, after examining the infant. "You cannot bring a githyanki to live with us."

"I could not leave it to be torn apart as my own baby was torn apart," responded Charybole.

"Why not?" shot back Baryomis. "When Zat finds out, she will kill it anyway, or order it killed."

"He has harmed no one," said Charybole, "and I will not allow harm to come to him."

"It is *githyanki!*" snapped Baryomis in frustration.

"*He* is helpless, and he needs me," replied Charybole, holding the baby even closer to her.

It didn't take long for word of the foundling to reach Zat. It seemed so unlikely for a githzerai to have anything to do with a githyanki, let alone adopt it, that she decided to see what was transpiring with her own eyes, so she made the pilgrimage out to the Witchlight Fens.

"Where is the aberration I have heard about?" she demanded, and while Charybole inspired friendship among those who knew her, Zat inspired awe and even fear among them, and those were strong emotions, more than strong enough to overcome loyalty to the young githzerai. Finally Zat got her answer, sought out and confronted Charybole, and commanded her to bring forth the foundling.

"What will you do with him?" demanded Charybole.

"It is my sacred task to protect the well-being of the githzerai," answered Zat. "If the babe is what I believe it to be, I will kill it, of course."

"If you do," replied Charybole with no show of fear, "*I will kill you.*"

"Githzerai do not speak thus to me," said Zat.

"No one speaks thus to me about my child," shot back Charybole.

"It is *not* your child," insisted Zat.

"He is now."

Zat frowned. "Do you not understand? We cannot allow a githyanki to live."

"This is an *infant,*" protested Charybole. "If I raise him, he will grow up to be githzerai."

"It will grow up to be githyanki, and this I cannot permit. The githyanki are the enemies of our blood."

"All I know about his blood is that it is red," said Charybole. "And if you spill it, then I will spill yours."

Zat stared at her. "You will not let me see it?"

"I will not."

"Nor slay it if it is indeed githyanki?"

"Nor slay it."

"You have made your decision," said Zat. "Now I must make mine." And she turned and began walking back through the series of portals to the Elemental Chaos and the genasi-ruled city of Threshold, where Zat held court.

Charybole saw the way the others looked at her and the infant, and she moved farther into the Witchlight Fens. She carved a spear for herself, and was never without it. She didn't know how Zat planned to strike at her adopted child, but there was never any doubt in her mind that sooner or later, probably when she least expected it, Zat or her agents *would* strike.

Two months passed peacefully, then three, then four. Each day she carried the infant out into the fresh air, each day she fed and cleaned him, and each day they bonded more and more closely. She named him Malargoten after a cousin who'd died fighting a mind flayer, and she lavished all the love and attention upon him that would have gone to her own child had she lived.

And when she had kept the foundling for six months, and she no longer saw horrors and potential death in every shadow, she was visited by just the kind of horror she had once anticipated.

She was sitting on the ground with Malargoten beside her, who was learning to crawl, when she heard the unholy high-pitched screech. She reached out, placed a restraining hand on Malargoten, picked up her spear with her other hand, and looked for the source of the sound—and found it not twenty feet away from her. The source of the cry was a bebilith, a huge, spiderlike creature straight from the Abyss, or perhaps some deranged fiend's nightmare, staring at the foundling with hate-filled red eyes. She knew instantly that it had come to do Zat's bidding, for there was no other reason for it to leave its demon-haunted domain.

She was frightened, for a bebilith, taller than the surrounding trees, is a terrifying thing to behold, but she got to her feet and stood between the spider and Malargoten, spear in hand, ready to defend the infant to the death.

And it will be to your *death,* a voice inside her head seemed to say.

"There are worse things than death," she replied with more conviction than she felt, and she planted her feet, ready to meet the bebilith's charge.

But it didn't charge. It seemed to know that she held a formidable weapon in her hand . . . and it was not there for her, but for the infant.

It began slowly circling to her left. She pivoted, always facing it. It moved to the right. She responded.

It charged directly at her, hissing and shrieking, only to stop just beyond the reach of her spear point. She glanced down to make sure Malargoten hadn't crawled in any direction, and kept her spear at the ready.

The bebilith feinted twice more with pincerlike appendages, and she knew it was studying her, analyzing her responses with more brainpower than any spider should possess. She, too, feinted an attack, then realized she'd made a mistake, for she'd shown the bebilith she was unwilling to move even a few feet away from the infant.

The bebilith approached once more, stopped when it was perhaps seven feet distant, took a quick step to the left, and when she turned to keep her weapon pointed at it, it spat out a jet of sizzling fluid, part fire, part web, that just missed hitting Malargoten.

"What was *that?*" muttered Charybole.

You have heard of the ties that bind? said the voice in her head, a voice she knew belonged to Zat, though it sounded nothing like her. *This is the glue that binds. Once it touches the githyanki, once it binds its hands together, binds it to the rock-hard surface of the ground, nothing will ever unbind it—and it will burn.*

Charybole knew she couldn't wait any longer, couldn't chance that noxious fluid touching the baby, and with a scream she raced toward the bebilith, prepared to trade her life for his. She didn't bother to feint, didn't attempt to protect herself, didn't waste a single motion or a single second. The bebilith hissed in fury and turned its full attention to her, its razor-sharp pincers reaching out to her, its obscene mouth dripping with vile-smelling venom.

She awoke as Malargoten lay against her shoulder, sleeping contentedly. She gently moved him a few inches away, sat up gingerly, and tried to remember what had happened.

The bebilith was sprawled on the ground three feet away, her wooden spear protruding from its eye, its hairy limbs curled in death, its massive body covered by the horrible liquid that passed for its blood.

She examined her arms, legs, torso, and found no wounds. She was sore, as if she'd been hurled to the ground in the bebilith's death throes, but beyond that she seemed very little the worse for wear.

Suddenly she remembered the webbing, and turned to examine Malargoten, but he was free of it.

Of course, she thought with a sense of relief. You couldn't have crawled over to me if you'd been hit with it.

She stood up, tested her limbs, and picked the infant up in her arms, holding him protectively, and turned her head toward distant Threshold.

"You have done your worst, Zat. My child and I are still alive, and your creature is dead. Let it end here."

And a silent voice was carried to her on the wind that came from Threshold, a voice that said, *It will end when the githyanki ends.*

If Charybole was sure of anything, it was that Zat did not make empty threats. She didn't know when the next attempt to kill Malargoten would take place, but she didn't waste any time before preparing for it. She created a bow, a quiver, and a large supply of arrows. Some she dipped in poison, some in other solutions to use against creatures that were immune to poison. She crafted a dagger and a battle-axe, and was never without them.

And one day, almost a year from when she had found Malargoten, a man appeared on the horizon—tall, tanned, heavily muscled, with a thick mane of wild black hair.

Humans didn't walk the Witchlight Fens alone, and she knew he must have been sent by Zat. As he began walking toward her, she nocked an arrow on her bow, waited until he was a hundred yards distant, and loosed it, aiming it to hit the ground a few yards ahead of him.

"That's far enough," she said.

"You are Charybole?" he asked.

"I am."

"I mean you no harm," he said calmly. "My race and the githzerai share no animosities. We make no war upon one another. Put your weapon away."

"Tell me why you have come, first," said Charybole.

"I think you know," he replied. "I have come for the githyanki."

"Whatever the reward is," she said, "it is not enough. Turn away or prepare to die."

"Before you fire your arrow, may I ask a question?"

"One question only," said Charybole. "And whatever it is, it will not soothe me into lowering my guard."

"My question is simple," said the man. "The githyanki are your enemies. Why do you risk your life defending one of them?"

Charybole leaned over, picked Malargoten up and held him above her head, and answered: "Does this look like an enemy?"

The man stared at the infant for a long breath, and finally shook his shaggy head.

"I have been misinformed," he said. "I am as formidable an assassin as my race has produced. I have defeated sixty-three men in mortal combat. There is no one that I fear, no nightmare creature that I will not slay if the price is right." He paused. "But I do not kill children, not even for gold. Go in peace, githzerai."

And it was as if the heavens were rent asunder. A single voice screamed *"NO!"* louder than the thunder, and suddenly the man was surrounded by not three, not four, but six enormous, lobsterlike chuuls, denizens of fetid waters and murky cesspools, their huge pincers clicking open and shut as they approached him. He fought bravely, never took a backward step, but they methodically began tearing him to ribbons. When he was blood-soaked, one eye gone, a gaping hole where an ear had been, the chuuls stood back, and Zat's voice said, *"Now will you do my bidding?"*

The man glared up at the sky with his one remaining eye and bellowed, *"No!"*—and the chuuls were on him again, and this time they didn't relent until there was nothing left of him but a few white bones and a damp spot on the ground.

Charybole stood her ground, an arrow in her bow, five more clutched in the fingers of her left hand, one for each of the creatures that smelled as foul and loathsome as their dwelling place, but one by one the chuuls vanished as suddenly as they had appeared.

She put her arrows in a quiver, slipped her bow over her shoulder, and picked Malargoten up in her arms.

"It is no longer safe here," she said as if the infant could understand her. "We must move every day, never sleep in the same place twice. I am sorry to force such a life upon you, but it is better than what Zat envisions, which is no life at all."

And so saying, she began walking farther and farther away from Threshold.

You can walk as far as you want, said the voice inside her head, *you can go to the heart of the Elemental Chaos, you can even descend to the demon-infested Abyss. It makes no difference. Wherever you go, I will find you.*

"Until he is bigger," replied Charybole aloud. "Then perhaps *we* will find *you.*"

But there was no response.

They remained in hiding for four years. Which is not to say that they found one secure place and remained there. Sooner or later Zat sniffed them out and sent her minions. Once it was a githzerai assassin, once another human assassin. Once it was a trio of half-fey, half-insect banshraes, once it was a bear, the most recent time it was a devil-spawned cambion, human in appearance but not in blood or powers, brandishing his hellsword.

Each time it seemed certain that this was the end for young Malargoten—and for Charybole, if she had the temerity to stand between the predators and their chosen prey, and of course she always did—but somehow, when the battle was done and the dust had cleared, it was the githzerai and the foundling who emerged alive, and their truly awesome foes who lay dead upon the ground.

"I do not understand it!" said Zat in tones of cold fury. "She is just a githzerai female."

None of her servants or sycophants had the courage to point out that Zat herself was "just a githzerai female."

"I have been trying to slay the githyanki foundling for almost five years," she continued. "Every single assassin and every single creature I have sent should have been able to accomplish its task. What is it about this Charybole? There is nothing in her childhood, nothing in her past, to imply that she should be able to withstand such assaults. *Nothing!* So how does she do it? Who has trained her to slay our greatest assassins, our most frightening creatures, with nothing but the primitive weapons she has created herself? Not only that, but she defeats them even when I send them in teams, even as she is protecting the githyanki child! How is it possible?"

There were no answers, of course, because no one knew how it was possible.

Zat sat perfectly still, staring into space, for five minutes, then ten more, then another twenty, until her retainers thought she had gone into some kind of trance, or perhaps even turned comatose. Just before they considered calling the wizards to see if they could bring her back to the here and now, Zat stood up.

"I had not wanted to take this measure," she said coldly, "but I will not be thwarted again!"

Charybole sensed it before she could hear it, and she could hear it before she could see it.

They had found a cave that was free of all other life forms; even bats seemed uninterested in it. It had been a hard trek and a long day, and the exhausted Malargoten lay asleep deep in the cave, free from prying eyes, and safe from whatever was approaching.

Charybole sat on the ground, her weapons laid out before her: a dagger, a sword, an axe, a spear, a bow, and twenty-seven arrows, half of them dipped in poison, half in things that were worse than poison. She was every bit as mystified as Zat that she had emerged victorious from her various conflicts. Still, whatever was approaching, she would not flinch, would not give an inch. She was ready for it, ready to once again defend the foundling who had captured her sympathy and her heart.

She didn't know what it was, but she knew it had to be big, bigger than anything else she had yet faced, because its approach actually made the ground shake. The wind changed, and suddenly she could smell it. It smelled like nothing she had ever encountered before.

The ground trembled even more, the acrid odor became stronger still, and suddenly it was standing there in front of her, its single angry eye glaring balefully at her. It was an astral dreadnought, Zat's ultimate weapon, a gargantuan creature whose gaping mouth was filled top and bottom with razor-sharp teeth. Its single eye was black, its tongue a dark blue, its armored scales reddish brown. Its strong arms ended in pincered claws that looked as though they had evolved for the sole purpose of holding githzerai helpless in them. Its lower body was serpentine, but it moved with speed and grace, and even the lack of legs did not stop the ground from vibrating as it undulated across it. Charybole stared at the dreadnought's body, trying to see how huge it truly was, but there was no end to it; its tail seemed to extend to infinity.

"And you are from the Astral Plane," whispered Charybole. "How did my race ever survive there next to creatures like you?"

She shot six, seven, eight arrows into it. It paid them no mind. She hurled her spear at it. It buried itself three feet into the dreadnought's chest. The dreadnought ignored it. She fired two more arrows. They had no effect.

Somehow she knew this wouldn't be like the other encounters. There was no way she could live through this. She wanted to check the cave, to see if Malargoten was awake yet, and if so to convince him to stay hidden, but she knew if she paid any attention at all to the cave's entrance the dreadnought would know where the foundling was, and it was for the foundling that it had come.

She picked up her sword and her axe and edged to the right, hoping that the creature would follow her. Once she had moved away from the cave's entrance, it paid her no further attention, and she quickly positioned herself between the dreadnought and the cave once again.

When it was within arm's reach she buried the sword in its side. She knew from the arrows and the spear that she couldn't kill it; her only hope was that she might somehow be able to cripple it. But though the sword plunged deep into the creature's scales, it had no more effect than her other weapons. She swung her axe, but the dreadnought reached out its pincered claw, caught her head in it, and squeezed. It was over in a fraction of a second.

The dreadnought uttered a scream of triumph and cast her lifeless body aside. It couldn't know it, of course, but that scream spelled its own doom, for it woke the sleeping foundling.

Malargoten walked to the cave's entrance, briefly rubbing sleep from his eyes. He saw the lifeless body of his adoptive mother, then turned to face her slayer.

The dreadnought saw its prey and roared. The foundling showed no fear, and stepped out of the cave. The creature reached out a pincered claw to grab him.

"No," said Malargoten softly, but with authority.

The dreadnought's claw seemed to strike an invisible barrier, and bounced off.

The foundling stared at the creature, his expression a mixture of fury and contempt. Finally he waved a hand and snapped a finger, and the dreadnought collapsed, convulsing in agony, and died.

Malargoten paid it no more attention. Instead he walked over to Charybole's body, stared at her crushed skull, and wondered what his people did with their dead.

◆ ━ ◆ ━ ◆

Zat sat alone in her quarters. She was troubled, and she was confused. The reports had come in: She knew that the dreadnought had killed the annoying female who had withstood so many of her minions . . . but she also knew that the dreadnought itself was dead, though there was not a sign of violence on its body. And there was no trace of the foundling. Probably the dreadnought had eaten it, but she felt uneasy not knowing for certain.

Suddenly she became aware of another presence in the room, not a physical presence, but a presence nonetheless. She looked around, and saw a shimmering in the air, a shimmering that suggested something tangible, something *more*.

"Who are you?" she demanded.

You know who I am, a voice said inside her head. *And you have made a serious blunder. For all of my life you have hunted me down like an animal. I was never in danger, of course, and until this latest attempt I was always able to protect my mother, even though she was not aware of it.*

"You are githyanki!" spat Zat.

I could have been one of you, continued the voice calmly. *Until now I bore you no ill will. But now you have killed my mother—*

"Your false mother," interrupted Zat.

The only mother I have ever known. You are safe for the moment, Zat. I will do nothing to you today, or this week, or this year. I will wait for my powers to mature, powers that could have served the githzerai. I wash my hands of your race, and my own kind will not have me after I have lived with yours. I will live apart from all living things until the time is right. And when it is, when I am invulnerable to the combined might of all the githzerai, I will return—and you, Zat, will be the first to know it.

She was about to reply, but before she could she sensed she was alone again.

She considered what she had heard.

Isn't it ironic, she thought bitterly, that by defending the githzerai race, I may have doomed it?

Well, then, was there a way to soften his attitude? Zat smiled ruefully. Would *she* give up plans of vengeance were their positions reversed? Of course not.

Finally, was there a possibility, however slim, that he was wrong, that a five-year-old githyanki child was *not* the most potent and invulnerable force within the Elemental Chaos?

She didn't hold out much hope for that—but suddenly she knew that she would spend as much time as she had before his return trying to find out.

Mike Resnick is, according to *Locus,* the all-time leading award winner, living or dead, for short science fiction. He has won five Hugos, a Nebula, and other major awards in the USA, France, Spain, Poland, Croatia, and Japan. Mike is the author of sixty novels, almost 250 stories, and two screenplays, and has edited more than forty anthologies. In his spare time, he sleeps.

THE FORGE OF XEN'DRIK

A Tale of Eberron

KAY KENYON

Ravon Kell slammed his shovel into the stony ground, cursing the hard jungle soil. They had already buried fifty slaves, and there was no end in sight.

The sun threw lashing rays on his back, cooking him in his rags, but the worst heat came from the ground itself, where the grinding magics of the genesis forge blistered the land, killing the jungle for a swath of a thousand feet around their prison.

Nearby, an orc guard wrinkled his snout at the stench of bodies. "Bury 'em three in a hole," he ordered the halfling Finner.

"That's against—" Finner started to protest, but fell silent as the orc loomed over him.

Ravon dug his hole deeper. Yesterday's slave uprising had been doomed from the start. An army officer in the Last War, he'd weighed the odds and had stayed out of the fray. It wasn't even a contest, here in this lost jungle of Xen'drik where no one knew there *was* a forge or slaves—both illegal under the Treaty of Thronehold.

Maybe the poor bastards knew the odds and just wanted to die. As the old marching song went, there were nine hundred and ninety ways to die. An orc's blade thrust being merely one.

He looked up at the massive factory: an arms mill the size of a fortress, soon to produce an endless supply of lances, shields, cudgels, maces, swords, crossbows, spears—not to mention magic-infused spike wire, lightning spheres, and thunder shock implements.

A genesis forge, by the Devourer, though one had not been seen in the world since the fall of Cyre, as they were forbidden by the Treaty of Thronehold. But those laws didn't apply in Xen'drik, a wild continent far from Khorvaire. Besides, a cloak of magic hid the forge. From the jungle, the misshapen fortress looked like nothing more than a vine-covered crag, not a hulking factory ten stories high, with massive iron walls studded with bulging armories and effluent towers disgorging steam and rank smoke.

At the top of the forge bulged the dome of the artificers' keep. There, mages with their diagrams, spells, and sigils directed the magical workings of the forge. They drew enormous power from stockpiles of dragonshards and from the latent magic of the very ground on which the forge rested—the ancient burial site of a race of giants, it was said.

Ravon spat. His task—the task of every other slave, guard, and artificer—was to bring the forge to working order, and by so doing, bring the world to war. As a captain in Karrnath's army, war had been his job, but he would never fight again. In the Last War Count Vedrim ir'Omik had thrown him in the dungeons, stripping him of his commission and very nearly his life. It was one thing to take his punishment like a man, and quite another to take it when innocent of the charges—charges trumped up by the count's favorite vixen, at that. Earlier in the war a few of Ravon's victories had come to the count's attention, but by the Nine Hells, he wished that Vedrim had never visited the battlefield with his entourage. The attractive lady had taken a fancy to the celebrated captain, he'd declined to bed her, the count had been led to believe otherwise, and now Ravon wished that for all he'd suffered in the dungeon, he'd at least had the pleasure of what he'd been accused of.

High up the outer wall, a flat ring protruded like a horizontally embedded plate. Two rings, actually, one within the other. They turned very slowly, in opposite directions, grinding the dragon shards—the raw material of the forge's magic.

On the outer ring, pacing slowly to keep the slaves in view, the forge master Stonefist glared down at them. Even among gnolls, he was especially ugly. Strutting up there on the outer ring, his presence filled the slaves with further dread, a fact that even the slow-witted gnoll well understood.

Finner pulled out a gourd from inside his shirt, offering Ravon a drink of hoarded water.

Ravon waved it away. "Drink it yourself."

"You first, Captain." Finner bent over with another of his coughing spells, but managed not to spill.

Ravon wiped the sweat streaming into his eyes. "I'm not your captain any more." He glared at Finner. "And I don't need a steward. Get to digging or that orc will put *you* in a hole."

The halfling still held out the gourd. "You'll always be a captain of Karrnath. Don't make no difference, in prisons or digging graves."

Ravon took the gourd, else there would be no shutting Finner up. Tossing off a gulp of water, he nodded at the halfling, getting a worshipful look in return. To his surprise, it shamed him. There was nothing left of him to look at that way. He'd left that man in the count's dungeons. They had beaten and tortured that man out of him, and then had made him do the same to others.

So, Finner, he thought, how do you like the real Ravon Kell?

Ravon entered the forge through the iron jaws of the front door. The inner maze of ramps and halls growled with a low throbbing, less heard than felt through the soles of the feet. The goblin who'd fetched Ravon prodded him with a spear. Ravon batted it away from the small of his back, heedless of the goblin's snarl. No one was going to cut him down before Stonefist said. Ravon's time had not yet come, and the goblin knew it.

He tramped up the stairs, leaving the guard to return to grave duty. Ravon had more freedom than most of the other workers. Stonefist had conceived the plan to save him for a showy death. Why waste the great captain of Karrnath on starvation or overwork? Maybe Stonefist's sadistic plan was ready to go, if the gnoll wanted to see him.

Second level, the rat pen. Gnomes and dwarves and half-lings ran in their caged circles, turning the great forge rings that wove the spell to cloak the forge from prying eyes. Every kingdom in Khorvaire would rise up to destroy the forge, if discovered. That wasn't going to happen, though Ravon, in his off-guard moments, hoped for it. Hope made servitude less bearable, a lesson he'd learned well in Vedrim's dungeon.

A female dwarf grown thin from the endless walk spat through her cage and landed a gobbet at Ravon's feet. "Think you're high and mighty, don't you? Foul slime!"

Ravon made a half salute. "Good day to you as well, Bisreth."

Others doing cage duty took up the catcalls. "Lackey." "Traitor." They thought he was in close with Stonefist–even *liked* the forge master. The very thought gagged him. It was true that Stonefist gave him the run of the place, within reason. Ravon provided entertainment for Stonefist—and banter the forge master had come to relish.

The thought festered that he was also a model slave, dependably doing what he was told. Once, he would have called such a man a craven coward. Well. Perhaps one day Stonefist would push him too far, and he'd show himself a man, after all.

Snapping whips in the air, the goblin guards silenced the rat pen outburst, ignoring Ravon as he passed through.

Arriving at the third level, Ravon found Stonefist waiting for him. The gnoll was seated next to a wall of the forge proper. The ten-story heart of the edifice sweated out a putrescent goo in spots. This was the bowel room, slave talk for the place where the forge shat out its weapons. Or would, come the word from on-high. Some high lord or other, but such things mattered little in the end. What mattered to Ravon was a decent death. He'd put more than his share of thought into choosing a good one.

Seeing Ravon approach, Stonefist kicked at the cringing slave filing the gnoll's toenails. "Enough!" he roared. She fled the room. At Stonefist's side stood an elf, the ever-watchful, the ever-grim Nastra, a bulging ring of colorful keys at her belt.

Noting Stonefist's daggerlike toenails, Ravon said appreciatively, "Nice job. Except for the stink. Need to wash those feet sometime, boss." Over the weeks he and Stonefist had fallen into an exchange of insults. The gnoll was doubtless stirred by verbal abuse from a man he could torture to death at a whim.

Stonefist grinned. "Maybe you lick feet?" He turned his foot to one side, then the other. "Lick clean?"

Ravon gave an elaborate sigh. "A slave's work is never done."

"No slaves!" Stonefist blared. "Slaves against the law."

"Well, if not slaves, how about *happy workers*?"

Stonefist roared a laugh. "Happy workers!" He socked his fist against the forge wall, leaving a dent. "Happy workers!" Even Nastra smirked. "Big boss will like happy workers," the gnoll said, his good mood growing.

"You never said who the big boss is, Stonefist."

"Hah! Big boss is . . ." His grin fell away. "But Stonefist don't tell."

A flicker of interest flamed high in Ravon. It would be good to know one's real enemy. But it was a soldier's instinct, and he was no longer a soldier.

"I save you from shovels, Captain," the gnoll said. "Not die of too much work. Stonefist save Captain for *commmmbaaat*," he said, as his eyes grew rapturous.

Nastra made a distorted smile.

"Maybe I won't do your combat," Ravon said lightly. He'd been wondering what he *would* do when Stonefist ordered him to fight. It might not be a bad way to die: Ravon against a few orcs and goblins. But then again, it would mean contributing to Stonefist's sadistic pleasures.

The forge master frowned. "Then Captain die. I cut your heart out."

No heart in there, Ravon thought, but have at it, you sack of pus.

The pleasantries concluded, Stonefist heaved himself from his chair. Ravon was a big man, but the forge master stood a foot taller.

"Stonefist show you a thing, yah?" Waving Ravon to follow, he lumbered toward one of the forge portals.

"Foul bitch," Ravon muttered to Nastra as she walked at

his side. Skinnier even than most elves, she still possessed a fluidity that might be called grace, if she hadn't been a sadistic freak of a gnoll's minion.

"I pissed on your bed this morning," Nastra crooned. "Think of me tonight as you dream." As she walked, her hundred keys clinked like bells.

"I *do* think of you. You perform all my delights, lady elf. Think of *that*."

She hissed in response. Oh, how the vile creature would love to carve him up a little with the handy knife on her belt. It was one of Ravon's few remaining pleasures to provoke her. Even Stonefist liked to see her taken down a notch.

They came to the egress gate in the forge wall, the place where the weaponry would soon pour forth. To Ravon's surprise, the process had begun.

A great, burnished sword blade, edges honed and glittering, protruded from a portal. The blade was emerging from the door so slowly that Ravon could barely tell it was moving. A tendril of smoke slipped out as well, as though the forge was passing intestinal gas at the effort. But it was still in testing mode. Ravon tried and failed to imagine the hellish environs of a fully enlivened genesis forge.

Stonefist eyed Ravon. "You fight my goblins with sword, yah? Kill and kill, to see if sharp?"

Stonefist had long promised Ravon a good fight with the forge's first product. A little celebration, as it were. With this weapon, by the look of the sword's ensorcelled iron, Ravon might last a few minutes even if out-numbered. But he said, "I'd rather fight *you*, Stonefist. Someone easy." He shrugged. "If it were up to me."

Stonefist's expression darkened. He bent over Ravon, pointing a meaty finger at his chest, his breath fit to knock

Ravon flat. "You kill goblins. You kill what I say you kill." His voice boomed. "You kill lady elf. You kill halfling Finner. Whoever Stonefist say!"

Lightly bringing the gnoll's attention back to the sword, Ravon asked, "When will it be ready?"

"Soon," the gnoll muttered. Then, regaining his mood, he said, "How you like sword?"

"Good so far," Ravon said.

Stonefist nodded over and over, muttering half to himself, "Took much dragonshards. Two years of dragonshards to make. Big pile. Now out come good-so-far sword! Ha!" Stonefist threw wide his massive arms. "Soon come big important visitor. He watch forge get born!"

That was news. The high lord coming. Ravon flicked a glance at Nastra, whose long and almost handsome face showed no sign of surprise, only a patient, cold longing to watch a captain of Karrnath fight to the death. Well, she hadn't overseen the killing of any slaves for a couple of days.

Ravon wondered who the big visitor would be. Wondered if he would live to see it. Hoped he wouldn't. "You'll need a bath, then, Stonefist," Ravon said. "With company coming."

Stonefist grinned, showing an impressive rack of teeth. "By Dolurrh, Stonefist miss you when you dead!" That brought on a fit of barking laughter. Even Nastra joined in, as ugly a mewling sound as Ravon had ever heard.

He heard Stonefist's guffaws all the way up to the fourth level, the slave barracks. Just before he turned into his quarters—by the grace of the Sovereign Host, a private cell—he heard keys jangling and turned to see Nastra slinking around the corner and down the crabbed and steep north stairs. Had she followed him, spying? He wondered where the creature was going. Nowhere to go, surely. This lovely forge was the end of the line.

Deep in the night, ear-splitting yowls erupted down the fortress corridor. Instantly awake, Ravon sprang from his pallet. From cell block eleven, he heard the rasping shouts of goblins and slaves chanting "Finner, Finner!"

Cursing, Ravon stalked down to the slave barracks in time to see a dozen goblins surrounding a bloodied Finner. One of them yanked a fistful of hair from Finner's head and, grinning, raised it aloft like a captured flag. The slaves stomped and hollered as Finner fell to his knees in a coughing fit.

In the tumult, no one saw Ravon stride in until he grabbed a goblin by his leather belt, holding him a foot off the floor, kicking and growling. He swung the creature around, slamming him into another goblin and clearing a wide swath.

His fit ended, Finner stared at the palm of his hand and a few bloody teeth he'd coughed up. By the Devourer, here was a fine mess. Ravon had promised Finner's lieutenant that he'd keep an eye on the young halfling. Finner had served tirelessly as the officer's steward despite a set of bad lungs that would have kept lesser men from service. Ravon owed it to the lieutenant, he supposed. The man had died in his arms on the battlefield.

Still holding the goblin by the belt, Ravon growled, "Anybody want this sack of shit?"

The goblins fell silent, their grins fading to resentful scowls.

"No?" Ravon flung the creature aside and walked over to Finner. The formerly cheering slaves now looked properly ashamed. To watch a fellow slave savagely beaten . . . Ravon shook his head, glaring at them. The urge rose to slay two or three goblins before the others fell upon him. But then, that would be too much like the old Ravon and it was so much easier not to be him.

He helped Finner back to his private quarters—a rat hole with a slit for a window—and dumped him in a pile of straw.

Finner gazed up at him, but this time without the puppy look. The beating bashed the puppy out of him, no doubt. Still, there was that *gratitude* in his eyes.

"By the Dark Six, get some sleep," Ravon muttered. Then, to escape Finner's groveling, he stalked into the cell warrens, the walls secreting the usual bubbling pustules like a body with the plague. Eventually he found some solitude on a balcony used for dumping refuse. He sat until a glimmer of dawn seeped into the jungle and the blasted ground near the forge. Fumaroles in the cracked land coughed up sulfurous wisps. On the far side of the clearing, an early morning detail was hammering away on something. A reviewing stand. Getting on time for the end of the world. But if the genesis forge was ready to deliver itself of millions of arms, and if it took two years of accumulated magical dragonshards to create half a sword, where were the stockpiles, the hoards of powerful shards and objects of enchantment? He'd dared to ask a forge artificer once, in a rare hallway encounter. The elite mage had wrinkled his nose at Ravon's odor and murmured, "Endless stocks, below. Endless."

He meant the giant graveyard. But somehow Ravon doubted there was enough enchantment below for all that would soon be rolling out of the genesis forge.

A noise startled him. Nastra stood at the door.

He turned back to gaze out over jungle. "So did your goblins report me?"

"Yes."

He shrugged. "Well, they started it."

There was nothing much to say to that, nor did she respond, but rather watched at Ravon's side as the jungle brightened from black to sewage green.

Below them, Stonefist had come out onto the turning rims and with his henchmen flung a helpless gnome off the ring to his death four stories below. Then another. The guards' laughter came trickling up.

"Stonefist's at it early," Ravon muttered.

Nastra remained silent for a moment, before saying, "How bad was Vedrim's dungeon?"

"Not pleasant. No hot and cold running water. Lousy food."

"I'll bet the count has especially creative tortures."

That was true, but he wasn't going to give Nastra any pointers. "It's an art with him."

Another gnome went sailing off the ring to his death. Nastra murmured, "It can make a monster of you."

He turned to her. "What can?"

She stared at him with cold, flat eyes. "Torture."

Was she accusing *him* of monstrosity? He stifled a guffaw. "What's *your* excuse, lady elf?"

"Each to his own, Captain." She nodded at Stonefist and his entourage, below. "You could save a few gnomes, though, if you had a mind to."

Ravon stood up, his peace shattered. "*I'm* not kicking them off the rings. That would be Stonefist, or are you blind as well as dumb?"

"Stonefist knows you're up here. He's throwing the workers off to goad you. Everybody has a breaking point. Our forge master wonders what yours is. Even the slaves are laying wagers." Walking off, she said, "I've got a few coins in the game myself."

When Ravon got back to his cell, Finner had washed out his second set of rags and hung them up to dry by the window slit. Ravon noted that the cell was newly swept as well. It almost looked decent.

Noting Ravon's scowl, Finner said, "It's what a steward does." Then he turned to pound the dust out of Ravon's mattress.

"Nine Hells." Ravon was now thoroughly stuck with Finner, all four feet of him, including his racking cough and broken ribs.

Finner turned to leave. "I'll fetch your breakfast."

"No!" At the halfling's wide-eyed look, Ravon muttered, "Tell them it's my gruel, but bring it up here and eat it yourself." Finner started to protest. "That's an order. A steward does what he's bloody well told."

Finner grinned with what teeth he had left.

One night a storm lashed down on the forge. Lightning erupted as though Eberron itself were on fire. It ought to have cooled the forge down, but it only succeeded in turning the warrens into insufferable chambers of steam. Unable to sleep, Ravon left Finner to his exhausted slumbers and walked out to lean against a corridor wall. The thunder was loud enough to wake the dead giants underground. Between bellowing cracks he heard a familiar jangling sound and looked along the corridor to see Nastra heading down the north stairwell— again. He followed.

Ravon was not a small man, but he had long experience with silent tracking, all the easier when walking on stone stairs in iron halls. He followed Nastra down the steps, open at the top but increasingly narrower as they continued down. It was a reckless thing, to follow her. She carried a small dagger at her belt, and he'd seen her use it. A blade at the throat . . . the hundred and twelfth way to die, and not as bad as some. Still, Ravon had a hankering to die with a weapon in his hand.

Call him sentimental. So Stonefist's promise of a fight with a bunch of his henchmen was always in the back of his mind.

Nevertheless Ravon followed Nastra to see what villainy she was up to. If she broke the rules, he could use it against her when she tormented Finner.

The elf slipped around another turn of the stairs, the descent growing hotter. By now they had surely passed ground level. Ravon hadn't thought there *was* anything past ground level, but down they climbed. Then, from around a landing, he heard a scraping noise.

Peering around the corner, he saw that Nastra had opened a door and, releasing the key back to her collection, she disappeared through it. The door clanged shut behind her.

He was not surprised when he couldn't open it. What surprised him was that when he touched the door, it burned his fingers.

It was the way of the hellish forge that the most interesting things happened at night. Executions, rapes, orc berserker outbreaks—but this night's entertainment was of a different sort.

A guard came for him, and Ravon tramped down to the bowel room at Stonefist's order.

When he saw the purpose of the summons, his heart quickened. Stonefist and Nastra were leaning over the forge maw, as though crooning over a newborn baby.

The sword was complete. Its hilt was heavy with cladding, but nicely wrought. The blade, perfect; the length, a good four feet.

Stonefist lifted it from the receiving tray, holding it up and turning the blade to and fro. "Commmbaaat," the gnoll rumbled. "Yah." He turned his gaze on Ravon. "You hold." He held the sword out, then withdrew it with a sly smile. "But not yet."

"My time has come, then," Ravon said, feeling a rush of relief like a window thrown open and fresh air wafting in.

The gnoll smiled. "When Stonefist say. Maybe tonight. Maybe tomorrow. Stonefist choose."

"But soon."

Stonefist squinted at Ravon, handing the massive sword to Nastra. "But Captain's death must be . . . special. Very sat-is-fying. Nothing . . ." Words failed him.

"Vulgar?" Ravon supplied.

"No vulgar!" the gnoll boomed gleefully, though Ravon doubted he knew what the word meant. "Nothing . . . quick," Stonefist finished.

Nastra locked the blade away in an armory drawer. Ravon realized that she was thinner than ever, wasting away, in fact. Maybe she was sick. The night was just filled with happy thoughts.

With the main event of the evening, the first weapon from the genesis forge, concluded, Stonefist looked for other diversions.

"Lady elf," he said slyly, "forge need more cage-walk. You get halfling Finner." He grinned at Ravon, actually drooling. "Night shift."

Ravon frowned. "He's already done his shift, boss."

"Missed work today." Stonefist put a finger to his forehead. "Stonefist remember. Missing shift."

"Two shifts in the same day will kill him." Ravon shrugged. "A waste of a worker when the very important visitor is coming."

Stonefist paused, processing this idea. Then: "Lady elf—you wake halfling."

Ravon kept his expression neutral. "Means nothing to me. You're the boss."

"Stonefist boss. *Vuulgaaar* boss, yah?"

"Yeah," Ravon said, giving an insolent salute.

Stonefist liked a few military flourishes. But he still sent Nastra up to the barracks.

Soon dismissed, Ravon rushed up the stairs to catch the elf. He found her at the door to his cell. "Nastra," he murmured.

She turned, her face a mask of indifference.

"What's he doing to you? You look worse every day."

Her eyes caught a glint from the everbright lantern high on the wall. "What's it to you?"

Ravon shrugged. "Just wondering why you want to be a lackey for our lovely forge master."

"Maybe I like the work."

That had occurred to Ravon, but he wanted to keep her talking. "Leave Finner alone, Nastra. Show a little mercy. Some day you'll need a favor."

She smiled, showing surprisingly clean teeth, not that it was a pleasant sight. "I thought you didn't care about Finner."

"I don't. But I made a promise in battle to Finner's dying lieutenant. I said I'd watch over his steward. Damned if I know why."

Her dark eyes held his. "It was a promise."

"Yes."

For a moment he thought she might be softening, actually affected by Finner's story. But no, the old sarcasm was at the ready. "Cry me a bucketful," she snapped.

She turned on her heel and stalked away. But to Ravon's surprise, she let Finner sleep in peace that night.

The next night, Ravon lay in wait for Nastra.

He hid in a recess by the north stairs and, true to habit, the elf skulked by and disappeared down. Nastra was hiding something, he was sure of it.

What he couldn't figure out was why he gave a damn.

In the last six months he'd learned not to care, even relishing the prospect of his own death. But then Finner had become his steward, and in Finner's eyes, Ravon had seen the reflection of the man he used to be. Nine Hells. One foot in the grave and now he had hope again . . . not a hope to live—no, never that—but hope to have absolution for all that he'd done.

By the Devourer's Teeth, he wished he'd never met Finner.

But now he was curious. Where did the sovereign bitch go on all these back stair excursions? A lover? His stomach turned at *that* thought.

He watched from a recess in the wall as Nastra stood before the hot door, fumbling for her keys. She selected a blood red one and, using it, went through.

Ravon plunged forward, catching the door an inch from closing. He worked the latch so that the elf would hear the mechanism click into place. Then he followed her down.

For down it was, a shaft of a stairwell now steeper than before—and hotter with every step. Here the walls streamed with foul excreta, slick and stinking. It brought to mind the question of *why* the whole forge, not just here, sweated a vile slime. It had always seemed natural to the misery of the place, but now Ravon thought it was something more, perhaps something far worse. The hammering heat itself was a mystery. But the forge was built on top of a graveyard of giants, and places of such ancient magic had a natural affinity for the dark places of Khyber, bringing its hellish heat close.

And down, still—with Nastra rounding the corners of the landings, and Ravon one turn behind, just catching a glimpse of her cloak as it disappeared. No lover down here. *Nothing* down here. His curiosity mounted.

Abruptly, the descent ended. Nastra was off across a murky cavern, roiling in noxious fumes. Ghostly rock formations jutted up from the floor while stalactites hung down from above, dripping goo . . . the very pus that infected the forge itself. Ravon followed the elf, the ground thrumming beneath his feet as though the heart of a giant lay just below.

A scream tore through the cavern, stopping Ravon in mid stride. The howl trailed off. He couldn't see Nastra, lost in the murk.

Voices. One horrid and low, the other a murmur. Nastra was with someone. That low, guttural voice sent a shudder over him. All senses on keen alert, he moved with practiced stealth toward the source of the voices, using rock formations as cover. That *voice*. Not human, not in any way normal. The list of possible creatures was short and exceedingly nasty; maybe best to slink away now before he risked discovery. Lying flat on the ground behind a massive rock, he crept forward to look.

A creature stood on a rock outcropping. A skeletal, flesh-wasted monster, some seven feet tall.

By all the Six, a death hag. Why had he pulled forward? The hag could probably hear his very breath if she wasn't so focused on Nastra. He was frozen now, lying flat, but exposed.

The death hag jumped down to where Nastra knelt, screaming, "My master does not wait! The baron of Cannith signifies nothing to such as us. My master does not wait for human lords!"

Then the hag slowly craned her neck, looking around. Ravon stopped breathing.

"Yes, exalted," Nastra piped up, bringing the hag's attention back. "Just a day, however. What is a day to your great master? It is nothing!"

The death hag screamed in frustration, raising her hands and wringing them. "A day, a day? You shall understand how long is a day, when my sisters cut a slit in you and slowly draw out your entrails!" The creature swiped her claws through Nastra's hair, snapping the elf's head back and forth. "We shall bring up the fires to feed the engine. Open the pipe! Let the sweet lakes of Fernia flow!"

Ravon heard the word *Fernia*, and his mind opened to a new and most unwelcome surmise.

The hag was still screaming, "Aye, Fernia longs to flow!"

Nastra quailed but answered, "Yes, Fernia shall flow, great one. The glorious day!"

Ravon's heart cooled at the growing realization. By all that was unholy, the forge needn't worry about running out of dragonshards. It was going to have Fernia. It would be fueled by one of the planes of the Elemental Chaos: Fernia, the Sea of Fire.

Because, he now realized, the genesis forge was sitting atop a manifest zone, where the worlds intermixed. But not even a death hag could create a pipe to extrude the Elemental Chaos . . .

Nastra looked up at the hag. "A glorious day it will be, but not yet, exalted one. Tomorrow. Stonefist begs the demon lord's indulgence for one more day—"

Her agitation growing, the death hag rolled her eyes fully around in their sockets.

Nastra went on, "—so that *his* master, the great Cannith personage, may arrive, may witness the event."

The death hag emitted a horrid ululation. She bashed her

right hand down on her own upper leg, shattering it. Somehow, the witch remained upright. Then she plucked aside her rags and touched her femur, healing it over with gristle. Calmer now after her outburst, the death hag grinned and yanked Nastra to her feet.

"*One day only*, sweetling. The demon lord shall wait *one day*. Then the fire comes up. The forge is born!"

"Yes, exalted lady. Tomorrow. You have my word."

The hag rasped, "What is your word to *me*?"

"Nothing," Nastra said. Then she met the hag's maddened gaze. "But it's all you've got."

The witch cocked her skull-like head, as though considering whether to eat the elf on the spot or save her for another time.

By the Sovereign Gods, Ravon had space in his mind to think, Nastra just talked back to a death hag.

"Leave me," the hag spat. "Return tomorrow and tell us Cannith has arrived. Then the gates of fire open!" With a ferocious leap she launched herself away, disappearing into the boiling smoke.

The creature was gone. Even so, Ravon waited a few beats before standing up to face Nastra. He swayed for a moment, temporarily weakened by having been in the death hag's proximity.

Spying him, Nastra's look revealed her dismay. The forge's secrets, or most of them, were now exposed. Her eyes flicked toward the vanished death hag. Then she waved him toward the end of the cavern where the stairs gave on to the audience chamber.

They stood face to face, eyeing each other. "So," Nastra muttered. "You know."

Ravon looked at Nastra's stringy face and stooped shoulders. Her visits with the death hag had eaten away her life force, until all that was left was this pitiful, wasted creature. He spoke in a stunned whisper. "You're going to unleash the Demon Lords."

"Not exactly."

His temper surged, and he pushed her against the stairwell wall. "No? Isn't the hag's master a demon lord?"

With surprising strength, Nastra pushed him away. "Nothing can unleash the Demon Lords. They are banished forever."

Ravon grabbed her arm, this time holding on with a fierce grip. "But they *aren't*. They've already found a way to unleash themselves. They've got you, Nastra, damn you to the Hells." He twisted her arm behind her back and she winced in pain. "I ought to kill you. The world would thank me for it."

"Go ahead," the elf whispered. "See if that stops the forge!"

Brutally, he threw her against the wall and stepped away, unable to execute her as she deserved. Through his contempt, he asked, "Why, Nastra? Why help the bastards?"

She slid down the wall into a crouch. In the gloaming light from the few brightglobes, she looked a bit like a hag herself. "For love."

He stared at her.

"The high lord of Cannith has my family. He'll kill them, mother, father, brothers, cousins. Merrix d'Cannith has already slain my sister." Her voice went very quiet. "Back when I first refused."

"Nice story. But you're not that important. Cannith could use any servant base enough, greedy enough, to do his bidding."

"Dragonmarked," she whispered.

"What?"

"I'm useful. My aberrant dragonmark. It shields me—just enough—from the powers of Khyber." She looked blackly up at him. "Even Stonefist can't survive down here for long. If you'd come much closer, you would understand."

He watched her carefully for signs of cunning. But oddly, he believed her. She had a gift. A twisted, awful one. And Cannith had tortured her family to be sure she used it.

"I'm sorry," he heard himself say. And he was, woefully sorry, about the hellish forge, the pact with the demons, and even Nastra's family. But pity was useless. It was anger that he needed. A righteous anger. He gazed into the smoke-laden cavern, imagining how all of Fernia would be harnessed for a new and bloody war. He felt something small and burning flicker in him, but wearily, he pushed it away.

Leaving Nastra crouched on the stairs, he climbed back to the upper realm. He hardly remembered going up the stairs, passing the hot door and, regaining the fourth level, entering his private cell.

There, on his bed, lay Finner. He was dead. Laid out, his rags smoothed, but not enough to hide the gouts of blood where he'd been struck through with a blade.

Pinned to the halfling's shirt was a note, almost illegible: *We tested sord blade witout yu. Work good!* It was signed with a bloody fist.

He knelt by Finner's side and closed the steward's bulging eyes. After a moment, his body trembling, Ravon rose to his feet. Rage filled him, flooded his mind, released his shackles. Where had he been these many months? Where had the fight gone, and the old Ravon Kell? He shook his head, as though clearing away a dream. The surge of power in his body, in his heart, told him he was ready now, to fight. All he needed was a sword.

A movement at the door. Nastra stood there. Her gaze went to Finner's body. "He didn't deserve that," she said. To his astonishment, she was holding out her ring of keys.

Ravon strode out the door, snagging the keys as he went by.

His steps were long but deliberate as he stalked past the cell blocks, his mind afire. He might not be able to fight Cannith or the demons or the hag, but there was one enemy he meant to settle with, and by Dolurrh, nothing was going to stop him.

When he got to the bowel room, no one was there except a couple of goblins, who backed away from him when they saw the expression on his face. Using the blue key he'd seen Nastra use, he opened the drawer where she'd locked in the sword.

Its weight was solid and lush in his hand. But he had no time to admire the forge's handiwork. He bellowed out Stonefist's name. Over the groaning of the forge's ugly heart, he heard his voice echo. The goblins crouched out of his way as he rushed into the corridor.

"Stonefist," he bellowed, "you ugly son of a sovereign bitch!"

He roared the gnoll's name again and again as he stalked down the halls with a warrior's tread, his footfalls deliberate, balanced, deadly. He knew how to enter battle. He remembered from the old days, which were not so very old, being only six months ago, back when he was Captain Ravon Kell, of his majesty's army. That Ravon Kell was back.

As he passed the twentieth cell block, a dwarf stood at the entrance. She nodded to him, pointing to the door far down the passage. Ravon understood. The forge master was on the rim. The forge master was out there throwing off slaves.

He flung open the door, letting the first light of day into the gloaming prison.

Stonefist was on the outside rim thirty yards away. Several large orcs kept him company. At the sound of the door opening, Stonefist let go of a human slave, letting him sink into a terrified puddle.

The gnoll turned to face Ravon. "Hah, Captain!" He noted that Ravon was armed. "You like sword, yes?"

"Yes."

Ravon had not moved from his place near the door.

Stonefist backed up slightly to keep his distance as the rim bore him slowly forward. "You like fight my orcs?"

"When I'm finished with you," Ravon said, "*then* I'll fight the orcs."

A slow grin crawled across the gnoll's face. Waving the orcs to stand back, he pulled a great curved blade from his belt, rumbling, "Stonefist finish *you*."

Ravon stepped from the doorway onto the inner rim as it moved in Stonefist's direction. He paced slowly backward, keeping distance from the gnoll as the two rings conspired to bring the combatants together. Between the rings was a furrow that would grind off a misplaced foot.

At the top of the forge a few artificers had emerged from the keep to look on.

Ravon hoped they would allow the fight to proceed. To fall from an artificer's bolt of power was the eighteenth way to die, and not unmanly, but not the noble end of hand-to-hand combat with an enemy like Stonefist. He stepped over the gap between the rims.

The outer rim was as broad as two gnolls lying end to end, but still there was little room to maneuver.

Ravon found his balance, feeling the sword in his hand like a magical extension of his arm. "The Demon Lords will teach you to lick their boots, Stonefist. Maybe you're too dumb to know that."

Stonefist grinned wolfishly. "Death hag and demon lord work for Stonefist! They open pipe to the fire. After pipe open"—he spread his arms wide—"it stay open. Nothing can close it, so artificers say. We no need hag or demon, then."

A double cross. Impressive, Ravon had to admit.

The forge master went on. "Stonefist invite hag up to rims and shove her in." Grinning, he pointed to the lethal gap. Then, raising his curved blade, he beckoned with a long arm. "Come to Stonefist."

Ravon didn't meet his opponent's eyes. In the stories, you boldly held the enemy's gaze, but in a fight you watched his chest for the first sign of movement, to gain a split second advantage.

A twinge from Stonefist betrayed a back-handed swipe, and Ravon's sword was there to greet it. He felt the shudder of the blow ring in the bones of his arm. He spun away and then around again, pricking the gnoll's upper arm.

Stonefist didn't feel it, not yet. But it riled him. "How Finner like new sword?" He lunged, missed, lunged again, as Ravon backed up.

Ravon feinted toward the gnoll's left side, then sliced his sword right. Stonefist sprang back. The gnoll was solid on his feet, and strong, but his blade was not as long as Ravon's. The forge master would die. But he was stronger than Ravon, so as much fun as the foreplay might be, it was time to finish it.

Behind Stonefist the orcs watched uneasily. They'd be the next fight, Ravon knew. He wasn't going to walk away from this battle, but he'd take a few of them with him.

Stonefist was swaying, warming up for his next lunge. "I give your eyes to the goblins for a meal!" he brayed.

Ravon shook his head. "But Stonefist, that would be vulgar."

"*Vulgaaar!*" Stonefist yelled in joy and rushed forward. Ravon jumped onto the inner rim. Then, the movement of the rim taking him past Stonefist's position, he hopped back on the outer one.

Now behind Stonefist, and before the gnoll could turn, he swung the great sword in an arcing slice at the creature's neck, knocking his head half off. It lay on his shoulder, the stump erupting with thick blood. Absurdly, Stonefist tried to put it back on, managing to tip it back into place. The forge master staggered around to stare at Ravon.

The gnoll stood as still as a rock outcropping, his gaze lit with understanding.

Ravon kicked a boot forward. "For Finner," he said, connecting hard enough to send Stonefist staggering backward. The gnoll teetered on the edge of the forge for a moment, then plummeted.

A roaring noise. The artificers sending a bolt of searing wind, no doubt. But then the roaring continued, and as Ravon became more aware of his surroundings, he saw that every window, door, niche, outcropping, ramp, and hole held a slave or five, and they were all cheering. The orc guards, who had started to approach Ravon, looked up in alarm.

The real battle of the genesis forge began at that moment as dwarves, gnomes, humans, halflings, and all the rest surged onto the rings, tearing the guards apart and throwing the pieces after their master. From above, the artificers sprayed bolts into the throng, burning many, but seeing the sheer number of slaves scrambling up the sides toward them, they retreated.

The traveling rim Ravon stood on had come around to the back side of the forge, and Ravon looked for a new way to enter the forge. He had another duty to discharge. Now that he was alive, after all.

Inside, chaos ruled as the cell blocks emptied, their occupants armed with pieces of wood, old iron implements, and broken bottles. Ravon heard the roar of dwarves taking command, directing the melee, even as their meaty arms swung improvised weapons against orcs and goblins. Carnage filled the halls, but Ravon stalked through, heading for the north stairs.

The shrieks and cries of battle receded as he rushed down, fumbling with Nastra's keys, looking for the red one, finding it. He inserted it into the hot door. Then down again, this time in silence, or in as much quiet as could exist in a manifest zone poised over the Lake of Fire that was Fernia.

When he arrived in the cavern, he was sweating heavily but still stoked from the combat. The churning madness of Khyber stirred his thoughts. That was good. When facing death, it was best not to be in one's right mind.

He shouted, "Death hag! By the Devourer, by the Dark Six! Death hag!"

Mists swirled around him. He bellowed again. "I bear a message for the lovely hag!"

The room stilled, as though his ears were stuffed with straw. He pivoted, looking in all directions, hating, like any warrior, not to hear his enemy, not to have every sense alert.

From behind came a singsong voice. "Sweet meat."

He spun. The death hag leaned over him, tall and spectral.

"I bear a message." He let his sword drop to the ground. If she would only listen.

"Speak your last words," she breathed, with breath like a month-old carcass.

"Listen until the end, hag, for your master will want to know."

"Oh, bold, bold." Her eyes rolled back and came around again. Ravon had to admire the trick.

The witch crooned, "I shall take your blood with especial pleasure. Sip, sip."

By Dolurrh, she was ugly. But he held her terrifying gaze and said, "I'm a bitter man. You may not find my flesh to your liking."

"I shall eat your tongue first, then decide."

He devoutly hoped she would kill him all at once and not save him for the occasional cannibalistic treat. He must remember to enrage her to that point. He'd always had a knack for annoying people.

Ravon hastened to say, "Here is the message from Stonefist. The baron of Cannith doesn't need you or your demon lord. Once you open the pipe, it will stay open. Cannith will ignore you. You've been duped."

The hag grabbed his shoulder, her nails strong as meat hooks. "Stonefist would not say so to such as you."

"You'd be right except I was in the process of killing him when he let it slip."

The hag screamed, smashing him down to his knees. "Where is Nastra?"

"I don't keep track of her. Sorry."

The death hag looked over his shoulder, peering into the caldron of smoke, watchful, perhaps desperate. Turning back to him, she yanked his hair, pulling his head back to expose his neck. "Bitch, bitch, bitch!" she howled.

"Know what you mean." His head was bent so far, he thought his spine would snap. He managed to spit out, "But the elf has her good points."

The witch hunched over him, her face very near, her breath vile. "You do not fear me, manling?"

With all that was left of his voice, Ravon whispered, "Not so much."

And he didn't. He was wholly occupied with trying to figure out what number his death was going to be at the hands of the hag. Was it the three hundred and eighth way to die, or the eight hundred and third? By Dol Dorn's mighty fist, it was *important* to know.

By the time he decided both were wrong and was wildly

recalculating, he found himself lying flat on the trembling ground, no one else in sight.

The death hag had gone.

Well. Perhaps his innate charm had won out.

As Ravon raced up the stairs, he felt the treads shaking beneath his feet. Splinters of stone fell from the ceiling.

The pipe. They were opening up a portal to Fernia after all. They didn't believe him. The hag didn't . . . but the shuddering continued, worsening. He barely got through the hot door as the stair collapsed behind him.

Summoning his last strength, he raced up the remaining flights. Somewhere above him the fight raged on, but even a battle could not drown out the booming roar of what was coming.

Charging through the halls, he bellowed, "Out, out! It's coming apart. Get outside!"

The forge itself heaved from side to side. And grew hotter with every minute.

Fernia was coming up. Not in a controlled pipe, he decided. It was coming in a flood, an eruption. It would blow the forge sky high. "Out, get out!" he roared as the slaves started to heed him. He grabbed a dead orc's pike and struck down a pair of goblins coming at him from a side hall. "Out!"

Then in a general stampede, those who yet lived raced from the corridors, cells, and crannies of the forge, heading for the door out. Bodies lay everywhere, orcs draped over dwarves and goblins over halflings, as though in a last embrace. The slaves rushed outward and Ravon followed.

Once in the clearing, he looked back to see gouts of fire erupting from the forge's window slits, and a pillar of purple smoke spiking up into the sky from the artificer's keep.

Even orcs gave up on the fight and stared. Then in a mass surge, they and everyone else turned and raced for the jungle.

Ravon noted a different group standing on one side of the dense forest. A large group of soldiers with their pack beasts also stared at the thundering, shuddering forge.

In their midst stood a lord, by his dress—a regal figure with dark hair and a chain of office around his neck. The expression on his face was one Ravon would never forget.

"Merrix d'Cannith," a voice spoke at his side. He couldn't see anyone. But it was Nastra's voice. "He came to see the forge open. Not fall to ruin."

"Hate to see him disappointed," Ravon murmured. The ground shook violently, as one side of the forge collapsed in a deafening crash.

Nastra went on. "I can extend my cloak around you. Perhaps invisible is best under the circumstances?"

Ravon saw that a large orc was making his way toward him. "If you wouldn't mind, lady elf."

"Not that I care about you," she said. "Never think that." The orc began to lope in his direction.

"Of course not. But we might fight our way to the coast. In case of drow. Orcs. Other riffraff. Two swords are better than one."

"Indeed," Nastra allowed.

In a swirl, the orc grew fuzzy to Ravon's eyes. The orc spun around, searching for his vanished prey. After a moment it stalked off.

Ravon felt Nastra bend an arm behind and slowly draw a sword from its sheath. She pressed its hilt into his hand.

The air split with a gargled roar. As they watched in frozen wonder, the top of the forge blew off in a gout of fire and iron. The sound engulfed the world. It was an angry blast from Fernia—but not to enliven the genesis forge, not in a controlled pipe. An eruption, sent by the minions of a demon lord to wreak death on his betrayers.

Baron d'Cannith beat a hasty retreat into the jungle as pieces of flaming iron, molten rivets, and doors red as newly poured ingots fell from the sky.

After the blast, nothing remained but a crater where the genesis forge had been. The jungle was set alight in places, but the eruption was done.

Ravon and Nastra turned and ran from the burning clearing. He let her lead the way, admiring her speed.

Catching up to her at last, he said, "We'll find your family. When we get to Khorvaire, we'll find them."

A quick glance at him. "Not that you care."

He shrugged. "Not in the least. But I figure I owe you."

She smiled. "A promise, then."

"Call it that."

They plunged deep into the jungle of Xen'drik, watchful for orcs, drow, stray goblins, Cannith's men, and a score of other enemies. It was a world Ravon Kell remembered well. It was good to be back.

Kay Kenyon, nominated for the Philip K. Dick and the John W. Campbell awards, began her writing career (in Duluth, Minnesota) as a copywriter for radio and TV. She kept up her interest in writing through careers in marketing and urban planning, and published her first novel, *The Seeds of Time*, in 1997. She is the author of numerous short stories and lives in Wenatchee, Washington, with her husband. You can read a first chapter of her books at www.kaykenyon.com.

ARENA OF SHADOWS

A Tale of EBERRON

SARAH ZETTEL

Kalev Shadowfall was having a bad night.

It had started out well enough. Gaining entrance to Duke Arisor's palace had proven trivial. This was peaceful, ordered Fairhaven, after all. The duke trusted the queen's law and the governor's vigilance. Kalev only needed to bribe one guard to leave one gate in the outer wall open. After that, he had scaled the palace's ivy-covered wall so swiftly not even the nesting sparrows stirred. The laughter and music from the grand reception in the ballroom covered any stray sounds he made, and the hired patrol tromping through the gardens had completely failed to look up to see the extra shadow moving across the stones. Duke Arisor had become too cavalier about his own safety of late. He was not the first of Fairhaven's prosperous citizens to assume that because the city was well-ordered, it was essentially safe. It was but one of his mistakes.

Another was selling information too sensitive to be allowed out of the capitol.

A few drops of oil and a thin blade had popped the next-to-useless lock on the study's window. Velvet draperies blocked off the sight of Kalev slipping down from the sill.

Kalev remembered thinking it was too easy as he stepped lightly down, not even rippling the drapes. He remembered wishing for a little challenge to add zest to the evening.

He also remembered thinking, Be careful what you wish for.

Because when Kalev peered between the drapes to make sure the study was empty, he saw a sprawling wreck of overturned furnishings and scattered papers surrounding the mutilated remains of a man dressed in emerald silk lying facedown in a large pool of blood.

Kalev swallowed his shock and made himself wait for a slow count of one hundred. No movement disturbed the gory scene. Kalev crept into the darkened room and crouched beside the man to ascertain that he was in fact as dead as he looked. That didn't take long. The back of the corpse's scalp was torn open, exposing the bloody skull beneath. The neck and shoulders had been shredded, leaving strips of flesh and silk dangling across the floor. The man's arms were broken. The smell of fresh slaughter coated the inside of Kalev's nostrils and left its sick, sweet taint on the back of his throat.

Kalev reached out and prodded the stiffening hands, checking the rings until he found the one he was looking for: the sigil of peridot and onyx that belonged to Duke Arisor.

Snickt.

Kalev spun to face the door, drawing his right-hand dagger from his sash, and found himself face to face with a dark-haired, bejeweled woman wearing a formal gown of topaz silk.

Her startling violet eyes darted from Kalev to the dead duke, the ransacked study, and to Kalev again.

The woman opened her mouth. Kalev crouched, ready to spring across the corpse and muffle her scream.

"*Blast!*" she exclaimed.

The woman shoved the door shut and strode into the chaos, kicking up papers around her ankles. Kalev, for one of the few times in his life, found himself startled past the ability to move.

The woman went straight to a massive bookshelf that, like the unfortunate Duke Arisor, lay toppled on its face. She dug her fingers underneath its edge and strained.

"Help me!" she snapped.

Kalev blinked. "Aren't you concerned I might be the murderer?"

The woman rolled her eyes. "If you'd done that"—she jerked her chin toward the duke's gruesome remains—"you'd be covered in blood. You're not. If you were one of that lot downstairs, I'd've noticed you." She looked Kalev pointedly up and down. His long black coat, black breeches, black tunic, gloves, and boots would indeed have stood out sharply in the ballroom. "And you'd've summoned the guard. You haven't. So, you're probably here to steal, which doesn't bother me, as long as we're not after the same thing."

"Admirably practical." Kalev bowed his head. She was wrong about his reason for being there, but there was no immediate need to point that out. Kalev stowed his dagger, stepped lightly to the other side of the shelf, and crouched down.

"On three, then," he said. "One, two, *three*."

A blur of midnight dropped down between them.

Kalev fell back, rolled over his shoulder, and came up on his feet, his dagger in his hand once more and a flush on his face for failing to look up in time like some lazy guard.

A stinking, humanish creature dressed in rags sewn with bones landed beside the duke's corpse. One hand brandished a notched short sword, the other clutched what looked like a golden statue of a cyclops. It bellowed wordlessly, revealing a mouth full of black teeth.

Skulk! Kalev leaped backward.

"Grab it!" shouted the woman.

"*What?*" cried Kalev, his voice embarrassingly shrill.

The woman snatched up a broken chair to swing at the skulk's head. The skulk ducked, howled, and raised its blade.

Then it jerked around and jumped head-first out the window.

The woman dived after it, arms outstretched. She missed by bare inches and sprawled full-length on the floor, sending up a flurry of papers.

A heartbeat later, shouts rose through the open window. Kalev shoved the curtains open and looked down at the crowd of guards gathered below. Some hared off into the darkness, presumably on the trail of the skulk, which had already vanished. The rest stayed put, probably waiting for orders.

"We need to clear that lot away, or we're never getting out of here," Kalev reasoned.

The woman understood at once. She scrambled to her feet.

"Help!" she wailed at the top of her lungs. "Duke Arisor is attacked! Oh, help!"

Attacked. Not murdered. The guard will come check the study. Smart. Below, an officer barked orders. Half the patrol headed for the walls, the other half sprinted toward the main doors, leaving the space under the windows clear.

The woman wasted no more time. She leaped onto the sill. There came a loud ripping noise and Kalev suddenly found a mass of topaz fabric flying at his head.

He knocked the bulky missile aside. When he could see again, the window sill was empty.

The sound of running feet in the corridor was very loud.

Kalev swung himself onto the sill, grabbed the ivy, and climbed down until he could safely let himself drop to the ground. He landed in time to see a faint flash of jewels in the lamp light as the woman scaled the outer wall.

Kalev set off at a run. He seldom lost his way, even in the dark, and quickly found the side gate again. It was still open. He was through and out into the street in time to draw a look of startled fury from the woman—now clad in breeches, boots, and a tight, dark tunic—as she gazed down at him from the top of the wall.

Before he could say anything, two massive hands yanked him off his feet and slammed him against the wall.

When his vision cleared, Kalev found himself pinned against the wall an inch off the ground, staring into the brutish face of a battered warforged. Essentially a living suit of armor, the creature had one massive fist cocked back and ready to punch Kalev's unprotected head.

"Sheroth!" The woman dropped lightly to the cobbles. "The target's this way!"

The warforged—Sheroth—growled, let Kalev drop, and lumbered after the woman. Kalev hit the cobbles, staggering a moment before he found his footing.

He stared after the retreating pair. What was going on?

The only way to answer that was to follow the woman and the warforged. Choosing the thickest shadows, Kalev ran.

Fairhaven was a city of wide avenues and tall spires, famed for its beauty. Duke Arisor controlled the majority of the spice trade on the river and, contrary to convention, had built his main residence close to the docks to keep an eye on his ships and his warehouses. Outside his palace, the district was low, mean, and twisted. The alleys Kalev ran through had more in common with a dungeon than a Fairhaven thoroughfare, and all of his senses were on high alert for footpads as well as for his quarry. Fortunately, this particular warforged hadn't been created for stealth, and Kalev, silent in his soft-soled boots, had no trouble following Sheroth's thudding footfalls as the warforged stomped over cobbles and packed dirt.

Abruptly, the lumbering footsteps ceased. Kalev skidded to a halt at the corner of a sagging timber and brick warehouse. Dagger ready, he eased himself around the corner.

Someone whimpered. Kalev's eyes darted left to see a pile of tattered darkness shifting on the other side of a darkened threshold. Kalev peered more closely and saw a slender girl staring back at him, tightly clutching a bundle of rags.

"Don't go back there," whispered the girl.

"Why?" Kalev stepped up to the threshold and crouched down in front of the girl. "What's back there?"

The girl drew a huge breath.

"Idiot!" cried a familiar female voice.

Kalev was snatched from behind and once more tossed against the wall. This time his head connected with the filthy bricks and stars exploded across his vision. When his eyes cleared, he saw the woman from the duke's study barrel past him and collide with the girl, knocking them both into the darkness of the warehouse.

"Don't!" cried the girl as she groped backward one-handed, clutching her bundle more tightly.

Kalev found his feet. The warforged filled the narrow alley juncture. Inside the warehouse, the woman . . .

The woman blurred and changed. Then there were two girls, one in rags, one practically swimming in the tunic and trousers the woman had worn. The first girl stared, eyes bugging out.

Then, that ragamuffin also blurred, and also changed, becoming an orc with heavy arms and a wide, grinning mouth, but still with the bundle of rags clutched in one clawed hand.

The second girl shifted, and then the orc faced an elf, slim and golden haired.

"Don't just *stand* there," rumbled Sheroth from behind Kalev.

Kalev gaped at the warforged, who wore a broadsword on his back and a morningstar at his hip. "What about you?"

"Too big." Sheroth looked down at him with glowing eyes. "Not too big to get you, though."

Kalev swallowed. It had not been his night.

Inside the warehouse, the two . . . beings . . . shifted and shifted again, becoming human, monster, male, female, beautiful, hideous, by turns. Two things did not change—the bundle of rags held by the one, and the clothing of the other. Which gave Kalev his target, whom had now shrunk to become a bearded dwarf in full armor.

Kalev gritted his teeth, hefted his dagger, and charged.

Kalev hit the dwarf with his shoulder and they went down together, rolling and grappling. Despite what Kalev's eyes told him, his hands felt no mail, or hair, just muscled flesh. Nails raked his face.

WHAM!

The building shuddered around them as Sheroth—a living battering ram—slammed against the doorway. Praying the warforged didn't bring the aging building down on top of them, Kalev stabbed down at his opponent. The pseudo-dwarf howled as the dagger struck home, and he kicked straight into Kalev's belly with both feet. The wind left Kalev in a rush and he catapulted backward. A second figure leaped over him, slim as a girl but with white skin and ivory hair tinged with lavender. The being wore the woman's tunic, trousers, and jewels, and wrapped its bare hands around the other shapechanger's throat. The shapechanger choked and growled, and reverted to a bundle of dark sinewy limbs and snarling hatred.

Wheezing hard, Kalev forced himself back into his fighting stance. The shapechangers spun round, grappling. Sheroth pounded the narrow doorway, making a deafening thunder over the fight. Kalev looked frantically for an opening as they rolled on the floor, snarling and screaming, and found none.

But he did spot the bundle of rags lying on the ground.

Kalev snatched up the bundle. It was heavy, and about the size of a loaf of bread. Gold gleamed under the tattered sacking.

"Who wants it?" Kalev held the bundle high.

The shapechangers froze and Kalev found himself facing two pairs of eyes, one murderous and dark, one furious and shining amethyst.

"Mine," croaked the skulk. "Mine or I kill it!"

Kalev had no time to make an answer. The other combatant took advantage of the skulk's inattention and gouged at its eyes with hooked fingers. The skulk bellowed and threw the other backward so hard she flew through the air and hit a pile of empty barrels with a cry.

"Vix!" Sheroth slammed its bulk once more against the doorframe. The whole building groaned. Wood and brick gave way with a splintering crash. Sheroth rocketed into the low-beamed space.

The skulk howled and leaped and Kalev found himself tumbling head over heels. He stabbed out, then felt his dagger catch and be ripped from his hand, followed by the bundle.

His arms were empty and the skulk was bounding for the much-enlarged doorway. Sheroth planted himself in its path, but it dived straight between the warforged's massive legs. Kalev tried to scramble after it, but tumbled over one of the barrels dislodged by Vix's impact and turned another undignified somersault to slam up against Sheroth's shins.

The skulk vanished into the night.

Sheroth shook his head and set Kalev on his feet. Then he shuffled past, almost on his knees he had to crouch so low.

"You all right, Vix?"

"Just about." Vix sat with her head in her hands, her wild white hair sticking out in all directions. When she looked up, she caught Kalev staring at her.

"You're a changeling," he said.

"And you're a fool." Vix spat blood and dust and wiped her pale mouth.

Kalev shrugged. "Possibly." He reclaimed his dagger and sheathed it. "But my name is Kalev."

She glowered at him with her bright amethyst eyes. Kalev knew some changelings didn't think of themselves in terms of human gender, but he couldn't make himself think of the pale being in front of him as a "he," much less an "it."

"Do you want to tell me what this is about?" Kalev gestured around the warehouse.

Vix shifted her weight uneasily and glanced up at Sheroth. Sheroth shook his heavy head.

"I've already saved your life," Kalev pointed out. "You at least owe me an explanation."

Vix eyed Sheroth. This time Sheroth only shrugged, the plates that formed its shoulders grating together.

Vix slumped forward, resting her forearms on her knees. "It's not that complicated. A piece of property was stolen. It was traced to Duke Arisor. I was . . . hired to get it back. Quietly."

"Hired?" Kalev arched his brows.

"More or less." The changeling rubbed a smear of cobweb from her pale forehead.

"And would I be correct in assuming this piece of property is more than just an ugly statuette?"

Vix studied her fingertips a moment before she met Kalev's gaze. "It's called the Memory Eye and it's a magical artifact. Other than that, I don't know, and I'm dead anyway, so it doesn't really matter."

Kalev arched his brow. "Dead?"

"Metaphorically speaking. I hope." Vix got to her feet, using Sheroth's arm to steady herself. "I can't believe I let it get away!" With surprising gentleness, the warforged laid a hand on the changeling's slim shoulder.

"Do you even know what that was?" asked Kalev.

"It was a skulk. Foul thing." Vix spat again. "Must have been a mesmerist. That kind can cast an illusion on its victims. A lot of people think they're shapeshifters, which just makes life more difficult for those of us who truly are."

Kalev nodded. A lot of people did not like or trust changelings, believing that their ability to change form made them inherently devious.

"But skulks aren't thieves," said Kalev. "They're predators. Why would this one give up the chance for a kill for this . . . what did you call it? Memory Eye?" Arisor had been involved in some shady dealings, but according to Kalev's information, he'd never dealt in magical artifacts.

Vix cocked her head toward him. "You know a lot for a sneak thief."

"So do you," countered Kalev.

"You never did say what you were doing in the duke's study."

"You said you didn't care."

Vix waved a hand, acknowledging the point. "Well, thanks for the rescue. Time we were going, Sheroth."

You're not getting away that easily, he thought. "We could help each other," said Kalev with a feigned casualness. "You want to find the Memory Eye. I want to find out why it was stolen by a skulk, and what Duke Arisor was doing with it in the first place."

"Why?"

"I'm insatiably curious."

Vix watched him carefully for a moment. "Why should I work with someone who's lying to me?"

"I'm not. I'm just keeping my own secrets. There's a difference. I'd think a changeling could understand that," he added.

Vix glanced up at Sheroth again. Kalev wondered how long the two had traveled together.

"All right," said Vix. "But I can't start yet. Meet me at the Arena of Unparalleled Wonder at dawn. I'll be coming off shift then."

Kalev straightened up. "You work at the Arena? I didn't know House Phiarlan hired changelings."

"Neither do they." Vix's form blurred and Kalev again faced the graceful, dark-haired woman.

"We'll see you at dawn." Vix picked her way through the ruined doorway and into the alley. Sheroth gave Kalev a hard glower before shambling after the changeling.

Kalev waited until the pair had vanished and nothing remained but the sound of the warforged's heavy feet. Then, using all the skill he had at moving undetected, Kalev followed.

The Arena of Unparalleled Wonder was House Phiarlan's greatest theater, and even by Fairhaven standards, an incredible sight. From the alley mouth, Kalev stared at the sparkling edifice. It took up an entire city block and its mass of glittering domes and crystal spires towered over its neighbors. At least one performance was always in progress on one of the dozen public stages or the six or eight private performance spaces. The finest actors and entertainers fought for a chance to play there. And why wouldn't they? Queen Aurala herself attended the shows at least monthly.

Kalev was not seeing the Arena from its best angle. He was watching one of the many side doors where Vix and Sheroth stood talking. He itched to know what they said, but dared not get closer. At last, Vix touched the warforged's arm in farewell, and went inside. Sheroth took a post beside the door.

The streets around were busy, as the cream of Fairhaven's society enjoyed a night's carousing. The place would have been a pick-pocket's paradise if not for the sharp-eyed members of the public guard standing on the street corners. Queen Aurala felt that if petty crime ran rampant through her capital, it would reflect badly on her work toward a peaceful, stable realm, and in this at least, her brother the governor shared her opinions.

Kalev considered his situation. He now had more than one mystery on his hands.

Despite Vix's assumptions, he was not a thief. He had been given the task of finding the skulk that was slaughtering the city aristocracy. Normally, such beasts were relatively easy to track, once you knew what you were looking for, but this one had not been exhibiting normal skulk behavior. Skulks were clever, but not subtle. They worked with none but their own kind, and they were cold killers, interested only in maximizing carnage. But after the third death, it had become clear the targets were not being chosen at random. Each one of the dead had recently provided the queen's intelligence services with information. Kalev had been in Arisor's study to search for signs the aristocratic smuggler might have gone into the information trade. Instead, he'd landed in this business with Vix and the Memory Eye.

Kalev fingered the medallion he wore beneath his shirt. Actually finding a skulk was a surprise. He'd expected to find a human trying to make the deaths look like a skulk's work.

My night for being wrong, he thought. But what did a skulk want with a magical artifact? And could it be coincidence that he and Vix both arrived at Duke Arisor's study at the same moment? Even if she was only a hired thief, whoever hired her might have more on their mind than retrieving property.

Kalev needed answers, and he did not have time to search the whole Arena for them, never mind the whole city. He made his decision and pulled out his medallion.

The day Kalev joined the Royal Eyes—the secret intelligence service belonging to Queen Aurala—he had been given this badge. The day he had been set on the trail of the skulk, the medallion had been given a spell. It would work only once, Keue Fourthmaster, the Eyes' quartermaster, told him. So he was not to waste it, or lose it. But for that one time, it would allow Kalev to see what he was looking for, no matter how many barriers stood between him and the target.

The problem was, if Kalev used it at too great a distance, he would not be able to determine the exact location of what he sought, and then the spell would be used up. The further problem was there might yet come a better chance, a greater need to see something. Kalev weighed the medallion in his hand and the decision in his mind.

Then, as he had been directed, he placed the gold disk against his left eye and murmured the words to activate the embedded spell.

The medallion grew warm against his skin.

"Who has the Memory Eye?" he whispered. "I need to see who has the Memory Eye."

Instantly, the world around him faded. The effect was dizzying. People became ghosts, and buildings thin mist. Only one thing remained solid—a black stain slipping down one of the Arena's great gilded domes. It clutched a bundle to its chest that, to Kalev's spell-enhanced gaze, glowed like a beacon. The skulk shambled across the roof, lifted a trap door, and jumped through.

And all the world was solid again, and Kalev was staring at the Arena with one eye covered.

The skulk was in there, somewhere. The skulk and Vix, who had spun him a story of blackmail and simple thievery. Kalev felt his jaw harden and he narrowed his eyes at Sheroth, standing straight and still in front of the stage door with its massive arms folded. Time was slipping rapidly away.

The direct approach, then.

Kalev took a deep breath and pelted across the street, dodging horses, carriages, and pedestrians alike. Sheroth looked up, and his jaw dropped.

Kalev didn't give him any time for questions. "Sheroth! The skulk's in the Arena!"

Warforged were fine tacticians and decent strategists, but Kalev had yet to meet one who could lie worth a damn. So Kalev was certain the surprise that stiffened Sheroth's stance was genuine. As were his next words.

"I have to warn Vix."

"It went in through a trap door in the roof, to the southwest of the smaller gilded dome," said Kalev quickly. "Is there any way you can check that out quietly while I let Vix know what's happened?"

"If it gets down into the bowels of the Arena, we'll never find it," Sheroth muttered, and Kalev held his breath until the warforged met his gaze. "Vix'll be in her dressing room.

Second stairs on your left going in, two flights up, first right, third door on the lefthand side. Got that?"

Kalev nodded and Sheroth went on. "Tell Vix I'll meet you at door twelve. Door twelve. Got that?"

"Door twelve."

Sheroth opened the door. "Quick."

Kalev nipped inside the Arena of Unparalleled Wonder, and into another world.

Kalev had attended Arena performances many times. He was familiar with the gilt and glitter of the front of the house, every aspect of it designed to amaze. This was nothing like that.

It was a world of timber, painted canvas, and shadows. All manner of effigies hung from fine black lines, looking disconcertingly like they were floating in midair. Ropes as thick as his wrist connected systems of huge pulleys. A steam elemental sat in a brass housing at the center of a complex conglomeration of wooden cogs and metal gears that drove shafts reaching up into the ceiling and down into the floor.

Actors and dancers in glittering costumes darted like butterflies between the stagehands in dark tunics and breeches. Burly men hefted boulders and pillars on their shoulders. The floor vibrated from the motion of feet and carts and machines. Humans and half-elves trudged back and forth, burdened by boxes or great piles of cloth, or hauled on ropes, or signaled up to the catwalks to the ones handling the massive glowing crystals that lit the stages.

Those catwalks made a network overhead that stretched farther out and higher up than Kalev could see. As his eyes adjusted to the dim light, he caught glimpses of stairways traveling up and down, and arched doorways leading to darkened corridors.

You could hide an army in here, Kalev thought.

Kalev was also very aware that despite standing in shadow, as the only one present without any clear purpose, he stuck out like a sore thumb. It was only a matter of moments before someone noticed him. He shifted his demeanor so he projected confidence and strode to the second stair on the left leading upward. As long as he didn't do something clod-brained, like getting in someone's way, he would probably be ignored.

He hoped.

The third door after the first right had the name Vixana Fairlight scrawled on it in chalk, a sign of how quickly things turned over in the Arena. Kalev knocked, but did not wait for an answer before he walked in.

Vix, in her guise as a dark-haired human woman, started to her feet.

"Get out of here!" she cried. "I don't need more trouble!"

"Neither do I, but . . ."

Footsteps sounded outside. Vix swore and shoved Kalev backward behind a folding screen draped with layers of dresses and cloaks. "Keep quiet!" she hissed.

The space smelled of old perfumes and powders. Kalev stepped back from the screen to keep his silhouette from showing, and breathed shallowly. He heard a faint swish as the door opened on well-oiled hinges.

"There you are, Vixana," said a rough male voice. "What's the news?"

"Nemar." Vix sounded anything but glad. "It's good. I've almost tracked down the . . . it."

So, this Nemar was Vix's employer. "*Almost* tracked it down!" Nemar exploded, then he seemed to remember he didn't want to be overheard. "I *told* you where it was!" he hissed.

"Unfortunately, Duke Arisor got himself murdered by a skulk," replied Vix evenly, but her voice was taut as a harp string. "Which stole your precious item."

"A skulk *stole* something?"

"Yes," replied Vix coldly. "Strange, don't you think? A creature that has no place in Fairhaven shows up and kills the duke shortly before I got to his study."

"None of your lip, thief." Nemar's voice turned truly ugly. "You swore you'd have it for me tonight!"

"I'll get it."

"You'd better." Heavy footsteps crossed the floor, cloth swished and wood creaked. Kalev tensed. He didn't want to show himself but he wouldn't stand by and let Vix be hurt. "You've got one too many secrets to fail, you and that warforged lummox."

"Leave Sheroth out of this!"

"I'll say what I like, *Vix*," sneered Nemar. "You just be sure you finish your job."

The door opened and shut, and footsteps walked away.

Kalev emerged from behind the screen. Vix said nothing, just sat down at the table of cosmetics and slowly began opening boxes and jars.

"Who is Nemar?"

Vix dipped her fingers into a paint pot and spread bright red cream across her lips. "He's the manager for stage eight. My employer."

"And your blackmailer, if I don't miss my guess. How'd he find out you were a changeling?"

"I took a fall one night," she murmured, watching her reflection. What's it like to stare into your own false face? Kalev wondered. "Almost broke my leg. The pain was bad. It's harder to hold a shape when you're hurting. He . . . caught me changing."

"And are you a thief?"

"I used to be." She wiped her fingertips on a towel. "No one hires changelings, so I fell in with a pack of adventurers. But I like living more than I like gold, so I came to Fairhaven to try to make a new start."

Kalev thought about the ugly snarl in Nemar's voice, and how he was the one who sent Vix after the Memory Eye. If a changeling thief was caught in a room with a corpse, how much further would the city guard look to find the murderer? "And Sheroth?"

"If you want to know his business, you can ask him," she snapped.

"I see."

"Do you?" She glowered at him in the mirror. Kalev made no answer, just met her gaze.

Vix blinked first. "I've got a performance." She got up and made to brush past him.

"You've got more than that," he said. "The skulk's in the theater somewhere."

"What!"

"It got in through one of the roof trap doors. It's in here, and it's got the Memory Eye with it."

For a moment, Kalev saw the changeling's pale coloring through the human's warmer flesh tones. "What in the name of all the hells is going on?" she demanded.

"That's a very good question," Kalev agreed. "Do you know what Nemar's connection to the Memory Eye is? Or Duke Arisor?"

Vix shook her head. "I never asked."

Then, thought Kalev, that's what I need to find out next.

Vix narrowed her eyes at him, as if she could read his thoughts. "Are you planning on *spying* on him?"

"I'm afraid I must."

He waited for her to protest, but she just sighed. "Don't get caught. I've got enough problems."

"I'll do my best. Sheroth's also on the case. He said to meet him by door twelve after your act. We can all rendezvous there once you get off stage, and plan our next move."

"You invite yourself along very easily." Vix snorted. "Why should we trust you?"

"Because you're in trouble, and there's no one else to help you."

Vix pressed her lips together in a hard line but he could tell she realized he was right. "My set lasts exactly fifteen minutes. I'll meet you at door twelve." She grabbed a spangled cloak and marched out the door.

Which left Kalev with one problem—how to find this Nemar in the Arena's labyrinthine backstage without being noticed and thrown out. He scanned the dressing room, hoping for inspiration. He found it on the broken writing desk that had been shoved into one corner of the dressing room.

Kalev buttoned his black coat all the way up to his throat and pulled his breeches out of his boot tops. He tucked his gloves into his pockets and dipped his right index finger into the inkwell. He plucked up a pen and ink pot and strode purposefully to the door. Now, if anyone spared him a glance, they would see nothing but a clerk, and who ever gave a clerk a second thought? It was almost as good as being invisible.

He emerged from the dressing room in time to peer over the railing to the main floor and watch Vix join a gaggle of sparkling costumed dancers all heading in the same direction.

"Now that's a beautiful sight."

Kalev jumped. A man stood beside him, a half-elf by the look of him. He'd moved into place so silently and easily, that for all his skills Kalev hadn't even noticed him. Then, Kalev realized he recognized him.

The half-elf was Gledeth Shore, the lead actor of the Arena. Kalev had seen him in his new drama less than a month ago, before the murders started. He had the fine-boned structure of a Valenar war prince combined with the lively energy of a charming human male. On stage, it was a lethal combination.

Kalev remembered his character of fussy clerk and sniffed.

Gledeth laughed and slapped his shoulder. Kalev flinched as if the blow was too hard, which only made Gledeth laugh harder. "Just don't get caught staring too long," he said, his eyes suddenly serious. "Or you might wind up in trouble." Then chuckling once more, he strolled off.

Kalev watched him go, thoroughly disquieted. What did the most famous actor in all of Fairhaven care what a clerk did or did not stare at?

Kalev wavered and cursed silently. He hunched his shoulders and shook his head so his hair flopped down across his brow, and started down the stairs. If Nemar was the stage manager, he would be in the wings, ready to line up the members of the dance troupe and give them their cue. Kalev would know the man as soon as he spoke and then . . .

"You!" shouted a furious voice. Kalev froze on the last step. A woman clad in a long black coat and carrying a huge ledger under her arm shouldered her way through the bustling stagehands. "Where do you think you're going?"

Then Kalev realized his disguise had a fatal flaw. No one spared a clerk a second thought, except, of course, another clerk.

Ten minutes, three flights of stairs, and half a dozen corridors later, Kalev found himself in the office of Mirias Jadering Phiarlan, a surprisingly stocky elf who wore his golden hair in a single braid that hung between his shoulder blades and displayed the great green earring that had given him his name. Kalev knew Mirias only by reputation, but that reputation was extensive. Mirias could make Kalev disappear so thoroughly not even the Eyes would be able to find his corpse.

Kalev sat beside the hearth in his office. Mirias's gaze bored straight into the back of his mind.

"So, tell me," Mirias said. "What brings you backstage at my Arena without ticket or invitation?"

Kalev crossed his legs, feigning relaxation. "There have been a rash of murders among the city's merchant aristocracy. I'm sure you heard."

Mirias nodded once.

"I am investigating these crimes. I have reason to believe they are connected to the Arena, and to the theft of a magical artifact known as the Memory Eye."

Mirias's green eyes narrowed.

"It was stolen from the study of Duke Arisor," Kalev continued, "who was murdered tonight, and now I find one of your stage managers is astonishingly eager to get his hands on it."

"Why is this any of your business?"

"As I said, I've been hired to find out the cause of the deaths."

"Hired by whom?"

Kalev smiled pleasantly and made no answer.

Mirias flexed his long fingers. "Nemar has bad luck at the gaming tables," he said at last. "He tends to . . . acquire objects of value and sell them. Good stage managers are difficult to find, so we have tolerated it."

"And now?" Kalev inquired.

"We may have to rethink this policy."

"In that case, I have a proposition," said Kalev. "Let me continue my investigations. If Nemar is behind the murders, I will make the problem go away, without anyone asking a single question, or casting any aspersions on House Phiarlan."

Mirias considered this. "I will give you one day. After that, I will take matters into my own hands."

Kalev inclined his head. "One last question. What is the Memory Eye?"

"The Memory Eye projects a copy of the last thing it's seen. For example, if it was on the main stage now, it would see Lady Daria Goldeneye in one of her most popular scenes. If its recall were activated, it would project that same scene so perfectly you would not be able to tell it from the original." He paused, attempting to gauge Kalev's reaction to this. "As such, it is very useful, particularly if a popular artist has fallen ill, or succumbed to a fit of temperament. The performance can go on and no one in the audience is any wiser."

Or demanding their entry fee refunded. "I can see where such an artifact would have . . . many uses," Kalev said. It could allow a person, say a stage manager, to be in two places at once. As he thought this, another face flashed in front of his mind's eye and Kalev found himself wondering if Nemar was working alone. The stage manager was already employed by House Phiarlan in one capacity, why not another? It was possible the story of Nemar's gambling debts was just that, a story. Mirias could very well be holding Nemar's leash, and the skulk's.

If House Phiarlan was engaged in a campaign against the Queen's intelligence sources . . .

Kalev got to his feet. "Thank you for your time. I will not forget this."

"Neither will I," said Mirias softly, as they shook hands.

"Where have you been?" Vix demanded. After his meeting with Mirias, it had taken Kalev almost another half hour to track down the street exit with the big white twelve painted on its black surface.

"Finding out about the Memory Eye, and about your black-mailing boss." And possibly getting led down a garden path. He looked around the alley where they stood. "Where's Sheroth?"

"I don't know." Vix wrapped her arms around herself.

Worry prickled Kalev too. Despite his brief acquaintance with them both, he knew Sheroth would never leave Vix waiting.

Kalev was beginning to see that whomever was behind this had spun an incredible web. The Memory Eye would allow them to be in two places at once, so they could work the social networks of the city and identify key information agents, but always with an alibi. Then, they could send in the skulk, who could hide in plain sight, to take out any agent who was getting too close to something important, or who might be about to change sides. Everyone knew skulks killed at random, so no one would ask why one person or another had been murdered.

But how was the skulk being controlled? Skulks worked for no one, obeyed no one, cared for nothing but death.

"We have to find the skulk," he said briskly.

Vix was not going to be so easily distracted. "Not until I know what's happened to Sheroth."

Kalev faced her. "Vix, if the skulk got a look at your true shape, it could have used it to lure Sheroth away from here."

Vix's eyes flashed amethyst. Then, she turned and started swiftly down the alley with Kalev following right behind.

They rounded the corner of the Arena, to a space filled with theatrical wagons painted with bright murals advertising acts and actors. Vix threw open a metal trap door set into the cobbles. Without hesitation, she climbed down a series of iron staples bolted to the wall. Kalev did the same. When he finally reached the floor, Kalev heard Vix speak a word he did not recognize. White light flared around her.

Kalev raised an eyebrow. Vix held up the glowing crystal for him to see. "We're all issued one. It's not safe to have flames burning unattended in here."

The room around them proved to be a storage space for fabric. It was lined with shelves stuffed with bolts of cloth in all textures and colors. Vix unlocked the door and let them into a hallway lined with doors.

"What are these?" Kalev asked as they walked into the corridor.

"Store rooms, mostly," replied Vix. "Doors to other stairs, to the work rooms, pump rooms, light rooms."

"How big is this place?"

"No one knows. There are rumors about whole families having lived down in these tunnels for generations." She ducked into another store room, surveyed the shelves, and reached one handed between two bales of fabric. To Kalev's surprise, she pulled out a spear made of a piece of black glass tightly lashed to a wooden shaft. She handed it to him and then brought out its twin.

"These rumors . . . ," he began, but she looked at him in a way that said quite eloquently she would answer no question that followed those words. Clutching his new weapon, Kalev turned away, but froze.

A trail of footsteps showed up plainly in the grime on the floor.

"Well, someone's been this way recently."

Vix held the crystal high and swore. "Sheroth."

"Are you sure?"

Vix pointed to the print of a huge, flat foot. "What else has a print like that?"

Kalev said nothing, just gestured with his spear, indicating that she should lead the way.

Following the faint trail in the dust, they traversed a series of ancient store rooms filled with the dusty detritus of the theater: pots and jars and crates, stacks of wood, coils of rope, folds of canvas. They passed through rooms filled with props, looking as if the contents of whole homes had been stacked in corners and piled on shelves. The corridor doors had been placed at strange angles, seldom directly across from each other, so each exit was a quarter turn from the entrance. The result was the uncomfortable sensation of going in circles.

Mildew permeated the stale air. A constant rustling accompanied them, and Kalev glimpsed the flash of red eyes as rats scuttled away from the unexpected light. Rickety stairways, their entrances half hidden by piles of debris or crates led them farther down. Kalev found himself quietly praying Vix's crystal didn't fail. Without the light, they'd be permanently lost in this labyrinth.

To keep his mind off that highly uncomfortable possibility, Kalev turned over the thousand questions that thronged his mind. What had convinced Sheroth to come down here? Had he truly followed a skulk in Vix's shape? But who controlled the skulk? How? It would have to be a powerful spell, or . . .

Kalev remembered the sight of Vix fighting the skulk, shapechanger facing shapechanger. Could a skulk mesmerist itself be under the spell of another kind of mesmerist? Someone who could not or would not enact their own murder. Someone who had a quick mind, and the glib tongue to cover any small inconsistencies.

Someone who had a predictable routine and could hide in plain sight, if they had the help of the Memory Eye . . .

They came to a stair that was stone rather than wood. They saw no more trail, but there was also no other exit from the room, so they headed down. It ended in a small space with walls of rough stone. Sewer stench permeated the draft that curled around Kalev's neck. Icy water leaked through the mortared joints and puddled on the ancient flagstones. For a moment he thought they'd hit a dead end, but then he saw a low crawlway near the floor.

Must go under the sewers, he thought.

Vix saw the crawlway too, and she held the crystal close to it, but the white light only penetrated a few inches into the stinking dark. Kalev looked at the changeling armed with her makeshift spear. "You'd better head back. I'll find Sheroth and bring him out to you."

"No," she said flatly, as he expected. "Sheroth has always stood by me. I'm not abandoning him to whatever's down there."

For a moment Kalev considered telling her who he was, and who he worked for. She was trustworthy. She could take a message back to his control for him, to let them know what had happened, just in case he never came out of this hole.

But all he did was nod once. "Then let's end this."

To Kalev's surprise, she let him go first, handing over the crystal without argument. Awkwardly, because of the spear and the crystal, Kalev crawled into the tunnel. It bent like a saddlebow and was coated with a stinking slime Kalev did not care to speculate about. His breath steamed in the crystal's light.

Finally, every joint aching, Kalev emerged from the tunnel into what he felt to be an open space. He held the crystal up high.

They stood in a strange, irregular chamber. Its filthy walls and ceiling curved sharply inward, making Kalev think it might be a juncture of sewer tunnels. Fetid heaps of dirt and refuse filled the many corners.

In its center stood Sheroth.

"Sheroth!" Vix cried as she emerged from the crawlway and darted forward. "What . . . ?"

"Get back, Vix!" bellowed Sheroth.

In the next heartbeat, the warforged drew his broadsword and charged, straight for Kalev. Kalev sprang to the side. Sheroth's momentum carried him past, but he pivoted faster than Kalev would have credited, and charged again.

"Sheroth!" cried Vix. "Stop!"

"He'll kill you!" Sheroth aimed a swing at Kalev's head. Kalev skipped back. He didn't dare parry. The spear's shaft would snap like a stick against Sheroth's blade.

"No! He's a friend!"

"He's a liar!" roared Sheroth.

If Kalev were facing a human, he'd just keep him on the run, using his speed to stay out of range and wear the other down. But he would wear down long before the warforged would.

Desperation giving him strength, Kalev hoisted himself one-handed up the pile of debris.

"Coward!" bellowed Sheroth as he charged again.

"Sheroth!" Vix leaped into his path. "What're you doing?"

"He's the murderer!" The warforged's eyes glowed with his outrage. "He killed the duke!"

"The skulk killed the duke!" Vix grabbed the warforged's raised sword arm and hauled down with all her strength. "Who told you this?"

Sheroth looked at her, momentarily paralyzed with confusion.

"I did," said a man's smooth voice, and Kalev was absolutely unsurprised to see Gledeth Shore emerge from the shadows, flanked by two skulks.

"What are you doing here?" Vix asked. Gledeth smiled indulgently down at her.

"He's a psion," said Kalev, not taking his eyes off Sheroth. "He's using his mind to control the skulks. He made them steal for him. He's convinced Sheroth you're in danger from me."

"So I very much suggest you get out of his way," said Gledeth to Vix.

"Sheroth's not going to hurt me," replied Vix calmly, looking up into the warforged's dull eyes and shifting, revealing her true form. "Sheroth will never hurt me."

Sheroth met Vix's amethyst eyes, and his body swayed.

Gledeth's eyes narrowed. "Hmmm . . . you may be right. Ah, well, Kalev, you'll just have to set your skulks on her."

The skulks roared and lunged forward. Vix screamed and stabbed out, catching one skulk in the shoulder. The skulk howled and reeled, and she pivoted on her heel to face the other sneering murderer.

"Kill them!" Gledeth shouted.

Sheroth plowed into the unsteady pile of debris that Kalev had climbed upon. Kalev leaped for the warforged's armored shoulders and bounced off, scarcely jarring Sheroth at all. He hit the floor hard, barely staying upright. Vix shouted again as both skulks charged her. She sliced one on the arm with her blade, sending it staggering backward, and with the back stroke slammed the butt of her spear into the other one's guts.

"They'll kill her!" Kalev bellowed to Sheroth. "You've got to do something! They'll *kill Vix!*"

Sheroth froze, just for an eye-blink. Kalev could practically feel the wave of power pouring from the psion, but it was not enough. It could not be enough to break such loyalty. Sheroth roared and turned, brandishing his blade in one massive hand. With the other, he grabbed the nearest skulk and tossed it aside.

Kalev faced Gledeth, spear poised. "Who are you working for, Gledeth?"

"You expect me to name my masters to you?"

Kalev smiled patiently. "You must be at your breaking point. You can't let the skulks go—they're just as likely to kill you as us. You can't let Sheroth go because he and Vix will take you down. If I want, all I have to do is wait it out, and you die."

The half-elf's eyes glittered. "Perhaps all I need do is wait until my skulks kill your pathetic allies. Then you are mine."

"You think I won't fight?"

"I think you don't want to," said the psion. "What I know is too useful to you and to your little queen. You need me to name my spy master. You know that you do."

He did. He wanted to bring Gledeth back alive, to see him questioned, to find out what the half-elf's plans were, why he had murdered, and who he was working for or with. It could be a threat to the whole of the realm and he, Kalev, could end it all, be a hero to the queen. If he could just capture Gledeth Shore alive.

Kalev swayed on his feet. "I . . . need . . . you."

Just then, Sheroth bellowed and stomped down on one of the skulks. There was a sickening crunch and squish as the creature's skull splintered beneath the warforged's foot.

Gledeth grinned and turned his shining eyes onto Kalev, in time to see Kalev's dagger flying toward him, but not fast enough to dodge before the blade embedded itself in his throat.

"But I want you dead more," said Kalev.

Gledeth gurgled and fell as a welter of blood spilled down the front of his silken tunic. Kalev turned in time to see

Sheroth grab the remaining skulk and hold it so Vix could run her spear straight into its wide-open mouth, slitting flesh and crashing through bone. The skulk gagged and gurgled and sagged, spouting blood, and Sheroth flung the creature away.

Vix and Sheroth faced each other, panting, shaking, their friendship unbroken, the slow understanding of true circumstances that comes after a battle washing over them. Kalev retrieved his dagger and wiped the blood and gore on Gledeth's sleeve before he tucked it back into his sash.

"Come on," he said to his comrades. "Let's get out of here."

Sarah Zettel is an award-winning science fiction and fantasy author. She has written nineteen novels and a roughly equal number of short stories over the past ten years in addition to founding the author cooperative Book View Cafe, practicing tai chi, learning to fiddle, marrying a rocket scientist, and raising a rapidly growing son. She is very tired right now.

WATCHERS AT THE LIVING GATE

A Tale of the FORGOTTEN REALMS

PAUL PARK

He lived with his own kind in the forest, away from the towns of the human world, because of what he was. But once a year since he was small he'd come away to the ruined city on the mountainside where his own people never ventured, nor full-blooded humans either, a place of old magic and old defeats. That first time he'd been hunting on the cliff top, and a wounded ram had led him far from home. In a bowl of mist and leaning stones he brought it down, a lucky shot with the small bow, but soon he heard the hounds yelping behind him. Before he could claim the kill he had been whipped away by men on horseback, shouting and cursing the mother who had borne him. Some dismounted and threw stones. Helpless, he had watched them pull the ram away, his arrow still lodged in its throat.

When he ran away it had not been in shame or fear so much as rage. Toward sunset he came out on the mountainside above the clouds and watched the red light cut across the rocks amid the tussocks of coarse grass. There was the fallen gate, its stone posts inscribed with runes he couldn't read, not yet. He approached, and came into the first of the ruined streets, the ruined houses built into the cliff side.

Carved statues lined an avenue. Some had lost their arms, legs, heads, but even so, he could see a vision of ideal beauty in the broken stones. He paused to study the statue of a boy about his age, yet more beautiful even than a human child, tall and slender, with long eyes and delicately pointed ears.

He stood at the lip of a stone pool, gesturing down into its depths, and in the last rays of the setting sun, the living boy squatted over it and saw reflected in its surface, as carefully as in any mirror, his own distorted features, his heavy jaw, protruding teeth, mashed nose, bulbous eyes under heavy ridges of bone. In such circumstances even the small attempts at decoration, the shards of broken glass that his mother had tied lovingly into his shaggy hair, appeared to mock him as they caught the light.

Then it was dark. He looked around for the door of a stone hall that still retained some of its roof. The black doorways seemed suddenly menacing. Who knew what ghosts and spirits prowled these ruins, who had died here when the city fell? Instead, shivering with cold, he stayed beside the pool, until the moon rose behind the shattered peaks, and moonlight struck the surface of the water.

That was the first time he had seen her. Every year since then he had returned, when the first full moon of summer fell into the water. He had changed since that first time, grown in stature and in skill, but she never changed. Always she stroked to the surface as if swimming up from underneath, from some submerged tunnel, he had thought at first.

Then, because he was a boy, he had worshiped her as a boy does a woman, worshiped her goodness, as he imagined it, striven to be worthy, and to fulfill every command. Later, full-grown, his shoulders tattooed with his clan's symbols of manhood, his ears pierced with iron rings, he had moved into another kind of worship, as she had stood with the water to her knees, her body clothed in wet silk, and a phosphorescent sheen that had followed her from the depths. Later still, reckless, he had staggered down into the pool, only to find himself enmeshed in weeds, while she pulled laughing away. "How ugly you are! How is it possible for a living creature to be so ugly? You disgust me—truly, you disgust me." But when he was exhausted and discouraged she came close to him again, and with flashing eyes she told him once more what he must accomplish to prepare himself. He'd done everything she'd asked.

These commandments, as if from a goddess, had led him far from his own people. Not for him the brawls between the clans, the comforts of marriage and children. Instead he lived with his widowed mother in the forest, away from the clan's hearth, despised, he imagined, by the purebreds in his village. With a dedication born of rage, he studied human lore. He learned the languages of men and other creatures. He studied old books by candlelight, and parchment scrolls from the libraries of the abandoned city. He spoke the words the goddess brought to him until the trees came alive. And in the spring he cut his totem stick from a piece of bone, and carved the length of it in a pattern of braided hair, and fashioned its knob in the shape of a wolf's head, with lumps of agate for its eyes.

On the night of the full moon he slept most of the day. His mother woke him for supper, as he had requested. Yawning, he sat down on a mossy rock in the middle of the stream, washed his body, shaved his face, combed his hair and knotted it with iron beads. Then he dressed himself in the clothes he had laid out the night before, his father's shirt, made from doeskin as fine as linen, salvaged by his mother after he'd left them, mended and patched over the years. The tribe wore furs and harder, heavier leather when they wore anything, but she had kept this human garment for the wedding of her half-human son.

Now she brought him porridge and blood sausage from the fire. She stood watching him, holding the food in the wooden bowl. Long before, she had learned not to question his choices, because it was common for the men in the village to abandon their old mothers and fathers to the wolves, the totem of their clan, when there were too many mouths to feed. But her son was a powerful hunter. Others claimed to see the deer and elk search for him in the meadows and the woods, and lay their horned heads in his lap.

"Haggar," she said.

He looked up, smiling into her coarse and wrinkled face, until he noticed that her eyes were bright with tears. "Don't worry."

"I'm not worried. But you are going far away."

He expected some sort of complaining then, and when it didn't come he started to say all the things that he'd rehearsed in order to forestall her: "I won't be long. I've left seven necklaces of iron cash. In the digging pit there's a wooden box with agates and opals you can sell in town. Humans love them for their games. The smokehouse is full of meat and fish."

But when she said nothing about any of that, he stood up to comfort her. "I won't go far," he said, which was a lie, the first he'd ever told her.

"There's my cousin," she said, referring to a girl in the village. "She waits for you."

When he put his arms around her, she relaxed into his chest. "Me, too," she said, fingering the bone buttons of his father's shirt.

Later, as it got dark, he left the encampment. Barefoot, he ran uphill through the woods. When the trees gave way among the rock piles, he clambered onto the ridge, then stood looking back for a moment at the firelight among the trees. It was the first night of the summer festival, and the men were lighting the bonfire in the charmed circle. They were already drinking their honey beer, and soon the women would dance to the rhythm of the drums, while the old shaman marked their foreheads from a bowl of blood—he'd never seen this ceremony. He missed it every year.

He stood on the ridge as the darkness gathered. "I know you're here," he said without turning round. The she-wolves picked their way over the stones, their heads low. He ran among them up the slope into the high meadow, among the red-star columbines. The wolves coursed after him but could not reach him, because as he ran he gripped his totem stick and muttered his evocations, until he could feel the coarse hair on his back and down his arms, and he dropped down to all fours.

Everything she'd asked he had accomplished, no matter what the sacrifice. Tonight she would understand that there was no remaining trace of the boy whose shape had so disgusted her. She would recognize how love had changed him.

Before moonrise he paused at the stone gatepost on the mountainside, whose runes, he now saw, spelled out a name, or else part of a name: CENDR. The remaining letters on the other side had crumbled away, and the post itself had broken into pieces in the coarse grass. The wind had died. Black clouds hung above him, obscuring chunks of stars.

And when he saw the sky glow silver behind the eastern

peaks, he picked his way down the avenue of statues, his feet delicate on the uneven stones. At the limit of his senses he could hear the noise of rats or rabbits in the empty houses; they would not show themselves. They would crawl into their crevices and holes, not knowing they were safe from him; he wasn't hungry. All day he had fasted, in preparation. Now finally he reached the rim of the stone basin and lowered his head to drink. But at the last moment he did not break the surface with his long tongue, and as the moon rose he saw his countenance reflected as in a mirror, his yellow eyes and cruel teeth. Baring them, pulling away his dark lips, he allowed his breath to trouble the water, while at the same time a small wind came out of nothing, following his secret command. It stirred the surface, sparing him the sight of his ugliness as he regained his mortal shape.

When the circle of the moon was bright in the water, he heard her laughter from the other side of the pool. She sat on the far lip of the basin, weeds in her yellow hair, which gleamed with phosphorescence. She was examining the bottom of one foot when she raised her head.

"Haggar," she said, her voice soft and musical, and he wondered if he'd ever told her his true name, and if not, how she came to know it. "So many years you've disappointed me. When I tell my friends, they laugh at me. But it's time to prove them wrong. I need your help. I have an urgent need. I hope things are different now."

So many years—nine years. During that time he had changed utterly in body and mind, but she had not changed. He stood in his leather breeches and his father's wedding shirt, his totem stick slung in his belt. Now she stood and beckoned, and as he stumbled forward, it occurred to him that he was older than she, or at least he looked older, a full-grown man.

And at the same time he thought about what she'd said: she needed him. What for? Need, he knew, was different from love, however similar they felt. And friends—what friends? He'd always thought she was alone in the world, last of her race, of the people who had lived here in this city, perhaps.

He paused, the water around his shins. She stood within a stone's cast away, one hand on her slim hip. She smiled at him, a mocking smile, he understood, and for the first time he listened to his doubts—he had learned much in the solitary study of his craft. He knew the evocations that summoned clouds and rain, and those that summoned lightning from the sky. He had his hand on the druidic chain of being that linked all beasts with the primal spirit, and he knew the evocations that would pull him closer to that spirit up the evolutionary links, so that he could find the dividing lines, and sink back down again into another body, bird, or fish, or reptile, or warm-blooded beast. And though he had the practical mind of his mother's people, he could not have learned these things without some knowledge of the rest, of other worlds or planes that joined to this one in small places, of the Feywild and the crystal towers of Cendriane, where the eladrin had once lived, tall and proud and slender, but blind in their suspicion that all other races were animals to be used. Worse than humans in that way.

"When I tell my friends . . ." Now suddenly he imagined her not as a solitary gift to him, but as an emissary from that world. He took a step backward, and at the same time watched the smile fade from her lips. How had she known his name, and not even his clan name but the secret name his mother called him? For an instant he imagined his mother's cottage in the woods, and heard in his mind's ear the drums of the summer festival, and saw the bonfire and the women dancing among the trees, among them Uruth, his mother's cousin, but younger than him, a sweet girl with big eyes, but not beautiful, not like this.

Her smile dwindled as she saw his doubts. She stood with her hand on her hip, while the moonlight spread across the surface of the water. "Catch me," she said, and she dived into the depths—the pool was deeper than it looked, he knew. With a cry, he dived in after her, struggling to follow, to seize her as she swam down. For an instant he thought he'd clasped her in his arms, but then she'd slipped down deep, her wet silk slippery as eel skin. The water was murky, suffused with light, and he saw nothing.

His lungs were bursting, but he held his shape. He knew this was a test, a last test, and if he failed it she would not come again. Last year he'd tried to follow her down, and in the hole at the bottom of the pool where the current changed and the water turned cold, he'd lost his nerve. Defeated, desperate, he had clawed his way up to the surface again.

But now he saw a glimmer down below, and imagined her small feet kicking through the weeds. He imagined diving down to her, touching her body with his outstretched fingertips as she twisted away. He imagined he would drown and die rather than lose her, and with all his strength he struggled grimly, even as he felt the weeds clutch at his legs. Below him in the phosphorescent depths of the pool he saw a shadow flicker, and with his lungs empty, his brain starved of air, he toiled down into the glow, first green, then blue until it burst around him, and he realized he'd been swimming upward to the light, and now had broken through the surface of another pool, under another sky.

And even so he might have drowned, because he found himself almost too exhausted to move, and too depleted to breathe, except he found the water shallow where he was. On his hands and knees, he dragged himself up a surface of smooth, blue-green tile until he lay at her feet.

The sunlight blinded him, it was so bright. The air was too rich to breathe. He had a vague impression of her standing over him, speaking not to him but someone else. "Humor me. I didn't choose him for his looks. Take him and put him with the others. Leave him his rags until we find him proper clothes. And be careful. He doesn't look it, but he has some skill. That's why he's here."

Haggar rolled onto his back, forcing his eyes open so he could peer up through his lashes at the azure sky, so terrible and deep. He forced his ears and nose to open, fuzzily aware that if he tried to protect himself from the intensity of colors, sounds, and smells that distinguished this place, he would lose any hope of commanding nature here, as he could at home. Ignoring the long hands that snatched his wolf stick from his belt, he murmured an evocation. Leaving his body to be mauled and harried by the eladrin, he cast his mind into the air until he hung suspended far above, and looked down with an eagle's eye on the small group of struggling figures at the edge of the tiled pool.

This projection of himself, this imaginary eagle, was not capable of astonishment. Otherwise he would have been amazed to see the extent of the ruined city below his claws, the height of the crystal spires that soared up past him. The city lay at the edge of a sprawling forest that had overgrown it in a twisting mass of vines. What remained were buildings of prismatic stone, many of them perfect and untouched, as if the inhabitants had been called away momentarily to attend to something important, and left their doors standing open. But other parts of the city bore the traces of the powerful explosions that had destroyed it many years before, circular craters that contained structures not just ruined but pulverized, blasted to their foundations. Within these circles nothing lived, in contrast to the teeming life that overran the rest, life not just vegetable but animal as well: panthers and rodents and feral pigs, as well as monstrous insects, made huge, perhaps, by the lingering effects of a forgotten war.

There were no birds above him in the high, unnatural, purple and blue vault of the sky. Below, the eladrin were wrestling his body into a cart. He counted three of them besides the girl, and as they bound his arms behind him, he could tell they were nervous and unsure. He knew it from the language of their bodies, and because they were rougher than was necessary—he was offering them the resistance of a sack of potatoes, or perhaps a sack and a half. Nor could he explain their vicious pokes and jabs as merely their natural contempt for him. No, the eladrin were in a hurry, and the horses, also, were skittish and shy.

He could not judge the time of day from the color of the light, which was too unfamiliar. He could not see the sun. But as he sank down into his body, tried to imagine the reason for their haste as they pulled the horses over the jolting stones, down the Avenue of Gods—this name came to him intact, a memory from old maps. He knew that, like the corresponding street in the mortal realm, it cut across the city toward the eastern gate, and was embellished by its own double line of marble statues—many objects here, he knew, had their own pale resonance in the land he had left behind.

He lay trussed-up in the back of the cart, considering his options. Now that he had his bearings, it seemed to him that even without his totem stick, much could be done. Whatever these people were afraid of, he could use that fear against them. He started with a few small guttural evocations, which his captors might confuse with the sound of him coughing or spitting—they hadn't blindfolded him or bound his mouth. No, they had underestimated him, which was why he'd not resisted them. But that would change now, he thought, staring at the girl's beautiful face as she looked up into the sky.

The breeze had freshened, and tendrils of dark vapor moved across the sky, while at the same time the front wheels of the cart fetched up against a root, whose heavy knee had split the paving stones. The driver spoke his own less-effective evocation as a single tendril broke out of the bark and grasped at the wooden rim like a weak, small, pale green hand—it was enough. Before the horses could pull free, a half-dozen more had clutched the wheel, while vinelike clouds clutched at them from above—the Feywild, Haggar thought, was responsive to him. The force of nature was overwhelming here.

The sky darkened. Soon, he imagined, a bolt of lightning would spook the horses; already they refused to move, shivering with their ears back, while the driver hacked them with his whip. Two eladrin warriors leaped out of the cart, and one stood guard while the other bent to cut at the new creepers with his sword. Neither of them had yet thought to connect him with what was happening.

The girl, however, was wiser. Alone in the cart with him, she bent over him. Her yellow hair fell over her face and he could smell the scent of her, a perfume like cinnamon or clove. "Listen to me, you bird-brained pig," she murmured. "Let me explain. In half an hour it will be dark. Sooner if you persist. Even in twilight, we won't last ten minutes here. Lord Kannoth will open up the gates of his black palace, and he will hang our corpses from the trees. He has an army of undead soldiers who worship him as a god. Do you want to play your stupid games with him?"

"Free me," Haggar croaked. His voice was ugly even to himself.

She bent lower, so that she could whisper softly in his ear. "You stinking lump of excrement."

Above them the sky was black, and a foul mist had gathered. Rearing up, screaming with terror, the horses yanked at their traces and the cart fell to one side, kept from overturning by the swarming vines. The girl stepped to the ground and stood erect. She raised her cupped hands, filled now with a greenish light that ran down her naked arms and over her body, soaking her clothes until she herself was a radiant torch against the darkness. She drew her knife and cut the horses free of the vines, and in an instant they were quiet; they stood trembling, patient, their eyes wide, their nostrils rimmed with foam. Then she bent to hack at the creepers that held the wheel, and Haggar could feel the cold edge of the blade as if against his own skin.

He rolled down against the side of the cart, and there he found his totem stick discarded and wedged in a crevice between the knotted slats; the eladrin had thrown it there, not respecting him enough to keep it safe. Rolling against the wolf's-head knob, pressing his shoulder into it, he snarled an evocation and felt his body change. He felt the bone absorb into his body. The ropes slackened, and he bit at them until they gave way.

He no longer suffered the edge of the girl's knife. Instead, she'd turned away from him, walked a few paces down the road to illuminate a wider area. Her arms were upraised, and the knife glowed in her left hand. In the mist, Haggar could see she kept at bay an emaciated pale creature taller than herself, while the other eladrin, the two soldiers and the driver, cowered behind her. Shaking himself free of the last knots, he bounded from the cart and moved away into the darkness, only to turn when he heard one of the horses groan, a low gurgle deep in its chest.

Both animals had sunk to their knees on the stone road. A hideous spider, larger than a man, crouched above them. Snarling and cursing, Haggar did his best to clear the darkness he had made, conjuring up a wind to blow the mist away, break apart the clouds. But he knew that whatever he did, he would find the day had sunk to twilight. Whatever creatures lurked in the catacombs and forests of Cendriane, their feeding time had come.

But there was a full moon here, too, or almost full, brighter than its counterpart in the mortal world. By its light, and the light cast by the girl, he could watch the spider wrap its kill in pale cords as thick as a man's wrist. In the other direction, toward the eastern gate, the way was blocked by a dozen or more of the undead, their bone-bleached skin luminous in the moonlight. Skeletal, with swollen heads and grinning jaws, they carried weapons of a type Haggar had never seen, swords that shone like crystal, and bows of yellow horn. One of them nocked a gleaming arrow, and in a moment the eladrin driver fell, shot through the eye.

Again Haggar paused, one forefoot upraised. This was not his fight. But then he saw another of the eladrin stumble to his knees, a sword through his belly. The final soldier was just a boy, and he fought bravely, his yellow hair matted with blood. But then one of the pale creatures pulled him down from behind, which left only the girl, twisting away from a behemoth with an axe, cutting him through the ribs and then shying back, her green fire diminished, almost extinct.

Haggar threw back his head and howled, and a single bolt of lightning hit the spike of the creature's axe, sending him sprawling. A peal of thunder shook the ground, and then Haggar was upon them, snatching the thin bones of the skeletons' legs. And when the girl fell, he seized hold of the collar of her shirt, gripping the fragile cloth in his narrow jaws, dragging her away. At the same time a miasma of fog seemed to spill out of the ground, and the creatures, disoriented, hacked and stabbed at shadows, while a freezing wind surrounded them in a sudden squall of snow. Haggar backed away from them, dragging the girl over the icy stones until they reached the gate at the base of the avenue, an enormous arch of carved and decorated marble, with friezes and embellishments of fighting beasts, and a squat stone eagle on each corner of the roof.

On the other side of the arch, the moon rode high and unimpeded above the forest's edge. Not knowing if she was alive or dead, Haggar dragged the girl out through the gate, out of the city, and immediately found himself returned to his common form, a lurching half-breed orc, gesticulating impotently with his totem stick while the fingers of his other hand grasped at her torn collar. Back through the arch he could still see the blizzard, but here everything was still.

Or not quite. There was a sound of melancholy laughter. Then a man detached himself out of the shadow of the gate, and Haggar understood without knowing that this was Lord Kannoth, archfey ruler of the catacombs of Cendriane.

He was a man of middle height, dark, delicate, and slender, and dressed in a jacket of wine-colored velvet. His only weapon was a flower, a lily at the end of a long stalk. Bending down over the recumbent girl, he touched the lily to her brow, her lips. His voice was light and mocking. "When I first saw you, I thought perhaps you were an enemy to be feared, some wild lycanthropic berserker out of Brokenstone Vale. But in the moonlight, as you perceive, these illusions have melted, and here we are, a simple eladrin maiden, a cowering orc, and me."

As he spoke, the snow died away on the other side of the arch. The mist dissipated, and as far as Haggar could see, the Avenue of the Gods stretched unimpeded to the blue-tiled pool. The wreckage from the fight had been pulled away. The stones were white as chalk under the moon.

"Tell me," said the archfey. "Now that everything is still, and if you can remember, and if you have the wisdom to speak, what is the impulse that has powered all this violence? Don't worry," he said, as Haggar crouched over the girl's body, stretched out his hand and then drew it back. "She is asleep, waiting for you to wake her. It is love, is it not? It is love that has caused all this."

He didn't deny it. In slumber, in the moonlight, all the anger and contempt that had disfigured her were bleached away. She lay on her back, her hair away from her face.

"And what about her? What does she feel? An orc and a fey maiden—I must confess to you, a story such as this could touch my heart."

Haggar shook his head. Lord Kannoth smiled. "But that might change. You must not give up hope. Don't be afraid—she cannot wake unless you kiss her lips."

Haggar looked up in wonder into the archfey's pensive face. Again he put his hand out, pulled it back.

"Boy," advised Lord Kannoth, "it is a token of my good will. But do not make me wait. For only a few more moments will I consent to be amused."

And so Haggar closed his eyes, leaned forward, and placed the lightest possible kiss on the girl's lips. Instantly she came awake, and when she saw him, she twisted away as if he'd burned her. She turned her face to the ground and spat. "Pig!"

Lord Kannoth laughed. "This boy has saved your life. Show some gratitude, my child. Pride is nothing, beauty is nothing, compared to the virtues of an honest heart. Believe me, this I know."

With his lily wand, he pulled the hair back from his feral, delicate face. And wherever the flower touched, the skin changed. What had been pale and pure, in a moment was scorched and ridged, grotesque and distorted, with ragged lips pulled back in a grin. "Child," he said softly. "What's your name?"

"Astriana, my lord," she mumbled into the dirt.

"Astriana, that's a flower's name. Accept your fate, Astriana, as I have accepted mine. This is your husband. Do you understand me?"

Tears glistened in her eyes. "Yes, my lord."

"Speak the oath in your heart, where I can see it. Good. Then it is done."

He stood and turned away from them. The moon slid behind a cloud. When it came free again, Lord Kannoth had disappeared.

"Come," Haggar said, after a moment. "Let's leave this place. It's not safe to stay here."

A hundred paces from the road, the forest waited. "No one will harm us," murmured Astriana. "Are you so stupid that you did not hear? He gave his word."

She was weeping into her fists. She crouched in the road as he stood over her, embarrassed. The air around them stood still.

"Are you so stupid that you don't understand?" she continued. "You're my husband now. Anything you ask, I am sworn to deliver, especially on this night."

"That is not the custom of my tribe," he said.

Moaning into her hands, she didn't hear. "I am carefully punished. All these months I've used my own self to entice you, everything I am—I knew what I was doing. Why else would you have come?"

Then she looked up, her cheeks wet, her eyes glinting savagely. "What do you want? Don't keep me in suspense. Whatever it is, I am bound to give it, as a good wife should."

Standing in the bone-white roadway, Haggar cleared his throat. He fiddled with his totem stick, picking with his thumbnail at the chunks of agate. "In my clan," he murmured humbly, "that is not the measure of a good wife."

She gave him a glance in which a moment of clear gratitude was immediately clouded with suspicion. "Easy to say. Are you so stupid that you can't understand what I'm offering you?"

He smiled, because he thought he understood how to disarm her. "Astriana," he said, and saw her flinch. "Woman," he amended, "this is what I want." Again she cringed away, as if from a blow. "I want to understand why you have brought me here, to this place. For nine years you made the journey to my world. 'Put him with the others,' you said, when I was lying in the cart."

She looked at him then, a long, slow stare. She wiped her nose on her hem and, eyes dry, clambered to her feet. "That's what you want?"

"That's what I want."

"I swear you're even stupider than I thought," she said, but then she smiled when he burst out laughing. "In the Feywild we are bound by our promises, you understand?"

He nodded.

"Then come," she said. "I'll tell you. It was not nine years for me."

She turned down the road into the forest. "What about your men?" he asked her. "Will you come back in the morning?"

"Who?" She shrugged. "They're gone. I hired them in the village."

"Even so. We should go back. One of them was just a child."

She gave him a look that suggested his stupidity had grown so powerful, it had become a force of nature like the ocean or the wind.

"Besides," he said. "We have no weapons."

"That's not the place to search for them." She gestured with her hand. Looking back through the gate, he could see an enormous figure standing in the roadway near where they'd struggled over the cart. His shape was human, but his size was not.

"We have no choice," she said. "Lord Kannoth has taken everything, all our strength. It's a tradition. His gift to us."

Now suddenly she was in a hurry. She turned and ran down the gentle slope, and he followed her. She had spoken the truth: there was no strength in him, no trace of his totem animal. Heavier than she, he labored to keep up, as if the air of this new world were too rich for him to breathe.

After a mile and a half, she stopped to draw breath under the forest's eaves. "How long?" he asked, after a moment.

"Until dawn tomorrow. It happened when I made my vow. It is the way of the eladrin, to come together without any skills or powers, as simple men and women on our wedding night."

He had the impression, now, that she was mocking him. "Don't keep saying that."

"It gives me no pleasure to remind you. Nine months, it was, not years. Nine months I cast my hook into that pool. You're not the only fish I caught."

"I suppose not."

She studied his face as if, he thought, she were trying to memorize his ugliness. "Why aren't you angry?" she asked. "I would be angry at the things I say."

They stood beside a stone pillar at the entrance to the forest. It marked the border where the bleached dust of the roadway and its verges gave way to the darkness of the trees. Where the paving stones gave out and the road became a rutted track, two enormous oak trees stood as sentinels.

"Kannoth's protection ends here," she said. She shrugged. "Even my knife is cold." She turned under the oaks and disappeared into the darkness.

He didn't know whether she was lying or didn't understand her own powers, but she retained some luminescence in the dark, a greenish glow that led him onward. Without it, he'd have had to pick his way like a blind man, because the canopy of leaves denied all but an occasional shaft of moonlight, and the path was muddy, and wound among tangled masses of roots. Soon the way steepened, and in some places they descended a cliff face among evergreens, clambering down over wet boulders. Rivulets of water fell around them, and Haggar was astonished at the fecundity of this place, the denseness and intensity of life. Every place he put his hand or foot, living creatures squirmed or flopped or skittered away, and the air was thick with bugs, which got into his nostrils and his mouth. In the darkness, sounds and smells assaulted him with an almost physical pressure, a profusion of squawking and chittering and grunting and croaking, of sap and ash and mud and rotting wood. But among all these he caught the tiny, evanescent perfume of cinnamon or clove, which he followed downward like a gleaming thread, hour after hour. Sometimes the scent of her would thicken, and he would find her waiting for him in some crevice or dell, her skin glimmering faintly.

And at these moments as they rested, she would give him partial answers to the question he'd asked: "I had to find some help," she said. "In the deep Feydark, where we are going, there is a portal called the Living Gate. For many generations, which means many hundreds of your years, a cohort of my people were its guardians. Over the years they relaxed their vigilance because the gate was shut, sealed in the old days. Even though we retain terrifying stories of the days before the seal was put in place, still over time these legends lost their urgency, sank into myth."

He stood beneath an overhang of gnarled roots while she bent to scoop up a handful of water. A beetle scurried up his neck and he slapped at it. When he looked down she had disappeared, and he clambered after her through the boulders. It was only after half an hour, sitting on a fallen tree trunk in a broad forest of oaks, that he heard the continuation: "So the traditions of the guardians became empty and ceremonial. It was a mark of honor at the Summer Court to be its captain. Last year a nephew of the queen achieved this post, a boy named Soveliss, and he used it to discover a way to break the seal, perhaps because he was curious about the world beyond the portal, the Far Realm. Perhaps for the glory of closing it again—we cannot question him, for he is dead, or worse than dead."

Her voice was a drifting whisper, and he had to lean in close to understand. She turned her head away. "Your breath stinks," she murmured softly.

The way grew steep again. In a crevice between enormous boulders, she paused. "At first, out of shame, he hid what he had done. He knew nothing of druidic lore, or any of our traditions. He was a boy flailing in the dark, and by the time he had confessed, most of my cohort was already destroyed. Nor was I able to recruit another, for the boy had been a favorite of the queen, and she refused to allow it. She was the one who suggested I go elsewhere, so as to find cruder folk. We are long-lived, and one of our lifespans is worth seven of yours."

"That is well known," grunted Haggar. "The arithmetic is clear," he added, and Astriana smiled.

"It was my choice to train you as I did," she said.

He remembered the long hours by himself, the years of study. "You didn't train me."

She shrugged. "But I provided the spark."

Then she was gone again and he hurried after, stumbling down through smaller trees with trembling leaves and pale branches, until he reached level ground, where he sank up to his shins in water, and his bare feet disturbed minnows and frogs.

When the trees gave out entirely, he strode though waist-high bushes in the swamp. The moon was down behind the hills, and the first red glow of dawn was in the sky. From this new vantage point, and under this new light, he saw he stood in a bowl among high hills with the forest all around him. He saw for the first time that the way they had traversed, wild as it seemed, was not untouched by ancient architects and builders, for here at the bottom of the bowl, rising up out of the swamp, he could see the remains of ruined buildings, the stone foundations of colossal structures. Following Astriana's footsteps, he soon found himself on the lip of a sinkhole which, though it was topped with mud and grass, and though rivulets of water coursed over its edge and fell in endless streams, revealed itself under the pink light as a gigantic cylinder of stone masonry, whose circumference was three miles or more, and whose bottom was obscure.

She stood on the brim of a waterfall, looking down. "We have arrived."

In the middle of this cylindrical well, rising from the bottom, was a tower, whose gabled roofs and turrets were far below them. A stone staircase spiraled down from where they stood, a quarter of the way around the inside of the well. It ended in a fortified buttress, from which a high bridge, a single wooden span, joined a crenellated terrace at the tower's top.

Astriana had already begun to make her way down the steps, and Haggar followed; there was no rail or balustrade, and to their left yawned the abyss, an open maw of darkness with the tower as its tongue.

But after a quarter of an hour, they stood on the stone buttress at the bridge's outer end. Guards kept watch there, archers with long bows, and halberdiers. The captain saluted as they approached the bridge. "Lady Astriana, when you didn't return, Lord Themiranth decided to go anyway. Past midnight we brought some of them up again—another failure. Your two were the only survivors, though one has died since, I think."

"And Themiranth?"

"He did not return."

He was speaking to her, but he was looking at Haggar, his nostrils wide, his lips curled in disdain. "Is this orc your prisoner or your slave? I've got a cage full of his stinking kind."

She smiled. "Captain, this is Archdruid Haggar, Magister of the Broken Pool, master of all druids in the mortal realm. He has agreed to help us. Is that not so, magister?"

At that moment, above them, the first rays of the morning sun touched the inside of the well, revealing tendrils of vegetation that hung down from its rim over the black stones. And as if touched by Kannoth's flower, Haggar felt his strength return. Astriana faced him, and in the new light he noticed things he'd never seen before, either in the darkness at home when he had met her at the stone pool on the mountainside, or in Kannoth's bewitching moonlight, which had covered everything it touched with a light as thick as paint, hiding as much as it revealed. She stood just his height, a fair-haired woman in ragged blue-green silk, barefoot, with muddy legs. Like all the eladrin, she appeared to have no pupils or whites to her eyes, which had a faintly yellow cast. Her wide mouth and forehead, her high cheekbones were beautiful to him—beyond beautiful—but at the same time he could see her flaws, the misshapen bridge of her nose, where it had been broken and reset, and the scar that ran over her cheekbone and her lips.

Suddenly embarrassed, he looked down at himself, the torn wedding shirt, which revealed his tattooed chest and shoulders, slick with sweat. " 'Magister'—that's a new one," chucked the captain. "Is this creature capable of speech?"

"It is you who should be silent," Astriana said. She turned, and Haggar followed her over the bridge into the tower. And she whispered to him as she walked through the guard chambers and tapestried corridors, so that he had to follow close behind her. "Among my people, it is customary for a man and wife to trade requests. You asked a question, and I answered. Now it is my turn. I want you to close this gate with me, and kill whatever creatures have crawled through from the Far Realm. Then it will be time for you to ask again."

"Anything I want?"

"Anything you want," she conceded, eyes fixed straight ahead. A pair of soldiers saluted, then drew back in surprise when they saw Haggar. "One more thing," she continued without turning around. "You are not to speak of Lord Kannoth, or refer in any way to the magic he cast over us, or of the promise I made. These obligations can only be dissolved by the Summer Queen at the Court of Stars, whom I will petition as soon as we have done our work. That will be enough of an opportunity for my humiliation, as if I needed to dissolve a marriage with a pig or a goat. No, be quiet," she went on, as he tried to interrupt her. "Among my people, my ugliness is already a legend. The part of a seductress was a new one to me, not one I could accomplish here. Doubtless I enjoyed it. Doubtless that was part of Kannoth's joke."

They had come to the center of the tower, a circular chamber that also contained a well, the interior echo of the colossal architecture outside. And in the middle of the well was an iron cage suspended from a hook and pulley and reached by an iron ramp. Without pausing, Astriana climbed the ramp and stepped into the cage, where she stood holding the bars. Haggar entered behind her, and at a nod from her, a pair of soldiers pulled the ramp away, leaving the cage dangling. Then another pair let down the chain; the cage descended down the length of the shaft, whose bottom was in darkness, invisible to Haggar as he peered between his filthy feet.

They passed storey after storey of iron balustrades, lit by glimmering lanterns. In time, Haggar guessed, they had penetrated below the foundations of the tower, and down into the rock. The air became damp and thick. As they descended, he felt his mood darken also. Astriana said nothing during all this time, but only stood with her hands on the iron bars, embarrassed, he imagined, at having revealed so much. Now that they could talk freely without fear of being overheard, she was silent. Nor could he think of what to say. "This is my duty as your husband," he ventured finally, "to close this gate?"

She shot him a look of agonized contempt. "If Themiranth is dead, it is a blessing. Not once has he followed my command."

A bell clanged and the cage jerked to a halt, dangling and groaning at the end of its stupendous chain. They hung suspended in a natural cavern, with stalactites and stalagmites the length of a man. Down below, a platoon of soldiers labored to secure them with long grappling hooks, and then to pull them to the edge of a metal structure, a wheeled staircase; when the cage grated against its iron edge, Astriana leaped onto it as if relieved not to be with him any longer in such an enclosed space, and sprang down the stairway, among soldiers very different from the eladrin in the upper tower. These were men in black armor, with hunched shoulders and heavy faces, stunted legs, and powerful arms.

They were inhabitants of the Feydark, Haggar guessed, firbolgs and goblins. One looked up, and he saw it was missing an eye. They clustered around Astriana as she descended the stairs, and she held out her hands, whether to welcome them or keep them at a distance, Haggar couldn't tell. They moved aside to let her pass, and she waited for him to catch up. "If the watch captain is right," she said, "we don't have time to lose. You will see."

Then she turned to speak to the one-eyed soldier in a language Haggar didn't know. "He says he's laid them in the antechamber," she summarized after a minute's talk. "Come."

They passed into a torchlit corridor, rough-hewn from the rock. And then through an iron door into a vaulted hall, at the far end of which two figures lay in nests of rags. Astriana hurried to them and went down on her knees.

One was alive and one was dead, as the captain of the watch had claimed. Astriana knelt over the living one, clasping one of her hands and pushing the hair back from her face. A smoking lantern hung from an iron stanchion above their heads, and by its light Haggar examined the corpse of the other, a tiefling, he saw, with bosses of bone along the crest of his scalp, and curling horns that rose up from his brow, one intact, the other lopped off at the base. The creature was dressed in jointed armor, and in his stiffened hand he still clutched a druid's staff, decorated with carved runes and also sheared off short. He lay on his back, and the straw and rags beneath him were soaked in his black blood.

Fascinated, Haggar studied the man's face, his curled, heavy beard, his red skin, paler now, he imagined, in death. He knew the history of this maligned and hated race, how ancient human families had sworn pacts with devils and corrupted their entire lines. "What did you promise him?" he asked.

Astriana didn't answer. The other woman was a shifter from the look of her, with a flat, feline face and jagged teeth. Hair grew on her cheeks and down her neck, and she was dressed in fur and leather. Or rather she had been, for she had ripped most of her clothing away with her long claws, and lay with her hairy body exposed. Her totem stick had fallen away from her and lay forgotten on the ground, a black shaft of tibia bone studded with uncut tiger's eyes.

She had raised herself onto one elbow and was talking to Astriana in low, urgent tones. Astriana scarcely seemed to listen, but instead she busied herself rearranging the bedding so the shifter could lie more comfortably. And when the firbolg captain strode in, she turned on him. "Didn't I ask you to take care of them? Bring her to my guardroom, to my couch. Give her water mixed with wine."

"Lady, she's a—"

"Do not tell me what she is."

Later, she brought Haggar to a square stone chamber cut into the rock. Food and water had been laid on an iron table—roast capon, pepper sauce, and bread. They sat on iron stools. "To answer your question, I promised I would fill his boots with gold."

"And her?"

"An invitation to the court of the Summer Queen at Senaliesse. The thanks of her majesty. You see," she said, biting into a bone, "you work for cheap."

"I would not have come here for those things."

"Don't I know." And then after a pause: "Themiranth was a fool, but at least he did me this favor. No one will question my decision to bring druids from the mortal realm. The tiefling. You and the shifter. You have a toughness that the eladrin have lost, most of us."

She grimaced, then continued. "Themiranth said it was because I was most at home with outcasts and degenerates. Creatures more like animals. He said it was because none of my own kind would look at me. Because of my ugliness."

He said nothing, even though he imagined this confession cost her a great deal. He watched her take a gulp of water from a crystal cup. At first he'd been embarrassed to eat with her, until he'd noticed how messy she was, licking her fingers, wiping her mouth on her hand. She'd changed into new clothes, soldier's garb that was heavier and plainer than the thin silks she'd worn in Cendriane.

"Eat," she said. "You've had nothing, and you need your strength."

The chamber was lit with magical lights that burned with a hard, white flame. They were set in niches in the walls. Haggar leaned forward on his stool and stuck his spoon into a wooden trencher: grilled mushrooms in black sauce. "What do you know of the Far Realm?" she asked. "The Living Gate, that's where it leads. No—'leads' is not the word I want."

When he didn't reply, she frowned. "I told you how to find the texts to study these things. Months ago—years ago, for you. Because I knew I wanted you for this. So try and talk to me. Try to be cleverer than you are. The Far Realm is outside of time and space—"

Haggar interrupted. "The words we use to describe these things, we can't control them."

Astriana looked at him, grease on her lower lip. "So?"

"So—nothing. This is what I took from what little I read, before I forced myself to stop: It makes us vulnerable to think about these things. Outside time and space—what does that mean? Objects and creatures that we can't perceive. What we see is only indirectly, by its effect upon our minds. And this is corruption. Creatures from this world that are pulled from their true nature and transformed."

Astriana stared at him, chewing slowly. "That razorclaw shifter," she said. "Hazel is her name. She told me Themiranth and the others are still alive down there. Mind slaves. Servitors of something called an aboleth."

"Did she see it? How does she know its name?"

She laughed. "I told her." Then after a moment: "The important thing is sealing the gate. These creatures, the aboleths, mind flayers, and their slaves. They will try to prevent us."

She kept chewing, pointing at him with her chicken bone. "You and me."

And when he said nothing, she paused, looked down. "Because you promised."

He cleared his throat. "When we have done with this, I won't be content with any knowledge or money or the worthless thanks of some archfey. The Far Realm is not the only thing that can't be thought of without damaging ourselves."

"So," she said, "you're saying we can use stupidity to protect ourselves. I suppose it's not so bad, to cultivate the minds of animals."

"It's what our people do," he said, not meaning orcs or eladrin, but followers of druidic knowledge from the dawn of time, before the higher races had evolved.

She smiled. The scar across her lips was livid in the dim light. "That's a lofty reason to have no plan at all. Eat," she said.

He chose a leg from the bowl of capon parts and brought it to his mouth, wondering if she could see his heavy teeth, the long tearing incisors, and if so, whether she'd grown accustomed to them. "Lord Themiranth and the others, I'm sure they were full of plans. Scholars of the Far Realm. Mind slaves now. After this, we won't think or talk when we fight against these creatures. Instinct only. Kick me if I have a thought." He stuck the leg bone in his mouth and snapped it off.

"I'll kick you anyway," she said.

After they finished, she left him for a few hours to rest. In a lighted alcove off the main chamber, he found a mirror set into the wall. Standing before it, he unbuttoned the remnants of his father's shirt and slipped it off, put it aside. He poured water from a crystal ewer over a linen towel and used it to clean his body, wipe away the mud that obscured the tattoos on his hairy arms and chest.

Like all shapeshifters, he wore only leather, which absorbed into his skin during the transformation, as did the bone of his totem stick. Doubtless Astriana at that moment was dressing herself in armor, choosing her swords and knives and spears, but he couldn't use any of that. Instead he stared at himself in the dim glass, while in his mind he allowed himself to climb the curving helixes of evolution away from his finished nature. These were the shapes he would take with him on this adventure, and he moved through them in the new air of the Feywild, to see if anything was different in this world.

He watched his jaw lengthen, and his neck grow thick and slope down toward his shoulders, which swelled first and then receded as he sank down to all fours—a wolf, the totem of his clan. It was his most comfortable shape, but he didn't stop there. Instead he increased the pace of transformation, while in his mind he scampered up the ladders: the coarse hair thickened on his forearms turned into plumage, while at the same time a web of skin stretched from his shoulders to his wrists, and his jaw turned cruel and sharp. And then his feathers receded into patterned, oily skin, and the scales spread from his nose as his legs fused together and his arms clung to his sides, and he dropped down before the mirror in a coiling heap.

But he was curled up asleep in his wolf's shape when she returned. She was dressed in the war garb of a shiere knight in the Summer Court of Queen Tiandra, an armor of overlapping scales, alternating blue and green, made from carapaces of insects, lighter and tougher than steel, and so tight and fine that they covered her body like a second skin. Her hair was brushed back from her face and held at her nape with a silver ring. She wore ridged gauntlets of silver mail and carried a mace in her left hand, while a long scimitar hung at her waist. In the dark alcove, her body seemed to glow.

"Time to move," she said, and he got to his feet and stretched, lowering his shoulders, letting his tongue loll out between his teeth.

He followed her through the studded door and down through a warren of deserted ward rooms and low-ceilinged corridors. In ordinary times, this place was full of life, the borderland between the Feydark and the surface world, where the fomorians of Harrowhame and the eladrin rangers of the woods maintained a queasy peace. This nest of warriors was now empty, but when Haggar and Astriana reached the endless staircases that led deeper into the guts of the rock, they found them packed with refugees, goblins and cyclopses and fomorians all crowding toward the surface, their possessions on their backs. And in their terror, all these pale citizens of the underworld had forgotten their differences, though they came from a dozen clans and races and competing powers. They waited in long lines so that they could pile on upward toward the sunlight, which many of them had never seen.

Hunchbacked women with bloated hands and faces carried their children on their backs, and they shrank against the damp, black walls to allow Haggar and Astriana to pass, the last guardians of the Living Gate. Occasionally they touched their foreheads or else murmured some vestigial token of respect before they bent to their burdens again and resumed their place in line. Now the wolf bounded ahead to clear the path, the long staircase that was lit not by torches or burning chemicals, but by glowing crystals in the rock, which shone blue and green and purple as they climbed down.

In time they came to Harrowhame itself, the dismal fortress of King Bronnor, built in an enormous cavern of quarried salt. They came out suddenly onto the salt floor, where the stone and iron ramparts rose above them. Here at least were light and soldiers also, the myrmidons of the fomorian king. From the citadel came the sounds of drumbeats and brazen trumpets, which echoed from the crystal walls. But the gates were closed, and there was no guard to acknowledge them as they crossed the salt plain under the battlements to continue their descent.

They entered a gigantic fissure in the rock, where the ground sloped downward. And here the world changed. Above, nearer the surface, the rock was cut, quarried, and dead. Here it was still alive, growing in a landscape as varied as any forest or mountainside. They climbed down through glowing forests of mushrooms. Animals lived here, snakes and lizards and rodents of all kinds, but also tiny deer and goats perched upon the rocks, and even a few pale birds. Flowering vines and creepers covered the distant walls, and hung from the stalactites above their heads. The air was lighter, richer here, and breezes wafted through the endless caverns, as if freshened from below.

The wolf loped ahead. They came to the shore of a black river and climbed the shattered rocks beside the waterfall.

Haggar picked his way over the stones and paused at the first man-made structure he had seen in hours, a guard house built from black cubes of pumice stone, and lit with a guttering lantern. "Who is there?" Astriana called.

Her armor glimmered green and blue in the darkness, and she raised her silver mace. A man staggered out the open door, a firbolg warrior dressed in leather armor, carrying his sword. "You're here," he said. "Thank the gods. I've stayed alone for hours, waiting for them to come back. They've taken all my men," he added, pointing with his sword to a hole in the rock wall, lit from within by an unearthly mix of colors.

"Who?"

"Themiranth and the others. What's left of them."

He was a big man. Sweat glistened on his pale skin. Raising his sword, making a gesture toward the depths, he said, "I was about to try again, one last time. There are too many of them if they come out in the open. But we can fight them in the tunnels, one by one."

"What's your name?" said Astriana.

"Garm, my lady."

"You're a brave man. Let's go down."

Finally they reached the environs of the Living Gate, that tiny portal to the Far Realm. Its diameter could be measured in eyelashes, yet even so, the substance that seeped through, less matter than deranged ideas, could poison a whole world. Once inside the last cave, they could see how all its surfaces were covered with a glistening slime, which sucked at their feet and made it hard to move. Yet it provided light for them; a mile and a half in, they saw the first of the aboleth's servitors, the eladrin guardians it had bent to its will. One of them appeared suddenly, standing up out of the shin-deep slime, where he had been lying full-length.

"Themiranth," Astriana breathed.

His skin was transparent now, his organs and blood vessels mottled and visible, his staring eyes wide with unthinking malice. He wore no clothes, carried no weapons, but waded toward them with his arms stretched out, trying to wrap Astriana in his slimy grasp. She hacked at him with her mace, which made a wet, squelching sound as it sunk into his flesh; Haggar didn't watch. He had already begun his transformation, climbing down the curving ladder in his mind, until his body had lengthened many times, his arms and legs had disappeared, and he was slithering through the mucus-covered rocks, past Themiranth and past the other eladrin servitors deeper down in the hole; they couldn't see him.

As he passed, he battered at their ankles with his blunt nose; one he knocked from his feet and encircled with his tail as he pulled himself along, crushing out of him or her what still passed for life. He let go, then swam down to where the slime was thickest, submerged in a paste or stew of half-dissolved corpses, until he found a corridor that was entirely packed with mucus, and he slithered through.

Just for a moment he saw the aboleth, with its wings and flanges and tentacles, its three red eyes in a vertical line; he closed his own eyes, closed his ears, let his mind sink down into its tiniest reptilian confinement, locked inside his flat little skull as if inside a prison made of bone, in the center of which he rolled his consciousness into a ball, as a prisoner might sit and hug himself on the floor of his cell, turning his face inward partly from despair, partly as a way to conserve his strength.

On the long dull surface of his body, along the smooth patterned skin of the great snake, he allowed himself to feel no sensation as he burrowed through the slime into the belly of the great beast, a belly that absorbed him as it allowed him to pass, and sucked him down into a landscape of inflamed viscera, mucus-encrusted tunnels full of parasites.

Even with his mind shut down, and sunk into his body as far as he could permit it without letting go of the synapses and ganglia that controlled his breathing and his heart, still he caught a vague impression of Astriana and Garm up to their knees in effluence, hacking and pounding at these parasites as they tried to drag them down.

Then Haggar was past them, and had slipped down through the submerged tunnels yet again, and glimpsed again the red eyes of the aboleth, and sunk through the membrane of its body once more.

In the heart's core of the monster he discovered the Living Gate, the portal to the Far Realm. Contagion seeped from it, a tiny valve of puckered flesh in the contracting wall. Another monster lurked there, floating in a substance that was neither solid nor liquid nor gas, a creature made of writhing tentacles around a single flaming eye. Daggerlike teeth circled its maw, and Haggar found himself drifting toward it in his natural form, naked save for his totem stick, which protruded from the bone of his forearm. It was as if this creature could perceive his true essence after all, and limit him to his weakest shape.

Gouts of fire burst from the monster's eye. But Haggar had his totem stick, and with it he began to stir the substance of the deep, grunting, muffled evocations as he did so, until the matrix that surrounded him began to move, assume a shape like a vortex or tornado; he was controlling it, as he would a cloud or a storm in his own world. The streamers of fire circled back, catching the monster in a net of its own flame, while at the same time the living gate spread open, and a single purple tentacle stretched through it. This was the mind flayer, the last of the horrors that awaited him here, and it searched for him diligently, penetrating through the ooze, grasping for his head. Doubtless just beyond the gate was the encrustation of the elder brain that was commanding this entire web of illusion and deceit.

He kicked away and it grabbed hold of him. Inside the prison of his mind, a long hand snaked through the bars, because he was afraid. He sat naked, curled up in the center of his cell, allowing the hand of the mind flayer to palpate his skull, searching for a place to enter. He felt a rush of emotion and sensation surge up through him, and his mind was full of pictures of the past and present and the future: his mother standing by the fire outside her cottage in the woods; the pool in the abandoned city on the mountainside, and Astriana standing in it with the water around her knees; Astriana with her mace held high, breaking the flesh of the slime-covered servitors, while he failed here, allowed the mind flayer to take him and destroy him, destroy them all.

But then with a last effort of his reptile will, he choked all that away, constricted the mental passages it flowed through, that sequence of images, and his mind went dark. Those processes of the brain and heart were what the creature fed on, and Haggar felt its grip loosen, its probing tentacle release its hold. Instead of struggling, he forced himself to relax, to welcome the touch of the jailer's hand upon his face. And the more he welcomed it, the more he emptied his mind of panic and regret, the weaker and less sure was its grasp, while at the same time he was climbing downward into a new reality, in which he stood in his wolf's form at the edge of a rocky, fetid pool under a blood red sky. Some kind of twisting mollusk was down there, a cephalopod with purple tentacles, and he stretched out his claws and ripped along its flabby, unprotected head.

He heard a scream, all the more horrifying for being silent and internal. He pulled back his paw. And then he found himself floating up through the spheres of illusion: the Living Gate with his naked body suspended underneath, watching the arm of the mind flayer suddenly retract and disappear, and the gate pucker closed. At that moment, as if the source of contagion was necessary for its life, the beholder shut its awful eye. And again at that same moment, Haggar found himself lying on his side among the mucus-covered rocks, his fur matted and greasy, his body aching and hurt. He licked at the air, and then after several panting breaths he stumbled to his four feet, and climbed and scratched his way out of the tunnel, to where Astriana sat among the stones, her armor coated with a glowing slime, her mace broken, her scimitar in her hand. Haggar crawled past Garm, the firbolg soldier, floating on his back, his face contorted in the rictus of death.

And then Astriana put her hand out and Haggar crawled under it, and allowed her to rub the soft fur of his forehead and around his ears. His tongue lolled out, and he licked her hands. She bent over him to put his face against her face, while he—not because he thought it was a good strategy, but out of simple exhaustion—allowed himself to find his natural shape again. His heavy head fell into her lap. She took her fingers from his hair, rolled him aside, and stood up hurriedly.

But later, after they had climbed back to the surface again, and after they had mounted the cage to the tower's roof, and after he had washed himself in the sumptuous quarters she'd assigned to him, he stood in front of the window, looking up at the sun as it rose above the rim of the great well. He didn't hear the door open, but he turned when she spoke. She wore a gown of green silk, open at the neck and throat, and her hair was loose around her head. "You know we are bound by our promises," she said.

"Then promise me. I want you to take me home."

Her head had fallen forward to accept his punishment. Now she raised her face to look at him. Her nose was crooked, and a scar ran down her cheek over her lips. "I promise," she said.

"And this will be my promise," he continued. "On the night of the full moon, I will wait for you, when the light strikes the surface of the water."

With his back to the window he couldn't tell for sure, but he thought he saw a blush pass over her cheek.

Paul Park has published eleven novels and a volume of short stories. His work has been nominated for the Nebula Award, the Arthur C. Clarke Award, the World Fantasy Award, and the Tiptree Award, among others. He lives in Massachusetts and teaches part time at Williams College.

BLOOD OASIS

A Tale of Dark Sun

KEVIN J. ANDERSON

Seawater moved against the hull planks like a lover's whisper. The yellow sun of Athas was bright, and a westerly breeze stretched *Horizon Finder*'s sails, guiding the three-masted carrack toward the seaport of Arkhold.

Unexpected spray whipped up from the bow, and Jisanne laughed. She had untied her long brown hair, letting it blow loose and free. She drew a deep breath with a sense of wonder that these sailors did not feel. They didn't understand how lucky they were to be there.

Captain Hurunn, a wealthy minotaur merchant with a large gold ring in one floppy ear, said, "A long voyage, a full cargo hold, even a net overloaded with fresh fish—time for me to settle down and enjoy my profits." Even when he was in a good mood, Hurunn's voice sounded like a gruff growl. From what little Jisanne knew from her brief previous visits to this glorious time, she doubted the minotaur captain would ever settle down.

With gentle reverence, she touched the opalescent crystal mounted to the compass stand. "The navigation crystal always finds its way back here." She was never sure how clearly the ship's captain and crew could see or hear her.

Hurunn snorted. "It's what the navigation crystal is for—to guide its owner home. It's a simple enough spell."

Jisanne shuddered at his casual attitude, forcing herself to remember that these people did not automatically hate and fear magic users, regardless of whether they were defilers or preservers. Whatever disasters had robbed Athas of this beauty had not happened yet. The world was still fresh and alive, as it Athas had been before its possibilities were stolen.

Horizon Finder entered the mouth of the harbor and crewmen gathered on deck, waving at the numerous fishing boats, feluccas, and galleys. They were all eager to get back to port.

High above, the elf lookout yelled, his already-thin voice an even higher pitch. "To arms—sea serpent off the stern! It's following us!"

As the crew scrambled to snag harpoons and bows, a fearsome triangular head rose up, streaming seawater from its golden scales. Its hinged jaw dropped open to reveal long fangs. A short distance away, a second monster rose up.

"That's *two* sea serpents, not one," Hurunn growled. "I need a better lookout for my next voyage."

The pair of serpents glided toward *Horizon Finder*, intent on attack. Seeing the swollen net of still-squirming fish suspended by a rope and winch above the stern, Jisanne had a sudden realization. "The fish—the serpents want the fish."

"Of course they want the fish. They always want the fish," the minotaur said, not overly concerned. "I was hoping we'd make it all the way to Arkhold, but these waters are infested with cursed sea serpents. A small enough price to pay."

With a deep bellow such as only a minotaur could manage, Hurunn commanded his sailors to swing the boom over the water. The sea serpents pressed closer to the dangling net, snapping at the spray in the carrack's wake. "Dump the catch!"

As twitching fish rained down, the serpents frolicked in the water, greedily feasting. From the rails, the sailors jeered at the monsters, and Hurunn complained—out of habit—about the money he'd just lost. The breeze picked up, blowing the ship safely into port and leaving the sea serpents behind.

Ahead, Jisanne stared at the thriving city. The fortress of a forgotten order of ancient knights sat atop the highest point overlooking the blue harbor. People had gathered down at the docks to welcome the sailing ship. A few ambitious traders even took small boats out to meet *Horizon Finder*, hoping to strike a sweet deal with Captain Hurunn before he reached the quay.

The minotaur handed Jisanne a flask of wine. "Here, to celebrate. Myself, I don't drink the stuff." He snuffled through his bull nose. "Clogs my sinuses."

She took a swig of the richest, headiest wine she had ever tasted. Everything seemed so unreal.

As the carrack tied up to a long stone quay, Jisanne saw the colorful market stalls full of fresh fruit. Musicians played instruments, their competing tunes a raucous clash of sounds. Jisanne took another drink of wine and glanced down at the pristine navigation crystal. Tears stung her eyes. She didn't want to lose any of this, but she knew . . .

As the scene around her faded, the moist salty air in her nostrils became harsh, sour, and dry. The puffy clouds in the sky shimmered into high blowing dust. The skirling music and the babble of marketplace sounds turned into the moan of desert wind.

"No!" But her cry was just a whisper, words lost in time. Jisanne clutched at the fabric of the world, digging deeper into the arcane magic, not caring where she found the power to hold on for just a few moments longer, but it was no use.

The blue ocean, the lush harbor, the vibrant city were all swallowed into dust. The waves became dunes, the horizon only an empty basin of powder, the Sea of Silt. Exposed by scouring winds, chains of ivory vertebrae and skulls with chipped fangs marked the long-desiccated carcasses of sea serpents. The minotaur captain, his elf lookout, and the rest of the ship's crew didn't notice they were vanishing. *She* was slipping in time, not them.

That Athas, that of the Green Age, was long gone.

Jisanne dropped to her knees on the deck of a skeletal wreck against a crumbling stone quay. Overhead, the bloated red sun was like an angry coal. The ancient flask of wine in her hand was as parched as the landscape. Next to her, propped up by a flat stone, rested a clay bowl half full of her dark, drying blood; the dull shard of the navigation crystal was immersed in the liquid.

Jisanne felt weak and alone, drained. She had powered the magic of the crystal by drawing on her own life force, not caring about the cost of her spell. She had restored the lovely, idyllic landscape of Athas for a time . . . too short a time.

And now she had to face reality again.

The crowds cheered in the stands of the Criterion coliseum, whistling, calling for blood. The spectators were all the same, regardless of their social status: powerful templars in special travertine seats near the sand of the arena, aloof patricians who whispered about Balic city business in between bloody combat matches, and unruly commoners crowded in higher seats under the hot red sun.

They roared their approval when Koram strode out of the gladiators' gate, wearing his white ceremonial sash with the sign of Dictator Andropinis dyed in red; he hated the sash, but was required to wear it. He adjusted armor made of sheets of petrified wood, then looked at the stands with passive disgust. These same people had cheered for him when he was elected a praetor of Balic, and they had likewise cheered when he announced his plans to liberalize the city's laws. Later, when the scheming foreign praetor Yvoluk, darling of Andropinis, disgraced him on false charges, the fickle crowds had cheered just as loudly. Then, after Koram had been shaved bald and thrown into the Criterion to battle monsters, they cheered again, expecting him to die . . . and now they cheered each time he emerged victorious. No one had expected him to survive for seven months in the arena.

The people of Balic would cheer for anything, Koram thought, so long as blood was involved. He felt no further loyalty toward them; he had already paid enough. Praetor Yvoluk had seen to that. Koram's wife and young son were already dead, worked to death in slave camps.

Emerging into the ruddy afternoon sunlight, Koram turned slowly and raised his bronze-inlaid ivory sword. Metal was extremely scarce, and good blades even scarcer; most of the other fighters considered him lucky to have a strengthened and embellished sword. But Koram would never consider himself lucky; he had earned this with blood.

As praetor in charge of the arena, Yvoluk could have warned him what sort of beast he would be fighting this day, but the evil templar liked to keep his surprises. Koram would defeat the opponent just the same. Otherwise it would be surrender.

The spectators continued to whistle and stomp. Koram stood in the shade of the stretched awning that covered the noble seats and part of the sand-covered fighting ground. In the pits below, handlers would force animals and monsters onto elevating platforms and turn them loose through trap-doors in the sand.

Koram heard the rumble of machinery, felt the sand tremble at his feet, and prepared himself. Since being sentenced to the Criterion, he had faced thri-kreen packs, drays, a raaig soulflame, and numerous warriors—human, mul, goliath, it didn't matter. Koram had slain them all because it was the only way for him to survive. He was lucky; he was skilled; he was determined. But he knew Praetor Yvoluk would give him no way out. He hadn't yet figured out how to kill the praetor for what he had done, but he never stopped trying to think of a way.

Koram saw something move beneath the arena floor, stalking him . . . a burrowing creature that sensed the vibra-tions of his movements. Koram stood absolutely still. Bored, the spectators in the stands shouted out catcalls, but he didn't budge.

In his special box, Dictator Andropinis sat on his throne under the awning, picking at his fingernails. He seemed an elderly man with a thin face and an intent expression, but he was not intent on the gladiatorial combat before him. When the dictator addressed his people, he exuded power. The sorcerer-king of Balic claimed to have been duly elected to his position several centuries ago—and who could gainsay him? Andropinis attended gladiatorial combats out of a sense of duty, not any real interest. Over the many years of his reign, the dictator had seen, and caused, enough death. Just then, he merely appeared bored.

Bursting out of the arena sand, a trio of gray-skinned anakores spat dust from mouths filled with needle-sharp teeth. He identified a large female with a hunched back and a line of thick, knobby protrusions, and two smaller, younger males with smoother hides and gleaming eyes. Anakores hunted in packs, and they would be a formidable team.

But he didn't need any assistance. He fought alone.

The first of the younger males lunged toward Koram, and he slashed with his ivory-and-bronze blade. The anakore swung a clawed hand, blinking its black eyes as if unable to see anything but dust, but its wide flat nose smelled him. As Koram danced away, the vibrations of his footfalls were enough to guide the monster.

The second male circled around and dove in as his companion retreated. Koram spun easily on the loose sand, jabbing again to drive the monster away. Then the older female let out a roar that sounded like an avalanche in a cave. In traditional anakore hunting behavior, one would knock a victim to the ground while others plunged forward to finish him. The female thundered toward him.

But it was a different ploy. Her challenging bellow had distracted Koram long enough for the two males to dart forward, attacking him from both sides.

He easily decapitated the anakore on his left, and the creature's body slid forward with its own momentum while the head went in a different direction. The other male crashed into him, but Koram slammed his armored shoulder into the monster's body, knocking it to the sands. With a quick, hard thrust, he skewered it through the chest.

The crowd cheered, but Koram did not acknowledge them. Dictator Andropinis continued to study his cuticles, never even looking at the combat.

The female howled and hurled herself at him like a boulder from a catapult. Koram barely had time to recover his balance and lift his sword. As she lunged forward, he swung hard and the bronze edge of his blade cut the anakore's shoulder. The creature dove again, burying herself in the sand and leaving only a spot of dark blood on the churned sand.

Koram turned in a slow circle, alert. The two males lay dead on the sand, twitching. He wondered who had caught these creatures in the wild and dragged them here to die in the coliseum. Everything died there, sooner or later.

Some gladiator showmen would have drawn out the battle, making the bloodshed last for most of the afternoon. The people saluted them as heroes, celebrities; those fighters reveled in the attention. Koram, though, didn't care about anyone watching him. He had killed two of the monsters, and he would dispatch the third just as easily.

The female anakore sprang out of the dust again with barely a ripple. Without a flourish, Koram slashed and cut a deep, painful gash along the monster's side. The female reeled, bleeding profusely, and staggered back, retreating from the gladiator. She stopped near the two dead bodies of the younger anakores, swayed and moaned.

Koram stalked forward but the female did not fight him. She touched the blood from her deep wound, then looked at her dead companions, letting loose a keening howl. "Merrrrrrrrcy," she seemed to say as she dropped her head toward the slain males. "My fammmmilleeeeee."

He hesitated, but knew she hadn't said anything of the sort. Still, anger and sickness rose up in him like bile. No one had given any mercy to his family, but he knew he could do nothing for this monster. The female would die here soon enough.

"The only mercy here is a quick death," he said, too quietly for the audience to hear. And without further spectacle, he drove the point of his blade through the monster's chest, ramming it all the way to the hilt to be sure of the kill. He jerked his sword back out, letting the anakore die without more pain. The big female collapsed beside the other two corpses.

The crowd applauded the speedy dispatch of the three enemies, but their response was lukewarm. Without bothering to cut off any of the monsters' heads as trophies, Koram stalked back toward the gladiators' gate and out of the sun. He was finished for the day.

The lean, bearded praetor stood under the stone arch, his face dark with anger. As Koram walked into the shadows of the tunnels, Yvoluk struck a hard backhand across his sweaty face. "Fight harder, worm dung! Perform for the people—earn another day of your worthless life! You make our opponents seem weak and passive when you kill them so quickly." His voice was heavily accented; Yvoluk had come from the east, an exile from another city, but he had made a powerful position for himself here.

Koram just looked at the man who had caused him so much pain. "Why don't you face me yourself in the arena? Then I would show you how much I want to fight."

Yvoluk raised his hand, threatening to strike him again, but Koram merely strode past and headed to the large underground complex of cells where the gladiators lived. It was not, and would never be, his home. But it was all he had.

Koram had been optimistic once; he had wanted to help the people of Balic. In the showy democracy espoused by the sorcerer-king, ordinary citizens were supposed to have the freedom to speak; they were allowed to run for the office of praetor, whether or not the Council of Patricians or Andropinis approved. Koram had been so naïve, so foolish.

An "unapproved" candidate who managed to be elected praetor typically met with an unfortunate accident before long. In his own case, Koram had asked too many questions in the first months, and Yvoluk had orchestrated his downfall, disgracing him with accusations of graft, turning public opinion against Koram, who had been their favorite only weeks before. Though there was no proof in the charges against him, the people did not believe Koram's vehement denials. He was arrested and stripped of his rank. His wife and son were sold to slave traders for a long march to work Tyr's mines, where they died within weeks. Koram was thrown into the gladiator arena, where he did not have the good sense to die. Seven months later, he continued to fight and kill.

His fellow warriors sulked in their rooms, brooding over their fates. Some oiled their muscles or strapped on armor in preparation for upcoming matches in the arena. A pair of dwarves sparred enthusiastically to hone their fighting skills. A newly captured goliath hunkered on a stone seat in his cell, rocking back and forth, holding his knees; his misery was even larger than his body. An insectile thri-kreen tracker, separated from his two psychically bonded clutch mates, recited poetry through stony mandibles to drown out the goliath's moans. The sandy, chittering thri-kreen claimed to be a nihilistic philosopher, and he accepted his undoubtedly short life as a gladiator.

Koram had befriended none of his comrades. They would be pitted against one another when monster combatants were in short supply, and if Praetor Yvoluk happened to notice that Koram cared for any particular gladiator, he would take great pleasure in arranging for a death match.

Koram sat on a stone bench and used oil, sand, and a scraper to remove the blood and grit from his skin. He no longer noticed the scabs and scars; all of his motions were mechanical. Another fight, another day.

Before he could lie back and rest on his pallet, however, a call to arms echoed through the barracks beneath the Criterion. Dimly heard through the stone block walls, the crowds in the stands roared with a sound that was definitely not cheering.

The gladiators stood, looking around in alarm; even the moaning Goliath climbed to his feet, keeping his head and shoulders bent so as not to strike his shaggy head against the ceiling. The two sparring dwarves stopped and listened. They recognized the sound of the alarm. "Balic is under attack."

The thri-kreen nihilist changed his song. "Today, our deaths may come in a different manner, but it is death nonetheless." Koram knew that the thri-kreen had been renowned as one of the most skilled trackers in his tribe, but his skills were wasted in the arena.

Though the guards had taken his sword, Koram painstakingly strapped his petrified wood armor on. Alarms continued to sound outside in the city, gongs and bells ringing. He didn't hurry.

With a clatter of boots and armor, soldiers marched along the stone-tiled tunnels, led by a dark-visaged Yvoluk. The goliath wrung his hands together and lurched out of his chamber. "Praetor! What is happening?"

Yvoluk's expression soured, as if an olive pit had caught in his throat. "The Skull Wearer leads an army of beast giants to the walls down by the estuary. They've destroyed one of the dictator's forts on the Dragon's Palate, and now they mean to take the city." At a signal from the praetor, the guards lashed their whips, making loud cracks against the stone walls. Yvoluk continued to shout. "Gladiators, our beloved Andropinis demands that you defend the city. You will be armed and sent to the walls. You are our bravest fighters. You will save Balic!"

"Why should we?" Koram asked. At another time, he would have been ready to leap into action, but his city had failed him.

Yvoluk curled his purple lips in a tempting smile. "You need incentive? Drive back the beast giants, and I will ask Andropinis to grant you your freedom. Fight for us this day, and you need never fight in the Criterion again!"

The goliath made a delighted sound, while the sparring dwarves squared their shoulders and grinned. The soldiers handed the gladiators their familiar weapons and rushed them out of the barracks and into the city streets. Koram intentionally wadded the sash that marked him as a fighter for Andropinis and left it behind on the bench in his cell.

The thri-kreen tracker matched Koram's pace, leaning over to whisper, "Do you trust Praetor Yvoluk to follow through on his promise?"

"As much as I would trust a footpath across the open Sea of Silt."

Behind them, the goliath moaned again.

From across the city, soldiers were mustering toward the wall that overlooked the dry estuary where hundreds of faded, dusty silt skimmers tied up to the docks. Yvoluk led the hapless gladiators to the top of the stone barricade, confident in his power.

A deafening tumult thundered from the harbor below. Koram and the gladiators gazed down upon a large army of towering monsters. Hundreds of beast-head giants waded the silt shallows, slogging through parched, pale depths that would have drowned any man. The giants' heavy armor weighed them down, but they plodded ahead, stirring up clouds of fine dust. Their heads were a menagerie of ferocious creatures, fanged feline predators, reptilian saurians, bloodthirsty lupine monsters, sharp-beaked birds of prey.

At the lead of the encroaching army stood a dominating figure, a huge giant with a necklace of skulls that dangled from a thick cord at his throat. The most fearsome of the beast giants, Skull Wearer supposedly drew power from the spirits of those he had slain—and he had slain many. With legendary animosity toward the civilized inhabitants of Balic, he had led many previous raids against the city, but Koram had never seen an army like this before. Dark energy thrummed around the giant leader as he let out a roar of challenge; the hundreds of beast giants marching through the silt echoed the shout.

"Skull Wearer has long hated Andropinis," Yvoluk said. "You must protect our sorcerer-king and save Balic!"

Below, the beast giants reached the docks, ripped the silt skimmers free of their moorings and smashed the hulls. Pressing their shoulders against the pilings, two reptile-headed giants shattered a sturdy dock, tearing it down. The attackers swarmed forward in a frenzy, wrecking all of the boats.

Most of the silt sailors had evacuated as the enemy army approached, but a last few men ran toward the gates, desperate to get inside. The Balic guards refused to open the reinforced barriers, despite the ever-increasing pleas. Beast giants grabbed the frantic sailors and battered them into ooze against the wall.

Skull Wearer shouted another challenge for Dictator Andropinis. More giants pressed forward like the waves of a long-forgotten tide. It seemed impossible that anyone could protect the city against such an invasion; Koram could see that he and his comrades would all die in the first line of defense. He glanced at the dwarves, the thri-kreen tracker, even the miserable goliath; they all realized the hopelessness of their position, as well.

Yvoluk raised his hands, filled with enthusiasm. "This will be your greatest battle—for the glory of Andropinis and Balic."

The praetor stepped to the edge of the wall, gesturing toward the giant hordes below. "If you survive this day, you will have your freedom. I promise." He seemed to expect cheers.

Koram reached out and gave the man a hard shove, toppling him off the wall into the press of giants. Yvoluk flailed as he fell, too astonished even to scream.

Koram had acted without thinking, sure he was dead either way. "I am through fighting for your benefit."

Seeing his action, the other gladiators immediately came to the same conclusion. The goliath rose up and battered soldiers on either side of him, toppling them off the wall. The thri-kreen laughed in surprise and delight, clacking his mandibles as he turned on the astonished guards, and the two dwarves began to fight.

In response to the unexpected turmoil above, the beast giants pounded on their shields, then hammered on the gates with stony fists like battering rams. A volley of spears arced upward, shafts as thick as small trees, and struck into the crowded guards and spectators.

The gladiators continued to fight atop the wall, throwing the Balic soldiers into chaos. Skull Wearer summoned the magic he had drawn from the ghosts of his victims, unleashing a dark thunderstorm of power against the harbor city.

Before long, Dictator Andropinis arrived with his escort, shouting out his own spells as he drew power to defend Balic. The air itself began to crackle and tremble as the surrounding trees and plants wilted, the ground turning as black as charcoal, its vital energy sucked away.

In the confusion, Koram turned his back on the front lines, waved his ivory-and-bronze sword to chase panicked soldiers and citizens out of his way. Some of his gladiator comrades fought anyone and everyone with great glee, giving their last great battle performance; others scampered away, seeking a place to hide.

Koram felt not a flicker of guilt for abandoning his city. He thought of the three anakore lying dead in the arena—his latest victims. He thought of his own family, killed through treachery. He had killed enough. He would not shed his blood to protect the sorcerer-king or his duplicitous citizens, nor would he stay and revel in the city's destruction.

He was done.

Koram made his way to the far exit gates that were not yet blocked. Before long, the city's back gates and side entrances would be clogged with citizens racing into the hills as they realized the true desperation of their plight.

He would set out into the wilderness and find his own path of survival. Considering what he had been through, he knew he would fare better alone under the dark sun of Athas than amidst the treachery of Balic.

Living aboard the petrified skeleton of *Horizon Finder*, Jisanne had the city ruins to herself. No caravans or silt schooners came this far south. Arkhold received no visitors except for the rare and foolish adventurer in search of forgotten treasures. Knowing how people were likely to treat a magic user, Jisanne hid whenever she saw a stranger; more often than not, the perils of the abandoned city drove them off before she had to worry.

Jisanne was on her own, just as she wanted to be.

Yet the desiccated place provided little for her survival. She caught rodents and lizards to eat; she set up scattered cisterns to hoard the reluctant droplets of water that rained down twice a year. But it wasn't enough, and she had to venture out on regular supply expeditions.

As the red sun lumbered over the grainy horizon, Jisanne stood on the ruins of the stone quay, facing the expanse of the Silt Sea. Her voice hoarse from thirst, she shouted a summoning spell for a floating mantle, one of the mysterious but gentle beasts of the deep wastes.

Her hands trembled and her head throbbed as she called upon the power. It would have been so much easier, so much faster, to steal the life energy of the surrounding flora and fauna, but Jisanne refused such shortcuts. She knew in her heart that the excessive and indiscriminate use of that sort of magic had wrung Athas dry. By using the navigation crystal, she had been able to visit the lush past, and she knew what the defilers had done to a healthy world.

Magic users were widely hated across Athas. All her life, Jisanne had tried to preserve the life of the world, never harming anyone, and yet, when her abilities were discovered, the people of Balic had punished her. As a hermit, far from any people, Jisanne was much safer. But the pain of her loss did not go away.

Answering her summons, the floating mantle appeared in a blurry brown corona of dust. The jellyfishlike creature drifted on the thermals, trailing thin tentacles to the silt. It hovered at the end of the stone quay, then lowered its enormous body to the ground so she could mount.

"Thank you for coming." Jisanne had no idea if the creature could understand her. Securing her sacks, pots, and supply pack, she climbed onto the leathery dome, grasping the ridges and nodules. Air flaps vented gas as the floating mantle exhaled, then rose into the air and propelled itself along, carrying her away from Arkhold and across the impassable expanse.

She ventured to the more fertile, and more dangerous, highlands of the Dragon's Palate as rarely as possible. The

Palate was close to Balic, and she never intended to go back home again. That was where happiness had been burned out of her—not by any defiling magic, but by human hatred.

Years ago, Jisanne lived in Balic with her older sister Selanne, who had a husband and two fine daughters. Unmarried, Jisanne helped wherever she could, often secretly drawing upon the power of the living to ease their existence. But she wasn't cautious enough. Jisanne was a preserver, not a defiler. Her magic was powered by the life force of Athas itself, but she never went so far with her spells that she hurt anyone or anything. Even though she knew full well the difference between what she did and the destructive magic of those with no regard for life, most common people didn't understand, didn't try, or didn't care.

Jisanne had ignored the rumors about her, the whispers when she and Selanne walked through the forum market, the way other people shunned their house. Oblivious, she had gone out one day to pick olives in a grove near a crumbling noble estate. Returning home at sunset with a full basket, she had found her sister's family murdered, the house burned. A mob had scrawled hateful words in the ashes—they had mistaken Selanne as a defiler.

Before they could come for her, too, Jisanne fled. She did not stop until she had reached the end of inhabited territory, and even then she kept going all the way to Arkhold. The mummified ruins of the abandonded port city seemed the perfect place for her.

Time had not lessened the pain of her massacred loved ones. Those nightmares remained as vivid as the navigation crystal's visions of ancient Athas. . . .

The floating mantle brought her to soupy mud flats at the shore of the Dragon's Palate. A thin stream trickled down from the foothills, where the scrub forest thickened. That would do.

She landed the docile beast near a dryer patch of thick grasses, and slid down its rubbery curved back. When she released it from her spell, the jellyfish creature floated away from the mud flats, heading back to the silt barrens. Her quest here would take some time and require a great deal of caution. The steep mountains of the Dragon's Palate were inhabited by ferocious beast giants; fortunately, a military outpost from Balic kept the giants busy.

Jisanne filled her water containers upstream, then placed the heavy jugs in a subtly marked cache, where she could retrieve them before she headed home. Then, with empty sacks tied at her waist, she explored the forest in search of edible berries, roots, mushrooms, fruits, and herbs.

A pang of loneliness stabbed her, but she had fended for herself so long. Only once had Jisanne let down her guard and trusted a stranger in the Arkhold ruins—and that lapse had nearly killed her. She had revealed herself to a half-elf treasure seeker who had looked so friendly, so earnest. The lone adventurer had captivated her with his story, his passion, and Jisanne had shown him the navigation crystal, had revealed to him the erstwhile splendor of Athas.

Jisanne had been so desperate for companionship that she had believed in him—until he had stolen the crystal. As the thief had run away with mocking laughter, taking a shortcut out onto the sands, a tentacled silt horror had grabbed him before he'd even realized his danger. Hearing his screams, Jisanne felt no sympathy. Later, she retrieved the navigation crystal from where it had dropped to the ground next to his corpse, and held it tightly. From that point on, Jisanne hid whenever she saw a human visitor.

As she filled her sacks with edibles from the forest, she took comfort in knowing the navigation crystal was hidden in a small pouch tied on the inside of her breeches. She had to exercise great care to avoid detection from the marrauding giants on the island; their main lair was to the north, closer to Balic. She was safe here, where she could hear, and hide from, the crashing approach of any plodding giant hunter.

She did not, however, notice the trap set by the band of feral halflings.

As she foraged, the small wild-eyed savages had stalked and surrounded her in utter silence. The halfling hunters scuttled ahead, lying in wait with their ropes and nets, and then they sprang.

The vicious little men hurled bolos at her, several of which missed, but one caught around her leg, and another struck her head, wrapping around her neck.

"Fresh human! Tender human!"

"Take her back to the village."

Jisanne clawed at the bolos—and then the halflings dropped a net on top of her. They pounced, driving her to the ground.

"Bring her to the other captives."

"If we have any left!" The last comment was met with cackles of laughter and howls of disappointment.

A stocky leader thumped his chest in triumph, and hefted a sword made from a giant's sharpened femur. "Another victory for Borodro!"

"But we *all* caught her, Borodro . . ." whined one of the younger halflings.

With a slash of his giant-bone sword, Borodro decapitated the complainer, and the severed head continued to whistle and grimace as it rolled on the dry leaves of the ground. The leader gave a snort. "Look, Delfi keeps complaining even without a body." The halflings' initial gasps of horror turned to laughter, cheers, and grumbling stomachs. "Bring his body back to the village," their leader ordered. They seemed satisfied with that.

Jisanne thrashed in the net, struggling to tear the tough strands. She didn't waste energy or breath demanding to be freed, since that would do no good. Everyone knew the cruelty of halfling raiders and slavers. She tried to work an escape spell, but failed; she was already weak and had used much magic to summon and control the floating mantle. She needed time and concentration.

"Tenderize her," said Borodro, "then let's get back to the village."

The halfling hunters fell upon Jisanne with sticks and clubs. She covered her head to protect herself, but the blows were too many. . . .

Some time later, she awoke, a mass of pain, trussed up and carried along as the halflings whistled their satisfaction. Jisanne clamped her bruised lips together to keep from making a sound. She heard shouts and cheers from more halflings ahead as they arrived at the village, a ring of stone houses that surrounded a stone pyramid.

Halflings were notorious slavers, and Borodro had said he kept other captives, though none were readily visible. The halflings dumped her into a small, filthy pen with walls made of twisted thorn branches. Her hands and ankles remained bound.

Jisanne tried to concentrate so she could gather power for her magic, draw power slowly from the surrounding plants and trees, perhaps even from the halflings themselves. If she garnered strength gradually, she might not alert the vicious little beasts to what she was doing.

She could have just ripped the power from the fabric of the world, stealing as much life force as required, but even to save herself, Jisanne was reluctant to destroy life by turning to the corrupting magic. The only time she truly defiled nature was to activate the navigation crystal, and that was . . . necessary. For now, she would find another way.

The halflings left Jisanne in the pen, focused on other interests, jabbering and chuckling.

"I'm hungry!"

"They better not have gnawed all the bones!"

"Save me a tender piece," Borodro said. The other halfling hunters dumped the decapitated body of their comrade on the trampled ground. "And start cooking Delfi. Throw in a lot of garlic so he doesn't taste gamey."

Jisanne realized that there were no other captives. Several human carcasses—mostly picked clean—were being roasted over a bed of orange coals near the stone pyramid. The returning hunters rushed over to the cookfire and squabbled over the remaining meat.

She felt a sickening wrench in her gut. Halfling cannibals were the worst.

Sweating, in pain from her contusions and cracked bones, Jisanne closed her eyes and began to concentrate on scraps of magic, pulling together any possibilities for her escape. She didn't have much time.

Koram walked away and never looked back at the Balic skyline. He did not listen to the mayhem as Skull Wearer and his beast giant army hammered the walls, did not flinch as sorcerer-king Andropinis fought back with arcane magic. He heard explosions, screams, a loud ripping roar . . . and he kept walking. It was no longer his battle; perhaps it had never been.

With his sword he cut the mooring rope of a fully stocked silt skimmer, then set sail out into the estuary. As a youth, in happier days in the great walled city, he had learned how to guide and levitate the skimmers on his impetuous adventures in the surrounding area. This, though, was no mere lighthearted expedition. He would never return.

The hot, dry breezes blew him past other coastal villages, then he turned east into deeper silt, crossing to the hazy highlands of the Dragon's Palate, where he hoped to live off the land.

After he beached the silt skimmer at sunset, Koram set up camp in the trees; he slept little, with his back against a sturdy trunk, as he listened to creatures stalking the night. He had no plan, no goal—and it felt liberating. Before, he had lived for his family, for his city, to make a better existence for all the citizens of Balic. He had worked hard and dedicated himself for people he cared about. And after his disgrace, he had been forced to fight and kill for people he hated.

Now all that was gone, the good and the bad. He owed nothing to anyone. He would heal, he would survive, and one day, perhaps he would find something else to believe in.

Next day, he continued to explore the island, finding the ruins of a Balic fort whose inhabitants had been slaughtered, probably by Skull Wearer's giants. He picked through the wreckage and took what he needed, but he did not want to stay at the site of a recent massacre.

Continuing his explorations, he encountered a commotion up ahead, shouts and snapping branches. He heard a halfling warrior party crashing through the forest long before he saw them. He decided they must be bad warriors to be so noisy and obvious . . . and then he realized they were chasing someone.

A young woman burst out of the trees, running wildly; her long brown hair streamed behind her. She looked battered and exhausted. When the woman saw Koram, they both froze. He had not intended to save anyone, and she looked just as reluctant to accept his help, but the yips, howls, and high-pitched curses of the pursuers drove her toward him.

"Halflings," she said, heaving great breaths. "I used my magic to escape . . . not much left now. And no time."

"Magic?" Koram tightened his grip on the hilt of his sword. "I have no love for defilers."

"I don't defile. I'm a survivor—so far. You'll come with me if you hope to survive."

Bounding forward with a speed and agility that belied his stocky body, the halfling leader raced out of the trees, waving his bone sword. He skidded to a halt, his eyes bugging out as he saw the armored gladiator, then he yelled back to the trees. "Hey, hurry up! I've caught another one!"

Brazen with confidence, the woman whirled to face the halfling. "Leave us, Borodro—and maybe we won't kill you."

Borodro laughed. "I have fifty followers right behind me!"

"I counted forty-five," she said.

He paused to tally them again in his mind. "More than enough."

Since he had done nothing to provoke the halfling hunter, had made no sign of even choosing sides in the dispute, Koram was taken off guard as Borodro threw himself forward like a rabid animal. With fierce and unhindered sword work, the feral halfling landed the first blow and chipped one of Koram's petrified-wood armor plates.

As a gladiator, Koram had fought many different opponents, so he adjusted his combat technique accordingly. His arena fighting skills took over, automatic and without mercy. He had not meant to fight again, did not want to get involved in this squabble . . . but he could not simply ignore this woman. If he had fought back earlier, if he had defended his family against the guards who came to take him, maybe he could have saved his wife and son. Koram parried the halfling's sharpened-femur sword with his own bronze edge, hammering so hard he splintered the giant bone. Borodro hesitated in surprise at the ferocity of the blow.

With a curled fist, Koram smashed the halfling leader in the nose, drawing forth a surprised yowl and a burst of blood. As the enrgaged Borodro threw himself against the gladiator again, Koram impaled him on his sword. The halfling collapsed, wailing as his blood poured out.

In the dense trees nearby, the remaining forty-five halfling pursuers heard their leader's death scream, then raised their own voices.

Koram held his sword and stood his ground; he did not even know who this woman was, but he was certain he could never defeat so many halfling cannibals.

The woman yanked a small pouch from her breeches and unwrapped it to reveal a rough shard of crystal. She looked up at Koram, wild-eyed. "No way around it now. I can use Borodro's life force before he dies, and I'll probably have to drain a dozen trees, too. But it's either defiling magic, or we both die."

Anger flared inside him. "I refuse to be part of defilement."

On the ground, Borodro coughed blood and wheezed out a death rattle. Wearing a grim expression, the woman knelt next to the dying halfling, working her hands around the crystal. "Normally I would use my own blood, my own strength, but this creature has already taken enough lives." She spat in the halfling's face to express her loathing, then she looked with greater sympathy at Koram. "You saved me. I'll save you. I'll take you to . . . a better place."

As she summoned the power to activate the crystal, Borodro wailed and writhed, then shriveled to dust. The grasses and weeds on the ground withered as the circle of defiling magic spread, drinking life energy from anything it touched. Tall trees turned brown, creaking, splintering.

Koram yelled at her, "I do not want—"

Then the first members of the halfling hunting party charged forward out of the trees, waving their weapons. They all looked hungry.

The crystal in her palm glowed as she finished her spell.

The world shimmered—and they were both in a different place. Koram's next breath tasted of moisture, life, flowers, and leaves. Nearby, a brook tumbled over mossy rocks on its way downhill. The shadowy monster-infested forest was now glittering with birdsong and gentle breezes. Even the sun in the sky was bright yellow, rather than a dull bloody red.

He stared in awe, then looked at the woman, demanding explanations. "Where have you taken me?"

The magic user shuddered in disgust at what she had done. The rough crystal in her bloodstained palm emitted a yellowish glow. "This is Athas . . . our world, before the sorcerer-kings and corrupt magic users wrung it dry."

"How did we get here?" The gladiator looked around, worried that Borodro's cannibal halflings had followed them through time. "How do we get back?" He had not intended to stay with this woman. The wounds and memories were still too fresh in his mind and heart, and he did not want to cast his lot with a stranger. It would not be fair to her, or to him.

The woman—who told him her name was Jisanne—looked down at the strange glassy shard she held. "Ancient sailors used this navigation crystal to take them home. This time period, this version of Athas, was the home of a powerful ship's captain." Though her skin was covered with bruises and she walked with obvious pain, Jisanne set off down the slope, following the stream. "I've brought us here. Look around you. Are you so anxious to be back in your harsh world?"

He found the fresh, green, *living* landscape remarkable . . . but its very strangeness was intimidating. "I have lost my family, and lost my interest. Little matters to me anymore. But I . . . will stay with you until I'm sure you are safe."

She regarded him with a hard expression. "I have taken care of myself for a long time, and I don't need a protector." She drew a deep breath. "But you are here with me now. I prefer this time and place, when the world was young and healthy—but my magic isn't strong enough to make it permanent. Come, we don't have much time."

Koram followed her down the slope to a wide blue river course—clear, swift-flowing water dotted with colorful sails of trading ships, oared dromonds from the city guard, even pleasure craft. He recognized it. "This is the estuary!"

"The way it once was." Jisanne led him along the shore. "This is how Athas was meant to be."

His heart felt leaden, wishing his wife and son could see this. "I suppose if we are trapped here . . . I would not complain." He could make a new home here, a new life far from his memories.

"It won't last." Jisanne scanned the shore, looking for something. "I stole life energy for this spell. Defiling magic is the only way to activate the navigation crystal, and it will fade soon enough."

He was uneasy with her casual use of the corrupting power, but he also knew that otherwise he would be dying just then, his body pierced with halfling arrows and blades. Jisanne had saved both of them. He owed her a debt of gratitude.

When he had turned his back on Balic, he had severed all ties, washing his hands of the evil government that had destroyed his family and the fickle people who had shown him no loyalty, no support. Though he had little to live for, once he'd left the arena, he did not want to die. Given time, perhaps Koram would find a reason that meant something—and someone who deserved it.

After they had rushed along through the peaceful forest, Jisanne let out a happy cry and hurried through the underbrush to a small rowboat tied to a drooping tree trunk. "Come, we must head south as fast as we can, while the spell lasts. Unless you'd rather travel across the silt?"

Though he didn't know what she meant, her urgency was plain. Koram climbed into the boat, took the oars, then guided them out into the fast-flowing estuary. "Where are we going?"

"South—to Arkhold. To my home."

After a lifetime of considering desolation to be the normal state of the world, he marveled at the bounty of water, the moisture in the air, the fractured-gold flashes of sunlight on the river's ripples. As he rowed vigorously, water splashed on the caked dust and blood on his skin; it felt cool and strange as the fresh breezes dried it quickly. A strange stirring occurred in his chest, and the weight on his shoulders seemed less heavy. Koram began to feel alive again.

As they made good time along the current, Jisanne told him her story, and he shared his own. She didn't seem at all astonished to hear of Praetor Yvoluk's cruelty or how the fickle people of Balic had so easily turned on him. They had done the same to her. Jisanne explained how ancient sorcerer-kings had abused dark powers, draining the world year after year, spell after spell, war after war.

"Defiling magic did this to Athas—and now I have used it to bring us back to a time before the world was destroyed." She shook her head in disgust at herself. "Ironic, isn't it? In order to visit an Athas untainted by the parasitical magic,

I need to drain more life force from the land."

"Either way, we are here." Koram rowed as hard as he could, carrying them far down the watercourse. They traveled for many leagues before the magic weakened. As Jisanne felt it fade, she urged him to pull the boat to the shallows.

With a wrenching disappointment, they watched the green shore and blue current curl and evaporate, changing from a verdant paradise to a barren brown wasteland. The Athas Koram was used to seeing. He felt suddenly hollow and lost, and he had to bite back a bitter cry.

The small boat ground ashore and fell apart with the sudden weight of age, disintegrating into dry and ancient splinters. The two found themselves in the rocks on the edge of a bone-dry canyon. "We'll have to walk from here. Arkhold isn't far," Jisanne said.

He hesitated, looking around at the stark rocks and dry desert. "I did not intend to stay."

She looked uncertain. "You saved my life. I prefer being alone, and I never said I wanted company. . . . But stay and rest. You can find your own path tomorrow."

Together, they trudged back to her skeletal ship, the dry docks, and the silt-buried old harbor city. He gave a gruff answer. "No place else to be."

Dust-shrouded Arkhold was dead, empty . . . and peaceful. When she and Koram reached her makeshift home aboard *Horizon Finder*, Jisanne fell into a deep, exhausted sleep. It took days for her to recover from the magic she had used, and so Koram did not leave. He tended her, brought her food and water, and kept watch against the ever-present dangers of the desert.

She could not shake the disheartened realization of how willingly she had turned to defiling magic to summon the past centuries of Athas. When possible, she would use her own blood to work the spell, drawing upon willingly surrendered life energy to trigger the crystal. A spell could be more permanent if not forced and stolen—but she had to use what she could. Jisanne knew she would do it again. Every moment she experienced in that long-lost period was worth the sacrifice, even if she had to steal the energy from other living creatures. It could rapidly become too easy. . . .

The gladiator from Balic wanted nothing from her, put no obligations on her, posed no threat. She had come to this place intentionally, hiding from her past; the other strangers she had encountered here were greedy, driven, dangerous. Koram, though, had cut himself off from the strings that bound him to his city and he had let the hot winds of circumstance blow him wherever they wished. And they had brought him to her.

While she continued to recover, Koram trudged off into the rugged land nearby. He returned a day later with three large iguanas he had caught, a pouch of leathery-shelled turtle eggs, and several wrinkled gourds that held water. If not for him, Jisanne doubted she could have survived.

For his own part, he also seemed to be healing just by staying with her in the empty quiet. The two kept their distance from each other, kept their silence, but eventually they talked more, surprised to find how much they were alike. Though the man carried no happiness within him, at least he seemed to find an inner contentment being there. In the evenings he would sit with her, and gradually opened up, talking more and more.

"I had to shut out all of my pain and anger just to survive in the arena. But I don't like to be so empty. When you showed me the past, you made me see how healthy this world once was . . . and could be again. Maybe my life can become whole again, as well." He hung his head. The bristles of hair had begun to regrow from his shaved scalp. "I will hold onto that hope."

With a wistful sigh, Jisanne thought of the glorious, vibrant past. "If we could return there, I would turn my back on all of Athas without a second's regret . . . the way you turned away from Balic."

Koram made a rumbling sound in his chest. "I would do it in a second."

<hr />

The peace could last only so long.

Just as the first flames of dawn scorched the Sea of Silt, a bellowing voice echoed through Arkhold. "Gladiator Koram, come out and meet your master—and your death! The smell of your treachery makes you easy to follow."

Belowdecks in the petrified old sailing ship, Koram recognized the voice, a sound that had come from beyond the grave. He leaped off his pallet and grabbed his sword, but did not have time to strap on his armor. Koram said to Jisanne, "Hide here. He doesn't want you."

She sat bolt upright, her eyes wide. "Who is it? Who tracked you here?"

"Praetor Yvoluk. He survived somehow. I suppose a soul as twisted as his cannot be easily crushed." He hefted his ivory-and-bronze sword. "If I kill him, I'll be back."

Jisanne took out the navigation crystal, drew a deep breath. "I am strong enough to use magic again. Let me help you fight him."

"That would be a waste of your life. Yvoluk has already taken my wife and son. That is enough." He stalked off and climbed the ladder out of the hold. He no longer felt empty and aimless. If he was going to face a hated enemy again, at least now he had a reason to fight.

He did not hear Jisanne whisper under her breath, "And *I* lost my sister and her whole family because I wasn't there to protect them."

Emerging onto the open deck, Koram saw a silt dromond bearing Balic's flag. Powered by a psionic helm, the large ship hovered above the dust, separated by less than a meter from *Horizon Finder*'s starboard bow. In the fleet maneuvers of Dictator Andropinis, Koram had seen these fearsome ships glide across the desert like giant sharks in the sky.

Smug, Yvoluk stood on the dromond's bow next to the thri-kreen tracker, the nihilist philosopher who had also fought in the Criterion; the chittering thri-kreen bobbed his rounded head, his faceted eyes gleaming in the bright daylight. "You see, Praetor—I told you I could track him." In his segmented limbs, the thri-kreen held the rumpled sash of Andropinis that Koram had left behind in his cell. Five more Balic soldiers stood behind them, armed and ready to fight.

When the tracker saw Koram's angry scowl at the betrayal, he shouted to the other ship. "It makes no difference. If we'd been pitted against each other, you would have killed me or I'd have killed you. It is nothing personal."

The words were dry as they came out of Koram's mouth. "I won't hold any sympathy or any grudge against you. My grudge is with Yvoluk."

The praetor's laugh sounded like splintering wood. "And my grudge is with *you*, Koram. You cast me to my death, but magic cushioned my fall. Unluckily for the beast giants, they have a strong life force. Using it to power my magic was as easy as poking a hole in a wineskin. I was nearly buried among the corpses I had slain." Behind him, the five warriors drew their blades and bows, ready to attack, but Yvoluk motioned them back. He seemed proud of what he had done.

"I crawled out of the zone of death just as Dictator Andropinis cast his own spell from the wall above. He unleashed such terrible magic that he felled dozens of giants, not to mention several hundred cowardly soldiers with a single spell. He called up a lava storm in the estuary, enough to send Skull Wearer and his minions fleeing. I barely scaled the wall myself." The praetor shook his head like a disappointed parent. "But you had already run away, Koram. You gave us quite a chase."

"Then I will save you further trouble. When you forced me to fight opponents in the Criterion, I had no reason to kill them. Now, though, I have all the reasons I need." Koram bent his powerful legs and sprang across the gap from *Horizon Finder* to the levitating dromond.

Jisanne was already rallying her magic as she emerged onto the deck. She saw Koram land on the adjacent silt dromond to face his enemy, yelling, "Fight me, Yvoluk! I have waited long enough for this."

The Balic templar just laughed. "And why should I bother fighting you when I have others to do so?" He motioned for his fighters, and three of the men nocked arrows to bowstrings; the other two lifted their short swords and crouched to charge.

With anger roiling through her, Jisanne stepped out of the shadows and began to work her first spell. Drawing energy from all around her in a quick rush, she felt the tension build within her. Her need justified whatever means she might employ, even defilement—fast, powerful, and deadly magic. "Leave us alone!"

Spotting her, the thri-kreen tracker gave an alarmed squawk and his small antennae lifted, twitching. "Koram sent a defiler against us!"

With instinctive terror, Yvoluk's warriors fired their arrows without any command from the praetor. Three shafts leaped out from twanging bows. One of the arrows clattered on *Horizon Finder*'s deck—but the other two struck Jisanne, one on the left side of her chest, the second in her abdomen. The impacts drove her backward.

With a howl, Koram thrust his sword deep into the traitorous thri-kreen's back, piercing the tan chitin; the thri-kreen's lower set of legs folded and he fell to his knees, dragging Koram's sword with him, caught in his hard shell. "Ah, so this is how it ends . . ." He whistled through his mandibles.

Jisanne gasped as her spell died around her. She tried to keep uttering the words, but only blood came out of her mouth, not the rest of the incantation.

With a barked command from Yvoluk, the soldiers fell upon Koram, five against one. Even as he struggled to tear his sword free from the thri-kreen's body, the warriors swarmed over him, thrusting and stabbing.

Lying in a pool of her own blood on the deck of *Horizon Finder*, Jisanne saw an image of her sister's family cut down by mob hatred. Yes, she did know how to use arcane magic, and now her own blood gave her all the power she needed to finish the spell.

The silt stirred beneath the levitating dromond. A line of ivory vertebrae moved in a serpentine ripple, and a pair of ribcages lifted up through the sand. Balanced on puzzle-pieces of stacked bones, two saurian skulls dropped open hinged jaws to brandish sand-worn fangs. The long-dead sea serpents both roared, a dry rasping sound that scratched through their hollow throats. Once so majestic as they glided on Athas's long-forgotten seas, the fossilized monsters now loomed over the levitating dromond. Jisanne clenched her bloodied fists, drove the monsters into action.

Yvoluk's warriors looked up and screamed, scrambling away from Koram. The praetor stared in awe, craning his neck up at the giant fanged skulls, then frantically worked his own spell to protect himself—but before he could finish, one of the skeleton serpents darted forward and chomped down. Lifting the bleeding templar into the air, the serpent shook him from side to side, bit him in half, then tossed the severed body off the dromond. Yvoluk was still gurgling as he sank into the silt.

Jisanne crawled to the side rail, lifted herself up, and extended a red hand toward Koram. On the levitating dromond, he was a patchwork of deep wounds, bleeding from numerous slashes and cuts, many of them surely fatal. She tried to call his name, but her lungs were filled with blood.

Koram dragged himself to the bow and somehow found the strength to make a staggering leap back to *Horizon Finder*. Jisanne attempted to catch him, and they both tumbled together. One of the arrow shafts snapped off inside, and the pain blinded her.

Even without her magical control, the skeletal serpents continued to attack the dromond. Ivory skulls smashed the planks, broke the hull, shattered the rails. The serpents seized the terrified Balic soldiers in their jaws, tossing bodies over the side or leaving them strewn across the deck. The dromond crashed, running aground onto the stone quay.

Jisanne and Koram held each other, barely hearing the screams and the mayhem. Drowning in the pain, she felt the magic fade. The twin sea monster skeletons raised sinuous bone necks as if in a salute, then crumbled into ivory shards in the dust.

Jisanne knew she was dying, and beside her Koram grasped her hand. His wounds looked even worse than hers. "Do you have the navigation crystal?" he said. "Take us back . . . to when Athas was alive."

With an effort she removed the worn object, wet fingers fumbling with the strings of the pouch. "The magic won't last. It destroys. It is what drained this world."

He leaned closer, his breath rattling. "Then I give you my life energy willingly—take it! I'd rather die there than in this place."

Jisanne cupped the navigation crystal in her palm. Each breath was like broken glass caught on fire; the arrow deep in her stomach was a grinding spear of ice that twisted in her guts. "Maybe with my life force, too, it will be enough to seal the spell permanently."

Koram could barely hold his head up. He was fading quickly. If she didn't act soon, the opportunity would be wasted.

Jisanne clenched her fingers around the crystal. Previously, she had filled a small bowl with her own blood, just enough to work the arcane magic. Now there was so much blood, but she felt so weak . . . and Koram was so weak.

She pulled the spell from her own core, stronger than ever before. Jisanne used everything she had, and everything Koram had. She scraped both of their existences until they were bone dry and empty, she pulled on any life force around them, the waning energy of the dying guards, the small burrowing creatures in the ground, every faint flicker she could find. Even the sand and dust turned dark. She had never called on so much life force to fuel her magic.

Her vision faded into static and grit, and she could see only the crystal in her hand. Jisanne tried to hold onto it, but the object dulled, then crumbled into small shards and glittering dust in her hand.

Destroyed.

Jisanne collapsed, feeling the weight of Koram beside her but no life there, and no life inside her either. . . .

Then the deck began rocking beneath them, and the bright sun beating down seemed to have a different quality. The air Jisanne inhaled was moist and salty—and as she sucked in a lungful she realized that the arrow wounds no longer hurt. The spell had worked after all!

With a loud snort, a deep voice grumbled at them. "I see you are back, lady magic user—and you have brought a fighter, too. He looks strong enough, but lazy. Lounging around on the deck—hmmf!" The minotaur captain stood over the two of them.

Koram picked himself up, touching his bare chest and searching unsucessfully to find his deep wounds.

"Are you going to sleep all day?" Hurrun put his powerful hands on his hips. "This ship has places to go—I am not running an inn at sea!"

Jisanne got to her feet and looked off the starboard bow to see the beautiful harbor city of Arkhold with its whitewashed buildings on the hills, the large marketplace down by the docks, the colorful sails of small fishing boats.

"We are glad to be here, Captain," Jisanne said. She felt more solid now than ever before, more *real* in this time.

Koram was amazed. "Please let us stay."

"All right, I won't throw you overboard just yet." The minotaur turned and stalked back toward the bow. "Just make yourselves useful."

Because they had surrendered their life energy voluntarily, perhaps they had twisted the nature of the defiling magic, and the navigation crystal had incorporated them into the past, into its memory of "home." Maybe they were really there, or maybe it was only a recorded vision that had an objective and persistent reality of its own. Either way, it didn't matter.

"This is our permanent place now, Koram," she said, convinced as she stood beside him. "We both made it so. This spell will never fade." They faced the sun—the golden yellow sun.

Kevin J. Anderson is a science fiction and fantasy novelist. His novels have appeared on national bestseller lists, and he has more than 11 million books in print worldwide. The prolific writer is well known for his immense contributions to the *Star Wars* and *Dune* shared worlds, and his solo projects (among them *The Saga of Seven Suns* septet of epic novels) have achieved tremendous critical and popular acclaim. Outside of novels, Kevin has also written numerous comic books.

LORD OF THE DARKWAYS

A Tale of the FORGOTTEN REALMS

ED GREENWOOD

Deadly Success

Flickering glows shaped two doors out of empty air, at either end of the large, dark room. The warrior strode through the one at the far end of the room, vanished in mid step—and reappeared stepping through the nearer glowing portal.

Where he immediately stiffened in mid stride to topple, spasming and thrashing helplessly—a strangled scream whistling through his working jaws—and crash face-first to the floor. His eyeballs burst, spattering the flagstones with a foul wetness that hissed into racing wisps of smoke, even before a larger flood spilled out of his mouth to join it.

The tall, slender man in black nodded in satisfaction. Six strong Zhentilar warriors had all found the same swift death.

Consistent results. His new spell was a success.

Smiling, he walked away.

Another Stormy Night

"My superiors at the temple? They think I'm trying to induce my brother to kiss the Holy Lash, of course. Which reminds me—you *will* embrace Loviatar before all other gods, won't you, Handreth?"

The wizard across the table gave her a mirthless half smile.

"I'll consider it," he said dismissively—then grinned, the bright, boyish flash of teeth Ayantha had known forever. She found herself grinning back.

"So, what brings a high-spells wizard from Waterdeep to cold, uncultured, mage-hating Zhentil Keep?"

"Coins, of course. Lots of them. And by 'mage-hating,' I presume you mean Manshoon and his magelings don't welcome wizards other than themselves?"

"I do. They don't. Walk warily, Han." She laid a long, barbed whip of many leather strands on the table, murmured a nigh-soundless prayer over it, then raised her eyes to his again and asked, "Who's your patron?"

"A merchant hight Ambram Sarbuckho—if you don't dissuade me from showing up at his doors, by what you tell me of him."

Ayantha shifted in her seat, supple black leather and tight strands of chain moving in ways meant to catch the eye, and gave him another smile. "So you sought out your little sister to learn how things lie here in the keep before taking service. I like that."

Handreth shrugged. "To rise to become a darklash of Loviatar—nay, just to survive this long, in service to the Maiden of Pain—takes wits. Wizards soon learn how hard it is to trust. You have wits, and I trust you. So here we are, in this vastly overpriced excuse for a highcoin drinking club, spending my gold. Speak."

His sister sighed. "We're not noble, so this is the best Zhentil Keep can offer us. Sit with your hands on the table, palms up. Please."

"So you can . . . ?"

"So I can lash you across your palms if someone comes into the room, to make them believe a darklash of the pain goddess is meeting alone with an outlander wizard for the right reasons."

Handreth put his hands on the table, palms up. "I believe I paid for a private room."

"You did. In the keep, there's 'private' and then there's 'private.' Again, we're not noble. Or Zhentarim."

Handreth nodded to signal he'd taken her point. Outside the leaded windows, the wind rose with a sudden whistle. Winter hadn't thrust its talons into Zhentil Keep just yet, but it was fast approaching, and bringing its cold with it. A time of whirling falling leaves, chill winds, and short, violent, icy rains. Puddles would form brittle skins of thin ice by night but melt every morn, for about a tenday. Then the snows would come, long before the Year of the Blazing Brand found its end.

"Ambram Sarbuckho is one of the wealthiest keep merchants," Ayantha told him, dropping her voice to a whisper. "He'll be given a lordship only if he joins the Zhentarim, though, and thus far he shows no signs of doing so. He's a glib schemer, always spinning little plots and swindles—and, I should warn you, he has hired an endless succession of serve-for-a-month wizards, rather than trying to buy the loyalty of one or two he keeps at his side for many seasons."

"So he's difficult?"

"*All* successful keep merchants are difficult, Brother. This one is open in his mistrust of everyone; he probably hires more informers than anyone in the city—after Manshoon, of course. He's . . . just as untrustworthy as he judges everyone else to be."

"I've done business with his factors in Sembia and Waterdeep, a time or ten. What's he known for, here at home?"

"A dealer in sundries, and importer of curios from afar."

"Huh." Handreth Imbreth grunted. "Someone a city ruler'll be suspicious of, right there."

His sister smiled thinly. "It's been a bare few months since Manshoon became First Lord of Zhentil Keep, his toady Lord Chess was named Watchlord of the Council, the priests of Bane started acting as if they were the watch, and we had eye tyrants lecturing us in our own streets. In Zhentil Keep, *everyone's* suspicious of everyone else. Watch your back, Brother—and never stop watching it."

"I thought Manshoon was yesterday's tyrant," Handreth muttered, "and some Lord Bellander or other is kinging it now, here in the keep."

His sister shook her head. "Folk in the streets believe that, and about half the merchants; the rest of us have wits enough to know Bellander's coup was staged by Manshoon himself. He's enthroned Bellander to be the target of those enraged by the new taxes and what's done by all swordsmen now making the lord's rule—*Manshoon's* rule, in truth—a thing of teeth, offering instant obedience or death. Bellander's a handsome, lecherous fool whose brains are about up to the task of outwitting yonder bowl of flower petals."

"Ah." Handreth nodded. "I'm familiar with the tactic; Waterdeep has seen it work a time or three, too."

Ayantha took up her lash, cracked it in the air, and brought it crashing down across the table. Handreth deftly plucked up his goblet before any wine could spill from it.

"We all know Manshoon's up-to something, and that he will move fast when he strikes," she announced, lashing the table again as the door opened and an impassive servant brought more wine, unbidden. She held silence until the servant withdrew, then struck the new decanter of wine aside, to shatter on the floor untasted.

Handreth nodded approvingly, and she inclined her head and went on.

"We just don't know yet what he'll do. All the spies we can pay—and keep alive, once we start paying them—tell us Fzoul, who speaks for Bane in this city, is still far too furious with the First Purring Lord to aid him in any way, though they'll end up working together eventually . . . and the beholders have told him bluntly, at least once, that he's on his own for now. My thinking is that they want to see if he can really establish rule over the city before they spend any more effort backing him."

She sipped the last from her goblet, set it down, and added, "Yet that just ensures he *will* do something; he has to prove himself, and soon, before all the lords he outraged at council manage to kill him off or just fill his platter with so many plots, coups, and small swindles and treacheries that he'll have no time to do anything but fight them off. So far, he's divided his time between summoning keep lords and merchants to private talks whereat he gently threatens them, training his ever-growing bands of ruthless warriors and magelings behind wards no one can penetrate, and spending days in seclusion, no doubt crafting dastardly new spells. We keep expecting his spellchamber door to open, and golems as tall as castle towers, and undead dragons with sixteen grafted-on heads to come bursting out and lay waste to the keep . . . but thus far, only he comes strolling out."

Silence fell.

Ayantha lifted an eyebrow. "Have I frightened you into scuttling back to the City of Splendors yet, Brother?"

Handreth smiled slowly, and his eyes began to glow red.

At the sight of that, the darklash hissed and stiffened, arching away from him in her chair.

Then she brought her lash around with vicious skill, letting the wizard taste it, right across his face.

His smile never changed.

"This," he told her, as her lash suddenly twisted in her hands, its strands leaping to coil around her neck and throttle her—then just as swiftly drop away, leaving her reeling in her seat, coughing and gagging, "sounds like fun."

The Spellchamber Door Opens

A tall, slender, darkly handsome man sat alone at the head of a long, polished table, his fingers clasped together under his chin. He was thinking, behind the faint half smile on his face that betrayed nothing.

In order to truly rule Zhentil Keep—not just lord it over the council—it would be necessary to break the power of the richest and most influential city merchants. Not to mention the hired wizards working for them.

The nobles he had already conquered, or could destroy at will. He just needed them to refrain from mustering arms against him and banding together while he dealt with the merchants.

The waylords. The sixteen men who could sway or cow all the other merchants and shopkeepers of the keep.

The sixteen who could not be throttled by surrounding their mansions and warehouses, and ruling the streets with sword and fist. The merchants whose mansions held Zhentil's Darkways, long-established magical gates linking those proud houses with certain mansions in Sembia. Allowing these sixteen to shuttle warriors, craftworkers, goods, and coins back and forth at will and in secret. Advantages that had won them all Sembian investments and Sembian backers whose aid they could easily call upon.

So "waylord" was a good name for them, even if only the Zhentarim called them by that name, or knew the sources of their power. To most citizens, they were merely the powerful merchants who dominated city life; folk to befriend and deal fairly with, who it was *very* unwise to make enemies of unless departing the city swiftly, never to return, and able to run far and fast. Sixteen men who shared a secret, but were a loose, often-feuding group, not a cabal or guild.

Yet true lords of the keep, for all that. Sixteen citizens who could quietly bring armies into the city without having to fight past the city walls or disembark at the docks.

They threatened the rule of anyone who sat on a throne in Zhentil Keep by their very existence. So they must die, and soon. The Zhentarim must seize and command their portals.

He had known this for years, but only now were his spells ready. Only now could he strike.

It was merely a matter of not putting a foot wrong in his swift, well-planned advance.

"If there is to be a Lord of the Darkways," Manshoon told the empty air around him, "let it be me."

He smiled at how much information he'd gathered by impersonating the wizard he'd just slain, Handreth Imbreth. Darklash Ayantha had screamed long and loud, and had proved every bit as tough as he'd expected. She should still be alive to scream for him a last time or two, when he was done here.

He reached out and pulled the cord that would tell his servants to open the doors and let his three most trusted underlings into the room.

"He wants to know all you can call to mind of the waylords, so start thinking," Sneel said unpleasantly.

Kelgoran glowered. One day, Lorkus Sneel would take a step too far . . .

"Don't ever make the mistake of thinking the Brotherhood's warriors are dullards," Cadathen warned Sneel, as calmly as if he'd been discussing unchanging weather.

"I don't," Manshoon's most accomplished spy replied coldly and flatly.

"Very well then," the wizard Manshoon trusted most—because, they all knew, his Art was far too feeble to challenge the master's—replied affably, "don't make the mistake of treating them as if they are. It will only turn to bite you, when you'll least be able to afford that."

"Spare me your granddam's advice," Sneel hissed. He turned to face the warrior again. "Well?"

Ornthen Kelgoran was a veteran of many skirmishes in Thar and beyond, a hardened warrior who had become wise to the ways of the crowded stone city of Zhentil Keep, and who was Manshoon's best slayer of those who crossed him. He smiled. "Well, what?"

Sneel sighed. "Don't be—"

"A dullard? Sneel, your arrogance is only surpassed by your inability to judge others. A serious failing in a spy, I'd say."

Before Sneel could reply, the warrior swept out one brawny forearm in a florid herald's gesture, a violent movement that made the spy flinch.

Kelgoran chuckled and began to declaim. "Most important among the waylords—those the rest will follow—are five men."

He held up one hairy finger. "Srabbast Dorloun, a dealer in textiles and footwear, and a greedy, coldly calm, burly mountain of a man. I know little of his hired wizard, Tanthar of Selgaunt, beyond an impressive reputation: scruples, powerful magic, widely traveled."

A second finger rose. "The importer of smoked meats and fine wines, Besnar Calagaunt, who reminds me very much of you, Sneel. Thin, apt to sneer—but unlike you, handsome and elegant. Unmarried, too, and a scourge of the ladies—but a devout follower of Loviatar who lives and works with two young priestesses of the pain goddess, Darklash Ayantha and Painclaw Jessanna. I expect he's covered with scars, under all those silken jerkins."

A third finger joined the other two. "Fantharl Halamaun, perhaps the wealthiest of the lot. He can afford *two* wizards of reputation: Ardroth Thauntan of Chessenta, and a handsome, mustache-twirling Tethyrian who styles himself Valandro the Mysterious and defends himself with three swords that fly around under his command. You can be sure the master pays special attention to *him*."

"Leave the wizards to the master," Sneel said coldly. "Tell me of Halamaun."

"Short, ugly, a glutton. Grasping and greedy—the man's a landlord and a coinlender, what more need I say?"

"His trades."

"Uh, builder. And repairer of most buildings in the keep."

"Very well. Your fourth?"

"Mantras Jhoszelbur. Trader in metals and ores, owns our biggest foundry, two weaponsmi—"

"Three. He owns three, and is busily buying out a fourth."

"Very well. *That* many weaponsmiths' shops, five ships I know of"—Kelgoran paused, one brow raised in challenge, but Sneel merely nodded, so the warrior continued—"two steadings where war horses are bred, reared, and trained, and a smallish coster or two. More interesting than all of that, though: Stormwands House. His own little school of wizardry, composed of the elderly mage Paerimrel of Amn and a dozen or so students, all young. They call themselves 'the Stormwands.' Jhoszelbur's old, short tempered, and—"

"Who are the most powerful of the Stormwands, the ones we must be wary of?"

"—ruthless. There are two Stormwands to beware: Rorymrar and Jonthyn. My men and I have gone drinking with them more than once, under the master's orders. They are . . . less accomplished than they believe themselves to be, but dangerous nonetheless."

"That's four. The fifth?"

"Ambram Sarbuckho, a—"

Four guards in full and gleaming black armor stepped through the tapestries in front of them, then drew the tapestries back and secured them with their chains. The full-face helms that kept them anonymous made their voices boom; the nearest commanded, "Enough. The master is not in a patient mood. Enter."

The doors were thrust wide, revealing a thin wisp of smoke that coiled and then rose like a snake about to strike.

The three men had never seen such magic before, but they knew better than to hesitate. They strode forward, right through the smoke, and the guards slammed the doors behind them and went to their crossbows, fixed by firing ports that pierced the walls of the room beyond. Their loaded and ready bolts were tipped with a poison only Manshoon would take no harm from—for the First Lord of Zhentil Keep was a careful man.

The Prize of Indispensability

Manshoon waved the three to the waiting seats at the far end of the long, polished table, and regarded them expressionlessly. These were his most accomplished servants, which meant they were adept at acting loyal.

Sneel, Cadathen, and Kelgoran—useful to him in that descending order, yet utterly disposable whenever the need arose.

"As Sneel has no doubt revealed without actually saying so," he said flatly, "I have decided to free Zhentil Keep from the tyranny of the waylords. Now."

He looked to his spy. "Begin subtly spreading word through our usual mouths that Halamaun is finally sick of Dorloun, and is covertly gathering hired bullyblades to start killing Dorloun's employees, suppliers, and clients whenever they can be caught alone."

He waited for Sneel to nod, then added, "You are also to start rumors that Jhoszelbur has decided to crush his longtime and increasingly successful rival Calagaunt. Further, you are to ensure that servants of all the waylords hear that the First Lord of the city is gathering power to decide who shall rise as lords in Zhentil Keep, and who shall be forced out of trade, the keep, and if need be, continued life. Then report back to me for additional orders."

Sneel nodded, but made no move to rise. The hint of a smile rose to Manshoon's lips.

"You are dismissed. Tarry not to try to overhear my orders to these two."

"Of course," Sneel replied, nodding low over the table before rising and smoothly making for the doors.

Manshoon waited for a signal—a single tap against the wall—after the doors had closed behind his departing spymaster. Then he looked at Kelgoran and spoke again.

"Gather your worst and most bumbling blades—those we need to test, and can easily afford to lose—for assaults on the mansions of Dorloun, Halamaun, and Jhoszelbur. Muster them at the warehouses, at the slaughterhouse, and at the Black Barrel; you choose which, for which. They're not to move, show themselves, or swing blades at anyone before I say so."

Kelgoran's nod was quick, and came with a pleased smile; he had already risen before Manshoon added, "Yes, you're dismissed."

The warrior's eager hastening brought a swift closing of the doors and the tap that followed them, leaving Manshoon and Cadathen alone together.

Whereupon the First Lord of Zhentil Keep drew a small, plain bone goblet from under the table, then an even smaller knife. Cadathen went pale.

"A renewal," Manshoon said calmly, drawing the blade along the outside edge of his hand. Dark red blood welled out, and he held his hand to let it run down his fingers and drip into the goblet, as he licked the knife clean and slid it across the table to Cadathen.

Who deftly trapped it with his hand, rose and went to the goblet, gave himself a similar wound, licked the knife, and set it carefully down beside Manshoon, his hands trembling slightly.

When the goblet was full, the master's murmured word and swift gesture would enact the blood spell. After they both drank, any harm suffered by Manshoon would instantly also be dealt to Cadathen.

White-faced, he whispered, "Why is this necessary, lord? Again?"

Manshoon smiled. "Call it a precaution that should hurt a loyal Cadathen not at all, but bestow upon a Cadathen of darker deed or intent a fitting traitor's reward. I need your silence, but also need you to know my plan, so you can adjust matters out in the streets and mansions to ensure it has the effects I desire. So heed well."

He cast the spell, they both drank from the glowing goblet, and Manshoon waved Cadathen back to his seat.

Only after the still-pale wizard was settled again did he add, "The waylords will be broken—or eliminated—by an enchantment I have just perfected, that will very soon be cast upon all of the Darkways. Anyone who passes through those portals thereafter will die, horribly and instantly, as my spell transforms all the blood in their veins to a potent flesh-melting acid."

Cadathen looked excited, but uneasy. "But will the Darkways not prove useful, in time to come?"

"They will. As doors that open when *I* want them to, not doors standing open always that can let sellsword armies hired in Sembia flood into the very heart of Zhentil Keep whenever some greedy Sembian or other decides our gems and metals make the keep worth the trouble of plundering. Even beholders can slay only so many sellswords before they get overwhelmed and hacked apart. And should such a dark day come, wizards like me—and you—will survive far less time than elder eye tyrants like Argloth or Xalanxlan."

Cadathen nodded, wincing.

"So traversing the Darkways will be fatal except when I remove my spells," Manshoon purred. "And only I will know when those times are. Making me too valuable for anyone who cares for Zhentil Keep to slay. I *love* being indispensable."

Windtatter Moon Rising

Rain had stopped lashing at the windowpanes, and there was moonlight at last.

A weary but very happy Lord Bellander rose on his elbows and gazed out the window.

"Ah," he murmured. "A windtatter moon."

"Indeed," replied the senior priestess lying bare and beautiful in the bed beside him. "It's why I'm here."

Bellander lifted an eyebrow. "Oh? Not for me?"

Bride of Darkness Orlpharla sat up rather briskly. "The Dread God revealed to Lord Holy Fzoul that the next wind-tatter moon would bring great peril to House Bellander. I'm here to keep you alive until morning."

"And after that?"

"After that, Lord Bellander," Orlpharla said coldly, "your survival is in your own hands. Our most recent visions suggest we'll be rather busy trying to keep Zhentil Keep from erupting into civil war."

———— ◆ ————

The Reapers Loosed

There arose heavy thuds of many staves and axes crashing against the doors, right on cue. His hired armsmen had timed matters rather well.

In response, guards shouted and came running; Manshoon smiled tightly and worked the spell that would make them *really* shout.

They did more than that. Some of them screamed and fled wildly through the mansion, crashing past tables and toppling sculptures and suits of armor.

The illusion he'd spun, of a beholder drifting menacingly forward, all of its eyestalks writhing, would circle the room he was in now.

The room where Waylord Fornlar Darltreth's Darkway flickered and glowed, now alone and unguarded.

His more important casting didn't take long; this was his tenth murmuring of the spell. When he was done, the Darkway blazed up brightly for a moment as if angered by his magic, then settled back down to glowing just as it had before.

The First Lord of Zhentil Keep gave it a sardonic salute and smile, and let his ring take him on to the next mansion.

Most of the waylords were elsewhere, gathered at Harlstrand House—whose wine cellar was the best, and feasting hall the grandest—to debate what to do about a certain upstart Manshoon and his rising power in the city. Sneel was very good at what he did; one waylord-shaking crisis, conjured up in less time than it took to eat a good meal.

He stood then in a rather colder room, hung with dark tapestries and occupied by another Darkway—and two astonished guards, who raised their spears and reached for an alarm gong.

Manshoon waved one hand and gave them slumber. His armsmen would need some time to hasten through the streets and reach the front doors of this high house; it would be best if no alarm was raised until their sudden assault on its doors.

This was all going very smoothly. He strode to where he could stand over the guards, and look to see if they had any useful magic he could confiscate.

"Let the reaping begin," he murmured aloud, "and the fortunes of the waylords wane."

◆ ◆ ◆

Interlude in Innarlith
"Outlander!" the High Constable of Innarlith roared, "Come forth!"

On either side of his broad, bright-armored shoulders stood a trio of impassive constables, their armor as gleaming as his own, wands ready in their hands. When one challenges a wizard, it is best to be prepared.

High Constable Lhoreld smote the door with his mace, a glancing blow that marked but did not dent it, yet sent an echoing thunder through the bedchamber behind that door. "Elminster!" he bellowed. "You were seen to steal royal paints and brushes, and bring them to this place! Thief, stand forth!"

The door swung open.

Out of the lamplit dimness beyond strode a tall, slender, white-bearded man, barefoot and in fact—the High Constable's eyes bulged—wearing only hundreds of smears of dried paint and a lady's diaphanous nightgown pulled around himself. He leaned unconcernedly against the doorpost in what could only be described as an indolent—even jaunty—pose.

"Aye? Have ye brought wine?"

High Constable Lhoreld went a little crimson around the temples, and his nostrils flared. On either side of him, his constables went from looking impassive to looking stern as they hastily leveled their wands at the man in the doorway.

"You stand in the Fortress Royal, wizard!" Lhoreld shouted. "In the name of the Spaerenza, Royal Ruler of Innarlith, I arrest you to face justice! You have stolen her art supplies—"

Elminster made a rude sound, and a ruder gesture. "Pah! I have *not*."

"Do—do you *mock* me, man?" The High Constable was incredulous. "The Spaerenza's paints are all *over* you, from head to toe! D'you think me *blind*?"

"Nay," Elminster drawled. "Merely stupid." He peered, to make sure none of the constables was clutching a decanter behind his back, then added, "Too stupid to bring any wine, at least."

"I'll not bandy words with you, wizard! I require your instant submission—on your knees, man, and hold out your wrists to be manacled! You'll be brought before Her Exaltedness for your punishment forthwith, and—"

"Punishment? Surely ye might want to determine my guilt, first? Or perhaps my innocence? Or has Innarlith no laws at all but the whim of its High Constable?"

Lhoreld was now purple and shaking. "Do—do you *seriously* mean to claim you did not steal art supplies, when sworn witnesses—over a score of servants and courtiers—saw you do so?"

"I do mean to make that very claim. I stole *nothing*. And *I* can produce my own witnesses to attest to my claim."

"Oh? Outlanders in your employ?" The High Constable sneered.

"No, personages that even a thick-headed windbag of a High Constable might have heard of. Let me begin with the Spaerenza herself. Then a certain Lord Wizard of the city, Uldimar Bronneth—ye may know him better as the Marquavarl; their son, Prince Hajorn, oh, and the Princesses Amaelra and Marinthra, too."

"Ah *hah*. You are aware that bearing false witness against the royal family of Innarlith is itself a very serious crime?"

"I am," Elminster confirmed, smilingly. "I believe ye'll find them happy to state my innocence in this matter."

The High Constable's utter disbelief was written very clearly across his face. "Oh? And I suppose the Lord Protector can speak for you, too?"

"No, I fear not," Elminster replied gravely. "However, both of his subordinates—the Dukes Henneth and Porlandur—were present, and can attest—"

"I'll bet they can." Lhoreld sneered. "I'll just bet they can.

In fact, wizard, I'm going to wager my career on that. If you can't get any of these worthies to swear your words are true, you'll wither away to bones chained to the coldest, wettest wall in the deepest of our dungeons, down where the rats go to die! I'll escort you there myself, without delay! Stand forth from yon doorway, or my men will smite you down!"

"Really," Elminster said reprovingly, like a kindly but disappointed mother to an angry child, "that won't be necessary—"

"*Wizard,* step away from yon door!"

With a sigh and a shrug, spreading open and empty hands, Elminster did as he was commanded, the constables smoothly surrounding him—whereupon the constable directly behind Elminster was imperiously swept aside by someone else coming to the door.

The new arrival was a tall woman whose fine features were known to everyone in Innarlith—from the coins in their purses, if from nowhere else—but who wore only a crown and a scepter. As she pointed that scepter at Lhoreld, it was already glowing.

"I *trust* you recognize me, High Constable," she said softly, ignoring the trembling, retreating constables to stare steadily at Lhoreld.

He went pale, fought to keep his gaze above her chin, then flushed and hastily looked away, stammering, "Y-yes, Great Spaerenza. I—"

"As it happens, Lord Elminster *did* spend the night with me. And my husband. After agreeing to my request, relayed by the Marquavarl—"

Right on cue, the Lord Wizard of Innarlith appeared in the doorway beside the Spaerenza. His nakedness was only partially concealed behind an unfinished portrait he was carrying, of an entwined naked couple whose features—though not yet entirely limned—were unmistakably those of the ruler of Innarlith and her husband. Straightening the painting, he gave Lhoreld what could only be described as a sheepish smirk.

The High Constable swallowed, looked at the floor, and firmly turned his attention back to what the Spaerenza was still saying.

"—to paint us, something that was overheard and applauded by all three of our royal offspring, and the Dukes Henneth and Porlandur, just as the Lord Elminster has informed you. I *trust* you will believe me, despite your reluctance to extend the same courtesy to him?"

"I—ah—uh—*yes*, Your Exaltedness! I—ah—most humbly apologize for—"

Lhoreld's clumsy attempt at groveling was interrupted by a soundless thunder that smote every brain and stilled all sound for as long as it took a bright blue mist to arise out of nowhere and wash through the Fortress Royal.

Everyone trembled from the sheer force of magic rolling through them, as lightning raced through the mist.

Hair stood on end, all over everyone's body, as the awed constables went to their knees, followed by Lhoreld and the Lord Wizard . . . and then, weeping in ecstasy, the Spaerenza herself.

They were all staring at two eyes in the mist, eyes the size of warriors' shields that were drifting nearer in the air, heading unblinkingly for the paint-smeared man who was still on his feet.

Elminster, you are needed urgently in Zhentil Keep.

"Goddess," Elminster murmured, going down on one knee.

The force of Mystra's divinity had driven the constables face-down on the floor, as the royal couple of Innarlith gaped at the great face now shaping itself out of the air.

Manshoon has altered the Darkways, making passage through them fatal. The dead include many of the Art, including accomplished mages like Ardroth Thauntan, Hoal of the Stormwands, and Handreth Imbreth of Waterdeep, the latest of Sarbuckho's hirelings. Mend this crime, El.

"Lady, I will," Elminster promised, rising and reaching a hand toward the bedchamber door. His robes, clout, boots, and belt of many pouches raced to him.

Wizards must not be slain out of hand, be they the cause of this or not—yet destroy not the gates.

Elminster nodded, boots in hand—as blue light flared around him, and he was gone.

And with him went mist, lightning, Mystra, and all.

Leaving the folk of Innarlith blinking at each other across a suddenly empty passage.

Rising unsteadily, tears still raining from her chin as if from a downspout, the Spaerenza gave her High Constable a rather rueful grin.

"I'd say it's a good thing you didn't actually arrest our guest, Lhoreld. It makes it far easier for all of us to forget any of this happened, don't you think?"

❖

An Unlooked-For Messenger

The alleyway was deserted, fortunately, but the cold and the distinctive reek—an unhealthy mix of smelting, woodsmoke from a thousand-some chimneys, and rotting fish—told him he'd arrived in Zhentil Keep.

"Thank ye, Mystra," Elminster murmured, hastily pulling on his boots. The goddess was, after all, why he had a deserted alley to dress in.

Right behind Fantharl Halamaun's mansion, too.

ED GREENWOOD
243

He went round to the front as he cast a hasty spell to make his garments smarter and darker, to go with the younger and more prosperous face he was giving himself. After all, a messenger from Halamaun's Sembian backers would either come through the Darkway, or seek entrance at the front doors.

The waylord's guards—two mountainous hulks in full armor overlooked by four crossbowmen who looked more than ready to fire—were expecting trouble.

"Emrayn Melkanthar, from Sembia, to see Fantharl Halamaun. Immediately," Elminster made crisp reply to the guards' challenge.

"The lord is not at home," was the flat reply.

"I'll await him in his forehall," he responded, just as flatly.

"We are to admit no one—"

"You will make an exception, or your master will be far less than pleased."

One of the crossbowmen vanished from the balcony above the doors, and returned with a handsome, richly dressed man with a styled and curved mustache.

"Valandro!" the Sembian greeted him, before the wizard could say a word. The Tethyrian frowned.

"I know you not, saer. Who are you, and how is it you know me?"

"I am Emrayn Melkanthar, and I am come from certain men in Sembia Halamaun does business with. Men who like to know with whom they deal—wherefore I was shown your likeness, and told you were Valandro the Mysterious these days, though I know you of old as—"

"*Enough*," the Tethyrian said sharply. Drawing two wands from his belt, he leaned over the balcony rail and said curtly to the guards below, "Let him in. I'll be responsible."

He hastened down to meet the Sembian, wands aimed and ready, but was seen to go quiet and fall into step beside Melkanthar, leading the Sembian away from the forehall and along passages toward the rear of the house.

When they reached the chamber that held Halamaun's Darkway, Valandro the Mysterious dismissed the guards there, closed the doors to keep them out and himself and the Sembian in, then stood like an impassive statue as Melkanthar strode slowly around the glowing portal, nodded, and cast a swift, tentative spell. Only to frown and cast another.

"There," he said aloud. "Manshoon's enchantment now no longer transforms the blood of users, but instead works on their minds, promoting one of the most feeble spells they already know how to cast—and making it the *only* spell they can cast. Vulnerability, but not instant death. Aye, that should do it."

He strode past the motionless and unseeing Valandro to the door, but was still reaching for its handle when it was flung wide, and four guards with leveled glaives thrust forward into the room, an angry Fantharl Halamaun right behind them.

"*Die*, foul Zhentarim!" the waylord snapped. "Not content to—"

"*Hold!*"

Magic lashed forth from the intruder with force enough to send Halamaun's guards staggering back, dropped polearms clanging and clattering.

"No Zhentarim am I," said the stranger. "I am of the Vigilant Ravens."

Fantharl Halamaun blinked. The Ravens were a powerful Sembian cabal that opposed Manshoon's rise to power, but he'd thought they'd not do anything beyond offering him bad prices and a chill welcome in Sembian markets.

"Your wizard Ardroth Thauntan died using your Darkway,"

the Sembian continued, "because Manshoon cast a spell on it that turns the blood of anyone passing through it to acid. I've countered his spell; it is safe to use again."

Halamaun glowered at the intruder, then nodded grudgingly. "I—I just heard from some fellow traders of their Darkways becoming deathtraps. You *know* Manshoon is behind this?"

The Sembian nodded. "By way of payment, Halamaun"— the builder stiffened, but the Sembian waved a contemptuous hand and continued—"suppose you tell me the name of one of Manshoon's worst, ah, enforcers. The warriors he sends to do his open slayings. I feel in need of some . . . sport."

Fantharl Halamaun drew his lips back from his teeth in a mirthless smile. "Ornthen Kelgoran. He won't be hard to find—he fears no man of the city who isn't his master Manshoon or an upperpriest of Bane."

"That will change," was the calm reply.

Neither knife nor spell tested Elminster's wards as he stalked out of Halamaun's house. He turned two street corners before he relinquished his hold over the mind of Valandro the Mysterious, leaving behind whirling confusion as to what Emrayn Melkanthar of Sembia had looked like.

Not that the Tethyrian would have much time to ponder. Unless Halamaun was far less scared than El had judged him to be, he would keep Valandro and his overdone mustache very busy spreading word to his fellow waylords of what Manshoon had done.

* * *

At the Drowning Hippocampus

In Zhentil Keep, richly dressed strangers attracted unhealthy attention in far safer drinking and wenching clubs than the noisome, dimly lit Drowning Hippocampus, so El altered his guise again, becoming a filthy, stooped old man in fittingly foul robes.

Besides, the Sembian's coins had served their purpose, buying the news of Ornthen Kelgoran's present whereabouts from several eager tongues. It seemed Kelgoran wasn't well loved, or was well feared, or both. Probably both.

Now, the man would either be dominating the bar with goblet in hand and tongue a-wag, or abed somewhere with a lowcoin lass. Or two.

El shuffled through the doors, into near darkness and an all-too-familiar din and reek of spilled drink, unwashed bodies, spew, and burnt cabbage. Why all of these places had to smell of scorched cabbage was beyond him, but . . .

To the owner of the first hostile glare directed his way, El mumbled, "Urgent message for Kelgoran—where be he?"

"Rutting in the back," was the reply. "Best wait for him to—"

El stumbled past, and down the hall his informant had nodded toward. At its very end he discovered a guard sitting against a door with a loaded crossbow across his knees.

That bow got aimed at his crotch with menacing speed. "Go away," its owner suggested tersely.

"Message for Kelgoran from Lord Manshoon," El growled back. "Still want me to go away?"

"How do I know you speak truth?"

"You'll know," El replied, thrusting his head forward, jaw first, "when Manshoon rewards you—either for helping me reach Kelgoran, or for being *less* than helpful."

He let two dancing flames kindle in his eyes, just for a moment, and the guard recoiled with comical speed, swallowing and trying to claw his way upright and seeking to slide sideways along the wall and out of the way, all at once.

"R-right the other side of the door, S-saer Zhent!" he offered breathlessly.

"Good," Elminster replied with a gleeful grin—as he plucked up the crossbow to aim it back down the passage, and trigger it.

Its loud *clack* was followed by a groan from the Zhentarim enforcer back down the far end of the passage, as its bolt sank deep into his chest.

Then Elminster kicked the door open and whirled the door guard around in front of him as a shield in one whirling motion, his hand clamped like a steel trap on the bones of the man's elbow.

The room beyond was almost filled by a bed. It was creaking as a naked, cursing, and very hairy man scrambled out from under a hissing-in-fear woman, reaching for his sword.

He stopped when El's spell took hold of his mind.

Almost absently El flung the guard into the coinlass as she came at him furiously, her hands like claws. There'd be time enough to compel her mind later—and the guard's, too, if need be.

Right now, he had something more urgent to do. His sudden arrival in the dark and raging cesspit of Ornthen Kelgoran's mind had alerted Manshoon, just as he'd expected.

Smiling savagely, El destroyed the First Lord's "eye" in Kelgoran's mind, searing Manshoon's magic swiftly enough to leave its distant owner not knowing who'd burst into his enforcer's mind, or why.

That should bring Manshoon out of whatever bed *he* was sporting in, right now, and set him to doing things that would add decidedly more fun to the unfolding proceedings.

The guard and the coinlass were still shrieking and tumbling on the floor when Ornthen Kelgoran burst past them, sword in hand but not bothering to snatch up and put on anything more than his boots, to hurry out into the streets with the strange old man.

The Zhentarim slayer was more than a little drunk, and was a cruel, unsubtle brute at the best of times, but he knew exactly where all of the waylords dwelt.

Under Elminster's mental goading, he loped through the streets with a no-longer-stumbling old man right beside him, heading for the nearest Darkway just as fast as he could.

Guidance Gives Out

Elminster shuddered at the sudden burst of mental pain, then sighed. It was too late; Ornthen Kelgoran was toppling, almost beheaded, his mind dying with dazing speed.

Elminster broke contact and let the Zhentilar fall, spraying blood as his head wobbled loosely on what was left of a thick, hairy neck. Thrice he'd held Kelgoran unmoving at each Darkway, to keep the man helpless as he altered Manshoon's slaying spell to his own.

This fourth time, the guards of Torlcastle Towers had been just a bit too swift and bold. He hadn't even begun the spell, yet here they were, with Kelgoran cut down and eight uniformed slayers charging at the one remaining intruder, howling all sorts of unpleasant things as their swords sought his life.

Elminster ducked away from one, almost collided with another who'd raced around to gut him from behind, and flung himself flat on his back. The startled Torlcastle guard stumbled over him, off balance and trying unsuccessfully to stab downward with a sword that was too long to draw back far enough to stab, and ran right into the guard who'd been hounding El.

Lying on the smooth, polished, cold stone floor, Mystra's man sighed and worked a spell that plucked all the guards off their heavy-booted feet and flung them at the ceiling high above.

They slammed into it with gratifyingly heavy thuds, swords and daggers fell from various hands—and then they all came crashing back down.

El stayed on his back amid the groans, knowing this wasn't done yet. He had to prevail swiftly, or servants and guards from all over Torlcastle's mansion would be in there, and readying crossbows, and he didn't have *time* for all of this foolishness—

Four guards came swaying unsteadily to their feet after their journeys aloft and back again; one of them even had hold of his sword.

Elminster rolled to his feet. "Keep back," he warned them. "I have no quarrel with any of ye. Just let me be, and—"

He knew his words were wasted even before he said them, but Mystra expected her agents to wield their Art with some sense of responsibility. Four guards came charging—and a fifth was crawling toward a fallen weapon, giving El a murderous glare.

Elminster sighed again, worked a simple spell, and watched as the closest guard got plucked to his death, hurled through the portal that would boil his lifeblood into acid at its far end. Well, certain Sembians *did* need fair warning of all of this.

That bought him time enough to use another spell on the others to fling them away into battering collisions with the walls of the room. Then he threw one into another, and hauled the crawler up off the floor to crash into the faces of two reeling guards.

Everyone went down, buying him enough time to circle around behind the Darkway, to where he could keep an eye on them all, and work the spell he needed to cast.

Fresh shouts came from the doors of the room as the portal flared, but Elminster's next spell had snatched him away out of Torlcastle Towers even before the crossbow bolts came singing through the spot where he'd stood.

He was in a hurry. Manshoon would be roused and at work by now, and a certain servant of Mystra had to find another Zhentarim who knew where the rest of the Darkways were.

And as every wayfarer knows, good guides are *always* hard to find.

Sitting Alone in Highturrets

Morlar Elkauvren was a waylord, and lived in a towering pile of stone, a great rising prow of tall windows, balconies, and spires that would look most loomingly impressive against the winking stars, to someone who had time to stand in awe.

Elminster wasn't such a someone, just now. It was enough that he knew Elkauvren and the location of his home— Highturrets, an apt name if there ever was one—and that somewhere in that vast mansion was a Darkway.

And if he knew his Zhentarim, word would have spread among them by now that some stranger was tracking down Darkway after Darkway. They would be hunting for this stranger, and massing defenders around each portal to watch for his approach—or, for the Darkways they didn't yet control, around the mansions that held such portals.

Which was why Elminster now looked not like a bearded man, but a slender, rather dirty young woman clad in a hooded cloak, high boots, and not much else.

"Warm you, saer?" she husked hopefully, to the parade of dark-armored men striding swiftly down her alleyway.

One of them whirled, sword half-grating out of its scabbard. "Get gone, sister!" he barked. "Well away from here, and come not back, or it'll be the last thing you ever do!"

Her reply was to duck her head, hiss angrily, and—once the Zhentilar were past—scurry hastily out of the alcove she'd been loitering in and flee the way they'd come.

"Who's yon?" someone barked, from ahead.

"A streetskirts," another man replied. "They've turned her out—let her go."

El paused for a moment at the cross street where those two Zhents stood, and murmured fearfully, "Which one of you is the wizard?"

Why?" the first Zhent snarled.

"F-for later," she quavered. "I was told to find him, another night, so I need to know what he looks like. Then I'll go."

Cold eyes measured her for a moment, ere the second Zhent turned and pointed. "There. He's called Cadathen. Likes redheads."

The coinlass shook back her hood and opened her cloak, flouncing just enough to make it swirl. Long, unbound red hair swirled, too, though the mens' eyes sought certain other revealed features.

"Thank you," she husked, before they could do more than grin, and hurried away. She didn't bother to tell them that her thanks were to Mystra, for the fact that the magic "she" was using could shift the hue of hair even faster than it took to pull open a garment.

She had to find a Zhent in armor about the same size as Ornthen Kelgoran, before the ring forming around Highturrets got completely settled. Ah—there!

"*You're* the one," she purred, throwing off her cloak to reveal her complete lack of weapons—and all her now-buxom charms—to the startled Zhentilar trudging along the street, his head down and his mood dark.

He gaped at her. "What, by all the gods—?"

"Take me," she hissed, whirling him into a doorway. "Here and now! I've been watching you for months, I'm crazed about you, I *must* have you! 'Twill take but moments, then give me your name, and I'll find you for longer dalliances on later nights! *Please*, my lord!"

Rather dazedly the Zhentilar ran a disbelieving hand down the warm, smooth flesh offered to him, then hurriedly started to unbuckle and unfasten. "Name's Vorl, lass! Watching me for months? Who *are* you?"

"Jahanna Darlwood, of the keep; my father's Brace Darlwood; seller of roof tiles and stone, and very wealthy . . ."

"Tell me later," Vorl snarled, shoving her back against the wall as his breeches sought his ankles. "We must be quick!"

The suddenly melting mask of flesh that smothered him as he tried to kiss it retained a mouth. As he sagged into senselessness, it agreed in a very different voice, "Aye, we must. Sleep now, lusty Vorl. I'll be tying ye to the door, I'm afraid; can't have ye racing back to reclaim thy armor before I'm done with it."

A few hard, swift breaths later, a man in a cloak was bound to the door—and his exact likeness was hurrying down the street in full armor, head down and hand on his sword.

"Vorl, you laggard," an older Zhentilar hailed him with a snarl, "where've you *been*? Rutting in doorways, all the way from the tavern?"

"Well, uh, yes," Vorl admitted, but his low mumble was barley audible, and the Zhentilar wasn't listening.

"Get *over* here, you lazy dog! We're to form a ring all around Highturrets—and your reward for being last boots in is getting to stand guard right *there*, hard by the jakes!"

"There" was an embrasure in the building's cracked and much-patched back wall, filled with rotting litter and containing a long-boarded-up door. It faced a matching alcove across the street, where a wooden bench with a hole in its seat had been placed over a large, square open shaft leading down into the infamous city sewers. Two unhappy-looking sternhelms were busy rigging up a blanket in a frame of spears, to serve as both a door and a wall for future patrons of the little seat, who might desire some privacy while they were sitting alone.

A jakes. It seemed the Zhentarim were expecting a lengthy siege.

Sternhelm Vorl growled a curse, because that would be expected, and trudged to his post, kicking aside the worst of the reeking, slimy refuse. He hoped he'd not have to wait long.

Mystra smiled on him; he'd barely had time to grow bored and cold ere the wizard Cadathen came in search of the jakes, blowing on chilled fingers and snarling some curses of his own.

If the Zhentarim mage was surprised that a Zhentilar sternhelm crossed the narrow street to hold the blanket open for him, he didn't show it.

He *was* surprised when the warrior stepped into the alcove with him, pulling the blanket closed, but only for a moment.

After that, he had no time left to be surprised about anything, ever again.

❦

As the Lord Mage Commands

"Cold, hey? Sitting alone over the sewers, I mean?"

Holding the rank of battle captain, Galandror dared to exchange such pleasantries with Zhentarim mages. Well, he'd not do so with the Lord Manshoon, but Cadathen was very far from—

"Too cold," the wizard said curtly. "We're not waiting the night through out here. Storm the gates."

Galandror and his fellow battle captain, Narleth, exchanged surprised glances, then nodded in unison. "By your command, Lord Mage."

Cadathen smiled and threw his shoulders back, like a pigeon about to preen. Obviously, he liked the sound of "Lord Mage."

Narleth used the title again, quickly. "The front gates, Lord Mage?"

Cadathen shook his head. "The rear. I'll destroy them with a spell, and the doors behind them, too. You get our blades in there fast, secure the chamber that holds the Darkway, then drive out everyone in that end of the mansion. I want no one creeping up on us while I set to work on it."

"Set to work on it, Lord Mage?" Galandror asked warily. There'd been no hint of this in their orders, and Lord Manshoon wanted them to be watchful for traitors everywhere. Among his magelings, in particular.

Cadathen gave both battle captains calm, direct looks. "I suspect our unknown foe who's seeking out Darkways is either hiding in them, or enspelling them to serve as scrying foci, so henceforth he can spy on the rooms that hold them, from afar. I need to cast a spell on the Darkway inside yon mansion, to see if my suspicions are correct. And all of us will have warmth, chairs to sit on, and whatever food and drink can be found in a waylord's mansion, rather than freezing our behinds outside on a dark street all night."

The Zhentilar nodded, reassured.

They collected their men swiftly, Narleth leading a dozen around to the front to bang on the main gates and hold Elkauvren's guards there while Cadathen forced entry at the rear of the towering mansion.

"Right," the wizard snarled, when Galandror came striding back to tell him all was ready. "Let's get warm."

He raised his hands, murmured something, and the night exploded in fire.

Guarding Flickering Silence

"Secure, Lord Mage." Galandror's tone was almost respectful.

Narleth had just returned and made his report. Only two Zhentilar had been killed, though Morlar Elkauvren would need to replace most of his house guards and a goodly number of his household servants. The cowering lord was shut up in his own guestrooms above his front gate, with watchful stern-helms to keep him there—and not one member of Elkauvren's household was both still alive and any nearer to the chamber that held the Darkway than the central feasting hall.

"Well done," Cadathen replied, turning to the glowing portal. "Now to make sure this hasn't been tainted by the foe's magic."

The two battle captains watched him closely, of course, but they were not to know that the spell he cast was doing no such thing, and instead was altering Manshoon's slaying spell into his own less fatal magic—just as they were not to know Cadathen was really the infamous archwizard Elminster.

Suspicion was clear on their tense, grim faces, but they visibly relaxed as nothing seemed to happen. Other than Cadathen stepping back to nod in satisfaction and tell them, "Our foe worked a magic so he could spy through this, just as I suspected. He won't be doing that now."

When nothing more happened, the two warriors relaxed even more—and soon threw daggers to see who would first go foraging in the kitchens and pantries, and who would first settle down to the tense, waiting boredom of guarding the empty, silently flickering Darkway.

* * *

Whispers at the Feast

Though Manshoon knew the waylords were meeting in a high house not all that far away, he kept all hint of his knowing any such thing to himself.

Here, in this grand feasting hall, he was a guest of the most powerful nobles of the city, and was taking great care not to remind them of his ruthless side or the mighty magic he could hurl. Nobles tend to dislike upstarts who threaten them—particularly upstarts who can destroy them at will. His presence was all about reassurance, building alliances if not friendships, and making common cause.

Not to mention establishing a firm alibi for himself, for when word spread of all the waylords slain or embattled, the survivors began to hurl their furious accusations.

Manshoon smiled and thanked his host for the excellent wine.

And why not? It held not even a trace of poison, after all.

His host, directly across the goblet- and platter-crowded table, was Lord Syal Amandon, the callow, bewildered-by-the-world son of Manshoon's onetime nemesis, the thankfully dead old snow lion Rorst Amandon.

Syal was swiftly falling under his sway, and Manshoon was anxious to keep matters that way. The other nobles— particularly old Hael and Phandymm—knew exactly what he was up to, but had thus far done nothing about it. He saw the anger and contempt glittering in their gazes, but they continued to say and do not the smallest thing to cross the

First Lord. Manshoon couldn't read them—long-established wealth bought wards and shieldings that subtle spells couldn't pierce—but he looked forward to any opportunity to learn what they were truly thinking.

He hoped one would arise before they were busily trying to put swords through him.

The three younglings were another matter. Lord Thaerun Blackryn, like Syal, was the pale shell of a more formidable sire. Young, hot-blooded, quick to boast, and cunning, he spent most of his hatred and energy trying to best and frustrate his rival, Lord Mindarl Naerh. Who did the same in return. Supercilious and swift-tongued, Naerh was a decade older than Blackryn—and every whit as ignorant of the world.

Belator, now, was a very different creature. As graspingly ambitious as Manshoon himself, and thus easily understood and used. With about as much safety as one "uses" a snake.

That left only Eldarr and his ilk; as old as Hael and Phandymm, but less keen of wit and far less self governed. They were the arrogant, red-faced ranting, patrician sophisticates every minstrel lampooned, the sort of nose-aloft old growlers that shopkeepers of the city thought all nobles were like. Which meant they could be ignored until it became necessary to crush them.

And Manshoon was growing adept at effortlessly crushing the Lord Murvyn Eldarrs of the world.

So it was with more than a little irritation—all signs of which were firmly kept off his face, for controlling his own face and voice were the first skills a far younger Manshoon had honed—that the First Lord of Zhentil Keep received an unexpected spell-sent message in his head.

F-first Lord?

The mind touch was wildly nervous and fearful. It was Joranthas, an aging Zhentarim too weak to be disloyal—and too weak to deal with much in the way of trouble. Which is what this missive would surely be about.

Lord Manshoon, I bring news. Joranthas was still frightened, but a little less frantic.

Yes? he thought back.

Ah, Lord, there's trouble at Wyrmhaven. I just . . . fled from there.

No doubt. Continue.

Ambram Sarbuckho returned from his meeting while our forces were still fighting his household servants to get to his Darkway. His bodyguards and hireswords had crossbows, and their quarrels were tipped with poison. Things went badly for our side.

Thank you, Joranthus. Get to cover.

Manshoon spent his flare of rage in a mental slap that both thrust Joranthas out of his mind and dealt the old fool a headache that should leave him reeling for days. He was icily calm a moment later when he turned to beckon Sneel from where the man stood like a servant against the wall.

"Forgive me, Lord Amandon," he said smoothly to his host, ignoring Lord Hael's glower of suspicion, "but I've just remembered that the servants who usually pump my water are ill; I must send my retainer to give orders to others to do their work, or the cook will have a dry kitchen long before morning."

"Of course," Syal said heartily, even before Sneel bent his ear to Manshoon's lips.

He kept his whispers short and simple. "Trouble at Wyrmhaven; Sarbuckho's back, and his men have poisoned bolts. Get Cadathen to crush them utterly. No excuses. Report back soon."

Sneel bowed low and hastened away, and Manshoon turned back to the table with an easy smile.

He wasn't smiling inside. Cadathen had to be victorious, or the Zhentarim would lose far too many minor magelings at Wyrmhaven—if they weren't dead already. More importantly, he dared not let Sarbuckho prevail, and become a clear example of successfully defying the Brotherhood. If the waylord won the night's fray, his victory would hearten many others into their own rebellions against the Zhentarim, large and small.

He ached to be racing to Wyrmhaven himself, to hurl spells to smash and rend Sarbuckho and his every last blade and servant—and instead he was stuck at this table, wearing an empty smile, and taking great care to use no magic at all over eveningfeast. Well, almost no magic.

Lord Belomyr Hael was starting to smile. Bane take Mystra, but the old wolf could scent his discomfort!

Hael was old, graying and growling, a worldly conservative—and right beside him, grandly adorned elbow to grandly adorned elbow, Lord Goraund Phandymm was an even older worldly and pragmatic conservative.

They were both smiling now, almost as if they could read his mind.

Could they?

But no, he'd worked spells a hundred times to check on that. They were just good at reading the smallest signs—tightness of lip, the briefest flash of an eye—but toothless old wolves for all that.

Down the table, Lord Samrel Belator helped himself to a decanter that was almost empty. Now *there* was a contrast: young, handsome, athletic, an embracer of new ways and ideas . . . Manshoon's real competition.

Well, such perils could be humbled—or killed—tomorrow. Tonight, he needed an alibi rather more.

Manshoon put on his best innocent smile, reached for the nearest decanter, and devoted himself to making empty small talk.

Cadathen would take care of things.

Cadathen would have to.

Orders Upon Orders

The man came through the curtains very quietly, but the two battle captains spun around, swords flashing.

"Halt!" Galandror barked, drawing his dagger and hefting it for a throw. Narleth came around the Darkway to flank his fellow Zhentilar, barring the intruder's path to the portal, and to Cadathen.

Then they recognized him and fell silent.

"I bring orders from the Lord Manshoon," Lorkus Sneel said, with just a trace of weariness. "Hinder me and face his wrath."

The battle captains lowered their swords a little.

"Cadathen," Sneel said, "you are ordered to gather all of the Brotherhood's forces you feel you need, proceed in haste to Wyrmhaven, the house of the Waylord Ambram Sarbuckho, and slay everyone there who resists you to take possession of the Darkway. Sarbuckho returned from Harlstrand House while our force was still fighting through the halls of Wyrmhaven, and his bodyguards used poisoned crossbow bolts. Our force is all dead or fled."

"Take me there," Cadathen replied promptly, "so you can tell the master what decisions I make, and how I fare."

"How you begin, rather," Sneel corrected him. "My orders are to report back to the master soonest."

"Very well." Cadathen fell into step beside him, calling back over his shoulder, "Battle captains, remain here and guard this Darkway!"

Even before they replied, he was through the curtain with Sneel, and hastening through the empty, echoing mansion, heading for Wyrmhaven.

◆ ― ◆ ― ◆

Rally and Betrayal

The handful of blood-spattered, wounded Zhentilar crouching in the cold alleyway were in pain, and angry. They snarled out a stream of curses as they told Cadathen they had fled for their lives, or been driven out of Wyrmhaven, leaving many fellow members of the Brotherhood dead inside. Ambram Sarbuckho was victorious.

Cadathen put his arms around two of the least disabled, gathered them to him, and whispered, "And you know *why* Sarbuckho defeated you? He was warned of your coming by the man who came here with me. Yes, Lorkus Sneel, the master's messenger. He betrayed you. He betrayed us all." He let go of them and strode off down the alley to find more Zhents.

Sneel strode after him—and Cadathen carefully didn't look back as a brief commotion arose behind him, a thudding and snarling that ended in a wet spattering sound.

When he did turn around, the two Zhentilar were following him, their swords dripping in their hands . . . and the huddled heap that had been Sneel lay still in the midst of a spreading pool of dark blood, in their wake.

Justice, mistaken or otherwise, was at least prompt in Zhentil Keep.

Smiling tightly, Cadathen beckoned the two men to him, as he came upon another knot of wounded Zhents. "Would you like to avoid the Lord Manshoon's wrath, and claim Sarbuckho's head before morning?"

There was a general murmur of assent. "What if I take myself into the forehall ahead of you, take down Sarbuckho's bowmen with my spells, then blast the doors open from inside to let you in? Will you be ready to charge into Wyrmhaven to finish the fray?"

"I'll say!" one Zhentilar replied.

"We're dead if we don't," an older one growled. "None of us can run and hide to where the First Lord can't find us."

That brought a general rumble of agreement, as more Zhents came trotting up to join the throng around Cadathen.

"Right, then," the wizard told them excitedly. "Charge the doors, after I bring them down. Until then, keep back."

He made two swift, complex gestures—and was abruptly gone, the space where he'd stood simply empty.

◆——◆——◆

War in Wyrmhaven

Elminster crouched low, the moment he felt the stones of the balcony beneath his feet. Being Cadathen was a bit of a strain; thankfully, he'd soon be done playing ambitious young Zhentarim.

Right after he turned, keeping below the balcony sidewall so the Zhentilar below wouldn't see him, he made the door that led into Wyrmhaven's fourth floor quietly melt out of existence. Then he hurried across the dark, deserted room beyond. The cold night air followed him.

From all he knew of Ambram Sarbuckho, alert warriors with crossbows would be massed in the forehall and every other room that had an exterior door. Zhentish mansions sported no ground floor windows, so defenders could concentrate where they were most likely to be needed.

Sarbuckho was a swindler from way back, and Elminster felt no compunction at all about blasting down men who fought for him.

So all he needed to do was get to the top of the great corkscrew staircase that spiraled down into the rear of the forehall, work a quiet spell, and stand well back.

As the floor heaved and shuddered, Wyrmhaven thundered and groaned all around him. A blinding flash flung a thick haze of smoke and dust into the air, and a rising roar from many Zhentilar throats told him he'd not only shattered the forehall and its defenders—he'd burst open its doors, letting them flood in.

Smiling, he waited until he thought the moment just right, and cast another blasting spell down the ruined stair, to claim Manshoon's men, this time. Then he turned and strode along the hallway, seeking a servants' stair down. He needed to get to Sarbuckho's gate and alter it, without greeting a poisoned quarrel.

In the eddying aftermath of his magics, he could feel the mounting pulse of the Darkway as he got closer to it. Elminster gave a jubilant little gasp as he saw that it stood unguarded, all of Wyrmhaven's guards gone elsewhere to fight the attackers.

He did what he had to do with swift ease, and teleported himself back to the alley. It was deserted, though a timid coinlass poked her head out a door to see if it was safe to emerge and seek business. At the sight of a Zhentarim mage, she hastily ducked back again.

El smiled thinly and started a careful circumnavigation of the embattled mansion, to make sure no Zhentilar got away. There should still be some poisoned quarrels left, if he knew his waylords . . .

Above all, he wanted no witnesses to tell tales about Cadathen or Sneel that would reach the ears of a certain First Lord of Zhentil Keep.

Neither his first circuit nor his second turned up anyone fleeing Wyrmhaven, where ragged shouts and the clash and clang of arms told him the fight was still raging.

That much vigilance would have to be sufficient. There were other things he wanted to do that night.

El stopped at Sneel's body, turned it over, and looked around to make sure no one was watching. Then he conjured a little light to see by and carefully shifted his own likeness to match the unlovely looks of Lorkus Sneel.

Dragging what was left of the real Sneel to the jakes he'd earlier thrust Cadathen's body down, he tipped Manshoon's best spy down into the sewers.

The eels would soon devour it, beneath the reeking waters and drifting filth, and—

His eyes narrowed. Instead of the wet, sloppy splash he should have heard, there'd been a distinct *thud*. Hurriedly he conjured light again and looked down.

Bobbing in the waters below was a dead man, face up and palely staring, several threads of red gore trailing from him into the waters around. It wasn't Sneel, or Cadathen for that matter.

It was Ambram Sarbuckho.

Elminster blinked. *That* fast, they'd got to him? Or was the Sarbuckho who'd come storming "back" to Wyrmhaven not the real Sarbuckho at all?

For a moment he contemplated just waving this mystery away and getting on with the business of undoing Manshoon's evil just as swiftly as he could. Then he sighed, waved that thought away, and teleported himself back to a certain balcony.

The room it opened into was as dark and deserted as before. Cautiously he stepped out into the hallway beyond. No guards, no one lurking with a crossbow . . .

Here, deep in Wyrmhaven, things had quieted down. A lot of the shouters and sword-clangers had, it seemed, perished, and the survivors were running out of foes to loudly fight with.

Up on this high floor there were no signs of life—or any evidence that the fighting had ever reached this far.

El stood against a wall like a thoughtful statue for a breath or two, pondering. If he were Ambram Sarbuckho, where would his grand personal bedchamber be?

High in the mansion, probably on this floor—for the levels above must be smaller expanses, broken by the separations of turrets and towers rising apart, and it seemed only wizards preferred such smaller, rounded privacies—and most likely toward the back of Wyrmhaven.

In other words, right this way . . .

As he went, El turned one of the rings he wore, to call up a protective mantle that would make him like smoke to metal weapons, and turn back many magics, too. He moved along the hall as quietly as he knew how.

It made a right-angled turn, to eventually meet with the end of a parallel hallway running down the other side of the main bulk of the mansion—and in the center of that cross passage was an alcove, whose back wall was a pair of high, rounded, ornate doors.

Trapped and guarded or not, they were what he'd been seeking. On the far side of them . . .

He drew off Sneel's boots, thrust his hands into them, and took a door handle between them, turning it. Locked, of course.

As he let the handle quietly return to its former position, he heard something he'd been expecting: faint feminine sobbing from the far side of the door.

Stepping smoothly to one side of the doors, he asked firmly, "Lady? Lady Sarbuckho? Are you in need of aid?"

The sobbing caught in a great gasping of breath and sniffling, then became a choked and tremulous voice replying in the negative—and furiously ordering him away.

Elminster frowned. Making no reply, he moved along the passage to its far corner, where he found what he'd hoped would be there: a much smaller, plainer, closed door.

It was locked, too, but a swift spell seared through it, leaving the lock holding a half-moon of door separate from the larger rest of it. El gently pushed that larger panel open and stepped inside, finding himself in a dark robing room lined with wardrobes. The weeping was louder now, coming from a gap in the wardrobes along the side wall, where a curtained archway obviously led into the main bedchamber.

Elminster peered through the gap where the two curtains met, satisfied himself that only one person was present—hunched over on the floor at the foot of a gigantic canopied bed, and trembling—in the room beyond, and glided soundlessly through the curtains.

His first act was to kick away the bloody knife in front of the sobbing woman. His second was to do the same to a black gem the size of his palm that positively *crawled* with magic. His third was to kneel swiftly and take her by the arms.

She raised a tear-streaming, bleeding face of misery to him, staring in fear. "S-sneel? *Here?*"

"No, I merely wear his shape. I'm not of the keep, Lady. Ye *are* Lady Sarbuckho, are ye not?"

She nodded, drawing her head up but spoiling the proud

movement by sniffing like a young lass getting over a tantrum. "Yavarla Sarbuckho I am, saer. Are you here to kill me for what I've done—or for my jewels, or for who I am?"

"I'm not here to slay ye at all. But tell me now, what have ye done?"

By way of reply, she shook her head and looked away, trying to jerk free of his grasp.

"Ye sent your lord husband down dead into the sewers, did ye not? Using yon knife, aye?"

Yavarla Sarbuckho went rigid in his arms, then sagged limply and whispered, "Y-yes."

"Why?" El asked, as softly as any comforting mother, gathering her against his chest.

She burst into fresh tears, in a flood of uncontrolled weeping, and struggled incoherently to say something through it. Elminster daubed at the blood on her face—one eye was swollen almost shut, and she might have a rather piratical scar down the line of her chin, if she lived long enough for things to heal—and murmured wordless comfort, rocking her like a child.

Eventually words came to her. "He-he—he burst in on me, in a rage . . . beat me! He'd learned . . . what I'd done!"

"And what have ye done?" El murmured into her ear, holding her tight.

Yavarla drew in one shuddering breath, and then another, fighting for control. "L-lord Manshoon came to me . . . alone. He was very kind, comforting, the very sort of lord I wanted—ohhh, kind gods deliver me!"

She burst into tears again, sobbing wretchedly, and Elminster rocked her and murmured, "Ye and the First Lord lay together, and he was kind and understanding and tender, and ye talked. He asked questions, like a kindly friend, and ye answered them, and he learned much about the Darkways, and

Lord Sarbuckho's dealings in Sembia, whom he traded with, and who else in the city used their Darkways in like manner . . . am I right?"

She managed a nod as she shuddered her way through hard breathing again, fighting her way out of weeping once more.

"Just now, thy lord husband burst in on ye in a rage, and tried to force ye to—what?"

"G-go straight to Manshoon, and touch him with the gem."

"Did he say what would befall then?"

"N-no. I knew. We both knew. He got it years ago from adventurers who plundered a Netherese tomb. When awakened, you touch it to the one you named when awakening it, and it will explode."

"With force enough to turn Manshoon—and ye—and probably most of whatever tall keep ye're standing in—to dust."

"Y-yes. It's awake now."

"So ye both knew he was sending ye to death. Ye refused, and he beat ye, and ye snatched out his own belt dagger and stabbed him . . . and he died. So ye stuffed him down yon garderobe."

"I did." Yavarla was past tears now. She stared at him almost defiantly. "And I regret it not at all. I have hated him for a very long time."

Elminster nodded. "With good cause, I have no doubt. Come—time is running out for us both." He pointed at the robing room he'd come through. "Choose thy two most favorite coverings—everything, from toes to top of head, mind; gems and underthings, main garments, and the cloaks and wraps ye wear when stepping out into snowstorms—and thy least favorite wear; three entire outfits. Bring it all in and toss it on thy bed. Be swift and quiet, and run right back in here if anyone sees ye through the ruin I made of thy robing room door. Do *not* flee out into the house beyond, or ye'll surely be slain. Brutally, by Zhentarim who have invaded thy halls, not by me."

Yavarla stared at him for a moment, then rushed into the robing room. Elminster went straight to the gem and sent it somewhere far away and safer. Then he plucked up the dagger, wiped it on a white fur rug that was already spattered with much of Ambram Sarbuckho's spilled blood, then kept the dagger and sent the rug on the same journey that the Lord of Wyrmhaven had recently made.

By then, Yavarla was done, and standing anxiously by the bed.

"Find thy most precious jewels, and all coins ye can lay hand on, that are in this room," El told her.

She held up a small coffer already in her hands. "N-no coins would he allow me, and his are locked in vaults down below, not here."

El nodded and waved at her to drop the coffer on the bed with the rest. She did, and he gathered up the thick coverlet, with its glossy shimmerweave skin around overlapped and sewn-together thick wool blankets, around all she'd gathered. The bundle was nearly as large as she was.

"Fight me not, now," he murmured, settling the bundle on one hip and sliding his other hand around her waist. "Hold very still."

She obeyed, and that gave his hands freedom enough to work a teleportation spell, and whisk them both to an alley that was becoming all too familiar.

We All Wear the Masks We Need

El looked up and down the gloomy alleyway. Seeing no one, he swiftly spread his bundle out on the filthy stones underfoot, in a spot where a shaft of moonlight fell fair upon it.

"Stand on that, strip, and get dressed in thy best," he ordered, hurriedly unfastening his own garments.

Yavarla was trembling as she stared at him, eyes large with mounting fear. "What—who *are* you?" she whispered.

"A friend," Elminster replied, his face and body melting and shifting under her stare, Sneel's rippling garments falling away or hanging limply.

Yavarla fought back a scream. A moment later, she stared at a woman of very much the same size and build as herself, a rather plain woman she'd never seen before.

"Is . . . is this . . . am I seeing who you really are?" she blurted out.

"Nay," the unfamiliar woman told her flatly. "We all wear the masks we need."

At that moment, Yavarla felt her own flesh beginning to creep and crawl . . .

She did scream and try to flee, then, but deft hands whirled her around, carried her back to the midst of the moonlight, and tripped her.

She landed hard on her knees, grunted in fresh pain, then shivered. It was *cold*, out here in the night . . .

"Hurry," her rescuer—captor?—said in her ear. "I'll help; what need ye first? Clout? Dethma?"

Feeling dazed, Yavarla gave in, getting dressed in greater haste than she had for many a year. She scarcely noticed that whenever she made a choice of garment, the woman—or was he really a man, as he'd first appeared?—donned one of the two like garments she'd not chosen. It was all done in panting haste, and she'd barely gained steady breath before she was fully dressed, cloak and all, and being towed firmly by the hand along the alley by her strange escort, who now carried a rather smaller bundle.

They came out into a street and turned right. Despite it being deep night, quite a few quiet, furtive folk were walking purposefully along, hands on weapon hilts, or meeting side by side with their backs to a building wall, where they could look this way and that while they muttered whatever business they were transacting. A few cloaked and hooded women silently parted their cloaks to show bare leg or hip at their approach, but made no reaction when they hastened on past.

The noblewoman shuddered, perhaps wondering if her future included becoming a desperate streetskirts. Elminster gave her no time to ponder; the lamps of the inn he sought were only a block away.

He tugged her close for a moment, to murmur in her ear, "For now, ye are *not* Lady Sarbuckho. In fact, Yavarla, ye have forgotten how to speak at all."

She made no reply, but went meekly with him and stood hooded and silent as the unlovely woman her escort had become briskly took a room for them both, snapping that they'd been forced to flee the place they'd been staying after it was "invaded by men fighting each other, with wizards and spells, too!"

They were behind a locked door and inside a warding spell stronger than any she'd ever seen cast before ere Yavarla caught sight of a mirror—and caught her breath, feeling herself on the verge of tears again. The face staring red-eyed back at her in the feeble light of the lone lamp was not hers.

"You have stolen my very self from me," she gasped.

"Only for now," the woman murmured from behind her, taking her under the arms as if to keep her from falling. "Sleep now, Yavarla."

And Yavarla fell down a great dark shaft into an endless rushing abyss of hatefully shouting, then gasping in pain and

horror Ambrams, a plunge from which there was no escape
. . . ever . . .

❦

New Lives, and Strangers to Go With Them

When Yavarla came awake, the light flooding through
the filthy window told her it was near highsun, and she was
lying in an inn bed answering questions. Whispering long,
detailed, involved answers about every Darkway she knew of,
and their owners, the names of the high houses that held those
gates, and the names and whereabouts within the mansion
walls of the chambers that held the flickering portals. Not
that she knew much, but she heard herself eagerly spilling
forth every hint and rumor and scrap of half-heard possible
truth she remembered, and far more than she ever knew she'd
remembered.

"You—you are using me," she gasped then, coming fully
awake and staring up into the eyes of . . . yet another stranger.

A bearded man whose eyes were sometimes as blue as a clear
day's sky, and at other times as silver-gray as a sword drawn in
a fog, and most of the time somewhere in between.

"Aye, I am," he replied gravely, "for it is needful. In return,
I offer ye a new life, far from cold Zhentil Keep and its cruel
lords and crueler wizards. Somewhere ye'll never have to face
death for slaying thy husband, or feel the sting of Manshoon's
betrayal—before that betrayal kills thee."

"I . . . I . . ." Something welled up in Yavarla then and burst
out of her, leaving her weeping as she thrust herself up and
bawled at him, "No! *Never*! I am *of* the keep, this is my *home*,
this is—Manshoon will never—"

Even as she said it, she knew otherwise. That cold and
gently smiling man would break her in an instant if she

stood in the way of his most idle whim. He had used her already, far worse than this man she did not know had used her, and—and—

Tears overwhelmed her again, and she covered her face with her hands and fought to cling to herself through them, fought until rage made her beat her fists on the bed sightlessly and cry, "I know how to do *more* than weep, damn all Watching Gods, I *do*!"

"Easy, lass," the man murmured, touching her cheek gently. The pain that had been there since Ambram's ring had laid it open vanished, and so did her grief, under a vast wave of weariness, followed by lighthearted cheer, a euphoria that came out of nowhere with the scent of lemons and vague visions of green trees and dappled sunlight and laughter . . .

"Magic," she said calmly. "You're using magic on me."

"I am. I want ye calm, Yavarla, and happy. Clear-headed to choose."

Yavarla drew in a deep, tremulous breath and said firmly, "I am calm. I can choose. And unless you intend to be my jailor, I tell you again: Zhentil Keep is my home. I want no new life far from here. I know full well how dangerous it will be, I know I love the First Lord but he loves me not . . . but I wish to stay. Even if it means my death, I am of the keep."

"So be it. Ye shall stay. Or rather, return to Wyrmhaven—if there's still a Wyrmhaven to return to—in a day or two, after I'm done causing a storm that may well sweep ye away, if ye are not kept safe. Think of this, then, as a vacation."

The light around Yavarla changed, and the bed beneath her became the cold flagstones of a stone floor somewhere in a forest under the open sky, with great old trees looming in a ring around her and stretching off into vast green distances beyond. The bundle of her shimmerweave coverlet lay on her shins, and a tall, beautiful, silver-haired woman was laying aside a harp to rise from rocks and bend over Yavarla in pleasantly surprised greeting. She wore foresters' leathers, and had none of the wrinkles of age that should go with silver tresses.

"Well met, lady. I am Storm Silverhand. The kettle is just boiling, and there will be hot buttered biscuits very soon. Will you take tea?"

Which was when Yavarla discovered she was ravenous. As she tried to smile and find words of answer, the woman bending over her was hearing other words in her own head.

Storm, this is Yavarla Sarbuckho, of Zhentil Keep. She just slew her husband, with good reason. Give her gentle slumber with thy spells and herbs, and keep her that way for this day and mayhap the next.

Storm smiled, inside her head. *Of course, El. If you decide what to do next for once, rather than just rushing out and doing it.*

Fair enough, Stormy One. Fair enough.

And it was. Moreover, the biscuits were delicious.

Done by Next Highsun

Thus far, this highsunfeast had gone better than he'd expected. Fzoul Chembryl's eyes told Manshoon clearly how furious the priest of Bane still was over Manshoon's seizing of power, but the First Lord's guest had obviously decided to be civil. For now, at least.

"I've never had any intention of deciding everything, and ruling the Brotherhood," Manshoon said carefully. "I want you to be—*need* you to be—a full partner in all decisions. So we are met not just to gorge ourselves on this superb cheese and harberry jelly—pray have more, won't you?—but to decide how to proceed next."

"In all matters of governance over the keep and the Zhentarim?" Fzoul asked calmly. "Or just in your—pardon me, *our*—war upon the waylords?"

"All, of course, but let us leave those decisions to later meetings, which I agree to hold at your behest and not mine, when this matter of the waylords is done with. First upon our mutual platter: Sarbuckho, and his defeat of our men at Wyrmhaven."

"You lost more than a dozen wizards, I've heard," Fzoul commented to the cheese he was slicing. "Let us begin by your trusting me enough to unfold clear truth about all of our losses. How many mages—and just how many warriors and spies can we add to that?"

"Ten and four wizards," Manshoon said quietly. "Five of accomplishment, the rest ambitious magelings or aging hedge wizards. Three or four spies—I'm still waiting for a certain man to report back to me. Almost twoscore warriors; the total depends on whether or not some recover. Sarbuckho's men used poisoned quarrels."

"Lorkus Sneel being that certain man?"

Manshoon nodded. "Do you know something of his fate?"

Fzoul shook his head. "Nothing. Truly. Well, I am for the utter destruction of Sarbuckho *and* his mansion. Present an example to anyone else contemplating any sort of challenge or resistance to the Brotherhood. Muster all we have for a very public assault in which Wyrmhaven is dashed to rubble. We hurl all our keep-shattering spells, and leave all loyal citizens thinking."

Manshoon's sudden smile was as bright as it was genuine. This was precisely what he'd been planning to do, priests or no priests. He liked the entire might of the temple behind it far better than otherwise.

They swiftly and easily agreed that Wyrmhaven's fall should be accomplished "by next highsun." Fzoul offered to set his upperpriests on rooftops to smite armsmen sent out to fight the Zhentilar—as well as any of the pitiful remnants of the city watch unwise enough to presume to challenge the authority of the Zhentarim.

It took but a few words back and forth for them to further agree to then sit back and wait for the cowed surviving waylords to suffer the effects of their portals becoming deathtraps. They would, of course, destroy any independent wizards who approached any waylord mansion, not wanting the waylords to be able to hire anyone who might be able to make the Darkways safe again.

"The waylords will fall, we'll rebuild the watch as ours, outright, and the council can meet as often as they like and say whatever they like," Fzoul gloated, over his sixth flagon of wine. "Zhentil Keep will be ours."

He was gratified by Manshoon's eager smile, and they clinked flagons together.

Fzoul Chembryl was enjoying this.

For this first time in far too many days, Manshoon really needed him.

Which meant no sly or savage attack would fall on him, here or elsewhere, for days to come.

More than that, the ever-mounting death toll among the Brotherhood magelings would give the Rightful Hand of Bane real say in the Zhentarim for some time to come; Manshoon was fast becoming one man, standing almost alone against all the might of the temple.

Alone indeed. Last night a beholder had come floating into Fzoul's private chapel, turning aside the guardian spells with contemptuous ease, to hiss a private message.

"Expect Manshoon to receive no aid from any of my kind in this fray over the Darkways," the eye tyrant had said. "We regard this as a test of Manshoon's strength and fitness to lead the Brotherhood. So fear not, Fzoul Chembryl—if Manshoon calls on us to crush you or your temple underlings, we shall not hear."

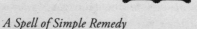

A Spell of Simple Remedy

"Keep back!" Elminster snapped as guards pounded up, glaives lowered and reaching for him. "I'm undoing Manshoon's evil, so all can safely use this Darkway again. Harm me, and you doom him, and all your livelihoods."

"*Back*, men!" a deeper voice rolled out from behind the guards. "Who are you, wizard?"

"Elminster," the bearded wizard replied—as the floor rocked under their feet, and distant thunder made glass lamps tinkle and the entire mansion shudder around them.

"What's going on?" the waylord demanded. "That's been happening most of the day, now!"

"Ambram Sarbuckho killed many Zhentarim last night. Manshoon is now busily destroying Wyrmhaven as a warning to all the rest of you."

"Meaning?"

El shrugged. "He intends to crush all who don't kneel to him. So, some of ye may elect to use thy gates to flee the keep, with all thy riches and retainers. Yet ye're Zhents, so most of ye will probably vow to fight Manshoon to the death. Me, I must use the time while Manshoon's indulging himself at Wyrmhaven to undo the fatal spells he worked on every last Darkway, to make them all safe again. So I'm off to the next one, now. Lord, ye have a decision to make."

A Warm Welcome

Yavarla swam up out of a pleasant slumber to find the sun warm on her face, and herself snugly wrapped up in her own shimmerweave coverlet. Storm had put her coffer in her hands and produced a soft pillow from somewhere to cradle her head. Yavarla could hear the beautiful, liquid swirling of her harp from off to her right, not too close, and smiled to herself.

She did not let that smile reach her face. Nor did she open her eyes.

This was all very pleasant, but it was a trap.

The man who'd snatched her out of Wyrmhaven last night was keeping her here, away from the keep, for reasons of his own.

She had to get back—to Manshoon—before any more time passed.

If this silver-haired harpist hadn't robbed her as she slept, she had the means to do it, too. Under the coverlet, Yavarla opened the coffer a crack with her thumbs, feeling carefully for the ring with the sculpted wing thrusting up from it.

There it was, amid everything else. Her wealth was untouched.

The harp music swirled, rising and falling. Storm Silverhand was strolling around the glade as she played.

Eyes shut, Yavarla worked to get that ring on her finger. She knew what she'd see if she looked over at the harpist. Those long, long silver tresses would be swirling and coiling like lazy snakes or stretching cats, curling leisurely in time to the music. The harpist's magic must be strong—so she, Yavarla, would have to be fast.

There! It was on, and snugged up against her knuckles. Close the coffer, think of the street in front of Manshoon's house, for it would be foolish to try to teleport into a wizard's home, with all the wards he'd have, and—

—Faerûn whirled around her—

—she was blinking in the bright sun of the keep, standing on the cobbles outside Manshoon's gates, her coffer in her hands. Grim guards were already lowering great glaives to menace her.

"I," she told them calmly, "am expected. Conduct me to First Lord Manshoon. Without delay, if you please."

The nearest guard inclined his head. "Lady, your name?"

"I am Lady Yavarla Sarbuckho. Wife to the Lord Ambram Sarbuckho, of the keep."

"Admit her," a young wizard's voice called down from somewhere above, and the great gates opened.

Yavarla kept a serene smile on her face as she was whisked up stairs and across polished marble halls and up more stairs, climbing ever higher. Twice her skin tingled, the ring on her finger burning her like fire, as unseen spellcasters probed her for magic. The second time, a man she'd never seen before stepped out of a door to bar her way and demand, "Remove your ring. No such magic in the presence of the First Lord."

"You," she replied coolly, "are not the First Lord. I have seen him—*all* of him—and I know."

Unimpressed, the man reached out for her coffer. After a moment, she put it into his hand.

"This shall be returned, unopened by me," he told her, his other hand still out. "The ring."

Silence fell between them, until she sighed, removed the ring, and dropped it into his palm. He bowed, indicated the door he'd come through, and glided away, murmuring, "Lord Manshoon awaits you."

Yavarla opened the door. The room beyond was a richly paneled study full of books and a massive table and high-backed chairs, like many she'd seen in the mansions of the mighty. Standing by the table was—her heart leaped anew at his dark, handsome looks, and the smile growing on his face—Manshoon.

"Lord, I came to tell you my husband is dead. I killed him last night, after he came to me wanting me to slay you. He—"

"*Yavarla*," Manshoon said warmly, opening his arms to welcome her.

As she rushed into them, fire kindled in his eyes.

With that same widening smile still on his face, he drawled, "Your usefulness is past."

Fire coalesced out of the air around her, binding her like chains—and then started to sear her.

"And you bore me," he added, as she tried to scream . . . but fell to ashes, instead.

His second spell kept even the smallest of them from reaching the carpet.

From a chair on the far side of the table, Fzoul Chembryl watched as the ashes roiled, then spiraled in the air like dark water going down a drain, and vanished.

Then he nodded approvingly.

A ruler free of entanglements is a leader free of weaknesses. He'd do the same thing.

He smiled crookedly, thinking of a certain rather eager priestesses back at the temple. He might soon have to.

The Time of Reckoning

At least this, Elminster thought rather wearily, was the last.

He'd told a seemingly endless succession of angry waylords what he was doing to their Darkways, and why—and now here he was in the luxurious black marble rear hall of Swordgates, looking up into the frightened face of Mantras Jhoszelbur . . . and he was done at last.

He straightened with a yawn, dusted his hands together, and told this last waylord, "I'm done here. If ye'd be rid of First Lord Manshoon, hounding him out of the keep is thy work to undertake. If ye prefer a life of slavery, let him proceed down the path he's chosen, and ye'll enjoy that status soon enough!"

Before Jhoszelbur could think of something suitably testy to snarl, El was through an archway and back along the passage that led to the rear door he'd come in by. He wanted to get clear of Swordgates before Manshoon finished destroying Wyrmhaven and came looking for other foes to reduce to rubble.

Guards scuttled hastily out of his way. El gave them a reassuring smile—no sense in having a few spears hurled at the back of your head, even if you did have a mantle to stop them—and then opened that door and ducked out into the alley beyond.

And the world exploded.

When he could see again, he knew what had happened. His mantle had returned half a dozen hostile magics to the various Zhentarim who'd first hurled them, then failed, overloaded by the onslaught.

Those backlashes were still causing various buildings where Manshoon's mages had been to slump or topple, up and down the alley—and the flood of still-rolling rubble had just swept him right back into Swordgates.

Thankfully, Jhoszelbur's guards were fleeing in all directions, not throwing spears, and there was no sign of any of the Stormwands.

Elminster fought his way free of all the stone—and then stiffened, as Mystra spoke briefly and firmly in his head.

Not that way, El. 'Tis time to teach Manshoon a lesson.

He sighed, looked longingly at the last Darkway he'd altered for a moment, then murmured, "As ye wish, Great Lady of Mysteries," and started walking briskly through Stormgates.

He strode the length of that sprawling, many-pillared stone mansion, raising a new mantle around himself as he went, to the front doors of Swordgates.

Jhoszelbur's house guards threw them wide at his approach, and Elminster strode out into the sunlight—and the welcome he'd been expecting.

Zhentilar javelins cracked and shivered on the descending flight of steps in front of his boots, and behind the massed black-armored horde of warriors happily hurling them, El saw baneguards advancing, upperpriests of Bane commanding them. More priests stood on roofs and balconies all around, and there were Zhentarim, too, some of them in the saddles of foulwings flapping and circling overhead like great black bat-winged toads.

The tripled-jawed aerial steeds of the Brotherhood croaked and hissed harsh unpleasantnesses to each other, their red eyes burning, eager to enter the fray.

Swordgates occupied a corner where two streets met, and similarly grand mansions lined both of those routes—high houses whose streetfront windows and balconies were crowded with priestesses of Loviatar, presumably aiding the Brotherhood to gain Manshoon's favor.

Manshoon? Ah, *there* he was, standing with Fzoul Chembryl on a high mansion balcony right across the road, ready to gloat as the lone wizard on the steps got destroyed.

The Rightful Hand of Bane held two dark rods in his hands, and Manshoon hadn't forgotten to bring a long, fell-looking staff.

"Oh, *dung*," Elminster said sourly, clawing in a pouch for

his least useful enchanted rings, so as to feed his mantle with *something*. This was going to hurt.

"Care, lords, I beg of you!" the owner of the mansion whose balcony Manshoon and Fzoul were standing on shouted then, from the room behind them. "If much magic is unleashed here, the destruction will be *ruinous*! Zhentil Keep's fairest houses could well be—"

Manshoon lifted one hand and made a lazy signal, without even bothering to turn around. The wealthy merchant gurgled in mid protest as his throat was slit, the ugly sound lost in Fzoul's thunderous, "*Destroy him!*"

The priest of Bane brought his arm down with a flourish, pointing right at Elminster.

Zhentarim, Banite priests, and priestesses of Loviatar all unleashed deadly spells, hurling them with glee, all wanting to be part of obliterating that lone figure on the steps.

Elminster's world became roiling flame, tongues of fire that swirled like white snowflakes in a roaring, purple-black darkness as the Weave was torn, Faerûn shrieked aloud, and he was plucked off his feet, shaken like a doll, and hurled—

Nowhere at all, as Mystra manifested all around him in an armor of eerie blue light, dancing sparks that dazzled the eyes with their hue.

Two huge and long-lashed eyes opened behind Elminster and drank in the darkness, and nine silver stars blossomed out of those sparks. Two of those stars darted into Mystra's eyes, and the other seven began to circle her slumped, pain-wracked Chosen.

Gathering all the magic hurled at him . . . and slowly, one spell after another, sending it all back whence it came.

The huge floating eyes of the goddess swept across the shouting Zhentarim army, regarding them with something like sorrow, then rose to meet Manshoon's astonished and outraged gaze.

As he stared at Mystra, and Mystra stared back at him, the First Lord of Zhentil Keep began to scream in terror.

Beholders appeared, rising menacingly into view over rooftops with their eyestalks writhing, gliding forward with fell intent—only to melt away in an instant. A moment later, every last foulwing faded to nothingness, spilling shrieking riders out of the sky.

The balcony where Manshoon and Fzoul stood broke off the front of the mansion it adorned and fell to earth, slowly and soundlessly. Clinging to it, the two mightiest of the Zhentarim bawled like babies, clawing at the stones.

It came to rest very gently, with no crash at all, but the two men pitched forward onto their faces, trembling in fear. Fzoul fainted, and Manshoon hid his face in his hands, daring only to peek between them.

He saw Mystra bend her will and power on the army at the foot of the steps. Baneguards vanished in bony silence, black armor was suddenly gone from hairy and horrified men, and spears and swords were swept away from their hands.

As they broke and fled, pelting away down the streets as fast as they could run, moaning and trampling each other in their fear, the goddess roared up into a spire of blue flame.

That great tongue of fire rose with a thunderous snarl, to tower high over Swordgates, to loom into the sky above Zhentil Keep and catch distant, awed eyes—then flashed, blinding many watchers, and—vanished.

On balconies and rooftops, down alleys and in windows, every last priest and priestess collapsed, all dashed senseless at once.

Silence fell. Mystra was gone.

Leaving Manshoon weeping and trembling, and a weary and wincing Elminster regarding him with disgust.

Stumbling in obvious pain, and trailing a scorched smell, El came slowly down the steps. Over the rubble, over the bodies of the trampled, over fallen weapons and spilled blood, across the street to where the First Lord of Zhentil Keep cowered.

Citizens were watching, peering from windows and alleys, from doors and from atop carts down the streets, as Elminster approached Manshoon.

"For years, ye have owed thy life to a promise," he told the leader of the Zhentarim quietly. "Ye almost threw that life away this day. *Try* to learn some wisdom."

On his haunches, Manshoon spun around and covered his ears, turning his back on the bearded Chosen.

Who rolled his eyes, drew back one dusty-booted foot, and gave the First Lord a solid kick in the pants, pitching him over onto his face.

Then Elminster stalked away, not looking back.

Face down in the dirt and furious, Manshoon snarled.

"I swear," he whispered, knowing how many eyes were upon him, "I'll slay you some day, Elminster. And work it so that as you die, you know full well who has slain you."

He kept still, hunched down. For now, though, he must play the overconfident fool, to avoid being destroyed by Mystra as too dangerous. Yet at the same time work, with infinite patience and contingency upon contingency, scheme overlapping scheme, toward ultimate triumph.

Oh, the things he could do without being hampered by Elminster's meddlings!

Hah, the things he could do *to* Elminster if the old bearded goat didn't have the goddess protecting him!

"There will come a day, Elminster of Shadowdale," Manshoon announced to his own spellchamber quietly, as he teleported back to its dark, deserted safety, "when *my* chance will come. A day when you aren't cloaked and armored in the favor of a goddess."

He turned slowly on one heel to look around at the quiet darkness. "And on that day," he added with a crooked smile, "Manshoon will laugh—and Elminster will die."

Ed Greenwood is the man who unleashed the FORGOTTEN REALMS on an unsuspecting world. He works in libraries, writes fantasy, science fiction, horror, mystery, and even romance stories (sometimes all in the same novel), but he is still happiest churning out Realmslore, Realmslore, and more Realmslore. Read more about Elminster in his novels *Elminster Must Die* and the forthcoming *Bury Elminster Deep*.

DREAMING OF WATERDEEP
A Tale of the FORGOTTEN REALMS

ROSEMARY JONES

He ran. He ran as fast as he could, through the mud in the yard, past the snarling hound lunging on the end of its chain, waking the two remaining hens roosting in the barn's doorway. Even the old barren sow, due for the butcher before the end of the fall, grunted and shifted in her dreams as he barreled past her pen.

He lunged for the ladder on the far wall and scrambled up it. One rotten rung cracked. He slipped, banged his knees painfully against another rung, but kept climbing. When he got to the top of the ladder, he flung himself face first into the musty old straw. There, safely hidden from the world, Gustin Bone gave way to the fury, sorrow, and regret that shook his ten-year-old body and howled like a lost soul.

A long time later, Gustin uncurled, wiping the tickling straw out of his hair and face. Then he walked across the ominously creaking floor to the open barn window and gazed across the moonlit farm, the most desolate and lonely place in all the world. His uncle was gone, nowhere to be seen.

"I'm going to die here," Gustin pronounced. And, liking the sound of his own voice echoing into the rafters, he shouted a little louder, "I'm going to grow old, die here, and nobody is ever going to know my name! It will be a tragedy."

Then he stopped. He wasn't quite sure that something could be a tragedy if nobody else knew about it. But he loved the sound of the word. He had learned it from the widow. She visited on a regular basis to clean out the farmhouse and scold his uncle about the state of Gustin's clothes and general hygiene.

"If you never come clean, boy, it will be a tragedy. Your mother, if she lived, would weep to see the state that you're in," the widow would say, flinging Gustin's shirts and breeches into boiling water while he sat shivering on a stool wrapped in a threadbare towel.

As little as he liked her cleaning methods, he was rather fond of the widow, who invariably ended her session of scrubbing by producing some type of biscuit or baked bread from her basket. But it wasn't her attentions to the mud behind his ears that made him screw his face into a frown and shout that night to the uncaring world, "I refuse to die here!"

No, it was the actions of his uncle—that woefully stupid, uncaring, altogether wrong man—that caused Gustin to scramble through the straw to unearth his mother's battered old trunk and thrust open the lid to pull out her even more battered knapsack. Finally, Gustin decided, he would fill that knapsack full and follow the road out into the wide marvelous world, all the way to Waterdeep, that City of Splendors. He had to go now, he told himself, before it was too late.

Only that morning he had smiled and chattered as he walked with his taciturn uncle to the village. Gustin filled the silence surrounding them with his own running observations on the birds in the hedgerows, the likelihood that the hens would survive the winter, and the oft-expressed wish that his uncle might adopt a kitten to keep the mice out of the barn.

"Farhinner's got a litter," Gustin informed him. Farhinner was the tanner and kept cats to keep the rats out of the leather. "Two tabbies and a ginger-stripe."

"Dog wouldn't like it," grunted his uncle.

Gustin shrugged, a ripple of the shoulders that he'd copied from Farhinner. He liked the man. Since the tanner had no sons, it seemed likely that he might be looking for an apprentice in a year or two. A stinky trade, none smelled worse except the butcher's shop, but it meant a room in the village and no farmwork. At the age of ten, Gustin already spent his days plotting ways to escape from the farm.

"There's strangers," said his uncle, stopping so abruptly that Gustin was two lengths down the road and several paragraphs into an argument in favor of kittens before he realized his uncle was not moving.

Then he blinked and saw what his uncle was staring at. There were strangers. Marvelous strangers emerging from the woods and skidding down the embankment toward the road. The first man was dressed in fantastic colors, with ribbons and feathers hanging from his broad-brimmed hat, and a long swirling cape that went all the way down to the heels of his highly polished boots. The dwarf following close behind this dandy bore a highly polished helmet on his head and sported a bright red beard cascading down his barrel-round front. The third stranger, also human and obviously male, wore leather armor, well cared for but marked with interesting nicks and scars. A long scabbard, very noticeable for its plainness, hung empty from his belt.

"Well met, my friends," cried the man with the broad-brimmed hat. "We are looking for a smith and an inn. For my friend has a sword in need of mending and we all have need of a place to stay."

Gustin's uncle shook his head and turned on his heel, as if he meant to walk all the way back to the farm rather than talk to the strangers. Gustin, however, was propelled forward by his own curiosity.

"You'll want to follow us into the village," he announced, ignoring his uncle wavering in the background. "We can show you the smith and the tavern. We don't have an inn. But you can probably sleep on the benches at the tavern." It was what laborers from the lord's fields did on the harvest days, if they'd drunk too heavily to find their way home safely in the dark.

"Any place with a roof would be welcome," answered the talkative stranger. "We'll take a stable or even a cow's shed tonight. I am Nerhaltan, my large friend here is called Wervyn, and the dwarf goes by the nickname Tapper."

The other two didn't say anything, but the dwarf Tapper glanced once, quickly, at the shadowed woods behind them. Gustin knew the track that they had been following; it led to old ruins, a little hill fort long since crumbled into a collection of tilting walls and a stair that climbed crookedly up to nothing. Village tales called the spot haunted but every child defied their parents and made their way through the woods to race beneath the high arch that once marked the fort's gate.

Gustin had run that race in and out of the ruins earlier that summer. No harm had come from it, although there had been a coldness about the place that he didn't like.

Behind him, his uncle sighed once and then gestured at the strangers. "It's not far to the village," he said. "We go slowly, the boy and I. Step ahead of us if you need to."

"We're happy for the company," said Nerhaltan, pacing alongside Gustin. "Your lad seems very bright for his age."

"My nephew," grunted his uncle.

"I'm Gustin," said Gustin. And then he proceeded to beguile the rest of the too-short journey with dozens of questions for the strangers: how far had they come, what type of sword had the fighter broken, did the dwarf carry a battleaxe, had they ever seen a dragon, did they know how far it was to Waterdeep?

The dwarf turned his bright eyes on Gustin when he mentioned Waterdeep.

"That's a long way from here," Tapper said. "What do you know about the City of Splendors, boy?"

Gustin paused, catching back his next question before it popped out of his mouth. His uncle had paced a little ahead of them, walking with the tall fighter, and the two were discussing the state of the weather and the possibility of a storm before moonrise.

"I have a book," Gustin whispered, reaching into his tunic and pulling out his most precious possession so a corner showed. "A guidebook to Waterdeep."

"Looks a bit chewed," said the dandy on the other side of him. "Like the rats have been at it."

"I found it in the barn," Gustin admitted, "in a pile of rubbish my uncle meant to burn." Papers and other items belonging to his mother, he didn't add. His uncle once tossed everything into the bonfire pit after he caught Gustin snapping open the locks on her old trunk and rummaging through it. But then the widow had stopped his uncle from dousing the lot with oil and started a shouting match about respect for his dead sister. Eventually papers went safely from the bonfire pit to the barn, because his uncle insisted that he wouldn't have "any of it in my house any longer. It will give the boy dreams! And you know what will happen then."

Gustin still didn't know what would happen, although he hoped it would take him far away from the farm like his long-lost mother. As for the dreams, they began the first night that he lay curled in his creaking bed and read the enchanting words "Waterdeep, a city of high adventures and dark dealings" by the light of a sputtering candle.

"Have you been to Waterdeep, saers?" he asked the dandy and the dwarf. Both shook their heads.

"Waterdeep is no destination for a poor man," said Nerhaltan. "I won't go there until I have gold in my pockets."

"Yet some say it is the place for a dwarf or a man to find the gold to fill his pockets," added his short companion.

"It takes gold to make gold," the dandy said. "That is why we are here, after all."

"Quiet," said Tapper, with a glance at Gustin that the boy pretended not to see.

They rounded the bend in the road. "Look, saers, our village," said Gustin.

Nerhaltan blinked at the collection of buildings circling a widening in the road. One large oak marked the center of the village, a brute of arboreal pride so big that none had ever figured out how to cut it down, and so the road split around it and the village circled it.

"Well," remarked Nerhaltan, "I have seen smaller. Let's hope the smith knows something about swords as well as farm tools."

The evening grew late. Past sundown was past his uncle's usual bedtime, but the three adventurers kept them talking at the tavern, insisting on buying them a meal and, for his uncle, a tankard of ale, in return for conversation about the village and the ruins up the road. Gustin did most of the talking and his uncle did most of the eating and drinking. Eventually Gustin's uncle slumped in his chair, snoring lightly before the fire.

Gustin felt no urge to sleep. His brain was fizzing with the stories that the three strangers told in return, about stolen maps and lost treasures, risks taken and rewards won.

"Oh, I wish I could go adventuring," he said, and then blushed at sounding so young. To cover his embarrassment, he reached for the slice of bread on his plate, crumbling it between his fingers and then making it disappear altogether in a shower of red sparks and a few tinkling notes of music.

Tapper's head reared back. "Well, now," said the dwarf. "That's a neat trick. Most small boys just eat the loaf to make it disappear."

Gustin shrugged. "It's just something I do to entertain the little children," he said, with all the pride of a lad who owned ten years of age. As far back as he could remember, he could make small things disappear or shift around. Such tricks made the widow laugh when she came to clean the farm and she'd taught him ways to twist his fingers and words to add sparks or dancing lights to the effect.

"Hmm," said Nerhaltan, also staring intently at him. "Can you do other tricks?"

"A few," Gustin admitted. "Like making my voice come from someplace else." That sentence caused the fighter Wervyn to start in his corner, as Gustin's voice sounded behind his head. Like Gustin's uncle, the big fighter had been dozing in his chair.

The dandy and the dwarf laughed. "Oh, very good. Do another."

"Do you have a cloth and a coin?" Gustin asked. This was a fairly new trick for him and he'd been practicing to impress the widow.

Nerhaltan pulled a handkerchief edged with lace out of a hidden pocket. Wervyn produced a well-worn copper coin.

With a few waves of his hand, Gustin passed the coin through the cloth. Then he crumpled up the handkerchief and shook it out empty.

"Humph," said the fighter. "And where's my money?"

"Why, in your pocket, saer, just where you had it," said Gustin.

The big man slid his hand under his vest and produced the copper coin again.

"Quick fingers?" the dandy questioned his companions.

"The boy never came near me," the fighter observed.

The trio stared hard at Gustin. "So, how did you do it?" Tapper said.

Gustin shrugged. "I've always been good at tricks," he admitted.

"A boy like you, a brave boy," began Nerhaltan, "could be a great help to us."

Gustin slid forward on his chair, eager to hear what the dandy had to say.

"Leave him alone." His uncle's flat voice, harsh and loud, startled them all. The man was awake and scowling. "No more tales. No more tricks."

His hand dropped hard on Gustin's shoulder. He pulled the boy out of his chair with one yank. "We are going home now. Stay away from us. Stay away from the boy."

"Uncle!"

"Saer," said Nerhaltan, following them into the twilight gloom outside the tavern's door. "It's growing dark. Let us buy you a bed for the night. We meant no harm and could perhaps come to some prosperous . . ."

"No!" shouted Gustin's uncle, lurching down the road, dragging a reddening Gustin after him. "No tales. No tricks. No more!"

Halfway back to the farm, his uncle's hand finally loosened enough on his collar to let Gustin wiggle free.

"I wanted to hear what they had to say," he protested, feeling very brave because the moonlight was dim and he could barely make out the deep frown scoring his uncle's face.

His uncle wheeled around, grabbing his shoulders, and shook him the same way that the farm dog would shake a rat when it caught one.

"Stay out of the village until the strangers are gone. If they come near, do not speak to them. Do not look at them."

"But . . ."

"And no more silly spells," yelled his uncle. "How many times must I tell you! No magic at all!"

"I only do simple ones to make people laugh," protested Gustin.

"No more!" roared his uncle. "And no more trips to the village. Not until you learn more sense."

They were in sight of the farmhouse. The dog set up a volley of harsh barks, awakened by his uncle's shouts. The farmer turned and yelled at the dog to be silent.

"Tomorrow, I'm burning your mother's books," he said in a quieter, more sober tone, turning back to his nephew.

"No!" Gustin sprang away from his uncle, racing toward the barn where her trunk was still stored.

"Including that daft guidebook you keep in your shirt!"

yelled his uncle after him. "Don't think I don't know about that! No more foolish tales, boy, no more tricks! This time, I mean it!"

◆━━━◆━━━◆

Upstairs in the barn, Gustin stuffed the battered knapsack as full as possible with his mother's papers, scrolls, and books. He would leave nothing behind for his uncle's bonfire.

Down the barn ladder he crept with more caution than he had hurled up it. The farmyard was a tangle of shadows. The hound shifted, paws churning in some dream of a hunt, and rattled its chain as he crept past, but the old dog did not wake. It knew Gustin's footsteps in its sleep.

Gustin was out the gate and halfway down the road before he stopped to consider where he would go. Everyone in the village knew him. His uncle would look there first.

The three adventurers had talked about going back to the ruins, just as soon as the fighter's sword was mended. After that, who knows where they would go? Waterdeep, as he had always dreamed, or some other destination equally splendid. Surely they would want a clever boy, a boy like him who knew more than a few magical tricks, to help them on their way.

Gustin turned off the road, following the track that led to the ruins. Being tired and mindful of the night shadows whispering through the tall grass, he decided not to go into the ruins by himself. Instead, he slid down into the bracken at the base of a tree, curling himself around the knapsack stuffed full of his mother's papers.

The three adventurers found him there, dozing in the late afternoon stillness and dreaming of Waterdeep.

The dandy poked him awake with one pointed toe. "What

ROSEMARY JONES
297

are you doing, boy?" he asked, but his eyes were bright with laughter and he looked as if he knew what Gustin would answer.

"I've come to help you to find the treasure," Gustin said as boldly as he could with grass sticking out of his hair and a few dry leaves itching their way down his shirt as he scrambled to his feet.

"How do you know we are looking for treasure? Or your help?" said the dwarf, and his face was harder and more suspicious than his companions.

"You said . . . last night . . . well, I thought," Gustin mumbled a little, staring at his toes, wondering if he'd been a bit rash.

"Of course, we are after treasure," said Nerhaltan. "What else would three like us be doing here? The boy's too bright for us to deceive." The dandy nodded high over Gustin's head at his companions. "We welcome your help, young wizard, welcome it indeed."

"I'm no wizard," Gustin quickly answered. "But I do know these ruins."

"Does your uncle know where you are?" asked Wervyn. The fighter looked concerned and frowned when Gustin shook his head. "Maybe you should go back to your farm, boy."

"Nonsense," answered Nerhaltan for him. "The boy's got too much adventure in him to be content on some farm. Lead on, lad, lead on. There's plenty for all if we can find our prize."

Gustin led the three men toward the ruins. The woods buzzed with the usual noise of a warm autumn afternoon, birds calling to mates, the deep rumble of frogs, the chittering of insects. It sounded so normal that Gustin paused.

"What is it?" asked the dandy.

Gustin shrugged. He felt as if a dozen ants were marching up and down his spine. A prickling of his skin unlike anything he had ever felt before.

"Are we going forward or going back?" said Tapper.

"Forward," replied the dandy, giving Gustin a slight shove between the shoulder blades. "Go to, sirrah, go to."

"There's something wrong," said Gustin.

"What?"

He shook his head. Suddenly he wondered if he should have listened to his uncle and stayed home. And then he was ashamed of his cowardice. Here he was, so close to discovering a lost treasure, and he stood trembling, afraid of a few birds singing in the tangled branches over his head.

Even as that thought tumbled through his mind, Gustin let out a great sigh of relief and enlightenment.

"It's the birds," he said to the three adventurers staring at him. "The birds. It's the wrong time of year. They should not be singing like that."

And the minute he said it, the woods fell silent. Not a cheep or a chirp could be heard.

The fighter drew his repaired sword out of the scabbard with a well-oiled hiss.

"It is close," he said to his friends.

Tapper peered from side to side. "Keep everyone together now. No one out of sight."

Gustin stared at the three now surrounding him in a tight knot.

"What is it?" he asked, with a sinking certainty that he would not like the answer he would receive from the adults.

"Nothing to worry about," said Nerhaltan with a strained smile. "Go on, boy, go on ahead. There's a hole, you see, down by the base of the wall. It's too small for us, even Tapper won't fit, but if you can wiggle your way in . . ."

A shout sounded to their left. It sounded uncommonly like his uncle calling "Gustin! Gustin!"

Out of habit, Gustin almost started toward the shouts, into the thickest part of the woods, but Tapper grabbed his shirttails and pulled him back. "To the wall, boy, to the wall."

Silence fell again. Gustin listened but he heard no more from his uncle. Perhaps he was turning away and searching toward the village road.

They reached the walls of the ruin. The place seemed colder than before and more menacing than he remembered, the shadows clustering at the base of the wall and making a gloomy twilight inside the roofless rooms of the abandoned fort.

High above his head, a kitten mewed, a lost sound. Poor thing, thought Gustin, it must have climbed the wall and gotten itself stuck. Fond of cats, he chirped, hoping to draw it into the open.

"Hush!" Nerhaltan clapped a hand over Gustin's mouth. "Don't call to it."

Gustin wiggled his way free and eyed the dandy with suspicion. "Why should I be afraid of a stray kitten?"

"Not a cat," muttered Tapper, nervously looking around. "It just sounds like a cat. When it's not trying to sound like your mother."

"Or a flock of birds." That from the fighter, who had put his back to the ruins' wall and was staring out at the woods.

"Now, about this hole," said Nerhaltan. There was a hole at the base of the wall, newly dug, as Gustin could tell by the fresh clods of dirt lining its rim. As the dandy had said, the opening was small, the stone blocks of the wall preventing it from being enlarged beyond the current opening.

Gustin went flat on his stomach and peered within. He snapped his fingers, concentrating on a useful spell that the widow had taught him, and made a light. The little glowing ball rolled away from his hand and dropped down the hole. It disappeared into a chamber located just under the wall.

"A safe room. All these little hill forts used to have them. A place to hide treasure," explained Tapper, leaning over Gustin's shoulder. "The original way in . . . well, we couldn't use that. So I came around to the other side of the wall and broke in through the roof. But it's too narrow a route for us to wiggle down and back."

The air issuing from the hole smelled stale, dank, and uncommonly like a grave to Gustin.

"Is something down there?" Gustin asked. For the end of his sensitive nose caught another scent, a stink like an animal, but no animal that he could identify.

"Nothing down there now," said Nerhaltan.

"Now that it is out here," added Wervyn. The fighter was facing away from the wall, looking up the broad stone staircase that wound around the tower to the guards' walk at the top of the wall.

"Go on, wiggle in." The dandy gave Gustin a little push from behind. "Look for a box, a little gold box with brilliants around the edge of the lid. That's all we need to pay our way to Waterdeep."

The late afternoon shadows stretched from the trees to the base of the fort, like long black fingers reaching for the adventurers standing over Gustin. "Hurry," said Nerhaltan. "We should be out of here as quickly as possible."

For the very first time in his ten years, Gustin wished that he was back at the farm and his uncle was yelling at him about his neglected chores.

He slid headfirst into the hole, plunging his arms in front of him like a swimmer to drag himself forward. His feet kicked the air outside until somebody grabbed his ankles—Nerhaltan, probably—and shoved him all the way in. Gustin slithered forward, concentrating on his light spell. A faint glow began to strengthen before him.

"What do you see?" The shout sounded very far away and muffled to his ears.

"Nothing!" he yelled back.

Then he popped like a cork from a bottle, tumbling out of the tunnel and onto the littered, stinking floor of the room under the wall. Piles of debris cushioned his fall. For which he was grateful until he put his hand onto the half-rotted corpse of a mouse. With a yelp of disgust, he rolled away, only to land on a much larger pile of bones that crumbled and cracked under his slight weight.

Gustin sprang hastily to his feet and spat a hasty command to his spell. By the glowing light that he now made float in the center of the room, he could discern rib bones, leg bones, and a few vertebrae. After a squeamish moment, he came to the conclusion that these were the remains of a lost sheep or, possibly, a calf. It certainly could not be a ten-year-old boy. After all, if somebody his age had gone missing from the village, he would have known. Even if it had been years and years ago. Or so he told himself firmly.

Gustin began kicking through the trash strewn about the room, looking for the gold box that Nerhaltan described. Nothing glittered or gleamed. After one quick turn around the room, he decided the search was hopeless and that he would rather be above ground, no matter what lurked among the trees.

Crossing back to the hole where he had entered, Gustin found that it was just out of reach. Even pushing the larger bones, dead leaves, and other bits of rubbish in the room into a pile under the hole didn't help. The material was too unstable. Every time he climbed up, the pile collapsed under his feet.

"Help!" he yelled. "I need a rope!"

There was no answer.

Gustin called again, louder and more urgent.

A faint cough sounded far above his head and then he heard Nerhaltan call, "Where are you, boy? Where have you gone?"

The dandy's voice was muffled and strangely distorted and, Gustin shivered despite himself, altogether too eager for an answer. Especially for a man who should know exactly where he was. After all, Nerhaltan had pushed him down this hole.

All the magic Gustin possessed tingled up and down his spine. Something was out there and it meant him harm.

Something sniffed at the hole leading into the safe room. Something scratched at stone and dirt, as if something too big for the hole was trying to dig its way in.

Gustin drew a deep breath and concentrated as he had never concentrated before. Then he opened his mouth and let his voice sail out and away from him, using the very same spell that had so startled the adventurers in the tavern. "Here I am! Here I am!" His words should be sounding from the very top of the hill fort's crumbling tower if his spell worked.

He held his breath, keeping perfectly still. Faintly, distantly, he heard the scrape of a heavy body moving away.

"We found a way but we could not use that," Wervyn had said. Not a lock, not a barred door, Gustin decided. But a creature hunting in the tunnels under the fort? Is that what had driven the adventurers above ground and to this second, futile attempt, using him to rob the safe room?

He dashed across the room, running his hands across the dank and soiled walls. Solid stone scraped his palms. He ran a circuit of the room, banging heavily against walls, kicking at the foundations, looking in the waning light of his spell for any sign of a door.

When he found it, he practically tumbled through it. Rotted wood painted to look like stone gave way before his frantic blows. He kicked a hole large enough to crawl through and found himself at the base of a bare stone stair twisting up toward the fort's main gate.

With as light a step as possible, Gustin speeded up the stairs to arrive, panting, at the top. By the slant of the shadows covering the courtyard, he had been below ground for barely an hour, perhaps even less. But he was acutely aware of the unnatural stillness of the woods beyond the ruins. Not a bird chirped, not an insect buzzed.

Above his head, he heard a cry, almost startling him from his crouched hiding place at the top of the stairs. Then he realized it was his own voice, still echoing among the stones: "Here I am! Here I am!"

"Where are you, boy? Why are you hiding?" A great shadow passed overhead as something huge and beastly clattered along the guards' walkway that ran across the top of the fort's wall. The voice was Nerhaltan's but the shadow cast by the dropping sun upon the weed-choked courtyard was too large to be that of the slender man.

Gustin crept under the broken arch of the main gate. He slid around the gate's main pillar, hugging as tightly to the wall as he could, hoping whatever prowled above him would not glance down.

The woods were very close, he told himself firmly. He only had to sprint a short distance with no cover at all before he could lose himself in the friendly shadows under the trees. Whatever hunted at the top of the wall surely could not leap down and catch him before he reached the trees. All these arguments made perfect sense in his head but he could not persuade his trembling body to leave the relative safety of the wall.

Then he remembered Nerhaltan pushing him down the hole with uneasy glances toward all sides.

Gustin stared in the direction of the hole where he first entered the hill fort. He could easily see the loose dirt piled outside the wall. Equally easily, he could make out the distinct shape of a man's boot leaning against the wall. It looked very much like Nerhaltan's leg. As for the rest of the dandy, there was no sign. Just the one leg leaning against the blood-splattered wall.

Fighting back the bile rising in his throat, Gustin prepared to run as he had never run before. Directly above him, he heard the beast cry out in Nerhaltan's voice, "There you are, clever boy!"

Another shout sounded across the meadow: "Gustin!"

Emerging from the trees, his uncle ran toward him, shouldering the heavy crossbow that he kept over the mantle for winter's wolves and other raiders of the chicken coop.

Behind his uncle strode the widow, her hands alight with flame. "Get down!" she yelled, even as his uncle dropped to one knee and fired an iron bolt over Gustin's head.

Gustin flattened himself in the weeds at the base of the wall. He heard the beast above cry out in pain, no longer disguising its voice, but screaming with a ferocious roar of frustrated bloodlust.

The widow spat out the words of a spell and long ropes of flame streamed from her outstretched fingers. The beast howled louder. The stench of scorched flesh and fur rolled over the gagging Gustin as he crawled as hastily as possible away from the wall.

His uncle reloaded the crossbow and shot again. The second bolt also struck home. The beast coughed and called out weirdly in the voice of the dandy: "Ah, the blood, the blood."

A heavy body crashed down from the guards' walk at the top of the wall. Gustin rolled over and stared down the length of his body. Framed between his boot toes was a hideous blend of a stag's legs with a lion's body and a giant badger's head. A tufted tail lashed from side to side as the wounded creature struggled to its hooves. It kicked out at Gustin but a blaze of fire from the advancing widow drove it briefly away from the boy.

Gustin scrambled to his feet. The badger head swayed back and forth, the open mouth blowing out a carrion breath that made him gag. Bony ridges lined the inside of its black lips, clearly visible, far too close to his nose.

Raising his own hands, Gustin repeated the spell being shouted by the widow. It was louder and longer than the one that she had taught him to light a candle. Smoke rather than fire blossomed at his fingertips. Cursing his fumble of the spell, he flung the smoke at the beast's eyes. Baffled and choking on the thick black smoke streaming from Gustin's hands, it wheeled around, racing away from Gustin to the safety of the trees.

A third bolt from his uncle's crossbow pierced the creature's throat. It tumbled over its hooves, crumbling into the grass.

With three strides, Gustin's uncle reached him and swept him up in a hard one-armed embrace. Then he dropped Gustin with a thump. "I told you to stay away from magic," he growled. "I told you to stay away from those men."

"Ah," said the widow, crushing Gustin in her own mint-scented embrace. "Leave the boy alone. How was he to know there was a leucrotta in these ruins?"

Gustin wiggled his way out of the widow's hug. "Where are they?" he said, looking around for the tall fighter and his dwarf companion.

"Run off!" snorted his uncle. "We saw them on the road."

"He's been searching for you all morning," the widow whispered in Gustin's ear.

"But why?"

"Because you are family," grunted his uncle, shouldering his crossbow and stepping around the dead beast in the meadow.

"That's worth something," the widow said, pointing at the leucrotta's body.

His uncle shrugged. "Send them out from the village to fetch it. It's magic and I'll have none of it."

"It wasn't magic that killed her," the widow said. "And it won't be magic that kills this boy."

His uncle shook his head and stomped off. The widow sighed. "There goes a stubborn man. It wasn't magic, that's what I keep telling him."

"Who? Who died?" But even as he asked, he knew the answers. It was as close to his heart as her book about Waterdeep.

"Your mother was always twice the wizard that I was," said the widow. "And restless with it. That farm was far too small to hold her. But it stole the laughter from him when she took to wandering. She was all the family he had."

"He has me." Gustin knew even as he said it that the day was coming when he would follow his mother's footsteps out of the village. The adventurers might have tricked him, even run off and left him, but it didn't make their tales any less appealing. He would go to Waterdeep and see the City of Splendors for himself.

"Make me a promise," said the widow as they walked through the woods. "The next time you leave, tell us both good-bye. Don't make her mistake and go running off without a word."

"I promise," Gustin said, and with a whisper of magic, he made his words echo from all the treetops.

Rosemary Jones is the author of two FORGOTTEN REALMS stand-alone novels, *Crypt of the Moaning Diamond* and *City of the Dead*. Her short stories can be found in the FORGOTTEN REALMS anthologies *Realms of Dragons II* and *Realms of the Dead* as well as other science fiction and fantasy books. For more on her latest projects, check her website at www.rosemaryjones.com.

TO CHAOS AND BACK AGAIN
JODY LYNN NYE

Bab threw himself into the ditch just in time. The foul, gritty red dust went up his nose and sifted into his curly brown hair, but he held his breath until the urge to sneeze passed. Not that anyone could have heard it, of course. He gripped his hammer until his fingertips could have pierced through the thick leather wrappings on the handle. The solid metal gave him comfort. Passed down from his grandfather's many-times grandfather, it was ingrained with virtues that helped him shape metal or slay enemies usually beyond the capability of a halfling.

His four companions stayed low as the file of chained orcs and goblins marched by, passing into the notorious Crossroads on the edge of the Chaos Scar. Whips cracked over their heads. The slave master in charge of the company shouted curses. Bab listened appreciatively to the language. Creative, he thought. A phrase or two like that would be useful to help keep the smithereens down while he was hammering metal on his forge in the middle of Wenly Halt. If he should ever see his forge or his home or the village again. A halfling like him should stay where it was safe, but he had no choice. All this was his own fault, sort of. He had been successful where others had failed, and that was the wrong thing to have done.

The tiny green thread tied around his wrist dimmed. He waited, counting to twenty before he raised his head.

The others sensed his movement rather than heard it. They were still within the hour affected by the silence charm given them by Priest Nock. Bab had three more of the precious blue beads still on the string around his neck. Besides costing a week's wages, they were made from mystical ingredients including a precious stone and a hair from his sleeping baby daughter's head, but he'd rather have them on hand than a hundred gems or an enchanted sword. While they were within the sphere of its magic, they could hear outside sounds, but no one could hear them. Three of his six had already been spent to get them past other perils in the wilderness. He guessed they would have no beads left to get them home again.

The lack of silencing spells would probably not matter. By the time they were through with their aim, he imagined, the question of getting home would be moot.

At least, if he didn't go back, he wouldn't have to paint the cottage again. Winter had been hard on the little house. The whitewash was definitely beginning to peel. But it was home. He imagined he could hear the swallows in the eaves chirping, his neighbor's dog barking, his wife Nomi nagging . . . the fond, familiar sounds that kept him going. He could get a day's worth of effort out of a good nag from Nomi. The woman had a gift.

Heartened by the memory, Bab gestured to the others. They scrambled out of the ditch one after the other: Adda, Scorri, Coran, and Legg. Legg's mouth was moving, though no sound came out of it. Then the charm elapsed. The bead burst and sifted into powder down Bab's chest. As it did, the old man's sharp whisper cut through the twilight air like a claw.

". . . I do not believe that I let you talk me into coming back here again! Not when we nearly died the first time. All of us! May your feet come apart between the toes! May your head . . . !"

"Shhh!" Bab hissed. "Don't say those kinds of things here when we're so close to the . . . You-Know-What! They might come true!"

Legg clapped a hand over his mouth. He was tall for a halfling, nearly a dwarf's height. He had meant no harm. Bab knew it. They were all feeling the strain of gritting their teeth while doing something no sane man would ever do—nor insane man either—unless there was no other way. But there was no other way. The glowing blue-green chunk of rock in the pouch on Bab's belt was a fact that gave them no choice.

Oh, the stone had sounded like a sending from the gods. The legend of the fallen star had been one that fathers told their little ones during the dark of the moon to make their hair stand up on the backs of their necks. Bab had loved those stories. He knew at least a few of them were true, since on a moonless night he could see the green fire in the skies to the west, over the cursed mountains beyond the king's wall. There were also weird beasts that turned up on the outskirts from time to time, misshapen creatures that looked as if they'd been born of two species at once: spider-squirrels, owl-cats, and a piteous thing that was part halfling, but no one in the village dared guess what the other part had been. The priest had given it water and said a blessing over it, but it had died. Monsters and other horrors had come out of the deep valley, tearing up the countryside. Most of them had been turned away from Wenly Halt, by force of arms or by the blessed well at its heart.

But after so many incursions the village folk had come to be interested in the sacred rock at the center of the legend. It had fallen from the sky, undoubtedly, because there were still those living who had seen it happen. Magical it was, because odd things began to happen, all springing from the kingdom to the west. It didn't take a scholar to put all the clues together. Power came from the sky, the realm of so many of the gods. It was there for the taking, as the legends said. Those who dared, won. And someone dearly wished, as fools will, that the people of Wenly Halt had some of the magic of their own—for the good of all, of course.

Bab rose from the edge of the road. Now that dawn had passed, they need not fear being jumped from behind. Instead, he and his companions could wreak fear in a few hearts. Halfling brigands were well known in the Crossroads, all brothers. He arranged a length of rag over one eye to masquerade as the eldest of the three chieftains and swaggered into the center of the throughway. The others scrambled to follow him. With their clothes dusty and torn they looked the part of the band of thieves. The deceit had worked the last time on the way in. Most of the humans and other things who lived in the Crossroads village were afraid of the halfling brothers—with good reason. Bab traded on the notion that people saw what they thought they saw. If they believed he and his men were those deadly, thieving brothers, then so be it. They certainly had stolen an item of value. Now they were sorry, and were desperate to put back what they had taken.

The elders of Wenly Halt had been the earliest to catch fire with the idea of having a piece of the fallen star. The village needed to defend itself against raids and attacks, and how better than to fight fire with fire? A rock had brought all that terror and evil to the cursed lands. What if they should secure a piece of it themselves? They'd have power, and to spare. Power in the hands of a halfling village? Sounded foolish when you said it out loud, but it had seemed like sense, a three-month ago.

Bab had thrown himself into the middle of the discussion. He hadn't heard any of the warnings that, for example, Dame May had voiced. "The star stone is evil!" she had cried. "A thing of darkness and mayhem!" The boarder who occupied her garden shed, Coran Halfway, agreed with her. He wasn't a halfling, but a half-elf, and a mage at that. He hardly spoke up in village meetings, so after the nine days' wonder of having an exotic stranger living among them, they treated him like part of the landscape. But for the elegant pointed ears, he could almost have been a halfling. He was shorter than Legg, with black curls and bright black eyes like a bird's.

No, Bab hadn't listened to a word. After all, until only a month or so before, he'd been in the wars under the generalship of humans and elves, four weeks' march from his home. Daring deeds were his daily responsibility. He'd crawled into orc dens and come out alive, with an advance in rank, a fearsome scar on his neck, and a trophy or two that he didn't show the kiddies, to prove he was brave and deadly. He had let himself be talked into leading the incursion to steal a piece of the stone, not that he had needed much persuading. Coran agreed to go along, to help protect the party. They and five others were feted as heroes until the day they set out for the Chaos Scar.

Vanity! It was like to kill a being. And it had. Two died, in fact. Of the seven of them who had gone in, only five had returned, and none of those unscathed. They'd outwitted wizards and fought monstrous creatures. But they had the stone, a thing of beauty, a smooth, imperfect sphere of blue-green twice the size of a halfling's fist. The village was jubilant.

For a while. Ah, well, they were so good at telling themselves what brave folks they were, to have snatched a piece of the sacred stone, that they ignored the signs. Dame May hadn't. She told them it was a Chaos Shard, and was full of peril for them. They should have listened to the witch.

So they used it to invoke protections around Wenly Halt. The mayor, who fancied himself a bit of a wizard because he was good at household cantrips, had used the stone. He declared that nothing should pass through its borders without permission. Well, it kept out the goblins that had been making nighttime raids on the henhouses and barns. Traders who liked to sneak in without paying the toll-gate fee were forced to stump up or spend hours more on the road marching toward the next inn. The mayor was well pleased with his magic-making.

Then the wind died down. No one noticed the eerie calm or the stuffiness that followed, not when the river dammed up at the same time and flowed all the way around the village like it was in a glass bowl. You could see fish swimming up against the edge and turning back again. A stag chased a doe straight toward town. Both of them rammed into the nothing that was there, and fell over. The children were like to laugh themselves to pieces over it, but it alarmed Dame May and those who were coming around to her point of view. Illicit lovers with their tunics half undone chased out of town by angry husbands couldn't get home again without help. One of them was the son of the mayor himself. In embarrassment, the mayor had to turn to Coran to undo that spell. Well, they made plenty more mistakes like that, not so easily remedied with a night in the stocks or a plate of meat scraps.

Halflings, as good, decent folk, never realized what kind of dark thoughts some of them had about the others. The last straw, or so the village saw it, was when on behalf of the Moot

Court, the monthly call for judgment, the mayor declared with the stone's power behind him, that "the truth shall come out, no matter what!"

So money palmed by a thief screamed to be put back in the purse of the victim. That led to a few beatings. The bruises on the ruffians' flesh spoke out in gasping, breathless voices as to the manner of their infliction. Then the dead rose to speak out against their killers. The trauma of having to face deceased loved ones nearly drove families to their own end. Bab felt that was what drove Adda to the final edge of madness, not that he hadn't been going there for a long time.

Bab glanced over his shoulder at the locksmith. Adda ought to have stayed behind in Wenly Halt, but the others felt he was a good luck charm. He was lucky, but lucky for himself, not for them, if you asked Bab, because things that happened to other people just missed him, almost every time.

Still, Adda had a knack with a lock, magical or otherwise. In fact, the bespelled pouch that held their unwanted treasure had been tied and retied more than once, Bab could tell. He hoped that it had not lost any of the charm that kept the smooth rock safe. It was just that Adda couldn't resist looking. Priest Nock said it was a holy madness, though under the auspice of what god, no one knew. No amount of Nock praying and bothering his own patron deity had proved enough to reveal it. Bab guessed that He or She was one of the ones who had gone insane from power, the very sound of whose name would result in the ground being heaved asunder—well, wait, that had already happened. But Nock assured them Adda was preserved by a benevolent god, not an evil one, as that who reigned in the Scar.

In the meanwhile, Bab and the others needed supplies, and maybe a rest. He swaggered toward the rough-beamed trading post where the human with one silver eye held court. Everything cost too much in the Crossroads because it had to be carried in by cart or enforced labor. A halfling couldn't trust any food grown in the polluted local soil. Water for the foul-tasting beer in the Poisoned Chalice pub had to be distilled three times, but there was plain water, drawn from a couple of decently deep wells. It cost a toll to fill waterskins at them, but it was necessary. Each of them carried enough journeybread in their backpacks for a month's wandering, in case no other food was available, but Bab hated to live on those dry mouthfuls for more than a few days. Still, it paid to be prepared. The last time they'd come, they ran out of provisions. He wasn't risking it again.

The Scar was full of perils. Not only thugs and thieves waiting for a chance to jump helpless travelers and deprive them of valuables, life, or both. On their first journey inward, they had come up on an underground temple that just oozed ill will and death, but Coran's prognostications showed that a star stone was hidden there, and they hoped to secure it.

It had, indeed, held one of the Chaos Shards, but the stone was not unguarded. At the heart of an arena smelling of blood, Adda had caught sight of a halfling woman in mystic robes seated upon a throne surrounded by armed male halflings, and he had fallen for her at once. She was a bonny one, to be sure, but a whistle of appreciation from Adda brought the entire bodyguard racing for him. They had only managed to escape by swiftness of foot and Coran spilling all his magic out in illusions.

The silver-eyed man in the trading post had thought the story wildly funny when they had stopped for provisions on their way home. Morgana, that was the halfling's name, took slaves and tore the guts out of living captives. She rarely traveled to the neck of the pass, but it was always bad news for someone. At least they'd gotten out alive that time. Bab kept his one uncovered eye roving to ensure that Morgana was nowhere in sight.

A fist-sized rock whizzed toward Bab. He jumped to one side, in plenty of time for it to pass. He drew his small sword and showed the most vicious face he could in the direction of the line of buildings.

"Who did that?" he demanded.

The answer was a rain of stones. Bab lowered his face so that the old army helmet took the brunt. He waited until the clattering stopped and looked up. A pebble bounced off his shoulder and hit him on the nose. His eyes watered with the pain. Mad cackling echoed in the air.

"Who's doing that?"

Bab heard at least three voices tittering. They sounded like insane children.

"I don't see anyone," Scorri said. She was their scout, a thickset girl with a long brown braid hidden down the back of her heavy hogskin tunic and spiked leather anklets above her hairy, bare feet.

No one in the road seemed to be looking at them, but more missiles pelted them. Coran threw up a hand and pebbles fell at his feet. Legg, magicless, got hit right between the eyes.

"Brats! I'll learn you to stone me!" Legg cried, shaking his fist. Sword in hand, he ran in the direction of the attack. The cackling receded ahead of him.

"No, Legg!" Bab shouted. The man was just too hot-headed. He could get them all killed!

He ran after Legg. The others fell in behind him. The laughter led them through the rough streets, on past the stinking heap of refuse behind the trading post, and into the narrow passage between The Poisoned Chalice inn and leaning, dilapidated hovels. They emerged in the rolling wasteland beyond the makeshift village's environs. Bab spotted Legg dodging between stunted trees and bushes.

"Do you smell that?" Scorri asked.

Bab took in a breath, then gagged. A stench like rotting bodies flavored with hot ash and bitter metal stung his nose. "He's here! Legg, Mordint's here!"

The tall halfling racing ahead of them heard and turned around in mid stride. His face was pale with fear as he headed back to them. The earth wizard was one of two beings that none of them ever wanted to meet again. Bab cursed. Why didn't they bring an army? Of course Mordint wanted to find them! The stone had been the center of his unholy labyrinth!

The rock-throwers had to be tempters, then. These malign little imps were a product of the roiling evil that came from the star stone. They harassed or lured hapless travelers into following them. Most were never found again. Those who returned told tales of having had to fight their way free of a dark maw full of tongues and teeth. Mordint used them to lure unwary travelers to use as gifts to the dark spirits. Bab had had a taste of being tied to a post as tentacles licked around his legs. That'd never happen again.

The stench grew stronger and stronger. The earth wizard had to be close by. Bab cast around.

"Where is he? Can we hold him off?" Bab asked.

"Touch me," Coran commanded. "Everyone come close."

The half-elf dipped a hand into the black satchel hanging on his hip and emerged with a bubble of green glass. It glowed and began to grow, casting its peculiar light on the scrub grass. Bab felt as if he were holding a great shield before him. Adda dived to the ground and wrapped his arms around

Coran's ankles like a snake. The sphere grew until they were all contained within it.

All but Legg. He hurtled toward them, knees pumping under his leather jerkin. Ten feet to safety. Five feet. Bab stretched out an arm to pull him inside. Legg reached for it.

And vanished into thin air. The wail of his protest died out like the tolling of a distant bell.

"Curse him!" Bab snarled. It was Mordint's favorite trick. If not for Coran's spell, the rest of them might have been scooped up, too. "Where have they gone?"

Coran lowered his hands and the bubble faded away. Scorri sniffed the air. She pointed toward the west. "That way."

"We have to go after him," Coran said.

Adda nodded. "He'll be beyond the five doors and the eight traps."

Adda meant Mordint's lair. Five days' hard walk to the northwest. Well, they were going there anyhow.

Bab groaned. He checked the pouch at his belt to make certain it was secured. "We'd better go get our supplies."

"We're going the wrong way," Adda insisted again, as they turned toward the sunset. "We have to go back again." He'd said that at least once a mile.

"We are not going near Morgana's temple," Bab said sourly. It was the second day since they'd left the Crossroads. "Not again, not ever!"

"She fancied me," Adda said, his round face lit up beatifically. "Those eyes of hers—lovely, like shining chestnuts. And her hair! And that chest!"

"All I saw was the necklace of shriveled eyeballs hanging on it," Scorri said sourly. "And none of those matched."

They were retracing an unwelcome path. Chuuls lurked in the murky waterways and thick mud in the channel to the lower side of the narrow, irregular road. Bab kept the others well clear of it. He had had enough of tentacles to last him a lifetime.

Sunlight was a weird green-blue this close to the king's wall, as if it had to filter its way through all the malignity of the star stones. They walked a thin ridge of land that rose like a lizard's spine above the muddy valley to the left. They felt exposed on the road, but things in the half-shadowed hollows were worse.

The halflings' footfalls were silent enough not to attract the attention of most creatures, though Bab worried about noise from Coran. He wore tall boots with thick leather soles that scraped and tonked against the gravel and stones underfoot. Bab had to restrain himself from turning around and hissing "Shh!" at the enchanter.

He spared a thought now and again for Legg. He hoped the older halfling was alive. What bad luck that Mordint had been in the Crossroads unknown to them and still angry! If they'd known, they could have returned the stone to him there. Now the advantage belonged to the earth wizard. They would have to meet him on his own ground. Bab feared the encounter, but it was more necessary than ever, to free his old friend.

Mordint's stronghold was still a couple of days ahead of them. Instead of the month it had taken them wandering the rift to find a star stone exposed enough to reach, this time they knew just where they were going.

To be fair, they had thought at first the lair was abandoned. Coran's fourth attempt at a finding charm said that a stone was to be found a hundred yards off the main path to the north, along a faint uphill trail in the sparse grass occupied mostly by clattering, bronze-shelled centipedes the length of a halfling's body, and brown snails as large as Bab's fist. The entrance was a U-shaped gap underneath spiny, blue-green undergrowth cascading down the north cliff face of the trench that the descending star stone had dug on its way from the heavens. The cavern smelled horrible enough that no one wanted to be the first to go in, but the urgency of the pointing spell said the stone was a powerful one. Their greed—yes, greed—made them brave the stench.

Bab wasn't sure what he had expected, but what they saw was nowhere near his imaginings. The vast room in which they found themselves soared at least ten man-heights to a colorful dome filled with light. In the center of the room, a carved fountain played, its bowls overflowing onto the mucky floor. His halfling sense of what made a good home site told him it must have begun as a true cave, a bubble in stone, but it had been worked into a marvel by who-knew-how-many pairs of hands. The shining gray-and-black streaked walls had been slagged into glass by the passing meteor, but the craftsmen who had followed etched out pillars and statues ornamented with carved swags, vines, and leaves.

Between the wall's decorations were mystic-looking emblems that none of them, not even Coran, could identify. Gems were set into the glass, but the pillars would have to have been demolished to remove them. It looked as though thieves had tried in the past, leaving scratches on the fine carvings but succeeding in dislodging not one stone.

The thick layers of green mold encrusting the walls and the ankle-thick mud on the floor showed that no one had likely inhabited the building for years except the animals they found there, like more of the giant centipedes that scuttled everywhere, including up the walls and along the ceiling, and enormous bull-headed frogs whose deep voices echoed off the mosaic vault above. Other things, including lost or forgotten treasures, may have been buried in the muck on the floor. Either way, it stank too much for any of them to want to root around and find them.

The charm indicated the stone they wanted was below them. Scorri scouted for a way, and led them to a place where the floor sloped precipitously downward. A marvelously ornate twisted post formed into the shape of a crouching man with a blocky head stood sentry at the top of the ramp. It had to be a staircase. Deep mud concealed the risers. Bab drew his sword and led the way, squelching through the slime.

When he touched the stair rail, the place came to life, literally.

Bab shook his head in disbelief at the memory. The man-shaped newel post had risen up, creaking and shedding dust. Its eyes burst into red flame. They lit upon the halflings. The stone man came toward them, swinging its arms. Bab had jumped back. The creature's fists slammed down on the stair where he had been standing only a second before. The companions ran down the flight, only to find the match of the stone man at the bottom, rising from the second post. Out of carvings along the walls came more men. Bab snatched the hammer off his back and pounded down on the nearest statue's foot. It cracked. The creature teetered over, still grabbing for him as it fell.

Bab and the others ducked and leaped to stay out of their way. It wasn't too hard; the stone men were clumsy and slow moving, but they were inexorable. Coran threw one enchantment after another trying to break the charm that gave them life, but it was just beyond his talents. Sometimes they paused, but always they came on. It was all Legg and Milner could do to keep them off the diminutive half-elf. They fled blindly into the darkness.

Slim, agile Dimon was a genius at lighting a lantern on the run. He had a flame going before they had gone a dozen yards. Bab almost wished he hadn't. The yellow light picked out pairs of multi-faceted eyes by the score. He called for the party to get into formation around Coran. Putting all of his power into his huge hammer, he swung into the midst of the enormous spiders, sending bodies and limbs flying.

They fought hard, slamming doors behind them, but always found more beasts and perils beyond. Adda noticed a loose stone in the floor before anyone else, keeping them from plummeting into a hollow shaft that seemed to descend to the center of the earth. Each of them leaped across the gap in turn. That was when Dimon ran into a web stretched across the corridor. They were cutting him loose when the master of the house turned up.

Bab's heart had almost stopped in his body. No mistaking a master wizard. The tall, austere man with the long, gray mustache arrived surrounded by a wreath of green light— and a stench that could kill a pig at a hundred paces. Bab didn't think anything alive could smell so bad, not even an orc—especially not a human. Mordint—they didn't find out his name until later—stank like a midden heap gone horribly bad. No wonder he lived as alone as possible, leagues away from civilization. He pointed his fingers, and lightning roared toward them. Coran got his wits together in time, though not fast enough to save Dimon. Bab still shuddered to recall his horrible death.

They fought in and out of doors that seemed to open on different rooms every time one ran through them. Bab remembered lots of shouting, especially by Coran trying to get them all back in one place. At last the half-elf got them together in a protective bubble, but not in safety.

The tall wizard had his beasts herd them toward the end of a long room lit by torches. Stone columns threw great shadows toward them like sinister fingers. Tied to one pillar by the wall was the remains of . . . Bab didn't like to guess what, or who. The manic laughter that arose seemingly from the walls chilled his blood. Then came the slap of damp, narrow feelers against their bodies like a combination of wet vines and dog tongues. One wound around Bab's neck, making him jump and shiver. He struck out at the thing he could not see, and felt the trailer slither downward and detach from his skin. The creatures could be killed! With a war cry, he rallied his companions to defend themselves.

He swung his grandfather's hammer, feeling it connect with invisible flesh. No matter how many of the invisible beasts Bab slew, more were behind them. Coran's magic was overwhelmed. The little enchanter went down and was held by things no one could see. Bab fought to help him.

Suddenly he was no longer in the midst of the beasts, but up against a pillar of stone. The evil wizard had swept him up by magic, and put him just where he didn't want to be. Legg appeared beside him, his sword arm plastered across his body as if he had just delivered a blow.

Before they knew it, five of them were against the columns, and tied there by magical bonds. The wizard began to chant. Bab and the others were once again crowded by the unseen creatures, all laughing and hooting in their ears. The carved stone dug into his back as he recoiled from them. His feet were engulfed by wet creepers. More lapped at his face. He was overcome with trembling dread. The wizard's chanting reached a crescendo.

In the midst of a thunderous pronouncement, Mordint went silent. Bab stopped struggling for a moment to look up in disbelief. The tall wizard's eyes rolled up in his filthy face. He toppled backward.

The next thing Bab knew, a knife blade was sawing up through the bonds of his pinioned arms. The rush of blood returning to his hands was more painful than the binding. Scorri, the only one of their number not to have been captured by the wizard, had struck him down. It had been a lucky stone from her sling that shouldn't have gotten through his defenses that hit Mordint square in the forehead. She cut them all free—all but Milner. The look on his still, dead face said that the fear had stopped his heart.

Without Mordint, the living defenders were more fearful, less organized. Bab used his military expertise to organize his people into a defensive position. Coran threw his most powerful enchantment on the prone wizard to keep him unconscious as long as possible. Moving forward behind each swing of Bab's hammer, they fought their way out of the pillar room. They still felt terrible fear, but survival depended upon ignoring it.

Keeping the enemy behind them, they fled in the direction of the stone. Adda managed to close and lock numerous doors between them and the stone men. Coran, running ahead of them with Scorri, called out to them in triumph.

The Chaos Shard was embedded in the wall in a very small chamber sandwiched between a reeking closestool and a cupboard jammed with decayed vellum scrolls that were of curiosity only as firelighters. Bab was frantic to get the Shard free of its setting and be on their way home again.

With the stone guardians pounding on the last of the doors, Bab kept urging Adda to hurry. Suddenly, the door burst asunder. The stone men tramped in, swinging their arms. Legg went flying. Just as the halflings were about to have to fight for their lives, Adda had let out a cry of joy. The stone had popped free.

The moment he did it, the stone men all fell down lifelessly. Bab stared unbelievingly, then came to his senses. He wrapped the glowing rock in a pouch. The survivors ran as if their feet were on fire out of the stronghold and didn't stop until it was a league or better behind them.

They returned to Wenly Halt heroes. The two lost half-lings were remembered fondly, and the town thought it had a treasure for the ages.

With the odd-colored sunlight beating down on his head, Bab reminded himself that he was not trapped in that dark hellhole any longer. It had featured often in his nightmares. He thought he could feel those tentacles on his legs again, almost as if they were real, the clammy grip tightening on his ankle . . .

Wait a moment, that *was* real!

He looked down. A gray claw was just closing on his foot. He knew what it was. Revulsion and fear turned his stomach upside down.

"Chuul!" he bellowed.

The hideous creature, part serpent, part bug, and part crab, slithered up the bank toward him. He seized his dagger and struck out at the pincer. It tightened and tried to pull him toward the ravine. The others drew arms and rushed to help him.

Fleshy creepers surged up through the mud as another chuul reared up its serpentine head. It seized Scorri's neck and pulled her off her feet, dragging her toward the edge of the path where the waving tentacles waited. Adda threw himself on it and chopped at it, spraying shiny gray blood around. Meanwhile, Bab hacked away at the claw holding his leg. The chuul hissed. It tried to latch on to his arm or throat with the other claw.

He darted his blade around, stabbing at random, so it could not guess his attack. It managed to thump him in the side of the head. He gasped, seeing stars. The beast outweighed them by several hundredweight. If it dragged them into the murky water, they were done for. The tentacles stunned victims so that they could be popped into the creature's maw without struggling.

"There's only a couple of them," Adda shouted, panting. He hacked at the beast with his dagger. Both he and Scorri kicked and struggled against the snapping claws.

Bab spared a glance to count limbs and realized he was right. But to say "only two chuuls" was like saying only two plagues. He dropped the dagger and brought his hammer around.

He smashed it down on the claw tugging him along the ground. Pieces of shell went flying. It was only a small chip compared to the size of the beast, but the chuul let out a high-pitched shriek. It darted for him with the other claw, dislodging Adda. Bab rolled as fast as he could, avoiding the hideous pincer. The claw nipped his ear and pulled a lock of his hair out. He bellowed in pain. It made another grab for him.

Adda jumped onto the other creature's back and hacked at its head, putting himself in reach of those deadly tentacles. It reared, trying to dump the skinny halfling into the murky water. Adda kicked it in the back of the head and jumped free. It took him around the chest with its claw, but it was the wounded one. Bab smashed at it with his hammer. Adda jabbed his chuul in the face. It dropped him and darted the second claw for his neck. Bab connected with his chuul's wrist. The claw loosened. He took the opportunity and kicked it the rest of the way open. He fell to the ground at its feet. It reared up, preparing to strike again.

". . . spirits of winter, heed my plea!"

Bab heard Coran chanting. A white object flew over his head and struck the creature in its armored chest. It stopped in mid grab. A clear, shining film covered it all over. It teetered and fell backward into the water with a titanic splash. Mud splattered the halflings on the bank.

"Ice won't hold it long, I fear," Coran said. His cherubic face looked drawn.

"Well done," Bab said, clambering to his feet. "Can you do it again to the other?"

"Not yet. Give me . . . time." The half-elf stood with his hands propped on his knees, panting.

"There isn't time! Scorri is nearly over the edge!" Bab ran to help Adda, with Coran stumbling along behind.

Swish! A gray tentacle made a pass at Bab's head. He ducked. A mere edge of it touched his cheek. He lost all feeling in his face. His mouth hung open as he gasped in air. He pounded at the chuul's shoulder as if he were beating a pot into shape. Scorri held onto the edge of the path, kicking to stay out of the water. Her face was turning purple. Adda clung to the claw arm. Gobbets of foul flesh flew, but he seemed not to be weakening the beast very much.

Tiny arrows of light peppered the creature's ugly face. It turned its head to look at Coran. One of the tentacles whipped out and caught the half-elf around the thigh. It dropped Scorri and started to reel in the enchanter. Adda ran to help the scout to her feet.

Conscious of the danger of touching the gray flesh, Bab ran after the small wizard, jumping up to strike at the chuul. His hammer bounced off its muscular sides, but he kept at it. The chuul slithered over the edge of the path and kept going. Coran was going to drown if they couldn't stop it.

Bab threw himself on his belly, grabbing for Coran's arm. The half-elf locked wrists with him. The chuul bellowed and kept going. It became a ridiculous tug of war, but Bab was determined not to let the half-elf fall into the muddy water. He braced his heels in the bank and held on. The chuul slithered over the edge, still pulling. Coran's face was pale. Bab thought his muscles were about to pull off his bones when the chuul gave a tremendous tug and submerged. Bab went flying backward on the churned-up bank.

He feared he had lost Coran, but the small enchanter dropped on top of him, knocking all his breath out. They lay nose to nose and gasped for a moment.

"Are you all right? Did it sting you?" Bab asked.

Coran rolled over and patted himself down. His robes were disheveled and stained, but largely intact. "All's well and in place." He displayed one stockinged foot. "It got my boot."

And indeed it had. Bab looked over the edge. The chuuls were tossing the leather boot back and forth like a ball, probably checking to see if a tasty morsel like the half-elf's foot was still inside.

"Come on!" Bab said, retrieving his hammer. "We need to get away before they decide that's inedible and they want the rest of you."

"No," Coran said, pulling his pouch around and feeling in it. "I need that boot! I can't walk barefoot like you halflings."

Bab groaned and plumped down next to Coran. Scorri and Adda all but crawled up to join them. The small wizard came out with a twisted thread.

"What's that for?" Adda asked.

"To snare my boot," Coran said. He spread the thread out on his palm and ran his finger along it. A ghost of the thread rose above them and elongated into a glowing rope with a noose on the end. It sailed toward the chuuls. He stretched out on his stomach. Bab and Adda held on to each of his legs. Coran wiggled the rope to try and catch the bouncing boot.

Bab sniffed the air. "Does that spell always smell so bad?"

"Never," Coran said, wrinkling his nose. Bab turned to the others. "Did one of you fart?"

Scorri looked outraged. "No! There's not enough devil's wind in *any* halfling to make that smell."

"Then . . . ?"

A shadow fell over them. Bab flipped over.

Mordint leered down on them. Bab gawked at him. The lanky sorcerer raised his arms. Clouds of flies buzzed around his armpits.

With his elf reflexes, Coran was the first to act. He flung his hand toward the sorcerer. Tiny silver darts flew in a cloud. Mordint dashed them away from his face. Coran screwed up his face and launched a cloud of white mist from his open palm. That made the grimy human recoil and bat at his eyes. The halflings scrambled up and started running away.

The path was no longer unoccupied, though. Bodies, weirdly misshapen creatures, blocked their way with spears and polearms. Before Bab could stop, he ran straight into a filthy, wild-eyed form.

"It's me!" Legg exclaimed, reaching out for him.

"No!" Bab shouted to the others, raising his hammer. "He made a zombie out of Legg!"

Legg moved in and knocked his arm upward.

"I'm not a zombie, you fool," he said, grinning. His teeth gleamed ivory in his mud-splashed face. "He hasn't hurt me. I told him why we're here."

Bab drew his hammer close to him and studied the other halfling. Under the layers of grime, Legg *looked* all right, but sorcery had deluded countless people before, and most of them were dead. He held the thread on his wrist close to Legg's face. It didn't glow. Bab tried it on the orc with the too-small helmet on his head standing beside his old friend, then on the hobgoblins and the who-knew-what-it-was snake-beast behind them. The thread burst into green light. Legg nodded encouragement.

"D'ye see? All he wants is his property back."

Bab nodded slowly. He turned around. His eyes traveled straight up the looming figure of the wizard who was suddenly at his back. At this close a range, Mordint's stench was near unbelievable. Bab breathed through his mouth. Very carefully, he reached into the pouch on his belt and removed the star stone. It felt smooth and cool, but hungry, as though it wanted to suck his soul out through his palm. Gingerly, he held it out to Mordint, who snatched it away and held it to his chest. The halflings stood trembling.

"Much better," Mordint crooned. The stone burst into brilliant blue-green light, casting a sickly shadow on the wizard's face. He raised the Shard over his head. "*Kasin!*" A beam of blinding white light lanced from the stone. Bab dropped to his knees. The beam passed over their heads and slammed into the nearby slope. Hot molten rock poured down the incline. Smithereens shot out in every direction. "Yes, good!"

He tucked it away in a pocket in his filthy sleeve. "Make ready!" he shouted. The ragtag force formed into an irregular square on the path.

Bab's heart was in his throat, but he managed to get words out.

"So, er, master wizard, why are we still alive?"

Mordint turned back to him and smiled, showing a mouthful of large, square, yellow teeth.

"You shouldn't be," the earth wizard intoned, his voice sounding like the knell of doom. "You're the cause of my present difficulty."

"Difficulty, master?"

"Yes!" Mordint scowled down at him. Thunderclouds formed around his head, and miniature lightning struck at his shoulders. "It is all thanks to *you* that I have lost my castle!"

Bab blanched. "Uh, how's that, master?"

For the first time, the mage looked discomfited. "When you removed the Chaos Shard from its setting, you caused my power to diminish. Without my stone minions I was too weak to defend it against the dwarf mage Hochster. How he heard of the theft, I don't know."

Bab blanched. Well, he and his companions hadn't been any too subtle about bragging about their conquest in the trading post, he recalled, but he didn't dare say so to Mordint. Word must have spread from there to this Hochster, whoever he was.

"No idea, master," he said, crossing his fingers, hoping the gods would forgive him the fib.

"I fought for months to dislodge him, but to no avail. I realized I required a force of my own to take it back. I went to the Crossroads to enlist willing soldiers." His eyes glowed like the Shard as he leaned over the halflings. "Welcome to my army."

"Oh, but surely, now that you have the stone, you don't need us," Bab said hastily.

Mordint stretched out a hand. "*Hoit!*" Coran's boot came flying and landed in the half-elf's arms. The tentacles felt around for it, then subsided into the mire with a *bloop*. "Fall in," he ordered them. "We have distance to cover. You know the way."

"Never!" Scorri sneered.

Mordint shrugged. "Then you'll die now." He raised a finger

and aimed it at the scout. She stood her ground, though her face went pale. Bab jumped between them.

"Hold on, hold on! We only came to return the stone, not fight, master."

"And that you will do," Mordint assured them. "The mystic force that placed it in the wall of my cavern should not have been broken by any force but mine. I want to see how you did it, so it cannot ever happen again. When my army rises again, you shall be free. You have my word," he finished grandly.

Bab doubted that. The halflings all looked at one another. They knew. The moment the stone men came back to life, they were all dead. Though they wanted to repay the debt, they didn't want to add their lives to the sum. But at that moment they had no choice. They fell in line. Bab had to think hard.

Mordint didn't have any stone men along, but his powers and his mercenaries were fearsome enough. His gnoll master sergeant marched them hard upland toward the underground fortress, with a whip over their heads to hurry them along.

"We can't work for him," Scorri hissed as they were hustled along the ridge road. "He's evil! You can smell it!"

"Can you think of an alternative?" Legg growled at them. "It's help or die!"

Mordint wasn't much for small talk. He didn't stop them from discussing anything they wanted. It was futile, of course. In the midst of his makeshift army, they couldn't get away.

Besides the soldiers they could see, including orcs, goblins, and hordes of slithering centipedes, were two enormous wagons driven by humans. One held food, and the other armaments and magical gear. Bab could feel the tempters around them, too. Once in a while an invisible tongue tasted his hand. Ugh.

It didn't stop him from making plans to escape when they could. He calculated all the weapons with any magical virtue they had at their disposal: Legg's bow, Scorri's sling, his hammer, and whatever Coran kept in his pouch. None of it amounted to much. Still, a good general kept everything in mind. You never knew what would save your life.

Mordint left Thangrik, the orc with the ill-fitting helmet, guarding them under an overhang while he issued orders to the others at a planning session around a bonfire. Bab could hear only a little, but it sounded like Mordint had thought his plan well through. He split his force into three smaller squads under the command of two bigger orcs and the snake-thing. With a look over his shoulder at the halflings, Mordint lowered his voice.

"He's talking about us," Legg said, shivering in his cloak. An attempt by Coran to start a campfire had been stomped out by the orc. Their food, which came from the communal pot tended by one of the disreputable-looking humans, was always cold by the time it reached them, but there was plenty of it.

"Aye," Bab said, trying to look at ease under the heavy-browed gaze of Thangrik and the worried eyes of his fellows. "Just thinking how he's going to keep his promise to us."

"Do you believe him?" Adda asked eagerly. Scorri looked up from her plate of stew with a scornful expression.

"As much as he deserves," Bab said. He shared a glance with Coran. He didn't want the locksmith going off on a crazy rant and drawing attention to them out of fear of death. Better to be gray shadows creeping in Mordint's shadow.

Even the halflings' sturdy feet were sanded smooth by the gritty roads by the time they heaved within half a league of the stronghold. The pathway looked different, notwithstanding the overcast sky showering it with misty raindrops. It had been straightened out and rid of its covering of rough grass.

Grumbling, Mordint sent a couple of invisible tempters to spy out the scene. The rest of them waited out of sight of the cavern entrance.

Though no one could see them, everyone could tell when they returned by the soggy feeling in the air. Whispers went through the ranks as Mordint conferred. Thirty dwarves were below ground, with the lord and master, Hochster, in the grand hall.

Mordint strode over to loom above Bab and his companions. They sprang to their feet. He carried a pierced bronze pot on a chain that belched yellow smoke smelling of singed hair. He revolved the pot over their heads and chanted in a tongue that made the skin crawl. When they tried to escape from the foul fumes, Thangrik and a couple of the invisible tongues prodded them back into place. Coran, still in control of his own actions, held up a spiked silver charm, but it was batted out of his hand by Mordint's next swing.

"I am not foolish enough to rely upon your word that you will do what I say," Mordint said as the half-elf scrambled on the ground to retrieve his amulet. "So heed my words. You will return my stone to its setting and place it exactly as you found it." He placed the blue-green rock in Bab's palm.

Bab wanted to protest that he would have done that anyway, but it was hard to speak with the smoke filling his lungs. He swayed on his feet. Mordint held his gaze with his mud-colored eyes. When he broke off to stare at Scorri, Bab felt as if something had been wrapped around his head. The wizard withdrew the censer and stalked away.

"It's a geas," Coran said gloomily. "We're fixed now."

"At least he didn't put a curse on us for after," Legg said. "We can leave if we want after we're through."

"If we can," Scorri said doubtfully.

"We will," Bab assured them, hefting the smooth stone in his hand. It felt just as unwelcome as it did the first time. "I don't know how yet, but we will."

The orc held them back while Mordint blasted open the entrance to the cavern with a spell that tore the earth back as if it were made of leather. Flanked by his force of orcs and other minions, he strode inside. Bab heard shouts of challenge and yells of pain.

Thangrik urged them forward and inside as soon as the threshold, or what was left of it, was clear. Bab almost hesitated before stepping inside. The smell of burning flesh and leather made his throat sting, but he forgot all about it when he saw what was ahead.

The place was *clean*. Apart from the debris of the explosion that had opened the door, the cavern was spotless. No more mold, mud, or grime anywhere. No wonder Mordint was outraged!

The author of his distress was obvious to them all. The earth wizard stood facing a stocky dwarf with linen yellow hair and eyes to match, braids to his knees and a beard to his feet. His own minions shot arrows at the invading orcs from behind the prone bodies of the stone giants that lay all over the floor. The two enchanters paid no attention to anyone but one another. They chanted at the top of their voices and threw handfuls of power, each seeking to destroy the other. A burst of fire flung by Hochster exploded over the halflings' heads. They hit the ground and took cover. Thangrik grabbed two of them by the scruffs and hauled them to their feet.

"Let's go," he said. "His magicness said you knew the way. Get moving!"

Coran had the presence of mind to put up a semblance of invisibility around them. Scorri led them around the walls as they dodged thrown furniture, severed heads, splashes of blood, and the edges of spells. Bab stayed at her shoulder, batting bodies out of the way with his hammer. Legg held his bow nocked in case anyone got in their way. Thangrik lurked behind them with his saw-edged sword, grinning like a fool. Bab sensed he was enjoying himself. He probably had orders to kill them all when they were done with their task.

The stairs were denuded of their newel posts, but Scorri was sure of herself as she went downward. The others followed cautiously on the immaculate stairs. Everything looked so different that Bab doubted his own memory of the place. He had to go by the ceilings to be certain they were even in the same building. The traps in the floor had been replaced by new paving stones, the cut marks still fresh on the surface. Scorri led them unerringly through the confusing maze.

They disturbed a dwarf with a long red beard putting a stack of clean white linens into the cupboard beside the stone's empty socket. He drew the huge axe at his side and came toward them swinging. Legg loosed an arrow that lodged in the dwarf's shoulder. It didn't slow him down at all. Thangrik waded forward, swinging. Legg and Scorri lent their strength to the battle.

"Help me! Hochster's men, help!" the dwarf yelled.

"Silence him!" Coran hissed.

Bab's eyes went wide. He remembered the remaining two beads around his neck. He grabbed one and flung it into the dwarf's beard.

"Hush!" he said.

The redhead's mouth moved but no sound came from it. His eyes went wide with despair. Thangrik grinned and stalked his now soundless prey. The dwarf took to his heels with the orc in pursuit. Coran and the others took up guard positions around the cupboard.

Adda stood at the empty gray socket in the wall, staring blankly at the stone in his hand. He looked up at Bab.

"I can't do it," he said.

"Course you can," Bab insisted. "Hurry it up."

"No, you don't see it," the locksmith said. "There's agony in there. Unbelievable agony."

"There's agony if you don't do it," Bab said. "We'll all die! Mordint put a spell on us."

Adda shook his head. "Death'd be less painful."

His usual scatterbrained expression was gone. He looked sane as a judge. Bab knew that was more dangerous than flightiness. But it was Adda's natural talent of undoing traps, puzzles, and enigmas that had made it possible to remove it. Was there any way to bring it back? Hating himself, he took the locksmith by his skinny shoulders.

"Adda . . . think how proud Morgana will be of you if . . . *when* you succeed."

Adda blinked a couple of times. "She will?"

"Aye, old friend. That beauty, all aimed your way. Think of it! You can tell her all about it."

Bab was both glad and dismayed, but the light went on in Adda's eyes. He hefted the glowing stone, almost smiling, and fitted it into the setting. The smile didn't leave his face even when terrifying blue sparks leaped out of the rock face and danced across his hands, leaving black streaks on his flesh. He turned the stone this way and that, as if it was a dial he had to set just right. The sparks went from blue to red to yellow. Adda's knees buckled. Bab put his shoulder under his arm to support him. Pain lanced through his body wherever he touched Adda. He was horribly sorry for the locksmith.

"Can I finish that for you?" he asked.

"No . . . yes."

"Leave it!" Legg said, over his shoulder. "You got the stone in place. That's all we promised!"

"No," Bab said. He could feel the yellow smoke rising in his lungs, but that wasn't what made him stand his ground. "It's not. If the stone men don't move, Mordint will know we didn't do what he asked. Besides," he added, "I keep my promises. We all do. That's why we're here, spell or no spell."

"I *hate* it when you're logical!" the older halfling snapped. "But you're right."

"Turn it," Adda said faintly. "Like the wards in a lock."

Coran and Scorri took Adda and helped him to sit down. Bab put his hand to the stone. It felt as if lightning shot through his body. His hair stood up and crackled on his head. He had made his share of locks, but they were big, hefty ones for securing cattle fences and the like, not delicate ones like Adda made. As he turned the stone back and forth, he felt what Adda had, the rightness as the Shard settled into its old place.

"I can do it," he said. "Get ready to run."

And it hurt like blazes, like handling a piece of hot iron without his gloves, but he was used to that. Forcing himself to forget the pain, he shoved the stone hard over to the right and felt it settle in finally and for all.

"Look out!" Scorri shouted. Bab turned in time to see a stone giant rising from the floor. It came toward him, its arms swinging. He dodged it and pulled his hammer around. His fingers were scorched black, but they still moved.

The halflings made for the corridor. Scorri took the lead and began to count off doorways. All around them, the stone men stirred into action, seeking to pound anything they could reach. Bab was determined that it would be orcs or dwarves they attacked, not halflings or half-elves.

They scaled the last staircase just as the newel post men were picking themselves up from the floor. The second one caught Legg with a backhanded swipe that sent him flying into a pillar. Bab threw himself at the giant's feet, hammering chips until the stone man toppled over.

In the great hall, Mordint and Hochster stood face to face. Stone guardians lurched around the room, taking vengeance on the dwarf warriors as well as orcs and hobgoblins. Bab signed toward the door.

Suddenly, he felt the mud-colored gaze upon him.

"Guardians!" Mordint yelled. "The prisoners!" He started to shout words in that harsh-sounding language.

"Curses be upon those halflings!" Hochster bellowed. He raised his hands and began to chant.

"I can't forestall both of them," Coran warned.

"Scorri!" Bab said. He yanked the last precious blue bead off the string at his neck. "Can you land this between those two?"

The scout was pale, but she unlimbered her sling. "I'll try," she said. She wound up and pitched it, just as the smoke of enchantment was beginning to rise around each wizard. The blue marble hit Mordint straight in the throat.

"Hush!" Bab bellowed.

And the center of the great room went suddenly silent. Mordint glared. He could shout no orders, nor chant spells. Bab didn't let his companions linger. They fought their way out past orcs and stone guardians, but as soon as they were over the threshold, they could outdistance anything but a spell. They ran for their lives.

The sun passed overhead and headed for the horizon behind them, but Bab and the others didn't stop until after they went past the place they had gone to ground the last time. They shared journeybread and a sip of brackish water in their skins, and just lay back on the spare grass to gasp.

"I've never been so grateful to be going home empty-handed," Legg chuckled. He'd lost the last two fingers on his left hand and had a bruise the size of his head on his thigh. Coran clucked over him and readied healing remedies, but Legg waved him away. "Never mind. Hardly use them. Still have my bow fingers. And my life, thanks to you, my friends."

"Bab did it at the last," Adda said.

"I'm proud of us all," Bab said. "Never again, no matter what foolish notions the elders have." He toasted the five of them with his waterskin.

"Let's get us a real meal at the Poisoned Chalice when we reach the Crossroads," Legg said. "I'll pay. Hang the cost! Couldn't be worse than Mordint's vittles."

"Aye," Bab said wearily. "I'll be glad of a sit down. No more excitement."

"No more," Coran agreed.

"Shh!" Scorri said. "Do you hear that?"

Bab nodded. There was the sound of many feet on the road, not far away. They gathered up their packs and scrambled up the embankment and into what small cover was afforded by the scrawny brush and gathering twilight.

A torchlit procession of humans and halflings stalked by. Their clothes were dusty and worn, but each of them was armed to the teeth with sword, buckler, and enough daggers to make them clatter. On the shoulders of six of them was a litter draped with blood-red embroidered tapestries and cushions. On them reposed a figure that made Bab's heart sink.

"Morgana!" Adda crowed, rising up from behind a bush.

He held out his arms to the halfling woman. "Remember me? I love you!"

The parade turned as one being to stare. Screaming, Morgana sat up and jabbed a point-nailed forefinger toward the locksmith.

Bab grabbed Adda by the shoulder and hauled him up over the rise. Exhausted as he was, he found the strength somewhere to run into the gloom. The others fell into step behind him.

With any luck at all, they could lose the horde somewhere in the Crossroads.

Jody Lynn Nye lists her main career activity as "spoiling cats." She lives northwest of Chicago with one of the above and her husband, author and packager Bill Fawcett. She has published more than forty books, including seven contemporary fantasies, five SF novels, four novels in collaboration with Anne McCaffrey, including *Crisis on Doona* and *Treaty at Doona*; edited a humorous anthology about mothers, *Don't Forget Your Spacesuit, Dear!*; and produced over a hundred short stories. Her latest books are *A Forthcoming Wizard* (TOR Books), *Myth-Fortunes,* her seventh collaboration with Robert Asprin in the *Myth-Adventures* series, and *Dragons Deal* (Ace Books), the third in Asprin's *Dragons* series.

THE DECAYING MANSIONS OF MEMORY

JAY LAKE

Character

The tavern bench creaked beneath Horn like a ship under sail. He swayed, listening to the wood pop and snap, knowing if he were afloat, he'd be leaking.

Leaking. Horn laughed at the thought. He'd leaked plenty in his day, and had the scars to prove it, by Set.

A pewter bowl of scrumpy sizzled before him. The truly rotten stuff, made from a ferment of windfall apples, brewer's yeast, and an occasional unlucky wasp. The cheap stuff, too. Cheap was definitely his milieu these days.

There had been a villa once, overlooking the sea. Pounding surf, pliant servants, and fine wines from distant islands.

He remembered watching the weather move over the Bight of Winds, tall clouds purpling on the horizon as forked legs of lightning strode the ocean. Silks billowed around him, water quivered in the Khaliki crystal vases, and he'd laughed at the powers of the natural world.

Bad idea, that. With age came wisdom. Sometimes wisdom came with an ass kicking, too. And nothing could kick ass like the whole world.

Horn pulled himself away from the decaying mansions of memory. That was an escape offering small improvement on the present moment. A present moment which unfortunately still included scrumpy.

Now *there* was a beverage of the gods. Small, bitter gods that resented the world and everyone in it. He stared into the muddy amber depths before summoning what served for his courage these days and grasping the bowl to drink deep, his entire two coppers' worth in as few goes as possible to get past the gag reflex.

Fate hung heavy in the silk pocket hidden inside Horn's ogre-leather vest. Squared off, with corners sharp enough to slice up a life. He could almost hear its voice mocking him, unless he was drunk enough to drown it out.

More scrumpy.

Once Horn had been a young man—human, mind you, no blood or brood mixing in *his* tribe—a fine figure of a warrior with secret talents nurtured deep in the Sacred Caverns so that people who did not look beyond a curved sword and spiked buckler were in for a nasty surprise.

Not that he wasn't a skilled fighter in his own right. He'd mastered finesse with point and sharp edge and bladed edge and even the butt end reversed in hand. He could wield the buckler as a second weapon with effectiveness that sometimes surprised even his teachers and the other young men of the tribe. Horn had hunted goblins, orcs, and ogrillons through the jagged hills west of the village since he'd been old enough to run alongside his older brothers and cousins with a stout stick in hand. He was used to cuts, bruises, even broken bones. Like all the young men of his tribe, he was toughened by life and custom and training until he was fit to be a sellsword among the coastal cities where sharp-edged young men with stamina and skill were always in high demand.

His tribe had fought their way out of the grinding poverty of the hills in the most literal sense possible.

But Horn knew he was something special. Feather, one of the oldest of the Old Men, had spent long nights under moons both brilliant and grave-dark showing him other paths. Wisdom, perhaps, but even more, what the casual observer might have called magic. Hill country wizard lore, in truth. And for all the shared, common bluster of his training at sword and fist, those times working with rare herbs and strange powders and the lights that danced in the seams of the world were never spoken of.

No ordinary sellsword, he. Horn had sworn a private oath on his fourteenth birthday that he would someday be master of a castle, a harem, and a legion of warriors. He'd sealed the rite with a solemn binding spell that made the very air crackle like winter ice on the rivers, followed by a bloody libation spilled from the palm of his own hand. Both sides of his nature, in other words.

The following month he'd gone down to Beggar's Cairn with the other young men to meet the hiring agents who'd ridden up from the swordmarkets of distant Purpure, High Canton, and Grandport.

The scrumpy went down hard as watered armor polish, tasting somehow of tin and leather in the bargain. Not that anyone drank scrumpy for the taste. Least of all Horn.

The tavern was, like all worthwhile bars, quiet, grubby, and sour-smelling. Good beer was brewed and sold somewhere in these lands, but this was not the place for it. So far as he knew, the tavern never closed. Rough-hewn tables, mismatched chairs and benches, a niggardly fireplace that heated nothing, a surly barmaid with a face so rough and pinched that even an orc would think twice before catching her about the waist.

Exactly how he liked his drinking.

The sun was nooning outside as decent men followed their ploughs or worked their forges or whatever the hell it was decent men did. Only the crippled veterans, hopeless vagabonds, and truly dedicated drunks like Horn were in their cups this early. Indecent men in an indecent place.

When had his world grown to include the idea of decency? Horn could no longer recall. The scrumpy was doing his thinking for him already. Which was, of course, the point.

He had too much to forget but not enough to remember. Fate was a bitter mistress at the best of times. It was an unwise mage indeed who ever trusted in her, for all that she was the patron of warriors when they stepped into the forest of blades that was the world.

Laughing on a pitching deck as the sea boiled over the lower rail. Blood ran in the scuppers, fresh-bright as it was washed away into the heaving bosom of the ocean. Horn traced the masts with bright fire for the sheer joy of watching his own fingers burst into flame. The surviving crew screamed their terror as his leathers sparked with the stuff, shadowed by the cresting waves that threatened to drive them under.

The sullen barmaid wandered past his table, very nearly flicking him with a sodden rag. "You're a sorry one," she muttered.

Horn focused on her through the bleary eyes of scrumpy and memories. A dozen replies hung in his head, but his tongue was too thick to spit them out, and he had no sword to back them up. Instead he went back to his drinking. Cheating fate was serious business.

Still the silk pocket hung heavy beneath his vest. Taunting, always taunting.

— ◆ —

Purpure had been a city founded by a mage of extraordinary ability, and it showed. The woman was long gone into death, transcendence, or whatever fate ultimately befell those paragons of power, but her influence remained in the breathtakingly graceful lavender towers that soared over the teeming streets. Down in the gutters, the city looked much like any other city in Horn's then-limited experience, but all he had to do was raise his eyes to be reminded of the glory of power undimmed down the long ages.

His daily life was far more gutter than glory. Somehow in the two years since coming down out of the hills, Horn had found himself at swordspoint far more than his more eldritch talents had been called for. He *looked* like a strapping barbarian to the eyes of the city-bred. The Purpureides treated him like one.

Still, it was work of sword and knife. Horn had learned much in the employ of Saanreich the Fat, merchant-adventurer. Saanreich collected interesting enemies almost as fast as he collected strange art and stranger artifacts from distant shores. Not to mention the cellars of his own city. The ethics of such a trade were beyond Horn's ken, but they were not his problem, either. His problem was to keep rude or troublesome strangers from bothering Saanreich the Fat.

That, he was good at. He grew more skilled, learning about city fighting, underground labyrinths, and their sorts of traps—stone, wood, blade, and bone. City lessons. The sort a boy in the hills might never learn. The sort that kept him alive.

But it was all fighting. And sneaking. Defending through offense, eliminating strangers as needful before they had a chance to become rude or troublesome.

All the while sampling the taverns and markets and bordellos of Purpure. He learned other lessons, was initiated into warmer secrets, lost the rough patina of the hills of his birth in favor of the slick, glossy hardness of the city-bred.

For a time, Horn had thought this made him tough. A better man.

Some lessons every boy has to learn for himself.

He belched. The air from his gut burned Horn's mouth. Sour stomach was an inevitable result of drinking scrumpy. He wished he had a hot loaf of good bread. Or really, anything to dampen the rankling smell and caustic taste.

The barmaid skulked past him again, frowning. "Yer a foul man," she muttered.

"Foul is as foul does." He spat the words out.

She gave him a longer look. Something gleamed in her eye, some spark beyond the sullen resentments of a tavern slattern. Horn stared back. Wordless, they locked gazes as intently as any pair of wizards stepping into a final conflict.

"Do I know you?" he finally asked. By giving in and speaking first, he'd lost the initiative, but Horn no longer cared so much what he lost.

"Foul is as foul does," she replied in a mockery of his voice and the hillman accent that scrumpy brought to the surface.

"Be off," he growled.

"Until ye needs something, eh?" She swished away, her skirts swinging in a way that unlocked other memories Horn didn't care for, either.

He'd spent two years among the orchards of the high valley of Taoimburra. The trees bore strange fruit—old men, of uncertain age and history, who did not so much teach as speak. Sometimes they spoke to the wind and the empty air. Sometimes they spoke to small groups of seekers who gathered around them. But they always spoke wisdom. Finally Horn had truly learned how to open the cracks in the universe and let in the light from beyond.

Light, that laid down a path for the greatest fools to follow.

Horn inspected his bowl of scrumpy. Nothing remained but apple pulp mixed with a few suspiciously chitinous bits. He traced a fingertip through the variegated sludge, but he wasn't that desperate. Not that he hadn't been so desperate at some times in his life, to be fair.

He looked up at the barmaid, who favored him with a knowing leer from behind the bar. Horn nodded, and with trembling hand laid two more coppers on the table. Something whined in his ear, but he could not tell if it was in memory or the present moment, so he ignored the sound just as he ignored the weight beneath his vest.

One night Saanreich the Fat became Saanreich the Exsanguinated. It was a terminal case of name change, brought on by Dark Reivers pursuing an ancient curse that had passed into the merchant-adventurer's hands along with a particularly fetching ivory nude of some unknown goddess. Horn had assumed she was a goddess, at any rate, given the excess of both arms and breasts beyond the usual norm.

The enemy infiltrated Saanreich's fortified villa in the Crowne Heights district of Purpure on a stream of sparkling smoke that only Horn's wizardly vision had seen. When he tried to rally his fellow guards, he'd been greeted with puzzled somnolence. When the Dark Reivers materialized in their bony, bladed numbers, Horn had fought them with both sword and spell.

He was the only person to leave Saanreich's burning villa alive. He used his recently acquired city fighting skills to escape the pointed attention of the Watch, who in that simple-minded way of policemen when confronted with a crime and a last man standing, put two and two together to get seventeen. Having killed two of the Watch on his way out in self defense, Horn knew he would not be returning to Purpure for the foreseeable future. A life of shipboard excitement urgently beckoned.

Within six months he was an officer aboard the armed trader *Wet Blessing*. Horn never did learn a mainstay from a jib sail, but he was a remarkably convincing negotiator ashore, whether serving as supercargo in a civilized port, trade negotiator on some forlorn beach, or temple raider in the odder corners of the Starfall Sea. Captain Arroxta had promoted him from hired muscle to fourth mate after Horn saved all their hides during the bloody, stupid business at Boiling Bay.

He never looked back, sailing with *Wet Blessing* four years, until Arroxta insisted on returning to Purpure. Horn jumped ship in mid ocean, preferring to maroon himself on an isolated archipelago than to leap into the teeth of city justice. His wealth he took with him in electrum chains strung with gems, small enough not to sink him and valuable enough to be worth the weight with which they encumbered him.

The wealth bought him nothing on a sand strip populated by coconuts and gulls, but in his time at sea, Horn had learned to look ahead.

The bar maid came back with another bowl of scrumpy, steaming fresh from the kettle, along with a calculating look in her eye. Horn stared back at her. He seemed to have forgotten how to blink. Once, that had been an accomplishment.

She laid the bowl down on the table with far more care than she spent on the ales that came in chipped or dented mugs. No one wanted scrumpy on wood, let alone the floor. It was too much trouble.

"You does know me," she whispered close. For a moment he saw something in her face, in her eyes that flashed green as spring in the hills where he had been born. Like someone else behind a mask of a face.

Horn felt an unaccustomed surge of energy. His fingertips sparked against the scarred wood of the table until wisps of smoke curled up. Old magic going to ground, that was all. He'd sold his spellbook to a university library several cities past. No one had wanted his soul, regardless of the exchange rate.

By now, everything in life was either coming or going cheap for Horn.

"You should be watching that, big man." She waved a damp towel at his fingers. The smoke whiffed away in the flap of the cloth. "Someone might notice."

"No . . . nothing to notice." The words stumbled out of his mouth like dwarves staggering from a collapsing mine—covered with dust and grimed with the darkness beneath.

"Of course." She flicked him with the towel, right across the cheek. Another spark rose. He slapped his own face, trying to tamp down the burning sensation, and nearly spilled the scrumpy. The silk pocket under his vest shifted, and for a moment Horn slid deeper into memory's snare.

Once he'd hired out to a goddess. Just once. Temples had been broken and priests slain. The little divinity was vanishing from the world, and had craved a final vengeance against her enemies as a grave-gift. Horn had gained three great gifts as his recompense, for the gratitude of even a dying goddess is worth its weight in kings.

Still, the work had not been worth the wage. By the time he was finished with the geas the goddess had laid upon him, Horn was soul-deep in other people's blood and a dozen villages lay burned to ash under a tropic sky.

"Fate," he told the scrumpy, and took a deep, deep draught to further drown the memories before they stole him completely away.

The scrumpy had no answer except to strip his throat raw and send his gut into open rebellion, even as it calmed his thoughts to a befogged nothingness that spun round and round faster than an angry dervish.

High Canton was a wilder city than Purpure. More importantly, writs of law were not exchanged between the two rivals, who had been fighting a slow, quiet war of gold and ships down the centuries. Hot, bloody wars were not so profitable unless you were the weaponseller.

Which High Canton was, in other parts of the Starfall Sea. The city had been built along the edge of a basalt escarpment where fumaroles smoked and crevices burped yellow smokes that could bring a man to his knees on the first breath and to his tomb on the second. Caves below the city were so hot that forges were not needed for some manufactures. The imps and fire elementals of the uplands were alternately contracted or coerced into laboring alongside the great muscled slave-smiths who served the lords of the Cantons. They turned out blades and arrowheads and siege engines by the shipload for sale wherever war sent men to buying such.

Horn had grown wiser and more subtle in the years of the passing of his youth. He rented rooms with an impressive entrance in one of the squared, tapering towers that dotted the city—his particular being the Tower of Bears and Swans. Local wags called it the Tower of Booms and Slams for the sake of the alchemist who held the upper floors. The boards between her and Horn were reinforced with copper and iron plating, while the roof was laid lightly enough that an explosion would not trouble the neighborhood with too many splinters and broken spars.

He made his living a while as a wizard, though his weapons were never far from his side. The justiciars of Purpure knew him as a sellsword guard. They would not be looking for him amid eldritch smokes and a gallery of reptilian skulls. Props, of course, for the magic of his home hills had been much closer to stock and stone, water and wind, than to the mannered incantations of the great schoolmen. Still, no one in a place such as High Canton, built on drama and cocksure display, would place faith in a wizard whose spells were quietly crafted from roots and colored clays and dank tinctures of leaves and flowers.

Horn paid his dues to the local Collegium. He wore the expected robe of midnight blue embroidered with silver sigils. And he quietly, so quietly, sought out older wizards sunken into their square-walled dens like urban hermit crabs and truckled from them one by one the secrets of their craft. His stock in trade was the learnings he'd acquired at the far edges of the sea, or sometimes his hill-and-hedge magic disguised with the endorsement of distance. Even more quietly, he worked his body, running across the lava fields and among the boiling sulfur pits. No one from High Canton went to those places except the occasional slavemaster. There Horn could battle imaginary demons and past foes, stretching his sword arm and pushing his muscles past the burn.

The work of maintaining two such separate sets of skills sometimes made him feel like two men. The reward was that he yet lived when others around him had died.

Justice from Purpure finally did come seeking him. Horn set fire to the Tower of Bears and Swans, took up his fattened spellbook—still written on bark and leaves as he had first been taught—and sent himself far away in a blaze of magic that very nearly snuffed the flames around him as it drew in power.

He woke to the barmaid pouring water on his face. Horn blinked the stuff out of his eyes, glad at the least that she had not dunked him in scrumpy. Men had gone blind for less.

"Enough for you," she said, her voice low and growling. "Three days at the bowl and you're still alive. 'Tis a miracle no one should be forced to witness."

Horn rolled away from her, pressing his face into the tabletop until splinters plucked at his lips. "I've witnessed too much," he mumbled. In the corner of his vision the barmaid moved, but she was different. More graceful. More powerful.

With a sudden sense of panic, he slapped at his vest. The weight of fate still hung there. Its silk was clammy and close now.

"I ain't taken it yet."

He tilted his head to look at her more closely—how did she know?—but the barmaid was walking away.

And she had grown distinctly prettier. He certainly wasn't any more drunk.

Magic, the blessed curse that gnaws at the soul and leaves a void in the mind into which too much that is alien and deadly can settle.

He'd known women beautiful enough to have launched entire navies for the sake of their faces. He'd known women who looked like the wrong end of an old sergeant after a hard day's training. But there had been only one Manxinnaea.

Her nose was bulbous and slightly crooked. Her eyes were the brown of a good businesswoman, as was her hair. No one would have mistaken her for a courtesan, which she wasn't; or royalty, which she was.

But she smelled like heaven, and she moved like a cat in a granary, and her attention focused as powerfully as any wizard's could ever hope to. Manxinnaea had been Horn's only love in life. When they had betrayed one another, something inside his heart had died.

Why was he thinking of her now? Fool, fool, fool. The barmaid had cast the oldest spell of all on him, a cantrip requiring only alcohol, sorrow, and time.

Wet and blinking, Horn stumbled away from the table to find the outhouse somewhere between the kitchen and the stables. The sun stabbed his eyes like a shining assassin. The air smelled odd, though after a moment he realized it was just fresh, or at least fresher than the fug within the tavern.

The world tugged at him like a child on its mother's skirt. Horn did what he came for and ignored the rest. The reeking darkness of the tavern held room for his doubts and the slow banishment of his memory.

Milieu

The old man's skin was the color of walnuts, and so wrinkled and scarred it very nearly could have served him as armor.

Horn had no intention of testing that assumption. He was here on different errands.

He had reached the Temple of Winds near the peak of Mount Eponymous, on the Lost Island of Ee. Not so lost, in truth, for anyone could book passage out of half a dozen ports in the southern extents of the Starfall Sea. Assuming a captain was willing to brave contrary winds and little chance of profitable trade to carry a lubber into seething waters.

Sometimes the name was everything. Romance, danger, a hint of riches. Or perhaps just a gigantic angle-sided building with hundreds of windows very nearly on the edge of a smoking crater from which a sullen red glow could sometimes be seen at night.

He'd approached the temple by climbing the Path of Ten Thousand Steps. Being who he was, Horn had counted. There were only 4,238 steps. Again, the name was everything. The Temple of Winds could have held hundreds of acolytes, priests, worshipers, and servants, but in point of fact he'd wandered the worm-haunted wooden hallways and galleries with their peeling murals for the better part of a day before locating anyone.

"You're not the chandler," the old man had said on first spotting Horn. He'd spoken Kyrie, the common language of traders and slaves all along these waters, but with an accent reminiscent of the hieratical tongues of distant Khappas.

"No," Horn replied. "I am a seeker of wisdom."

The old man squinted, taking in Horn's scars, motley head of fire-scarred hair, and ropy muscles. "Looks like you haven't found it yet, or you'd have learned to stay out of trouble." He wheezed with asthmatic laughter at his own wit.

Horn shrugged. His skin was less tortured than his host's. "Trouble finds me. I end it, one way or another."

Another snort from the old man. Then: "We have wisdom in great supply here. Libraries full of it, scrolls stacked a hundred high. Were you looking for any particular sort of wisdom?"

Ignoring the sneer in the old man's voice, Horn carefully offered the answer he'd been working through for weeks, months even, since embarking on this particular journey. "I have gained power and lost purpose as I have traveled through my life. I come to you seeking direction, which is, of course, the cardinal characteristic of the wind."

"Actually, the wind mostly just blows," the old man muttered. "It cares not for direction."

"Yet here is where you stand against the wind and watch the world," Horn replied.

Something gleamed in the old man's eyes. "Our secrets are not so secret, are they?"

"You are the rumor in a dozen ports, and the whisper in half a hundred more." That was almost true.

"Come, then. I will show you our world-watching. Then you can decide if you really wish to ask for direction here."

"The ship on which I hired passage will not be back for at least three weeks," Horn said. "I may as well learn something in the meantime."

"A practical man, I see."

At nearly forty years of age, Horn hoped he'd learned something from life. He followed without comment.

The temple's paucity of acolytes and servants showed in the dust and grime lining the hallways. Elaborate doorways carved from teak or mahogany punctuated their progress. Their friezes were cracked and split from a lack of polishing. Red pillars lining the corridors were fading to a dusky melon color, streaked with smoke. Most of the lamps were not only unlit, but also in obvious disrepair.

It was like seeing a great lady of some earlier generation reduced to face paint and ill-fitting dresses. Horn could appreciate what this temple had once been, and might someday be again if it found patrons and worshipers.

Eventually they arrived at an enormous open space that rose through all the nine stories of the temple. It was like a high, wooden cave. Each level had a railing carved and painted to represent old battles between gods and monsters, though these were now as cracked and faded as everything else. Five stories below, at the bottom, the floor was occupied by an enormous map.

Horn stared down at it. He realized he was seeing the Starfall Sea at the center of the map, but there were countries and waters beyond its borders that he'd never known of. It was magnificently detailed, as if he looked down upon the world itself.

That thought made him consider how the hairs on his neck prickled. Slowly, Horn realized he *was* looking down upon the world itself, at least in a sense.

"The wind sees everything, sooner or later," the old man said softly beside him. "It carries word and deed across rivers and mountains and oceans."

Breath stuttered in Horn's throat. "Here, you listen to the songs it sings."

"Listen and take note."

He studied the map. "That is not a work of hand, is it?"

"Prayer and study and ancient miracles bound into place." The old man grasped Horn's arm with a grip of iron. "Far greater men than you have come to steal the secrets of how we do this thing."

"I come to steal nothing. Only to ask." Horn had the distinct impression that if he looked hard enough, he'd find the Lost Island, and the Temple of Winds, and a great gallery with two men looking down.

He could see every place he'd ever be able to reach in his lifetime. That thought made Horn feel very small indeed.

After a while, the old man spoke again. "Most don't want to see what lies before them."

"I have fought," Horn said distantly. "Fought with sword and spell. I have been the red knight of slaughter. I have called down fire upon my enemies. I have killed half a hundred men, countless orcs and goblins, and dozens of stranger enemies. I can magic the fish from their shadowed realms alongside the riverbanks, and I can face down an army if I find it needful. I know what lies behind me. Seeing what lies before can guide my steps in new paths."

"Or the oldest ones." Another grip of the arm, this more of a friendly tug. "Come with me. It's nearly time to eat. You stay here too long, you will lose yourself in the map."

A dozen monks gathered in a corner of what had once been an enormous refectory. The kitchens beyond were dark and quiet, their great clay ovens with the dragon mouths long gone cold, or even cracked. Iron pots hung like the helmets of ogres in those old shadows.

These men had made a stew in a warming fireplace in the dining area itself. They gathered around the one surviving table from what must have once been scores of tables. All were as old or older than Horn's guide, and all shared the man's hard-used air. They seemed more like veteran warriors than elderly clerics.

His appearance caused no comment at all. Clearly they'd known he was here. Some signal passed silently between them? Or perhaps just the wisdom of anyone who knows his own house well.

Horn took a bowl, shallow and oblong with tiny feet beneath, then followed his old man's example of scooping out a ladle or two of the stew, along with a piece of flatbread still steaming from its own little pot-oven in the fire. Each monk had brought his own spoon, so Horn just slurped from the bowl.

A minute or two later, he realized that all the bowls were the tops of skulls, carefully sealed and lacquered. No one else seemed to care, so Horn kept his own counsel. The dead did not worry him overmuch. Besides which, he had not killed the people whose heads these were. They would not haunt him.

They ate in silence, except for the occasional grunt or raised eyebrow. Horn got the impression of a conversation taking place. One that had long since transcended the need for words. He maintained his own silence out of politeness as well as a sense of caution.

As the bowls were set aside, one by one the monks came to sit before Horn. Each spent a few minutes studying his face from a close distance. A quiet staring, intense, strange. As if his future were being read from the bones beneath his skin.

After their study, the monks one by one nodded at him, then nodded at his guide, then drifted off into the dusty shadows of the Temple of Winds.

Finally only Horn and his monk remained together in the refectory. He felt a distinct sense of abandonment. Like a ship drawn up on a beach, left to woodworms and dry rot. Or, indeed, this building.

"Paths," the old man finally said. Shrewd calculation crossed his face. Horn was certain that was a deliberate display.

Finally, Horn spoke up for himself. "I had purpose once."

"You would do better to petition the Raven Queen"

Horn shrugged. "Where would I find Raven Queen? With her demense in Lethrna, she cannot be found ensconced within a temple, or in the mumbling prayers of priests."

The monk nodded. "Fair enough. But neither does the wind care for your purpose and your future. As soon inquire of the tides, or seek wisdom among the rocks."

"People do those things."

"Are they any wiser for it?"

He had to laugh. "I have seen little so far in my life to lead me to believe that people are any wiser for *anything*."

"Yet here you are, many weeks' sailing from your home, wherever that may be."

Horn thought of the distant hills of his birth with a small pang of regret. Most of his fellow sellswords had long since gone back, settled down with a village girl, and begun the serious business of breeding the next generation of boys. He was fairly sure that neither Feather nor any of the other Old Men had ever expected to see him again.

"Home is where my boots are," Horn finally said.

"Some would name that a sad fate."

"I have seen the world."

Now the monk shrugged. "So have I."

What was this scarred old man trying to tell him?

Horn tried again. "Given that I seem unable to petition the Raven Queen as you suggest, is there another path?"

"Some things change a man slowly. Journeys. The passage of years. The love of a good woman. Imprisonment." The monk paused a moment. Horn sensed he was speaking from experience, looking back at his own paths. Then: "Some things change a man swiftly. War. Disease. Shipwrecks. The love of a bad woman."

"Change is inevitable."

"And that is what you crave. The inevitability of change." The monk leaned close, as his fellows had. "Have you ever encountered a true artifact? From the First Cities, or the Old Gods, or out of the treasure houses of the greatest mages of history?"

Horn frowned. He was familiar with the concept of artifacts, mostly from his studies with the wizards of High Canton within darkened rooms among its square towers. "It is possible that an old master of mine handled such, but for my own part, no."

"One way to think of such items is as change itself, distilled into the palm of your hand. Even something as simple as a wand can change the user. You have found this in your own experience, I am confident."

Nodding, Horn agreed. He could remember certain spells, certain secrets, the learning of which had reshaped his view of the world. On occasion, abruptly so.

The monk tapped Horn's chest. "Then to find your purpose, you might consider seeking out one of these artifacts. Not all of them are in strongrooms and locked boxes."

"You have something in mind?"

"We know where many things in this world are to be found. The Map of Winds is an artifact in its own right. Many secrets whispered under the open sky find their way here."

Horn was wary, on his guard at this. "Everything in this world comes with a price."

"Of course." The monk smiled, like evil dawning. "We have need of something wrongly taken from us long ago. Fetch this item back from where it is held today, and we will place fate in your hands."

Knowing he was committing himself blindly, Horn let himself step forward. "What is this thing, and where do you need it fetched from?"

Melee

It took him more than a year to fight his way back to the Temple of Winds. Along the journey, Horn took wounds of the body and soul. He slew a white dragon, losing the tips of two fingers and most of his hair from its icy breath. He bargained away the life of an entire village for passage through a high trail defended by ogres.

In a glacial cave far higher up a mountain than Horn had ever hoped to climb, he found the Rod of the Eight Winds embedded in a crystal sphere guarded by four enormous nagas. After dispatching them, he skinned them and traded their hides to the ogres before passing through the smoldering ruins of the white dragon's village on his way back to the temple. The ship on which he bought passage was attacked by pirates, three of the waterfronts he visited were set ablaze in his time there, and near the end of his journey Horn came down with a hacking cough that threatened to carry away his life.

Seen another way, the Raven Queen had opposed him at every turn.

It was as if she knew everything he did was fighting toward an attempt to force her hand in granting Horn a purpose.

In the last port, the one from which he could take ship to the Lost Island of Ee, he took a room so he could rest and ride out the worst of his cough. The Rod of the Eight Winds was concealed in a ceramic globe he'd had fashioned not long after securing it, and covered with poorly crafted paste gems to discourage thieves from becoming too creative. It was well enscorcelled, too, of course, but Horn could handle those without endangering himself.

It was himself he was concerned about.

The room was a dusty, dormered section of attic on the third floor of a dockside tavern. He had a tiny round window through which he could see the tops of masts, smeary and bobbing through the grimed and spotted glass. Horn slept on a rope bed with a rag mattress, and was forced to spend some of his healing energy on cantrips to battle the bedbugs and beetles that contested possession. The only other furnishings were a miserly whale-oil lamp and a tiny chest that he'd avoided, preferring to keep his few belongings in the bed with him.

Otherwise the room was rotted boards and cobwebs, not unlike the interior of the Temple of Winds. Except, of course, for the lack of carvings, and the paucity of red pillars.

For almost a fortnight he lay there, stripping rags from the bed to cough into until they were too blood-soaked to use any further. For them, he used the despised chest to dispose of. The tavernkeep's boy brought him water and a slice of bread every day. On that, Horn's life depended.

He would be cursed before he would send for a doctor, though. They were as crazed as alchemists, and less trustworthy than the maddest of priests. A decent cleric with healing prayers would have done him, but Horn had never followed a god any further than strictly necessary for self-preservation. Besides, no one in this port knew him well enough to stand and plead his case before any altar.

Finally one day someone new came into the room. At first he thought it was one of the girls who plied their own warm commerce a floor below, with shrieks and moans that kept Horn awake the nights his own coughing did not suffice. She was a thin woman, dark-skinned in the manner of these southernmost ports, with eyes the color of the inside of a lime. Her wrap was dyed in patterns, colored purple, dark blue, and black.

Horn gripped his dagger close. The sword was overmuch trouble, and he was far too sick to manage a decent spell—even the cantrips against the tiny, biting monsters of his terrible bed exhausted him.

If the woman was there to rob him, he was not sure he could stop her from her work.

"You seek what does not belong to you." Despite her appearance, the woman spoke the hillman's language of Horn's birth, sounding just like one of the village girls he'd known in his youth.

"A sending," Horn gasped. He wondered if there were any point in calling out for aid. His chest shook, another terrible cough building up.

"Not a sending." Her voice was a gentle chiding. "Always present."

Horn took a shuddering breath, fighting the cough to get the words out. "My life belongs to me."

"Actually," she said with a smile, "it does not."

Her hands briefly caressed his chest, then the woman was gone, though Horn could not remember the door closing. When he awoke later, his breathing was clear for the first time in weeks.

It was time to return to the Temple of Winds. He adamantly refused to speculate on who had visited him, or why, though he burned a small offering of thanks on the dockside cobbles that next evening.

Horn found himself winded climbing the Path of Ten Thousand Steps. Or even four thousand, two hundred and thiry-eight steps.

He was ashamed.

Since leaving this place, he'd crossed mountains and oceans, slain a white dragon, faced down ogres. But even healed of his wretched, wracking cough, he was still weak. The week of sailing to reach the Lost Island of Ee had not improved his health. Too many rough seas. Too much bad food.

The old monk waited at the top this time. An unseemly glee seemed to have taken possession of his lined, scarred face. Horn felt suddenly impatient with the old man. Irritated, even.

Or was that just his own fear at being given the power to choose his path?

"I have come," he announced. Utterly unnecessary, but it was the sort of thing one said in such moments.

"You have succeeded, I trust," the old monk said. "Or you would not have returned so soon."

"Soon? I have been gone for several seasons."

"Some quests take years. Or lifetimes."

Lifetimes, plural? thought Horn. When he was young, he'd considered reincarnation unlikely, as well as probably too much trouble, given the karmic debt one was said to accrue. As he grew older, the idea of coming back for another try seemed less foolish, but sadly no more practical. "My quest took thirteen moons."

It occurred to Horn that standing on ceremony would be pointless. The monk wanted greed, he could have greed. Horn merely wished to sleep in a bed that was neither rolling under him nor filled with biting insects swimming in his sweat. He unslung the padded leather bag in which the ceramic globe was nestled. "Here. It is yours. I took some pains to disguise the rod. It's embedded in a crystal shell. That's how I found it."

With that, Horn pushed past the monk and into the Temple of Winds. He quickly located the monk's cell he'd used for the three weeks when last he was there. Bare wooden walls, a ceiling with a faded painting of a thousand-eyed demon, and scant furniture. He'd seen better prisons, though this room had no lock on the door or guards in the hallway. The same threadbare linens lay rumpled on the straw mattress, under months' worth of the everpresent dust.

He took a few moments to shake them out, then remade the bed, slipped into it, and slept the sleep of the blessed.

The next morning, Horn went to the refectory on his own. Usually there was rice soup for breakfast. Sometimes even a few eggs harvested from nests in the abandoned upper stories of the temple, or from the cliffs outside if one of the monks had been particularly in need of exercise.

Three of them were eating when he arrived, including the old man who had been his guide. In his time there before, Horn had never been offered any names. Nor had he heard the monks use names in their rare, brief conversations. They were just old men in an old temple.

Unsure whether or how to push the question of his compensation for retrieving the Rod of Winds, he settled for a skull bowl of congee and a somewhat withered peach. Horn ate in silence until his monk spoke up.

"You have walked the world, and brought us what we asked."

Horn nodded. His mouth was full of the pasty rice stew. He quickly swallowed.

"It is time for your reward." The monk reached within his robes to lay a small ivory box in front of Horn.

He studied the offering carefully. It was not much larger than the palm of his hand, and a finger's width in thickness. The outside was covered with shallow carvings that reminded him of the art sailors made on walrus ivory or whalebones. The patterns were difficult to comprehend, something between thorny roses and things with far too many teeth.

Looking slightly to one side of the box, Horn called upon his years of training in the magical arts. Eyes that had peered through smoke and spell and scattering learned to see what was truly present, rather than what only seemed to be. It was still a box, still strangely carved, but it practically vibrated with the energies it contained—human energies formed under a working hand. This did not have the slick sheen of divine apparition.

"Powerful magic here," he observed quietly. Some spellcaster had spent a good portion of his lifetime constructing this thing.

"You seek a powerful reward," said the monk.

Horn picked up a chopstick and passed it close to the ivory box. Nothing. No spark, no smoke, no vibration or light.

Very gingerly, he touched bamboo to ivory. Again, quiescent. Where he might have expected a bit of flash and drama, he was encountering only, well, ivory.

The monks smiled as they watched. Clearly they would be no help to Horn. He was the great swordsman and master spellwright—it was up to him to sort this out.

Which was, in truth, fair enough.

Another careful stab with the chopstick provoked no additional reaction. Horn laid the utensil aside and reached for the ivory box. The monk had handled it without incident, after all.

Something clicked slightly as he lifted it. The weight and balance of the box shifted. It was only a container, not a thing in itself.

Looking over it in his hand, Horn saw how an inner box could be made to slide out the end of the carved shell. It was no different from the card boxes that soldiers and sailors sometimes carried in their kits.

Card boxes . . .

"You people," he breathed. "This is the Deck of Many Things."

"Fate in your hand." The monk was positively grinning now. "Your choices are your own. Everything lies before you. Every path is in your hands."

"Bastards," Horn said.

The old men laughed at him before wandering off into the dusty shadows of their temple home. He heard the fading echoes of their mirth for a while.

Consequences

Horn racked his brain for whatever he might have read or heard about the Deck of Many Things. The monks had never shown him a library—they were obsessed with their map, and with listening to the wind—so even if he found one, he doubted it would contain much to aid him in understanding such an item.

Everyone knew the general gist, of course. The Deck of Many Things was a campfire favorite, for storytelling and idle boasting. Most people wouldn't know what to do with a magic wand or a flaming sword or a crystal ball or many of the other legendary magic items and artifacts that supposedly littered the world.

But cards? Everybody understood cards. A metaphor for life, how the king ruled all but the knave snuck in beneath the queen, and the ace at the bottom could trump the very top. Colors and numbers and a swift flick of the hand could turn the fate of your last piece of silver, or make you a rich man indeed on a hot, lucky night.

He had to admit it: cold fear blew through him. All magic was balance. Who needed reincarnation to believe in karmic debt? Unwise or unlucky wizards learned fast enough how much one paid for one's mistakes. One sometimes paid more dearly for one's successes.

What he could recall of the Deck of Many Things strongly suggested a balancing act between bright blessings and arrant curses. What would he draw if he opened the ivory box? The keys to a kingdom? Or just as likely his own ruination.

The other piece of lore that came bubbling upward was the idea that he must commit to a number of draws from the Deck before he began. Horn wasn't certain that was a rigorous rule, or simply a sensible rumor.

He'd never been a great risk taker. Study and practice had always been his way. That and careful planning. But what had he expected from these monks? Mystical guidance?

One could not plan for this. The Deck was worse than that time when he'd sought vengeance on behalf of the dying goddess Karrehein. It was wild power in his hand.

If Horn had been a praying man, he would have prayed. If he'd thought for a moment that the monks might give him practical advice, he'd have gone begging for their words.

But this was for him.

A day later, his chest still weak, he went to the top of the Path of Ten Thousand Steps and looked out across the ocean. Bottle-bright and the color of polished glass, it heaved and sparkled as only a great mass of water can do. No ships were visible, just water to the horizon. Great, swale-bellied clouds passed slowly overhead.

Behind him the volcano stank and muttered. The winds of the world came here. He could find no better place to seize his fate in his hands.

Feeling both foolish and very much in danger of his life, Horn raised the ivory card box toward the sky.

"I shall draw down three cards," he said in a firm voice before prising open the little ivory drawer.

They lay within. Pasteboard, like any card, but slick and firm and overwhelmingly solid in appearance. Freed of their ivory enclosure, the cards positively reeked of magic.

Horn picked at the deck, flicking out a card from the middle.

He turned it in his hand.

The world changed.

Throne

A villa, overlooking the Bight of Winds. Technically a castle, though without moat or curtain wall, and it would not stand up to much attack at all. At the foot of his patio was a drop to pounding surf. Horn was well supplied with pliant servants and fine wines from distant islands. He was happy there, and everyone loved him.

The only thing that gave him pause was the ivory box he always carried in a silk sling beneath his robes. What the Deck had given, the Deck could take away. Horn still had two more draws, though now he wished he'd stopped at one. Was he supposed to just hold onto the deck like this? Or should he have simply drawn the three cards in a fan?

No answers came to him, and life was good, so Horn tried not to worry overmuch. He lived at the villa for several years. The weather was kind. Ships called at his dock just often enough to bring news and goods. Horn sent for his wealth, stashed in banks and strongrooms scattered across a dozen ports, and from time to time considered either hiring himself out or going adventuring.

It should have been boring, but was not. Rather, the villa was pleasing to the eye and soul. He eventually grew accustomed to the well-earned rest from his labors.

One day a cockleshell boat with an ivory hull and a single lateen sail the color of a dead man's eyes made his dock. Horn watched it a while from the patio, a slim stemware glass of wine in his hand. He did not recognize the ship but felt vaguely disturbed by its color and form. Eventually Moneo his majordomo approached him.

"Sir, you have a visitor." After a pause, the man added, "A lady, sir."

Horn knew his staff would have approved if he'd taken a wife and become a true lord of the estate. This stretch of coast along the Bight of Winds was a wild country, dotted with a few small fishing villages. No king or prince extended a writ along these particular waters or shores. The villa itself was safe largely in its isolation—there was not sufficient trade here to attract pirates or bandits. He could have raised a flag, bred some strong sons, and founded his own ruling line. Raiders might have been a problem for his grandsons.

So a woman caller was of interest to Moneo and the other servants. A woman caller was worrying to Horn, however.

"Show her in," he said. "I will receive my guest here on the patio. And tell Cook to lay on a feast fit for a prodigal." He had an uneasy notion just who was come to visit.

She came walking out, short and thick-bodied in the manner of the people of the coast here, but her eyes were the color of the inside of a lime, and her robes were dyed in patterns, colored purple, dark blue, and black.

Horn knew her immediately. "You came to me once, when I was sick unto dying in a distant port."

"Yes." She nodded, and he felt wind upon his back and buzzing in his ears. "You seek what does not belong to you." Despite her appearance, the woman once more spoke the hillman's language of Horn's birth.

"Not a sending," he said, remembering their conversation before. "Always present."

"Always." She cocked her head, and he had never seen a more beautiful woman, for all her common looks. "Yet you tempt me." A blunt finger tapped at his chest, clicking against the ivory box beneath his own robes.

"It is time for me to draw another card, is it not?"

"Far past time." She smiled, and he felt the stars shift in their courses. "With age comes wisdom. Or at least experience."

Realizing he would not be a guest at his own feast that evening, Horn took out the ivory box. He tugged open the tiny drawer to turn another card from the center of the deck.

The world changed.

Ruin

The tavern bench creaked beneath Horn like a ship under sail. He swayed, listening to the wood pop and snap, knowing if he were afloat, he'd be leaking.

He realized he'd had that thought before. His memory was playing tricks. Or the scrumpy was.

Which was the point here.

He stared up at the barmaid as she swished past. Her skirt was made in dark, muted colors—had it been so earlier? The woman favored him with a sidelong glance, her expression somewhere between wise and malicious. He turned his head to watch her tend to a pair of tables by the fire.

Finally she made it back over to him. "Out of money yet?"

"I don't know," he answered with unfortunate honesty. "Out of scrumpy yet?"

Her laugh held a curious edge. "We'll never run out of scrumpy when there's the likes of you in the world."

"I wanted . . . more." He wasn't sure if he meant more than scrumpy, or more than what life had given him in the world. The mansions of memory had grown crowded in his head, haunted by regrets.

"You seek what does not belong to you."

Those words, so familiar. And had she just spoken Kyrie, or another tongue from too long ago when he was young and the world was colored with hope?

Horn peered closer. Her eyes were green. The color of the inside of a lime. "It's you," he said. "You healed me once. You threatened me once."

Now her smile bordered on joy. Around them, the reeking, smoky tavern seemed to recede into abstract distance. "And I have come for that which I have been cheated of."

Horn slipped his hand inside his vest, touching the ivory card box in its silk sling. He drew that box out for the first time in . . . how long? There wasn't any way to be sure. The path of his decay had been as gradual as it had been inexorable, since drawing the second card.

The ivory card box lay in his hand. Malevolent. Powerful. The old monk's great joke played upon him.

Fate.

"This was always yours, was it not?"

With a nod, she said, "And you have held it far beyond your time."

He extended his hand. "Here. Take it."

"Three times you said you'd draw. Three cards to chart a path through life." She leaned close, her eyes sparking. "Draw the third, little man, and return to your life."

Horn could hear the click of the dice that made up the multiverse. Beneath the struggles of gods and men and monsters, behind the powers of magic and prayer and bared blade, chance governed all.

The box came open easily enough. The cards slipped into his hand. The pasteboard again seemed slick and heavy. Horn considered simply tossing them into the air, as if they might fly away like little birds. Instead, vaguely aware of the clink of tankards and the murmur of voices, he thumbed a third card from the middle.

Conclusions

Horn had grown into an old man of no little power and persuasion. The hills of his birth suited him fine these days. Like Feather had so long ago, he picked a boy every few years who showed a certain, special spark and took the child aside for training. The tribe traded in sellswords raised to the purpose, but their true power was in the quiet thread of wizards spawned down the generations.

Some nights he sat vigil in the high caverns. Some days he hunted alongside the young men with their tagalong brothers and cousins, for the sheer joy of the chase and the kill. Some evenings he found a high rock and looked down upon the plains that led toward the coast, and recalled Purpure, High Canton, the Lost Island of Ee, and so many other places his feet had touched.

But always he went back to his hut. There Margaine, his green-eyed foreign wife, awaited him after her own days of seeing to the sick or wounded, and teaching the little girls.

It was enough.

As for the card he'd never turned, it hung on the wall of his hut in a leather bag. Some nights it twitched, or even glowed—magic trying to escape. If he'd not been a wizard of some power in his own right, he would have been overwhelmed years before.

The barmaid had laughed when he'd palmed the card and slipped it into his vest. Then she'd left with him. The ivory card box remained behind, innocent trap for the next man. Nothing more had been said about cheating, or what belonged to whom. He was never sure if she retained the aspect of the Raven Queen, but Margaine's eyes always sparkled that curious color.

Some day he would turn the card. Some day he would know what fate he had removed from the Deck of Many Things.

Just not today.

Today, his path was his own. Today, the mansions of his memory gleamed once more. Today, he would not flip the last card.

Jay Lake lives in Portland, Oregon, where he works on numerous writing and editing projects. His 2011 books are *Endurance* from Tor Books, and *Love in the Time of Metal and Flesh* from Prime Books. His short fiction appears regularly in literary and genre markets worldwide. Jay is winner of the John W. Campbell Award for Best New Writer, and a multiple nominee for the Hugo and World Fantasy Awards.

MANY ROADS LEAD TO NEVERWINTER™

RETURN WITH
GAUNTLGRYM
Neverwinter Saga, Book I
R.A. Salvatore

NEVERWINTER
Neverwinter Saga, Book II
R.A. Salvatore
October 2011

CONTINUE THE ADVENTURE WITH
BRIMSTONE ANGELS
Legends of Neverwinter
Erin M. Evans
November 2011

LOOK FOR THESE OTHER EXCITING NEW RELEASES IN 2011
Neverwinter for PC
The Legend of Drizzt™ cooperative board game
Neverwinter Campaign Setting

HOW WILL YOU RETURN?
Find these great products at your favorite bookseller or game shop.

DungeonsandDragons.com

THE ABYSSAL PLAGUE

From the molten core of a dead universe

Hunger
Spills a seed of evil

Fury
So pure, so concentrated, so infectious

Hate
Its corruption will span worlds

The Temple of Yellow Skulls
Don Bassingthwaite

Sword of the Gods
Bruce Cordell

Under the Crimson Sun
Keith R.A. DeCandido
June 2011

Oath of Vigilance
James Wyatt
August 2011

Shadowbane
Erik Scott de Bie
September 2011

**Find these novels at your favorite bookseller.
Also available as ebooks.**

DungeonsandDragons.com